Dear Reader,

Thank you very much for picking up my new novel, *A Mother's Sacrifice*. The mother of the title is Martha, a character I really admired as I was writing her, but I certainly gave her a lot of challenges – I hope you like her as much as I do and find yourself intrigued by her story.

I do love to hear from you wonderful readers, so please do visit me on Facebook www.facebook.com/JennieFeltonAuthor or follow me on Twitter @Jennie_Felton for my latest news!

Love,
Jennie x

By Jennie Felton

The Families of Fairley Terrace Sagas
All The Dark Secrets
The Birthday Surprise (short story featured in the anthology
A Mother's Joy)
The Miner's Daughter
The Girl Below Stairs
The Widow's Promise
The Sister's Secret

Standalone
The Stolen Child
A Mother's Sacrifice

A Mother's Sacrifice

JENNIE FELTON

Headline

First published in Great Britain in 2020 by
HEADLINE PUBLISHING GROUP

First published in paperback in 2021 by
HEADLINE PUBLISHING GROUP

1

Cataloguing in Publication Data is available from the British Library

ISBN 978 1 4722 5648 5

Typeset in Calisto by Avon DataSet Ltd, Arden Court, Alcester, Warwickshire

Printed and bound in Great Britain by Clays Ltd, Elcograf S.p.A.

Headline's policy is to use papers that are natural, renewable and recyclable
products and made from wood grown in well-managed forests and other
controlled sources. The logging and manufacturing processes are expected
to conform to the environmental regulations of the country of origin.

HEADLINE PUBLISHING GROUP
An Hachette UK Company
Carmelite House
50 Victoria Embankment
London EC4Y 0DZ

www.headline.co.uk
www.hachette.co.uk

To my dearest daughters, Terri and Suzanne.

With all my love, and heartfelt thanks for all you do for me.

Acknowledgements

First, a huge thank you to my lovely family, who are always there for me. And my good friends – you know who you are.

Then, as always, to Kate Byrne, my brilliant editor at Headline, and Rebecca Ritchie, the most wonderful agent. You are both the cream of the crop!

Thanks also to the team at Headline, including Faith Stoddard, Alara Delfosse, Siobhan Hooper, Martin Kerans, Rebecca Bader and Isobel Smith. Without all your hard work my books would never make it on to the shelves!

And, lastly, I guess I should thank the World Wide Web for making very diverse bits of research so much easier than it used to be when I first began writing as Janet Tanner.

Prologue

Hillsbridge, Somerset – 1906

Sergeant Love was in bed and snoring loud enough to wake the dead when something disturbed him. He shifted restlessly, thinking that Alice, his wife, must have given him a poke in the ribs as she sometimes did to try to put a stop to the regular droning that she likened to sleeping in a farmyard.

'Leave me be, can't you?'

But now Alice's hand was on his shoulder, shaking him.

'Wake up, for goodness' sake, Will. Can't you hear there's somebody at the door?'

'What?' He rubbed his fist over his chin to wipe away the dribble that had run from his open mouth.

'Somebody's at the door!' Alice repeated impatiently, and simultaneously the knocking that had woken her came again, loud and insistent.

'Oh, bugger.'

Sergeant Love struggled to a sitting position, rolled out of bed and reached for his dressing gown.

That was one of the drawbacks of living above the police station. You were always at the beck and call of anybody who wanted a policeman, whatever the time of the day or night it happened to be.

By the light of the moon that was streaming in through a gap in the curtains he could see that the hands of the bedside clock were showing twenty to three, and that surprised him. He'd have thought Constable Sparrow, who was on night duty, would have been in the office, having a cup of tea and making up his notebook. The town was usually quiet at this time of night. Perhaps Sparrow was out on his bicycle making a last round – or perhaps the dozy bugger had fallen asleep at his desk. That wouldn't surprise the sergeant. Sparrow had looked even more lethargic than usual when he'd come on duty at ten.

Sergeant Love thrust his feet into his highly polished black boots, not bothering to lace them, and made his way down the stairs, through the small living room, and into the lobby. The door to the little office was open – no sign of Sparrow there – and before the sergeant could unlatch the door the hammering began again.

'All right, all right, I'm coming!' he called grumpily. If it was young tearaways having a laugh, they'd catch the rough end of his tongue.

But it wasn't young tearaways. On the doorstep, her hand raised to knock yet again, was a middle-aged woman he recognised as Martha Packer, landlady of the Three Feathers, a pub at the very outskirts of his patch. And if her insistent knocking had not told him that her reason for being here was that something very serious had occurred, her grim expression certainly did.

Sergeant Love sighed inwardly, seeing the remainder of his night's sleep disappear 'down the Swanee', as he described it, and thinking that he wouldn't mind betting that whatever Martha's problem was, it involved her son, Garth.

* * *

2

The Three Feathers, several miles outside Hillsbridge on the road to Bath, had been owned by the Packer family for as long as anyone could remember. Successive generations had served beer and spirits to the hardened drinkers of the nearby villages, at first from what had once been the front room of their home – a sizeable house with a cottage adjoining, and land that stretched to the surrounding fields and woods – then later, the ground-floor layout had been tinkered with so that there was a lounge as well as a public bar and a snug. Seb, Martha's husband, had also built a skittle-alley in one of the outbuildings at the rear of the property so that the Feathers, as it was known, could raise a team from amongst their regulars to play in the local skittles league.

Less than a year ago, Seb had died in a tragic accident that had devastated the family. His will had left everything to his three sons, Garth, Conrad and Lewis, but it was still Martha who ran the business and served behind the bar.

In her late forties, she was still a handsome woman, evidence that she'd been known for 'a stunner' when she was young. Though there were now broad streaks of silver in what had once been a fine head of coal-black hair, her face was remarkably free of lines and wrinkles, perhaps thanks to a tendency to plumpness, and her posture as upright as it had ever been, with no hint of the rounded shoulders or widow's hump that afflicted many women of her age.

As for her nature, it was ideally suited to her role as a pub landlady. Although her manner was friendly, warm and welcoming, she could also be formidable if the occasion warranted, as any customers who became rowdy or overstepped the mark soon learned to their cost. Life had dealt Martha some hard blows; besides losing her husband, she had buried four children – three who had died in infancy and one stillbirth – but somehow

3

the terrible losses had failed to break her. Instead they had made her stronger, so that now a core of steel lay beneath her generally pleasant demeanour.

This was the Martha Packer Sergeant Love knew – strong, resilient, optimistic. But now, as she stood on the doorstep of the police station, erect as ever, her face was ravaged, and her hands, tightly clasped around the bone handles of the tapestry bag she held in front of her like body armour, also spoke of something very wrong.

'What's up then, Mrs Packer?' he asked.

Her chin rose; she hesitated for only a moment.

'I need to talk to you, Sergeant.'

Another brief hesitation.

'I have just killed my son.'

Chapter One

St Peter's Workhouse – April 1896

'Jeannie – hush, my love. Don't cry, please!'

Eleven-year-old Ella Martin rolled as close as she could to the edge of her narrow bed and reached across to her little sister. There were eight beds in the dormitory and luckily Jeannie occupied the one next to her.

'I want Mammy!' Jeannie's voice was thick with tears.

'I know. So do I. But you mustn't cry. Miss Hopkins will hear you and then . . .' Ella broke off, not wanting to put into words what would happen if the housemother was disturbed. Children who cried at night were silenced with a rag soaked in chloroform to keep them quiet. And it did that all right. Not so long ago one girl had gone to sleep and never woken up again. Her bed, next to the door, was still empty, and Ella was terrified the same fate might befall her sister. 'You don't want to make her cross, do you?' she finished.

'N-no . . .' Eight-year-old Jeannie's sobs softened into hiccups and snuffles and her fingers curled round Ella's, gripping them tightly.

'You'll see Mammy soon. When she's well again,' Ella

whispered urgently, trying to ensure that Jeannie didn't start crying again in earnest.

'Really soon?'

'Yes.'

But she knew it was an empty promise. Here in the work-house families were separated, wives from their husbands, children from their parents, boys from girls. Siblings did get to see one another for two hours each afternoon when they were taught their lessons, either by the local rector or Miss Owen, who had once run a dame school in a nearby village. But it was only on Sundays, when they attended church, that the children had any contact with their mothers and fathers, and next Sunday was a whole week away. Six long days and nights. Even then, if Lilah was still ill they wouldn't be allowed up to the infirmary where she was being looked after for fear of spreading germs. They hadn't been allowed there today, and they hadn't been allowed to visit their father when he was dying of the lung disease that had cost him his job in the pits and the house that went with it – the reason the family had ended up here in the workhouse.

Ella's greatest fear was that her mother might follow him to an early grave. She had never been in good health since giving birth to Jeannie and Ella had only faint memories of the strong, fun-loving woman who had used to take her for long walks in the fields and woods behind their home, play hide-and-seek with her while she buried herself in the laundry basket or crouched behind the sofa, and sang her to sleep at bedtime. She'd been only three years old when Jeannie was born. But when Daddy had explained to her that Mammy wasn't well and needed help with the new baby she had been eager to do her bit.

She'd taken soiled nappies to the soaking bucket and prodded them in with the wooden spoon Lilah kept especially for the purpose, and sat beside the crib, rocking it gently until Jeannie fell asleep, however long that took. Later, as Jeannie grew, Ella had kept her entertained when Lilah was tired, or forced to take to her bed, even preparing food for them, albeit mostly jam sandwiches or bread and dripping.

As time had gone by Lilah's health had improved, but since they had been forced into the workhouse the awful conditions there had weakened her again, her reserves of strength eroded by the hard physical work, often in the laundry or the kitchens, and the cold and damp that permeated the place – even in summer the chill still emanated from the old stone walls. Ella had seen her grow thinner and paler, and during this last bitterly cold winter she'd developed a chesty cough that she couldn't seem to shake off, which had worried Ella, though Lilah tried to reassure her that it was nothing that some spring sunshine wouldn't cure.

Since the weather had taken a turn for the better this week, Ella had been in hopes that she'd see some improvement in her mother when they met in church on Sunday. But it wasn't to be. Instead she was worse, and sick enough to have been taken to the infirmary, so that Ella and Jeannie hadn't been able to see her at all. No wonder Jeannie had been in tears on and off for most of the day, Ella thought. She'd felt like crying too, and still did.

But at least Jeannie was quiet now, just sniffling occasionally, and when at last the snuffles stopped and her breathing became even, Ella whispered a little prayer of gratitude that the danger of her being quietened with a chloroform-soaked rag had passed – for now, at least.

Her hand, which Jeannie had been clasping tightly, had gone through the stage of pins and needles to being completely numb, but she had been afraid to move in case she disturbed her sister and set her off again. Now, however, she inched closer to the edge of the thin straw mattress so that she could reach across with her other hand and gently prise herself free of Jeannie's fingers. Success. She rolled over on to her back, rubbing life back into her hand, then pulled the coarse blanket up as far as the neck of her nightgown – any higher and it would make her throat itch – and closed her eyes. But with all her worries about Mammy churning round in her head sleep felt as far away as ever.

Would she be all right? Would she get better? Or – the thought was so terrible it ran a shiver through her body and made her feel sick – might she die as Daddy had? If she did, Ella didn't think she could bear it. And what would become of her and Jeannie? Ella felt as if all the cares of the world rested on her young shoulders.

A solitary tear escaped and rolled down her cheek and she turned her head to brush it away on the worn pillowcase. Crying would do no good. Somehow she had to be strong, for Jeannie as well as for herself. But oh – it wasn't easy! And her bitter disappointment at not seeing Mammy today wasn't helping either.

How, she wondered miserably, could a day that had started off so well have ended so badly?

Because it was Mothering Sunday the children were excused their morning chores for once so that they could go out to gather the wild flowers they would give to their mothers during Matins. Ella and Jeannie were both so excited that not even the icy cold water they had to wash in, stripped to the waist, for their morning ablutions, or the porridge and dry bread that made up their breakfast, could dampen their spirits, though they still sniffed enviously at the delicious aroma of crisp bacon rashers that wafted their way from the table where the staff ate. When the meal was over and they'd helped clear away the dishes, they were escorted out of the workhouse grounds and across the road to the open countryside beyond.

It was a beautiful spring morning, the sky the clean-washed blue of April and scattered with fluffy white clouds, the crisp air full of the fresh sweet scent of dew-wet grass. At first, given a little freedom, the children scattered, taking the opportunity to run about in this paradise, so different to the workhouse exercise yard, where a high wire fence divided the boys' section from the girls'. Then, when Miss Sparks, the assistant mistress who had accompanied them, reminded them sharply why they were here in the meadow, they began hunting for wild flowers to make their posies.

Cowslips, buttercups and daisies nestled amid the rough tufts of meadow grass, clumps of primroses blossomed on the banks, and violets peeped out from the moss around the roots of trees. Ella picked some of each, careful not to damage the delicate stalks, and soon had enough to make a pretty posy. A little further on, in a copse that bordered the field and the river beyond, she spied a cluster of bluebells, and was just making her way towards them when Jeannie came running up to her.

'Look, Ella! See what I found! Isn't it lovely?'

She held out a long-stemmed dandelion.

'Oh – not that one,' Ella said, wrinkling her nose.

Jeannie's face clouded. 'Why not?'

Ella realised that Jeannie had never had the chance to learn about wild flowers – or butterflies and bees, for that matter. She'd been scarcely more than a toddler when they'd been forced to come and live in the workhouse, and never roamed the fields and meadows with Mammy as Ella had.

'It's a weed. We called it a wet-the-bed,' she explained gently. 'You don't want that one.'

'But it's so pretty! It's like the sun!' Jeannie protested.

Ella shook her head, smiling, and sighed.

'Oh, go on then. If you think Mammy will like it.'

'She will! I know she will!'

Jeannie was probably right, Ella thought. She'd like anything Jeannie had picked especially for her. But wild garlic grew here beneath the trees – the air was full of the smell of it – and Ella didn't want Jeannie picking any of the pretty little white flowers because she thought they looked like stars.

'Don't touch that, Jeannie!' she cautioned as her sister made a beeline for the plants. 'Your hands will stink all day. And so will Mammy's if you give it to her.'

'Come along now! Time to go back!' Miss Sparks was calling and clapping her hands.

Reluctantly the children abandoned their treasure hunt and headed in her direction, some – eager to please – making haste, some dawdling. But a small knot of three boys, two big and one little, ignored her altogether, and it looked as if a fight was starting between the two older ones.

'Leo! Arthur! Stop that!' Miss Sparks called, but again she was ignored, and the scuffling only worsened as they fell to the ground, rolling over and over, punching and gouging.

Miss Sparks hitched up her skirts and ran towards them with surprising speed, followed by some of the boys who were eager not to miss a good fisticuffs, while the girls hung back, looking frightened. Not so Ella. Leo Fisher, one of the combatants, was her best friend in the workhouse.

They'd first formed their alliance last summer when they had both been assigned tasks in the garden – Ella a flower bed where she was to deadhead the roses and do some weeding, Leo to dig the vegetable patch and prepare it for planting. Ella had hit a problem with brambles that were invading the rose bed and in trying to remove them she'd scratched her hands and arms so badly that they were bleeding. Leo had noticed, and when the supervisor wasn't looking, he'd come over and helped her cut the brambles back.

'Just give me the nod if there's something you can't manage,' he'd said.

'Thanks.' But she knew she wouldn't call on him. If they were caught they would both be in trouble – especially Leo, who would almost certainly be thrashed with a split cane. But he'd taken that risk today, and she was really grateful. Here in the workhouse acts of kindness were in short supply.

From that day on they'd always exchanged a smile when their paths crossed, and chatted when they had the chance. Ella learned that he was a year older than her, and an orphan who had spent his whole life in the workhouse. As their friendship grew she came to think of him as the big brother she'd never known, but about whom Lilah had often spoken. Mark was his name, and he had died before she was born, when he was just a baby. She'd often wished things had turned out differently and he'd lived to grow up. He would be there for her and Jeannie, looking out for them, making her feel safe, taking some of the burden off her shoulders. But now there was Leo, filling the empty space in her life that Mark would have occupied.

When winter had come and there was no work for her to do in the garden, Ella had seen him mostly only through the wire fence when they were sent out to exercise, or in the classroom, but that happened less frequently now, as Rector Evans who taught the older children had recently singled him out for private tuition. Ella missed him, but took consolation from the fact that there was no risk of him getting into trouble for helping her with her sums, as he had once, when he'd been sitting next to her and seen her struggling, by passing her a slip of paper with his

11

workings and the answer written on it. She'd quickly hidden it beneath her exercise book, but she'd been terrified for the whole of the rest of the lesson, knowing that if the rector found out they'd be severely punished, either with a beating, or, worse, locked for hours in the hell-hole that was the punishment room – bitterly cold, damp, with not so much as a glimmer of daylight, and probably nothing to eat or drink.

When she'd next seen Leo in the exercise yard she'd whispered to him through the fence that he must never do such a thing again, but he'd just grinned and winked at her, his clear blue eyes sparkling like sapphires, and she wasn't convinced he wouldn't risk it.

But that was Leo all over. Kind, clever – his hand was always the first to go up when a question was asked in class – easy-going and fearless. Despite being tall, and quite strong from the hard physical work he had done in the garden during the summer, he wasn't one to throw his weight about or get into fights, even though he was often taunted for being an orphan with no family of his own, or teased about the colour of his hair. 'Ginger' they called him. But Ella thought it was the loveliest shade of red-gold she had ever seen.

Now, as she ran towards the scene of battle, Ella wondered what on earth had happened to involve Leo in such a violent punch-up. Admittedly, Arthur Durbin, the boy he was fighting with, was known for being a bully, but she couldn't imagine what he could have done or said to rile Leo so.

A few moments later she found out.

Eddie Thomas, the little five year old who had been beside them, had now retreated from the scene of the fracas and was watching from a distance, tears and snot running down his freckled face. Taking pity on him, Ella stopped and dropped to a crouch on the springy grass beside him.

'It's all right, Eddie,' she said. 'Nothing to cry about. Just the big boys being silly.'

Eddie rubbed his hands across his face, leaving streaks of dirt and pollen.

'He's got my flowers!' he wailed.

'Who has?' Ella asked.

'Arthur Durbin. He took them away from me and wouldn't give them back. And then . . .' he began to sob again, 'and then he stamped on them!'

'Oh, he shouldn't have done that,' Ella said, shocked. But she understood now why Leo had gone for Arthur. He would have been infuriated by the boy's cruelty.

By now Miss Sparks had separated the scrapping pair, and was chastising them both equally. Ella knew Leo would never snitch on another boy, however much he might deserve it, and certainly Arthur wouldn't own up to what he had done. If anyone was to save Leo from certain punishment for standing up for little Eddie, it would have to be her.

She grasped the child's hand.

'Come on, Eddie. Let's go and tell Miss Sparks what happened.'

He looked up at her, his lip trembling.

'If you tell her, I expect she'll let you pick some more. And I'll help you.'

The boy brightened at once, wiping his eyes with the sleeve of his shirt, and Ella led him over to Miss Sparks, who broke off her rant at Leo and Arthur and turned impatiently to Ella and Eddie.

'What?' she asked, so sharply that tears started to Eddie's eyes again.

'Arthur took Eddie's flowers and stamped on them,' Ella said. 'Isn't that right, Eddie? Leo was just standing up for him.'

Miss Sparks looked to be on the point of ridiculing her, but there in the grass, flattened by the boys' rough and tumble, lay the unmistakable evidence. Cowslips, celandines, even another dandelion or two lay there, crushed and ruined.

'Is this true?' she demanded of Eddie.

The little boy nodded miserably and cringed against Ella, clearly afraid of what Arthur might do to him for dobbing him in.

Ella put an arm round his shoulders. 'I told him you'd let him pick some more, and I'd help him,' she ventured.

Miss Sparks hesitated for a moment, then relented. 'Very well, if that's the case. But be quick about it. Leo – you can help too as long as you stay out of trouble. And Arthur . . .' she grabbed the bully by the collar of his shirt, 'you come with me. We'll see what Mr Yarlett has to say about this.'

Mr Yarlett was the master of the workhouse, and a figure to be feared.

As Miss Sparks started back across the field, dragging a red-faced Arthur along with her, Leo turned to Ella.

'Thanks,' he said, rubbing his cheek. A bruise had already begun to darken and swell, but apart from that, and his shirt hanging loose over the back of his trousers, he looked none the worse for the scrap. 'You saved my bacon there. But you shouldn't have. You might have been for it for speaking out of turn.'

'I wasn't going to let Arthur get away with it and see you in trouble,' Ella said, blushing a little at the praise from her hero.

'Well, we'd better get on with picking these flowers before she changes her mind,' he said, and the smile he gave her made her heart sing.

Leo had helped her out so often; at least now she'd been able to do something for him in return.

* * *

Back at the workhouse the children were lined up for inspection to make sure they were clean, tidy and presentable. Then the girls formed a crocodile with Miss Hopkins, the housemistress, at the front, and Miss Sparks bringing up the rear. The boys, supervised by two of the masters, followed. Of Arthur there was no sign. Perhaps he'd been locked in the punishment room, Ella thought. But she wasn't going to waste her pity on him. What he'd done had been cruel; picking on a boy half his size, stealing the flowers he'd gathered so lovingly for his mother and wantonly destroying them was unforgivable. If he had been put in the punishment room perhaps he'd think twice next time.

The adult inmates were already in church, a dejected bunch in their drab clothes, sitting in the pews halfway down the nave. The children were ushered in behind them. They always arrived just a few minutes before the service began; the longer they had to sit still and wait the more likely they were to be disruptive, in the opinion of the authorities. As they filed into their places some of the adults turned round, seeking out their own child for a wave and a beaming smile.

'Where's Mammy?' Jeannie whispered anxiously, tugging on Ella's sleeve. 'I can't see her.'

'Neither can I . . .' Ella bowed her head as Miss Sparks shushed her into silence, then quickly raised it again, scanning the rows of women for a glimpse of Lilah. Now that they'd turned back to face the altar it was difficult to tell one from the other in their workhouse uniforms and with their hair tucked into mob caps. But she felt sure Mammy wouldn't have turned away without having made eye contact first. A worm of anxiety wriggled in Ella's stomach.

Where *was* she?

15

The service began and as Ella continued to try in vain to locate her mother her anxiety grew. The other children were singing lustily – one of their favourite hymns, 'All Things Bright and Beautiful' – but Ella could only whisper the words and she scarcely noticed the beautiful floral decorations that adorned each window sill and filled every hollow in the great stone pillars that ran the length of the church, even though the rector drew attention to them. Beside her, Jeannie too looked worried, her small face solemn, her lip trembling.

At last it was time for the children to present the flowers they'd gathered to their mothers, who were now assembled at the back of the church in the large open space between the porch and the font. Ella was certain now that Mammy wasn't here – she would have seen her when she'd filed past the pew where the children were sitting – and sure enough as she and Jeannie moved into the aisle Miss Sparks drew them aside. As the signal was given for the line of children to move off she put a restraining hand on each of their shoulders.

'Not you two. Your mother isn't here – she's not well.' Her voice was almost lost in the triumphant music swelling from the organ, but both girls knew what she had said. They'd known it already.

Jeannie gave up the struggle to control her wobbling lip and began to cry, and Ella could feel tears pricking behind her own eyes, but she blinked them back, her fierce pride refusing to allow her to cry in front of Miss Sparks and the entire congregation.

'Hush up now, Jeannie,' Miss Sparks whispered urgently. 'And go back to your seats, both of you.'

As she ushered them back into the pew, Ella could see Leo two rows behind them. As an orphan he had no one to give flowers to either, and had remained in his seat. Now he caught Ella's eye with a questioning look.

She gave a small shake of her head and mouthed the words: 'Mammy's ill.'

'Oh no!' he mouthed back.

Usually a sympathetic word or look from him could cheer Ella. Not today. Once again she bit back her tears and concentrated on trying to comfort her little sister.

Now, lying on her thin mattress with sleep refusing to come, Ella relived every moment of the day that had begun so well and ended so badly.

When the service was over and they had all filed out into the spring sunshine, she had approached Miss Sparks, still clutching her posy.

'Please, miss, can we take our flowers to Mammy when we get back?'

'I shouldn't think so. She's in the infirmary,' Miss Sparks said shortly.

'Please!'

'It's not my place to say yes or no,' Miss Sparks said. 'You'd better ask Miss Hopkins.'

She turned her attention to marshalling her charges into line, and Ella, nervous but determined, went back to the church porch where the housemistress was talking to Rector Evans. She was a formidable figure in her long black cloak, which Ella always thought made her look like a great black crow as it flapped around her angular frame. Iron-grey hair was drawn back into a severe bun and topped with a black felt hat, and a face that Mammy described as 'enough to turn the milk sour' completed the daunting picture. Beside her, Rector Evans looked like a big bird too in his own black cape, only perhaps with his white vestments showing at the neck and hem he looked more like a magpie. *One for sorrow* . . . Ella shivered. There was something about Rector Evans she didn't like at all.

As she approached the pair, Miss Hopkins swung round, glaring.

'Where do you think you are going?' she demanded. 'Rejoin the others at once!'

Gathering her courage, Ella stood her ground. 'Our mammy wasn't well enough to come to church today. Please, could we see her later on so we can give her our flowers?' She held out her bunch imploringly, and added, 'Miss Sparks said to ask you.'

'That won't be possible,' Miss Hopkins said shortly. 'She is in the infirmary, I believe.'

'I know. But . . . it is Mothering Sunday, and we picked them specially . . .'

'I suggest you lay them on one of the graves. Or take them into church and leave them in front of the statue of the Virgin Mary. But whichever it is, do it quickly. You're holding everyone up.'

Ella wasn't going to give up so easily. She didn't want to put her flowers at the feet of a plaster statue or on the grave of someone she'd never known. She wanted to give them to Mammy. Especially if she was ill. Especially if, as Ella feared, this might be the last Mothering Sunday when she'd be able to give her flowers.

'Jeannie has some too,' she said, nodding in the direction of her sister, lined up and waiting in the crocodile with the other children. 'She's going to be so disappointed if she can't give them to Mammy. And they'd cheer Mammy up. Make her feel better.'

'Ella Martin!' The housemistress's voice rose threateningly. 'Do as you have been told at once, or—'

Rector Evans interrupted her, placing a hand on Ella's

shoulder. 'Couldn't an exception be made in this case?' His tone was conciliatory. 'It is Mothering Sunday, after all, as Ella says.'

Ella cringed at his touch, even though she was grateful for his intervention, and she held her breath, hoping Miss Hopkins would change her mind. The housemistress was 'sweet on' the rector, she'd heard some of the older girls say. But although Miss Hopkins' tone softened to one approaching sycophancy, her words were unrelenting.

'You understand, surely, Elijah, we can't have children visiting the infirmary unless they are sick enough to need treatment themselves. They carry all manner of germs.'

'I suppose that's true,' he agreed regretfully. 'But things being what they are, couldn't one of the staff take the flowers to the mother?'

'Would that make you and your sweet little sister feel better, my dear?' he asked, but Ella couldn't help noticing his eyes were on Jeannie.

She wasn't surprised. It was probably because of her sister that he'd spoken out on their behalf. Jeannie was a favourite with everyone. Petite, fragile almost, with her fine fair hair and skin and turquoise eyes fringed with long dark lashes, there was something almost fey about her, as if she belonged not to this world but an enchanted grotto. Beside her, Ella felt clumsy and plain. Being three years older it was only natural she was going to be bigger, but she had never been dainty as Jeannie was, and her colouring, though similar, was far less striking, her eyes muddier, with flecks of brown, her eyelashes stubbier, and her hair several shades darker.

Now, however, she was grateful for the effect Jeannie seemed to have on everyone.

'Thank you, it would,' she managed.

'Very well.' Unsurprisingly, Miss Hopkins was all too anxious to appear reasonable and even kindly in the rector's eyes. 'You can always be relied upon to find the solution to a problem, Elijah.' She turned to Ella. 'Give the flowers to Miss Sparks when you get back to St Peter's and tell her I have said they are to be taken to your mother, with your love. Now, run along, there's a good girl.'

Her tone was honeyed but her cold grey eyes were flashing daggers at Ella, who knew she'd pay for it later.

And so she had.

'How dare you embarrass me in front of the rector?' the housemistress had stormed at Ella before ordering her to hoist up her skirts and administering three stinging slashes to Ella's bare buttocks with her split cane.

Ella made not a sound. She wouldn't give the horrible woman the satisfaction. And when the beating was over she looked up to meet Miss Hopkins' eyes defiantly.

'Let that be a lesson to you, or it will be the worse for you if there's a next time,' the housemistress warned her.

Now, hours later, her buttocks were still stinging, but it had been worth it. At least she'd managed to get the flowers to Mammy.

Or had she? For all she knew Miss Sparks had kept them for herself. Oh, she wouldn't have kept Jeannie's. The little girl had managed to crush them in her hot little fists when she'd got so upset so that they were wilting and the petals falling off. Not that Mammy would mind – they'd be just as precious to her as the most perfect bouquet. But Ella's . . . they had still been fresh and pretty. Just the thing to brighten up the room Miss Sparks shared with three other female staff members . . .

But no! She mustn't think like that. If she did she'd choke up again. The flowers had reached Mammy, she told herself. And

Mammy would be well again soon. Next year, on Mothering Sunday, she and Jeannie would be able to give her their flowers themselves.

Ella closed her eyes, determined to think only positive thoughts, and before long tiredness overcame her and, like Jeannie in the next bed, she slept.

Chapter Two

In spite of the warm sunshine outside it was bitterly cold in the classroom. It almost always was. The thick old stone walls emanated the chill and damp that had seeped into them throughout the winter and never quite warmed up or dried out.

Sitting behind her desk on the wooden form that she shared with her neighbour, Ella shivered, though not just from the cold. She hadn't really stopped shivering since Sunday, a tremble in her stomach that spread through her veins and on to her skin, so that her whole body felt quivery like a half-set jelly, and constant anxiety was a lump in her throat that made her feel sick.

Mammy was still in the infirmary, and Ella knew she wouldn't be able to sleep until she knew she was on the road to recovery. At the moment there seemed to be no sign of that, according to what she'd been told.

She dipped her pen in the inkwell and tried to concentrate on the sums Rector Evans had set them on the blackboard, but the figures blurred before her eyes, and though she knew today's problems were well within her capabilities, she felt sure she was making silly mistakes.

It wasn't helping, either, that the rector seemed to be watching her. Even though her head was bent over her exercise book she could feel his eyes on her, and if she glanced up she could see she was right. Why it was so unsettling she didn't know, but it was. There was something repulsive about the man, with his fleshy lips and jowls that quivered above his clerical collar, and his big flabby hands with fingers like overstuffed sausages.

She shouldn't feel like this about him, she thought. He was a good man, he must be if he was a priest. And he'd talked Miss Hopkins into allowing the flowers they'd picked to be taken to Mammy, even if they hadn't been able to do it themselves. But she couldn't help it.

'He gives me the creeps,' she'd said to Leo once when they were managing a surreptitious chat through the wire fence in the exercise yard.

'Why's that?' Leo had asked.

She'd thought about it. 'For one thing, I don't like the way he smells. Sort of musty and funny . . .'

Leo had laughed. 'You're right there. But he's all right really. He's helping me a lot. Says he thinks I might be able to get a scholarship to a posh school if I work hard.'

'Oh – you're not going away, are you?' Ella's heart had dropped like a stone. The thought of Leo not being here was unbearable.

He'd shrugged. 'I expect it's all talk. But really, he's not so bad when you get to know him.'

'I suppose,' she'd said doubtfully.

But now, in the classroom, with his eyes constantly on her, she was feeling uncomfortable all over again. And even worse, when the lesson came to an end and the pupils were filing out, he drew her aside.

'A word, Ella.'

Was she going to be told off for not concentrating on the lesson properly? Ella supposed she deserved to be. But when

23

they were alone, the smile he gave her was benign, and not at all like the prelude to a wigging.

'You're a clever girl, Ella, but you're not being stretched enough,' he said. 'In class we have to go at a pace that suits everyone, and I can't give you the attention you deserve. I'm going to suggest to Mr Yarlett that I give you some extra lessons.'

'Oh!' Ella was startled. 'Like Leo, you mean?'

'In a way, yes. Not with him, of course. He's a year older than you, and I'm preparing him for an entrance examination to a good school. He can go far, that lad. But so could you, with the right tuition.'

'You mean . . . you'd put me in for an exam?' Ella asked, daunted by the very thought of it.

'No. I'm not sure higher education is for girls.' The rector smiled indulgently. 'But there are other paths you and your sister could take, with a little help from me. You're what – eleven now? That gives us two years before Miss Hopkins will be looking to find you a position – as a scullery maid, more likely than not. You're worth more than that, Ella, and so is Jeannie. But let's concentrate on you for the moment. If you make the progress I think you can, I'd be happy to recommend you to the governors of the church school as an assistant there. In time, you could well become a teacher yourself, or a governess. Now, what do you say to that?'

It had never occurred to Ella that when the time came for her to start work she could ever be anything more than a maidservant, considering herself lucky to leave the workhouse behind, even if it did mean getting up at the same unearthly hour, carrying out similar menial chores, and still having to share a room, maybe even a bed, with the other maids. The very idea of being able to work with children, helping them with their reading, writing and sums, picking them up when they fell over and tending to their grazed knees, comforting the little newcomers who were missing their mammies – it sounded like a fairy tale, something she would never have dared to even dream of.

She wished she would be sharing the extra classes with Leo, though she knew she'd struggle to keep up with him. The thought of being alone with the rector made her uncomfortable. She supposed she'd have to sit next to him while he coached her, and smell that horrible smell that made her feel sick. But if it meant that she would have the chance of working in the church school, then it would be worth it.

'I'd really like to work with children,' she said.

'And you'd be prepared to attend extra lessons, and study in what free time you have?'

Ella nodded. Though what free time he was talking about she didn't know. 'Yes.'

'Good.' The rector smiled at her. She didn't like his smile, either, she realised. It made him look self-satisfied rather than friendly. 'Then we'll begin next week. I can spare an hour following the class lesson. And by then we'll have had the burial . . .' He broke off, adjusting his expression to a serious one. 'I'm very sorry about your mother, Ella. I will be praying for her, and for you and Jeannie, that you may find comfort.'

Ella stared at him for a moment, uncomprehending. Then a trickle of ice ran down her spine and her knees felt as if they would give way beneath her.

'What . . . ?'

What do you mean? she had intended to say, but the words stuck in her throat.

The rector frowned. 'Haven't you been told?'

Ella's stricken face gave him his answer.

'Oh dear, oh dear. Then it falls to me to break the sad news.

Your dear Mama left us in the early hours of the morning to be with Jesus.'

The room was spinning around her, shock making her weak and dizzy. She swayed, and the rector caught her by the arms, lowering her into the chair behind the teacher's desk and pushing her head down between her knees.

'Oh, my child . . .' His voice was sympathetic now, though Ella could not hear his words over the buzzing in her ears as the blood rushed back into her head.

When at last she straightened up, she realised he was crouched beside her.

'Mammy's dead?' she whispered.

'I'm afraid so. She died very peacefully in her sleep. You and your sister should have been informed. I assumed you had, and that was the reason you were finding it difficult to concentrate on your classwork. This is shocking . . . shocking.'

'I was worrying about her. I knew she was really bad, but I didn't know . . .' Tears filled Ella's eyes and ran down her cheeks, and for once she did nothing to try to control them. 'I didn't know she was . . . Oh, Mammy! Mammy!'

The rector put an arm around her, pulling her into his shoulder. With her face buried in his cassock the smell she detested was strong, but now Ella was scarcely aware of it. Mammy was dead – nothing else was registering. Not even that, really.

It shouldn't have come as such a shock to her – wasn't it exactly what she'd been afraid of? But it had. It had! And the finality of it was like falling into a bottomless pit.

She'd never see Mammy again. Never feel her arms around her. Never hear her laugh or sing. Never . . .

The tears flowed, hot and salty, stinging her eyes and burning her cheeks, and sobs shook her thin frame with every breath she drew.

Mammy . . . Oh Mammy . . . No! No! No!

After a few minutes her chaotic thoughts and emotions began to crystallise and she raised her head, turning her red and swollen eyes to the rector. 'What . . . What will happen now?'

The rector fished a clean white handkerchief out of the sleeve of his cassock, wiped her face gently, then handed it to her so that she could blow her nose. 'In what respect, my dear?'

'Everything! What will happen to Mammy?'

'She'll be given a Christian burial and laid to rest in the workhouse cemetery. I shall officiate, of course.'

She nodded, biting her lip. 'And me and Jeannie?'

'You will be looked after just as you have been ever since you've been here. Until you are old enough to leave us and go out into the world. It's one of the reasons I'm eager to begin our extra tuition as soon as possible. So that you will be well prepared to find some occupation that will ensure you are never forced to return.'

'But what about Jeannie? I can't leave her here all on her own . . .' The tears began again.

'Don't worry about that. It's a long way in the future yet. By the time you leave she will be almost as old as you are now.'

'But she's . . .' Ella didn't know how to put into words the feeling she always had, that Jeannie was somehow vulnerable, and not just because she was three years younger. Then another thought struck her.

'She doesn't know about Mammy yet, does she? How am I going to tell her? I can't do it! I don't know how . . .'

'Don't upset yourself, Ella. I shall see to it that Miss Hopkins speaks to her immediately. I fail to understand why she hasn't already done so.'

No! Not her! Not that horrible, cruel woman! The words were

27

loud inside Ella's head, as if someone outside herself was speaking to her.

Ella squeezed her eyes tight shut, cutting off the tears and gathering her courage. The housemistress would state the facts baldly, without an ounce of compassion or sympathy, she knew that only too well. Jeannie was going to be devastated whoever gave her the news, but Ella knew she couldn't allow her to hear it from Miss Hopkins.

'No.' She said it aloud this time, her voice tremulous but determined. 'She's my sister. I've got to be the one to tell her. I'll find a way somehow.'

Rector Evans nodded slowly. 'Very well, if that is what you would prefer. It's very brave of you, Ella.' He placed a hand on her shoulder again. 'Would you like me to be there with you?'

Ella bit her lip hard. For all that she disliked the rector, he was being very kind, kinder than anyone else had ever been in this horrible place. She nodded slowly. 'Would you?'

'Of course. Wait here and I'll fetch her.'

'Her lessons will be over by now, I expect,' Ella said.

The little ones were taught by Miss Owen in another classroom, but sometimes, if they were restless, they were allowed to finish early.

'I'll find her, don't worry.'

Left alone, Ella twisted the rector's handkerchief between her hands, wondering how best to break the news to Jeannie, and another solitary tear rolled down her cheek. She brushed it away impatiently. She didn't want her sister to catch her crying. Somehow she had to be strong for both of them.

A few minutes passed before Rector Evans was back with Jeannie, whom he'd found sweeping the floor of the dining hall with a broom almost as tall as she was. Her small face was clouded with apprehension; she might be only eight years old but Ella suspected she had already guessed there was bad news to come.

The moment she saw Ella, Jeannie ran to her, grasping her knees and gazing at her fearfully. Ella put her arms around her little sister, hugging her.

'Jeannie . . .' Her voice faltered, the words refusing to come.

'Jeannie, your sister has something very sad to tell you,' the rector said, his tone suitably doleful. 'You must be a brave girl, as she is.'

Again, Jeannie's eyes, full of panic, met Ella's, and the older girl swallowed the knot of tears that was constricting her throat.

'It's Mammy, Jeannie. She's gone to be with the angels, the rector says.'

Jeannie's mouth fell open, her eyes widening. Then her chin began to tremble and she pushed Ella away as if she could distance herself from what she was hearing.

'No!' she cried. 'No, she can't have! She'd get well, you said. You promised!'

'It isn't within your sister's power to promise such things,' the rector said. 'It is the Heavenly Father's will that prevails.'

Ella's heart, which felt as if it were being ripped out of her body, seemed suddenly to turn to a block of stone, hard as the rocks that edged her flower garden.

'So why do you tell us to pray if it does no good?' she demanded, her small face ravaged with grief and despair. 'What's the point if He doesn't listen?'

'He hears you, my child. And He will comfort you.'

The rector was well used to uttering such platitudes to grieving members of his flock; they tumbled from his lips without any real conviction. But he had long ago learned to conceal any doubts he might entertain, just as he had learned to control, and hide, the dark urges that sometimes assailed him, and for which

29

he asked forgiveness not from a confessor but, alone in front of the altar of his church, directly from God.

Assuming his most pious expression, he reached out to lay his hand on Ella's head, as if imparting a blessing.

A face peeked around the door. It was Miss Owen, who had been teaching the younger children this afternoon. She had been shocked to learn from Miss Sparks that little Jeannie's mother was dead – a terrible thing for any child, but especially one as delicate and vulnerable as Jeannie – and as she passed the schoolroom and heard the rector droning on in the voice he used for sermons she had decided she would do what she could to comfort the sisters.

'My dears.' Ignoring the rector, she crossed the room and put an arm round each of the weeping children. 'Why don't you two come with me? We'll find somewhere nice and quiet and sit down for a bit.'

Dazed, grief-stricken, Ella and Jeannie did as she suggested.

'Can we see Mammy, please?

The thick fug that had dulled Ella's brain, so that each thought had to be pulled out like a thread through cotton wool, had cleared a little, though her thoughts were still random and disjointed.

Miss Owen had taken them to an empty office, fetched strong sweet tea and even a bag of biscuits, and stayed with them, offering what comfort she could. Now, at Ella's request, her brow furrowed above her wire-rimmed spectacles.

'I'm not sure that's a very good idea, Ella.'

'Why not?' Ella's lips thrust into a stubborn purse. 'Is she still in the infirmary?'

'No, she will have been taken to the mortuary, and that's no place for children.'

'I don't care where she is,' Ella said. 'We want to see her, don't we, Jeannie?'

Jeannie nodded, sucking on her thumb.

'And could we take her some flowers? We weren't allowed on Mothering Sunday.'

Miss Owen shook her head sadly. 'It's not for me to say. But are you quite sure you're ready for this?' She gave Ella a deep, questioning look, her reservations about the wisdom of this clear in her eyes.

'Yes,' Ella said determinedly. 'We're sure.'

Miss Owen rose, still looking anxious. 'Then I'll see what I can do.'

When she had left the room Jeannie clutched at Ella's sleeve. 'What will she look like, Ella?' Her voice trembled with trepidation.

'Like she's asleep.'

Ella wasn't at all sure about it. She'd never seen a dead person, but it was what she'd heard people say. She hoped it was true, and in all honesty she was apprehensive herself. But she couldn't let them bury Mammy without seeing her one last time.

At last Miss Owen was back, and both girls raised expectant eyes to her face.

'I have permission to take you to the mortuary,' she said.

'And the flowers?' Ella wasn't going to let it go.

'Not today. It will be dark soon. But you can pick some to lay on her grave when she's buried.'

For a brief moment it looked as if Ella was about to argue, then she nodded, apparently satisfied.

'Come along then,' Miss Owen said.

The mortuary was cold and dank, the air thick with a vile odour that Ella had never smelled before and never wanted to smell

31

again – sickly sweet, with overtones of disinfectant. It made her feel sick again, and she pressed her hand over her mouth and swallowed the bile that rose in her throat. Miss Owen had remained in the corridor outside, handing them into the care of a male orderly, but as they stepped into the cavernous basement room Jeannie tore her hand away from Ella's and fled, back the way they had come.

Ella hesitated, wondering if she should go after her. But if she did, she might not be allowed back, and she was desperate to see Mammy. Miss Owen would take care of Jeannie whilst she did what she had to do.

The orderly led the way across the flagstoned floor, past big wooden tables that were stained like the chopping board Mammy used to use when she was cutting up meat for a stew, to a trestle on which lay an open box. Ella wasn't tall enough to see inside from here, but her heart was beating an uneven tattoo so it felt as if it was going to leap right out of her chest. Along the way the orderly picked up a stool, and set it alongside the trestle.

'You ready then?' he asked.

He lifted Ella, his big hands almost circling her waist, and steadied her on the stool.

Without even realising what she was doing, Ella had closed her eyes. Now, taking a long trembling breath, she opened them.

The coffin was made of cheap, thin wood, and lined with the same kind of rough material as their bedsheets, and a flimsy lid with Lilah's name chalked on it rested against the trestle, but Ella noticed none of that. All she could see was Mammy, still and white as a marble statue, with her hands crossed over her chest. Two pennies lay on her eyelids, so that they were hollow copper pools instead of the greeny-blue that Ella and Jeannie had inherited, and her nut-brown hair spread across the thin pillow was still mussed from tossing and turning in her infirmary bed, and dull and lifeless as Lilah herself.

She doesn't look as if she's asleep, Ella thought. She looks . . . as if she's not really there at all. The body in the cheap coffin was no more Mammy than the workhouse nightgown that was buttoned to her chin.

But empty shell or not, it *was* her, or all that was left of her. Tentatively, Ella reached out and touched one of Mammy's hands, then quickly withdrew it. Cold! So cold! Ella looked away, fighting to control the confused emotions that were not at all what she had expected to feel, and noticed the way the sheet was raised over Mammy's feet, as if it were hung over the end poles of the clothes horse. This shocked her too.

'Had enough, then?' The orderly's tone was rough but kindly, and he made to lift Ella down.

'No.' With an effort Ella regained control of herself. 'I have to tell her something first.'

The man stood aside. He often talked to the dead himself, alone here in the mortuary.

'Go on then.'

Summoning all her reserves of courage, Ella covered Mammy's cold hand with her own, and this time it didn't seem so bad.

'Don't worry, Mammy,' she said softly. 'We'll be all right. And I'll look after Jeannie, I promise.'

I know you will. It was as if Mammy had spoken loud and clear inside her head.

Tears rose in Ella's throat; determinedly she swallowed them. She didn't want the orderly to see her cry – and if Mammy was somewhere nearby, watching, she didn't want her to see them either.

'God bless, Mammy,' she whispered, and with one last look

at the marble cast of the mother she loved, she turned to the orderly.

'Thank you. I'm ready now,' she said.

The burial, such as it was, took place two days later, not just for Lilah, but also an old man who had died the following day.

Ella and Jeannie, carrying the flowers they had been allowed to gather that morning, followed the coffins to the workhouse cemetery, holding hands tightly, and with Miss Owen walking beside them. Ahead, leading the procession, was Rector Evans, his white surplice billowing in a stiff breeze. Behind him walked the wife of the man who was to be interred. There were no other mourners. The other inmates could have attended if they so wished, but no one did. Though Lilah had been well liked, the bleak ceremony was all too clear a reminder of their own circumstances, and the old rhyme: 'Rattle his bones, over the stones. He's only a pauper nobody owns.'

Fittingly, the sky had clouded over and the first few drops of rain fell as the rector intoned the time-honoured words and tossed a handful of earth on to the cheap wooden box. Not so long ago this had been unconsecrated ground, but now it had been blessed he felt comfortable conducting the last rites in the same way as he would in his own churchyard.

Miss Owen had suggested the girls should each tug one flower out of their posies and drop it on to the coffin, then place the remainder beside the pile of earth that would be shovelled back into the grave. She nodded to them, indicating that this was the moment. Ella released Jeannie's hand to do just that, and the cowslip fluttered down and came to rest on the coffin at the very spot she imagined covered Mammy's heart.

'I love you. I always will,' she whispered, then squeezed Jeannie's hand. 'Your turn.'

But her sister's face was distorted with anguish, the posy crushed between her tightly fisted hands. She wailed, the most heart-rending sound Ella had ever heard, dashed the posy to the ground, and took to her heels, running as fast as she could across the uneven ground, tufted with weeds, and between the mounds of old graves.

Miss Owen ran after her, catching her easily when she tripped and fell headlong. Ella looked down once more on the wooden box that contained her mother's earthly remains.

'I have to go, Mammy,' she said softly. 'Jeannie needs me.'

Then she turned away, setting off towards her distraught little sister and hoping she could find some way to comfort her.

That night, when the lights were put out and the dormitory door closed after the housemistress, Jeannie climbed into Ella's bed.

'Jeannie . . . you shouldn't . . .'

But she didn't have the heart to turn her away, and in any case she wanted her sister close just as Jeannie did. The two girls cuddled together, Jeannie's tears soaking the neck of Ella's nightgown, but at last her snuffles quietened – tired out by grief and the horrible events of the day, she had fallen asleep.

Still wide awake herself, Ella's thoughts returned to Mammy, and in the darkness she seemed to see Mammy's face as she had looked in her coffin and remembered with a shiver just how cold she had felt. She must be even colder now, lying in her grave covered by all that dank earth. The thought was so dreadful she almost cried out, but somehow she controlled herself. She mustn't wake Jeannie. She mustn't upset her again. Her sister was her responsibility now. Somehow she must find the strength to keep the promise she had made to Mammy; somehow she must make sure Jeannie didn't suffer any more than she had to.

And she would! She would! No matter how many nights she lay awake seeing Mammy's dead face in the darkness, no matter how many days she had to devote to looking after Jeannie, whatever it cost her, she'd do it.

Ella pulled her sister even closer, letting the warmth of the small body warm her so that the ice in her veins thawed a little. She was beginning to become drowsy when she heard the creak of the dormitory door; her eyes flew open and her heart thudded into her throat as she saw a shadowy figure in the doorway, holding a lamp aloft.

Oh no . . . please no . . .

Hardly daring to breathe, she waited, expecting the blanket to be wrenched from their entwined bodies at any moment.

But when she risked a peep again the figure with the lamp was gone and she heard the click of the door closing again. Either they'd been lucky enough not to be seen, or the mistress, whoever it had been, had decided to leave them be this once.

Whispering a prayer of thanks, Ella closed her eyes, and this time the image of Mammy was as she had been before the sickness had claimed her. Smiling, warm, loving.

As she drifted towards sleep Ella fancied she felt a hand smoothing her hair away from her forehead, and a feeling of peace filled her. As she looked out for Jeannie, helping her in any way she could, Mammy would be beside her. Watching over her. Watching over them both. It was all she could hope for, all she needed to strengthen her for the days, weeks and months that lay ahead. And it would be enough.

Chapter Three

The Three Feathers – April 1896

On the nights when the skittles team was playing a home match, the public bar of the Three Feathers was always much quieter than usual, and tonight was no exception. Instead of the usual buzz of chatter, the silence was broken only by the rumble of falling skittles carrying across from the alley on the other side of the yard, together with the roar of approval from the other team members and spectators when someone scored a hit that brought down all nine pins at once or succeeded in wiping out a last lone skittle. In the nook beside the fireplace old Percy Green and his brother Maurice sipped their pints and puffed on their pipes, sending clouds of fragrant smoke wafting across the room, and Minnie Weaver, who had once, long ago, been known for obliging clients with her favours behind a hedge or against a wall in return for a shilling or two, sat alone at her usual table surrounded by the three hessian bags she carried everywhere with her. What they contained, no one knew, or asked. Minnie drank far more than was good for her and had gone a bit daft in the head, folk said. Whatever, it was a fair conclusion that no one would be seeking her services nowadays.

Behind the bar Martha Packer was also alone. Her husband Seb, landlord of the Three Feathers, was also a key member of the skittles team, which played in the local league. Later, when the match was over and the players and spectators poured back into the bar, queuing three deep for pints of beer, pickled eggs and pork scratchings, he'd be there to help her serve, but for the moment he was needed elsewhere. The team was doing well in the league and Seb was a high scorer, who often managed a 'spare' by wiping out all nine skittles with his first balls so that the third gave him a further shot at a full board.

As another roar went up on the other side of the yard, Martha smiled to herself. It sounded as if things were going the way of the home team, and she took pride in the success, as well as the standing which the Feathers enjoyed in the locality. She loved the pub, loved the warm and friendly atmosphere, loved being here at what most often felt like the very heart of the village of Fossecombe, and knew in her heart, though she was too modest to ever say as much, that she had contributed to its success, managing to be welcoming to the customers while at the same time standing for no nonsense from them, while Seb would go to any lengths to avoid a confrontation. To think that she'd started out here as a barmaid almost twenty years ago and was now the landlady was a source of enormous satisfaction to her.

From the very beginning she'd enjoyed the life, so different to the soul-destroying monotony of stitching gloves at the factory in Hillsbridge where she'd worked since leaving school. She'd defied her horrified parents to take the job, determined to escape the whirr of the machines and the surly, slave-driving overseer, fed up with being shut indoors when the sun was shining outside, and having to work with nineteen other women and girls. Not all of them were catty gossips, of course, but the sprinkling of those that were soured the atmosphere. And they had showed too much interest, too, in trying to discover the ins and outs of the apparently abrupt end to her relationship with Joe Hill, her sweetheart, who had disappeared off the scene some six months earlier. That was something Martha had no intention of talking about and the job at the Feathers had provided her with a welcome escape from all that.

Nowadays, the pub was the centre of her world, encompassing everything she held dear. Seb, her husband and her rock. Almost sixteen years they'd been married, and she'd never once had cause to regret it. Her three sons, Garth, fifteen now, and working as a labourer on her brother Ernie's farm, Conrad, at eleven, a sensitive dreamer, and Lewis, just eight, who was, she sometimes thought, already more mature than his two older brothers put together. Here, too, were precious memories of the three children she had lost in infancy and the one who had not even lived to draw breath. Teddy would have been thirteen now and Dicken twelve had they not succumbed to whooping cough within a week of one another when they were toddlers, and Lily, her only daughter, had been three years old when she'd contracted measles and followed her brothers to their grave. Her death had hit Martha the hardest of all – her little girl, pretty as a picture with her dark ringlets, blue eyes and winning smile, dainty as a fairy in her pink pinafores and slippers with matching ribbons in her hair. Martha had looked forward to sharing things with her she'd never be able to share with the boys, but it wasn't to be. For a time she'd been terrified of losing one of the others too, but her prayers had been answered, and though she still carried the lost children in her heart, and laid flowers on their graves on their birthdays and the anniversaries of their deaths, she counted herself lucky. At least she still had three healthy boys who had survived the most dangerous years, and now, barring accidents, would grow to adulthood.

Martha wasn't thinking of any of that now though. She was wondering if she'd take the opportunity of the lull to pop out to the kitchen and set the copper on to heat the water they'd need for washing glasses at closing time. Lewis would be in the kitchen with his nose in a book and he could run in and tell her if it came to the boil, though she'd warn him not to try to take it off the heat himself. He wasn't big enough or old enough to handle it safely and neither Garth nor Conrad would be there to help him. Garth had gone out for the evening with his pals – Martha dreaded to think what they might be getting up to – and Conrad was earning himself a shilling acting as sticker-up for the skittles match.

Just then, however, she heard the rasp of the door that opened on to the street as it scraped over the cobbled floor. A customer at this time of the evening when a home skittles match was being played was unusual, but whoever it was would want serving. As Martha waited expectantly the inner door opened and a man came in, big, ruddy-faced, with a growth of dark stubble on his chin, though what hair was left on his head was streaked with grey. It was her brother.

'Ernie!' she exclaimed, surprised. 'What are you doing here?'

'Well, that's a pretty welcome and no mistake!'

Because he was a farmer, Ernie Wells, three years older than Martha, had to be up at the crack of dawn and he liked to be early to bed. It might be only just before nine in the evening, but for Ernie that was late to be out and about. And he wasn't one for visiting pubs either, even his sister's, though he was fond enough of a jug of cider or a tot of whisky at home. His ruddy complexion wasn't all down to weathering, Martha sometimes thought.

'It's not like you, that's all.' Martha flashed him a warm smile. 'It's nice to see you though.'

Ernie perched on one of the bar stools. 'I'm not sure you'll say that when you hear what I've got to say.'

Martha's smooth brow furrowed, her dark brown eyes narrowing. 'Is something wrong? Lizzie, or one of the children?'

'No, nothing to do with them. I wanted a word with you about Garth.'

'Oh.' Martha's heart sank.

Much as she loved her eldest son, Garth had always been something of a worry to her. Right from babyhood he'd been a rascal and into everything, but he was such an adorable child it was hard to be cross with him for long. As he grew older the scrapes he got into were of course far more serious, but still he employed his undoubted charm to escape punishment.

If he and his pals played knock-out-ginger or left a parcel with a length of string attached in the middle of the path, hiding in the bushes and jerking it away when a passer-by went to pick it up, it was never Garth who was caught and given a hiding. If he got into a fight, it was always the other boy who was blamed for starting it. If he cheated at marbles or conkers, he was a past master at wriggling out of it; if he secretly swapped a duplicate cigarette card for one he wanted for his set when his friends weren't looking, he slipped away before anyone noticed they had the wrong card. And if he was caught stealing biscuits or apples, he always had an excuse – he'd taken them to give to a beggar, or one of the Baker children, who were perpetually hungry because their family was poor as church mice as well as ragged and filthy.

Sometimes Martha despaired of him, but she loved him dearly and always made excuses for him to Seb – to avoid him getting a hiding for his naughtiness – and to his brothers, who were often frustrated and cross with him for his devious ways.

As he approached school-leaving age she fretted constantly at the thought of him going down the coal mines, which was really the only option for local lads. Seb said it would be the making of him, and he'd probably be started on the screens, sorting coal in the colliery yard. But she knew it wouldn't be long before he was sent underground to work as a carting boy, and she couldn't bear the thought of it. Carting was a terrible job, and meant crawling along the narrow and faulted seams on all fours, dragging a putt of coal by a rope that encircled the waist and was attached to a chain and hook, known as the guss and crook. It was dangerous work because besides the seams – too low for pit ponies – there were also the steep inclines – 'topples' and 'dipples' – to be negotiated, and if a carting boy lost control of his heavy putt he could be dragged down and thrown clean over the top of it. One boy she knew of had died after scraping the whole length of his back on the roof of the dipple, tearing away great chunks of flesh.

Even if Garth escaped something so disastrous, his waist would be rubbed raw by the encircling rope, and the coal dust that got into the wound and into his veins would leave scars that would never completely disappear. It broke her heart to think of her handsome son marked for life, and she worried too about the coal dust he would inhale that caused the lung disease so many old miners suffered from.

Eventually, unable to bear the prospect any longer, she'd gone to Ernie, her brother, and begged him to take Garth on as a labourer on his farm. To her enormous relief he'd agreed, albeit reluctantly – he was a tenant farmer, and could ill afford to pay another wage.

'Don't worry about paying him, Ernie,' she'd said. 'I won't take anything from him for his board and lodging, so whatever he earns he can keep for himself. If it comes to that, I'll reimburse you for his wages.'

'And what would Seb have to say about that?' Ernie had asked gruffly.

'Just leave Seb to me. The Feathers is doing all right, and we've kept Garth all his life so far, we can go on doing it for a bit longer. Believe you me, I'd do anything to keep him out of that darned pit.'

'Well, if it means that much to you, our Martha, I'll take him on,' Ernie had said. 'But you can forget about giving me anything to cover his wages. You know as well as I do it would only cause trouble, and it's a bad job if I can't do something to help my sister out.'

Garth hadn't been too enthusiastic about the idea either. He didn't want to become a farm labourer any more than he wanted to be a carting boy. But he didn't really have any option, though he made up his mind that he'd be keeping his eye out for something better, and if nothing came along he'd leave home when he was old enough and seek his fortune in Bath, Bristol, or maybe even London. But for the time being, at just thirteen, he supposed he was best off at home in a comfortable bed with his mother putting food on the table and doing his laundry, and for the moment that was the way it had stayed.

He'd been working on the farm for just over two years now, and Martha had thought he was settled there. She'd stopped worrying about him so much, though she was still concerned about what he got up to when he wasn't under Ernie's eagle eye. That was the trouble with Garth, you never knew what he would get up to next. And now here was Ernie, come to see her when it was past his bedtime, wanting to talk to her about Garth, and not looking too happy about it.

'Can I get you a drink?' she asked.

'I'll have a drop of Teacher's, if you're offering.'

She measured a double into a glass and set it on the counter.

'Well, whatever it is you've got to say, you'd better spit it out,' she said, bracing herself.

Ernie took a gulp of his whisky before speaking.

'Well, there's one or two things I think you ought to know. For starters, I caught him in the hay barn the other day with Polly, our dairymaid, and you can guess what they were up to.'

Martha's jaw dropped. 'What? Our Garth? Never! He's only fifteen . . .'

Ernie grunted. 'Old enough, Martha. Surely you can remember what boys are like at that age, because I certainly can. Always after whatever they can get their hands on. I can mind you coming running home one day in a right old state because Teddy Jackson tried to get inside your frock.'

'That's true enough.' The afternoon when Teddy Jackson, a big lad, already six feet tall and broad with it, had grabbed her from behind, pressing her back against him, with his hands kneading her breasts and pulling at the buttons of her blouse, was etched in her memory as clearly as if it were yesterday. It had been her first encounter of its kind, and she had been so shocked and upset she'd never quite forgotten it, though she knew now it hadn't really counted in the great scheme of things.

'Well, if that's all it was . . .' she said.

'I'm not so sure it was.' Ernie took another gulp of his whisky. 'They'd both been missing some time, long enough for me to go looking, and from the state of them they'd been doing a bit of rolling around. Polly's hair was all messed up, with bits of straw in it, and I could swear Garth were doing up his trousers afore he came down the ladder.'

'Oh my goodness,' Martha said, shocked all over again.

'I'm not having that sort of goings-on,' Ernie said firmly. 'I had a few words to say to them, I can tell you. Told them they'd both get their marching orders if such a thing ever happened again. And I think Lizzie spoke to Polly too. But I'm thinking Seb ought to give Garth a talking-to about what might come of it if that's what he's getting up to.'

'I'll see to it.' Martha had no intention of telling Seb; she'd deal with it herself as she always did where Garth was concerned. She pointed to Ernie's glass, which was almost empty. 'D'you want another one?'

Ernie hesitated, thinking of his early start in the morning, but considering what he still had to tell Martha he thought he could do with it.

'Go on then. Just a drop. And you'd better put a spot of water in it.'

Martha poured another measure, hoping Seb wouldn't notice how much the bottle had gone down. He wouldn't be impressed by her giving away the profits, even if it was for her brother. She added a splash of water from the jug that stood on the bar and pushed the glass towards Ernie.

'There you are then. And I'm glad you told me, even if I'm not best pleased to hear it.'

Ernie took a swig of the whisky.

'Trouble is, Martha, that's not all. There's something else. Now, I've got no proof of this, but Lizzie's been missing money out of her purse.'

An icy chill trickled down Martha's spine and immediately she was on the defensive.

'So if you've got no proof, why are you telling me?' she demanded.

'Because the fact of the matter is Garth's the only one who's been in the house today aside from me and Lizzie and the kiddies. And it's not the first time it's happened, though it's the first I've got to hear of it.'

'Perhaps Lizzie's made a mistake – it's easily done,' Martha said. 'I often forget what I've spent and think I've got more than I have.'

'Not our Lizzie. She can always account for every penny.'

'Oh!' Martha scoffed. 'She's got to be perfect, of course.'

'Now don't let's get nasty about this, Martha,' Ernie said evenly. There was no love lost between his sister and his wife, he knew, but he wouldn't stand by and have Lizzie bad-mouthed. 'I'm telling you because I thought you ought to know. I haven't spoken to Garth about it myself – I know he'll only deny it – but I reckon you should. And you can tell him that if he doesn't mend his ways he'll find himself out of a job. I'm not standing for his nonsense any more. Not even for you, Martha. Comes a point—'

'Yes, all right. I'll talk to him.' There was still an edge to her voice, though she was making an enormous effort to be conciliatory. The last thing she wanted was for Ernie to refuse to have Garth working at the farm any longer. 'And I'm sorry if he's been giving you trouble. I'll do my best to make sure he behaves himself from now on.'

'The problem is his middle name is Trouble. This today was just the last straw.' Ernie drained his glass. 'I'll be making tracks, then. But mind you tell him . . . if things don't change for the better . . .'

'I know. Thanks, Ernie. And . . . I really am sorry.'

When Ernie had finished his drink and left, Martha turned to the spirit shelf and poured herself a large gin, her hand shaking. She seldom drank, unless a customer insisted on buying her one; like Seb she was all too aware she'd be drinking the profits, and in any case she didn't want to make a habit of it. But goodness me, she needed one now!

As if the tumble with the milkmaid wasn't bad enough, Ernie's accusation of Garth stealing from Lizzie's purse was worse because she already had suspicions of her own that she'd been missing money and had tried to dismiss them. Rascal he might be, but she hadn't been able to bring herself to believe he'd actually do something like that – stealing from anyone, let alone his own family.

Now she could no longer get away from it. Though she'd flown to his defence, her stomach had turned as she'd faced the truth – Garth was a thief. And who knew what else he might be capable of?

A roar from the skittle-alley interrupted her racing thoughts. While she'd been talking to Ernie she'd lost track of time; now it sounded as if the match was over. At any moment the rush would begin. Martha downed her gin in one gulp – she didn't want Seb to catch her drinking – and put her glass beside the sink. Then she forced a smile and turned to face the crowd of men pouring into the bar from the skittle-alley.

Tired though she was after a long day which hadn't finished until she and Seb had washed dozens of glasses, wiped down the bar and the tables and swept the floor, Martha couldn't sleep. Garth had come home whilst they were still clearing up and gone straight upstairs to his room; there had been no chance to speak to him alone, and in any case, Martha hadn't yet decided the best way to approach what she knew would be a difficult conversation.

As the grandmother clock at the foot of the stairs struck two she was still wide awake, her thoughts chasing one another in never-ending circles, and the knot of anxiety sitting in her stomach like a lump of undigested food.

This was what she'd always been afraid of, that Garth's misdemeanours would only get more serious as he grew up. That he had bad blood in his veins, and that nothing she could do could change that. Heaven alone knew – she'd tried. A sense of utter helplessness and despair engulfed Martha. Who knew where it would end?

Beside her, Seb was snoring gently. If only she could talk it over with him as she did everything else, she thought. There were no secrets between them, but this one subject was never discussed. Never had been in sixteen years of marriage. And the silence was part of an unspoken agreement. Garth was her problem and hers alone. Somehow she had to deal with the consequences of what had happened all those years ago.

Staring into the darkness, Martha remembered.

Chapter Four

Hillsbridge and Fossecombe – 1879

None of it would have happened if Joe hadn't left Fossecombe. Her life would have turned out quite differently. If he'd been ready to settle down they'd no doubt have married, had a family, and brought them up in a miner's cottage. At least, that was the way Martha had always hoped it would go. He'd given her a pretty ring the birthday before last, and though he hadn't said it was an engagement ring, and hadn't corrected her when she put it on the third finger of her right hand, it had meant the world to Martha. Perhaps it wasn't real silver, perhaps the greeny-blue stone was just glass, but to her it was precious.

Though he was a couple of years older than her, she and Joe had been sweethearts from schooldays. Martha was head-over-heels in love and had no doubts but that Joe was the one she wanted to spend the rest of her life with. But by the time she was nineteen and Joe twenty-one, things were changing, and not for the better.

At first, when he began making excuses to see her less often, she had been afraid he was seeing other girls. In fact, nothing could have been further from the truth.

Joe had always been fond of placing a bet on a horse or the result of a football match and he liked to visit Ticker Bendle, the bookmaker, himself, rather than writing his selection on a scrap of paper and giving it to one of the bookie's runners – lads who waited outside the public houses on paydays when the teams of miners shared out their earnings. One Saturday afternoon, whilst loitering in Ticker's office, he'd met a friend of Ticker's who was also involved in the world of betting, but in a much larger and more lucrative way. He ran an undercover gambling club in the basement of a seedy hostelry in Bath, and invited Joe to pay him a visit one evening. Intrigued, Joe had put the idea to one of his pals, Mark Freeman, and the two of them had taken the club owner up on his suggestion.

Mark had lost all his money that night, and after one more visit to try – unsuccessfully – to recoup his losses, had decided it wasn't for him. But Joe, who'd been luckier, was hooked. He took to going to the club two or three times a week, but before long his luck too had turned and he reached the point where he could no longer afford to continue with what had become an addiction.

It was then that Percy Jacobs, a loan shark and a friend of the club owner, had stepped in. Stupidly, Joe had taken his money, careless of the huge interest rates Jacobs charged, but his luck had refused to change for the better. Eventually, as his debts grew, the threats began. Pay up – or face the consequences.

Worried as she had been about the change in Joe, Martha had no idea of any of this until matters came to a head.

Joe had called at her house unexpectedly early one evening, and suggested they go for a walk, and something about the way he said it, and his whole edgy demeanour, had warned her that this wasn't going to be just a casual stroll and a kiss and a cuddle in the long meadow grass. And she was right.

'I've got to talk to you, Martha,' he said when they were well away from the houses.

Her heart sank like a stone tossed into one of the river pools. He was going to tell her he'd met someone else, didn't want to see her any more. It was what she'd been afraid of for weeks now, but that didn't make it any easier.

She said nothing, waiting for him to break the news she was dreading, but when he spoke, what he had to say came as a complete shock.

'I've got to get away for a bit.'

'Away? Where?' she asked, her voice rising.

'I thought maybe London. Wally Reed went up there and he says there's plenty of work to be had.'

'But . . . you've got a job here . . .' she said, confused.

He snorted. 'Such as it is. I never intended to stay down the pits for ever, you know that, but when I made a move I wanted to be able to take you with me.'

The spark of warmth that came from hearing those words was quickly engulfed in her confusion. 'Then . . . I don't understand, Joe. Why now? What's the rush?'

His eyes fell from hers; he looked almost ashamed. 'I've just got to. That's all.'

A glimmer of insight pierced the fog that had numbed Martha's brain. 'Are you in some sort of trouble?'

'You could say that.' He still wasn't looking at her, and he kicked at a loose stone on the path with the toe of his boot.

'What sort of trouble?' She reached for his hand. 'You can tell me.'

He jerked his hand away. 'No, I can't.'

A horrible suspicion tasted like bile in her throat. 'You haven't got some girl in the family way, have you?'

'Course not!' he said sharply.

51

'Then what?'

For a long moment he was silent. Then he turned to face her, gripping her by the wrists. 'If I tell you, you've got to promise me you won't tell another soul. Will you promise?'

She nodded, knowing now that the expression she'd seen on his face was indeed shame. 'Promise.'

'All right. Well, I've made a bloody mess of things. Got myself in a hell of a pickle.'

He huffed breath over his top lip and continued, haltingly telling her about the gambling, the debts, the threats.

'Jacobs will come after me, make no mistake. Set his heavies on me. I'll end up in a ditch or a dark alley unless I get the money to pay him off, or do what he wants.'

'And what does he want?'

'For me to thieve for him. Burgle some of the big houses round here. He's already got a gang of poor suckers like me doing the posh addresses in Bath, even threatening rich-looking blokes on the street with knives and stealing their wallets and watches. Anything to keep him off their backs. So now you know. I've been a fool, and now I've got to pay for it.'

'Oh, Joe!' Martha was too shocked to be able to string more than a few words together. That he could have got himself into a position where his only choices were turning into a common thief or ending up beaten half to death was almost beyond belief. But Joe was desperate, no doubt of that. And her father had always said that putting bets on the horses, though harmless in itself, could be the start of a slippery slope. 'It's a fool's game,' was his mantra. 'In the end the bookie always wins.'

'When are you going?' she asked at last.

'Tomorrow. I'm catching an early train. Then . . . well, we'll have to see how it works out. But I couldn't go without seeing you first, saying goodbye.'

Goodbye. Such a horrible, final word.

'Couldn't I come with you?' Martha asked impulsively.

Joe hesitated, and the hesitation warmed her heavy heart. Then: 'I don't think that would be a very good idea. I don't want you sleeping in some shop doorway or on a park bench, and that's what I'll be doing until I find a place to stay. Perhaps, later on, when I've sorted myself out . . . if you still want to, that is.'

'Of course I'll want to! If you want me . . .'

'You know I do. There's never been anyone else for me, Martha.' He pulled her into his arms, kissed her. 'You never know, if things quieten down here I might be able to get home to see you. And if I get settled in London, then we can think about making a fresh start there. But for now . . .' He pulled away slightly, looking deeply into her eyes. 'Remember, not a word of this to anyone. I don't want anybody to know what a fool I've been, especially Mam and Dad. I've just told them I'm off to look for a better life. Mam's not happy about it, but it would kill her if she found out the truth. Just stick to that story, all right? I'm trusting you, Martha. And now I've got to go.' He pulled her close again. 'Look . . . I'm really sorry . . . I never thought it would end like this.'

'I know.' She buried her face in his neck. 'I love you, Joe,' she whispered.

'Yeah. And you.' It was the closest a man could be expected to say the three magic words, and as if to make up for it, he kissed her again.

'Will you be all right getting home on your own?' he asked.

She nodded, tears constricting her throat.

'I'll be in touch.'

Yet another kiss, deep, meaningful and full of promise, and then he was gone.

Martha watched him walk away, the tears running freely down her cheeks now, conflicting emotions tearing her apart.

It wasn't some other girl that had been the cause of his strange distant behaviour over the last weeks. It was a stupid obsession with gambling; he wasn't the first to fall into that trap, and he wouldn't be the last. But it meant he was off to London, leaving her behind, and she didn't know when she'd see him again. For a while at least she would have to be content with the occasional letter – knowing Joe, she couldn't imagine that he would get around to writing very often – and her hopes and dreams. The days would stretch ahead endlessly, the evenings lonely. And the secret she'd promised to keep would be an unbearable weight on her shoulders, making the loneliness more complete.

But he loved her. He'd more or less said so, and he'd talked of a future together. He hadn't just left with no explanation, he'd confided in her, trusted her with his awful confession.

Somehow Martha managed to feel heartbroken, bereft and happy all at the same time.

At a bend in the road Joe turned, raised his hand in a last wave, then disappeared from sight.

Martha set off for home, hoping the tears would have dried on her cheeks before she met anyone who might notice.

Joe had been gone for almost a month when Martha heard of the vacancy at the Three Feathers.

Algie Packer, the landlord, had fallen down a flight of stairs, breaking his leg in two places, and Maud his wife had never taken to her position as landlady. She hated having to make small talk to the customers, and the smell of beer and tobacco smoke often gave her what she called 'sick headaches' that forced her to take to her bed. Seb, their only son, was having to run the place more or less on his own, and he'd decided to advertise for a girl to help behind the bar, wash the glasses, and be of general assistance. A girl, he'd reasoned, would be more willing to carry out the menial tasks than another man, as well as being an asset in keeping the customers happy.

The moment Martha walked into the bar he knew he need look no further. Not only was she easy on the eye with her dark hair, glossy as a lump of freshly hewn coal, brown eyes and a winning smile, but also her manner was open and friendly, she seemed sensible and capable, and not the sort to be afraid of hard work. She'd be sure to become a favourite with the regulars, he thought, and most importantly she'd found favour with his mother, who had insisted on vetting the applicants.

'She appears to be respectable, and that's the main thing. We don't want a girl who's no better than she should be, giving the place a bad name,' she'd said, before adding cryptically: 'Or leading you astray.'

Seb had laughed. 'Oh, for goodness' sake, Mother, I think I'm past the age for being led astray.'

'No man's ever past that,' Maud retorted tartly, and Seb had just shaken his head and laughed again; he was used to his mother, who had found fault with every girl he'd ever walked out with.

He was twenty-five now, with the reputation of being a confirmed bachelor, though this had less to do with his mother's disapproval of his choice of lady friends and more with the fact he'd simply never yet met anyone for whom he was prepared to sacrifice his freedom. The moment a girl began to hint at wanting a ring on her finger was the moment he backed away and moved on to pastures new. Why anyone would want to tie themselves down to a wife and a brood of children who had to be provided for was beyond him.

55

Until he met Martha.

On the day that he interviewed her he sensed she was somehow different. What it was, he couldn't have said, but something about her fascinated him, and after she had left he couldn't get her out of his head.

Much as he would have scoffed at any such suggestion, Seb Parker had, for the first time in his life, started out on the rocky road to falling in love.

Working closely together, it wasn't long before Martha and Seb struck up a friendship.

On Martha's part that was all it was – an easy-going companionship between two colleagues. Joe was still the only one for her; she lived for the letters she received from him, brief and infrequent though they were, and still missed and longed for him every day. He'd found himself a job as a window cleaner, it seemed, at some official-sounding establishment she'd never heard of, but it must be a huge building, she thought, because he had said that every time the job was completed it was time to start all over again. There were never any passionate declarations of love, but she didn't expect any. That just wouldn't be Joe. It was enough for her that he signed off 'Love, Joe', and added a kiss.

For Seb, however, it was very different. The initial attraction he'd felt for her had only intensified, so that she was constantly on his mind. When they were together the pull was so strong he could scarcely take his eyes off her; when they were apart all he wanted was to see her again. He could scarcely believe what he was feeling and it disturbed him, frightened him almost, used as he was to being able to remain detached.

What *was* it about her? he asked himself impatiently. Yes, she was good-looking, but so were most of the other girls he'd walked out with. Yes, she was warm and friendly, but that alone couldn't explain the way she made him feel. Perhaps it was that he knew she had a sweetheart – she'd mentioned him once or twice, saying his name with a sort of defiant pride. Could it be that he was seeing her as something of a challenge? The first girl who hadn't been anxious to get his attention? The sweetheart clearly wasn't on the scene at the moment; when he'd asked her if he didn't mind her working every evening, she'd simply replied that he was away, but given no indication where or why. Maybe he was a soldier or a sailor, Seb thought. Or maybe he was in jail. That would explain her reticence.

Or maybe he didn't exist at all. Perhaps she'd made him up for some reason of her own. Whatever. There was something she was hiding, he felt sure. And the intrigue only added to the attraction he felt towards her.

He'd make a move and see how the land lay, Seb decided. If she knocked him back, so be it. But if she didn't . . .

He didn't want to think any further than that. At least, one way or another, it would put a stop to this obsession that was beginning to get to him like an itchy rash he couldn't scratch.

One afternoon in early June when he'd locked the door at closing time, he took a last tray of empty glasses into the kitchen where Martha was elbow deep in a sinkful of hot soapy water.

'That's the lot,' he said, setting the glasses down beside her.

'Thank goodness for that!' Martha lifted a hand dripping suds and wiped her forehead with the sleeve of her blouse. 'It's like an oven in here.'

It was true. For the last couple of hours the sun had been shining directly into the window over the sink, and the copper for boiling the water had intensified the heat in the tiny kitchen.

Seb saw his chance.

'We could go and sit in the garden for a while,' he suggested. 'Have a drink, and wait for it to cool down a bit before you have to walk all the way home.'

In the moment before Martha replied, he thought she was going to turn him down. To his relief, she didn't.

'Good idea,' she said. 'Just let me swill these glasses out, and I'll leave them to drain.'

'I'll get the drinks,' he said. 'What would you like – cider?'

'Just a half.'

He headed back into the bar feeling pleased with himself, filled two glasses, and took them out to the small garden on the other side of the courtyard at the rear of the premises. There was a wooden bench there and a small table. The recent good weather had dried out the bench, sodden throughout winter and a wet spring, but when he'd set down the glasses of cider he felt it anyway to make sure he didn't need to fetch a cushion for Martha. It was fine, the old wood warm to his touch.

He went back to the kitchen. 'All ready when you are then.'

'Just finishing.'

Martha plunged her hands back into the water, then jerked them back out again, gasping.

'Oh!' Blood had begun to seep out of her middle finger and quickly became a stream. 'Oh – how stupid! The carving knife. I forgot it was there . . .'

Seb grabbed a cloth from a peg beside the sink. 'Here . . . use this.'

Martha took it, wrapping it around her injured finger, but it wasn't long before the cloth was soaked through.

'Oh, this is ridiculous!' Martha unwrapped the cloth, found a fresh place, and wound it round her finger again.

'I'll see if I can find a dressing. There should be a first aid tin in the bar.'

Seb hurried off, and came back with an old tea caddy stuffed with lint, cotton wool and gauze. He cut a length off each with a pair of kitchen scissors.

'Right. Come here.'

Obediently Martha held out her hand – there was no way she could manage to do it herself. Seb took it, whipped off the drying up cloth and quickly applied the dressing, pressing hard on her finger until he was able to tie the strip of gauze tightly over it, finishing with a double knot and a small bow.

'Let's see how that goes then,' he said, replacing the first aid items in the tea caddy. 'We might need to do it again before you go home. That's a deep cut, and fingers always bleed a lot.'

'Thanks.' Martha held her hand aloft, impressed by the neatness of the dressing. She wouldn't have expected a big man like Seb to be so deft. 'How could I have been so stupid?'

'Easily done,' Seb said. 'Let's go and have that drink. You could do with it, I expect.'

'Good idea.' Martha, who had been leaning against the big stone sink, pushed herself away, and swayed slightly.

'Hey – are you all right?' Seb was beside her in an instant, his arm going round her shoulders.

'Yes . . . fine . . . just a bit dizzy, that's all . . .' Embarrassed, she drew away.

'Have a drink of water.' He poured some into a clean glass, handed it to her, and watched while she took a few sips. 'Better?'

'Fine, honestly.'

But he took the glass from her and put his other arm round her shoulders again. 'Let's go and sit down for a bit. I'm taking your water with us. It'll do you more good than cider.'

This time she didn't protest. The dizziness was passing, but his arm around her felt good, safe. In the garden he settled her on the bench, sat down beside her and passed her the glass.

'When you feel better, I'll walk you home.'

'Honestly, there's no need,' she said, embarrassed again.

'We'll see about that.'

'Seb – don't fuss! It's just a little cut. Anyone would think I'd chopped my finger off.'

'Lucky you didn't.' He reached for his cider and took a long pull, and for a few minutes they sat in silence. Then he put his drink down and gestured towards one of the outhouses. 'Did I tell you I'm thinking of turning that one into a skittle-alley? If Dad has no objection.'

She looked at him, surprised. 'No. What a good idea!'

'That's what I thought. We can field a team in the Hillsbridge and District League. I want to put this pub on the map, Martha. We're in a good position here, right on the main road to Bath, and we've catered just for the locals for too long.'

Martha thought about it. 'You're right. It's perfect for passing trade. It might be worth thinking about doing snacks – nothing fancy, just something a bit more than pickled eggs and pork scratchings. Crusty bread and cheese and pickles, perhaps. Or sausages.'

Seb laughed. 'Shut up – you're making me hungry! But seriously – it is a thought. It would mean more work for you, though.'

'I'm not worried about hard work,' Martha said. 'I'd love to see the Feathers thriving. I'm guessing your mother wouldn't have wanted to get involved, but you've got me now.'

'We'll talk about it again when you're better,' Seb agreed.

'I'm better now! That was just a funny five minutes.' To prove it, she reached for the glass of cider Seb had put ready for her and took a sip, examining her bandaged finger as she did so. 'See? The cut's even stopped bleeding, by the look of it. Come on – let's start making plans!'

* * *

'So that's your boss, is it? And walking you home too.'

Elsie Wells, Martha's mother, had been shaking a duster out of the front room window when she'd seen the two of them walking along the track – despite her protestations, Seb had insisted on seeing Martha safely home – and though she'd drawn back, not wanting to be seen watching them, she'd made sure she got a good look from behind the curtains at her daughter's employer.

'I cut my finger and came over a bit faint,' Martha said. 'He wanted to make sure I got home all right.'

'He went to all that trouble just for a cut finger?' Elsie gave her daughter a sharp look. 'Are you sure that's all it was?'

'He's kind like that.'

'Hmm. And not bad-looking either. Quite a catch, I'd say.'

Martha's finger was throbbing now and she didn't feel like having this conversation. 'You're not trying to matchmake, I hope, Mam. Because if you are you're going to be disappointed.'

Elsie folded the duster and put it in the cupboard on top of a tin of beeswax furniture polish. 'You could do worse.'

'Mam . . . you know very well I'm promised to Joe.'

Elsie straightened, looking her daughter in the eye. 'And he's where, exactly?'

'In London. You know that.'

'Gone off for no good reason and left you behind. Never been back once to see you. Only writes to you when it suits him.'

Martha looked away, wishing she could explain. But she couldn't. She'd promised Joe.

'If you ask me, it's time you started looking elsewhere if you don't want to be left on the shelf,' Elsie said tartly.

'I'm going up to change out of my work clothes,' Martha

said, anxious to end this conversation and making for the door. 'Seb's given me the evening off, and I want to get into something cooler.'

'If you've got any sense you'll make sure your sister doesn't get to meet him,' Elsie called after her. 'She wouldn't think twice about setting her cap at him, and you'd have missed the boat.'

'She's welcome to him,' Martha called back, but for some reason the very suggestion had touched a nerve. Ivy, her younger sister, was an incorrigible flirt, and as she was also very pretty she was never short of admirers. Whereas for Martha there'd never been anyone but Joe, Ivy had walked out with half the boys in Hillsbridge, and it was generally acknowledged she could get anyone she took a fancy to.

As Martha unbuttoned the white blouse she wore for work and slipped out of her ankle-length black skirt, Elsie's words were still niggling at her.

What is it to you? she asked herself, annoyed by the unfamiliar feeling that might almost have been proprietorial jealousy. Seb and Ivy were both footloose and fancy free; she was not. As she'd said, she was promised to Joe. He was the one she'd always wanted and always would.

So why was she suddenly feeling this way, irritated and a bit put out?

Martha threw open the bedroom window and leaned out, letting the breeze that had sprung up cool her hot cheeks. Seb had been kind to her, shared his plans and dreams with her, and she was flattered. That was all. And she wouldn't even think about how gently he'd dressed her injured finger or how nice it had felt when he'd put his arm around her.

She turned back into the room, crossed to the dressing table and picked up her precious ring, which she never wore to work for fear of losing it when she had to take it off to do the washing up.

'Don't worry, Joe, I'm here for you,' she said softly as she slid the ring on to her finger. 'And I'll wait for you however long it takes.'

'How's the finger?' Seb asked when Martha arrived for work next day.

'Sore, but I expect that's because it's beginning to heal.' She opened the larder door, unhooked her frilly apron from its peg and slipped it on. For some reason she felt a little shy in Seb's presence today, but she was also enthusiastic about the plans they'd begun to make for the Feathers and it gave her the ideal excuse to cover her confusion. 'Did you get the chance to see what your mam and dad thought about us doing snack meals?'

'I had a word with them this morning over breakfast,' Seb said. 'They've got no objection, so I reckon it's full steam ahead. And they're happy for me to convert the outhouse into a skittle-alley too – as long as I take responsibility for clearing out all the rubbish that's stored in there. I thought I'd make a start this afternoon after we close.'

'I could help you,' Martha offered.

'It'll be dirty work. You don't want to get your clothes mucked up.'

'Haven't you got some overalls I could borrow?'

Seb laughed. 'Martha, I'm a good bit taller than you, and bigger round. You'd be lost in them.'

Martha wasn't going to give up so easily. She was enjoying having a project to work towards too much. 'What about your dad? He's more my size.'

'Well, if your mind's made up, I'll ask him.' He glanced at

the clock; the hands were just about to point to midday. 'Better open up first.'

'I can do that.'

By the time she'd unlocked the door, let in and served pints of beer to the two old miners who had already been waiting outside, Seb was back.

'I've sorted you some overalls and a shirt to go underneath if you're still set on the idea at two o'clock. But I'm warning you – they've seen better days.'

'Just as long as they cover me up,' Martha said. 'I'm not vain.'

Another elderly man came in. When Martha had served him he took his pint over to the corner table where the first two were enjoying a smoke and a chinwag and Seb, who had been checking the bottles of spirits, turned to her.

'By the way, to my surprise Mam said she wouldn't mind baking the bread for your snacks if you'd see to buying the cheese and pickles.'

'Oh, that would be good!' Martha said enthusiastically. 'The smell of fresh bread would be sure to whet a few appetites. But we still need to make it known what we're planning before I start buying loads of stuff that might go to waste. Test the water, if you like. I thought I'd try to make a poster to stick up on the bar. Or a blackboard. That might be easier. My brother's children have one – if they've grown out of playing with it he might let me have it.'

'Good idea. It shouldn't be too difficult to get hold of one. And if we really want to spread the word we could put an advert in the local paper . . .'

Excitement prickled in Martha's stomach. 'This is really happening, isn't it?'

'Too true.' He smiled at her. 'Between us, we're going to put the Feathers on the map, Martha!'

64

* * *

Seb hadn't been exaggerating when he'd said the overalls had seen better days. She got changed in the kitchen with the door firmly closed though he had already gone across the yard to the outhouse. She tucked the shirt in as best she could and fastened the bib and brace over it, then rolled up the legs, which were several inches too long for her, to just above her ankles. Her mother would have a fit if she could see her now, Martha thought, smiling to herself, but she was enjoying herself.

As she crossed the yard Seb emerged from the outhouse dragging a rusty mangle.

'Well!' he said with a grin. 'You're all togged up with nowhere to go, I see.'

'Don't you dare laugh!' Martha retorted. 'And you're a fine one to talk. You're not exactly a fashion plate.'

'I'm dressed for work.' He pulled the mangle back against the brick wall of the outhouse where he had already stacked a couple of chairs, their rush seats fallen through, and a chiffonier missing its drawers and with a door hanging off. 'Goodness only knows how I'm going to get rid of all this stuff.'

'I could ask my brother if we could borrow his horse and cart,' Martha suggested. 'He's a farmer.'

'It'll take a big cart and a strong horse,' Seb said, wiping his forehead with the back of his hand.

'He's got his hay wagon and a couple of carthorses. If they can manage a load of hay, a few old bits of furniture should be a doddle. What else is in there?'

'Come and have a look.'

It was dim inside the outhouse, with only one window and the open door to let in the light, and it smelled damp. Seb pulled out a tin trunk and dust flew, tickling Martha's nose.

'You can see what's in there for a start.'

Martha dragged the trunk outside the better to see what she was doing as well as to escape the dust. When she lifted the lid a strong musty smell wafted up, and this time she couldn't help sneezing. The trunk appeared to be full of old clothes; Martha gingerly lifted the topmost item with two fingers and a thumb – it was damp and sticky to her touch, the satin bodice discoloured and brittle. Beneath the dresses and undergarments were old sheets, also damp and yellowed. She closed the lid with some relief – something else for her brother Ernie's hay wagon.

She went back inside, began to pull out a large cardboard box containing what looked like old pillows, but the cardboard felt as damp as the old clothes had, and as she moved it the bottom fell out and feathers crawling with mites and chewed-up scraps of paper, cardboard and cotton spewed out across the floor.

'Looks as if the mice have been at it,' Seb said.

Martha squealed and jumped back, alarmed at the thought of a mouse running over her feet.

'Hey – it's all right!'

'I know!' she snapped, feeling foolish. 'You just startled me, that's all. I'm not afraid of a mouse.'

'No? You could have fooled me!'

'I wish I hadn't offered to help you! You've done nothing but laugh at me. And I could do the same to you, believe me. You've got the most enormous dirty mark all across your face.'

'Really? Well, if you were a friend you'd clean it off for me.'

'Oh, Seb! Why are men so hopeless?' She fished a handkerchief out of the pocket of the overalls. 'Come here.'

She reached up to scrub at his cheek, and before she knew what was happening his arms were around her waist, pulling her close, and his mouth was perilously close to hers. Something strong and sweet twisted inside her, followed swiftly by a rush of panic. She placed both hands on his chest, pushing him away.

'No! Don't! Please!'

He released her, backing away and raising his arms in submission. 'Sorry . . . sorry . . .' A rueful grin lifted one corner of his mouth. 'I guess I got it wrong.'

'I like you, Seb. I like you a lot. But . . .'

'It's all right, you don't have to explain. I like you too, Martha, but I shouldn't have pushed my luck. I should know you're not that kind of girl. And you've got a chap, haven't you – lucky bugger.'

'I have, yes.' For some inexplicable reason she was trembling.

'So – I'm sorry. I shouldn't have done that. You're not going to walk out on me, are you? Because I'd hate to lose the best barmaid I could wish for because I let her know I fancy her.'

'Seb . . .' This was spiralling way out of control.

'Are you? Going to leave?'

'No, of course not. Don't be silly . . .'

'Phew.' He pretended to wipe sweat from his forehead. 'Still friends?'

'Let's get on with this clearing out,' she said. 'Have you got a broom? I'll sweep this lot up.'

'I'll do it. Why don't you go and make us a cup of tea?'

'Good idea . . . And by the way, you've still got a dirty face.'

It was her way of trying to ease the awkwardness of the situation. The last thing she wanted was a strained atmosphere between her and Seb. But it wouldn't be easy to get back to their former easy-going companionship. She knew now why she had felt oddly shy seeing him today. And she knew that the panic she'd felt when he'd almost kissed her had stemmed partly from her own feelings. For two pins she'd have let him.

Her confused emotions running riot, Martha headed for the kitchen to make that cup of tea.

Chapter Five

Within a few weeks word had spread that the Feathers was now making tasty snacks, and the clientele began to grow with people travelling to and from Bath stopping by or even coming specially as it was the only hostelry in the area offering this kind of service. Martha had enlarged the menu, adding sausages, hotpot – a large casserole made on a Thursday, which was heated up each day to ensure it didn't go off and cause upset stomachs – and even liver and bacon if ordered in advance. Maud Packer had offered to do the cooking in her own kitchen, more enthusiastic about anything to do with the pub than Martha had ever seen her. As long as she didn't have to deal with the customers she was happy to do her bit and contribute to the family business.

Preparations for the skittle-alley were taking much longer – Seb was trying to do most of the work himself to save expense. The outhouse was cleared of rubbish now, but he'd had to point some of the old brickwork and repair the roof in a couple of places. Now in every spare moment he was busy sanding down old railway sleepers to lay the alley.

After the initial awkwardness, things between him and Martha had, on the surface at least, returned to more or less the way they had been before he had attempted to kiss her. It hadn't been mentioned again, and Seb hadn't done or said a single thing to make Martha uncomfortable. And yet she was. She was aware of him as she hadn't been before, unable to forget the way she'd felt in that moment before she pushed him away or the emotional turmoil that had followed. If their hands brushed accidentally her nerve endings prickled at his touch and colour rose in her cheeks; if he came up close behind her to reach for a bottle or a glass she felt his presence, solid as a rock, even though there was no physical contact. And sometimes she dreamed about him, that they were walking hand in hand and he was smiling at her, that cheeky grin that made her stomach flip over. She would wake feeling ridiculously happy, and then the guilt would come rushing in.

Though nothing had happened between them, though she would make sure it never did, she knew she was betraying Joe all the same.

Perhaps she should leave the Feathers, she thought. Take herself well out of the way of temptation. But it wasn't that easy; she couldn't be without work and her position at the glove factory would be filled by now even if she had been able to face going back there. And besides, she didn't want to leave Seb in the lurch. His father would never be able to work behind the bar again, and she hated the thought of a new barmaid stepping in to run the project that had given her so much satisfaction, and perhaps making a horrible mess of it.

No, she'd just have to try and forget what had so nearly happened between her and Seb, put it out of her mind. And as soon as Joe sent for her, she would. She was promised to him; he was her future and always had been. It was just loneliness that was making her feel this way, clutching at any port in a storm.

As for Seb, he would probably have run a mile once he'd had his fun with her. If she had let him. Wasn't that his reputation? Love 'em and leave 'em.

So Martha carried on as usual, throwing herself into the business she was building, and hiding her feelings for Seb along with the guilt that accompanied them, and quite unaware that Seb was doing the very same thing.

It was an evening in late July when a carriage drew up outside the Feathers and the three men Martha was to come to dislike intensely rolled into the bar for the first time. One was over-weight, with the long side-whiskers popularly known as 'Piccadilly weepers'; one small, slight and balding; and the third, much younger than his companions, was powerfully built and with dark good looks that suggested a Mediterranean heritage. Flashily dressed in bowler hats, sack coats with velvet collars and patterned trousers – either striped or checked, with braid side seams – they caused something of a stir amongst the regulars, who eyed them suspiciously and muttered disparaging comments into their beers.

The three men stood for a moment taking a good look around, and Martha half-expected them to turn around and walk out again, dissatisfied with the humble surroundings. Then all three approached the bar.

'Good evening, gentlemen.' Hiding her surprise Martha greeted them with her usual welcoming smile. 'What can I get you?'

'Three pints of your best bitter, sweetheart.' It was the overweight man who spoke and given his well-to-do appearance, Martha was surprised by the coarseness of his voice.

'And whisky chasers.' The slightly built man, whose sack coat was draped across his narrow shoulders, spoke with more educated tones. 'What do you have?'

'Teacher's?' Martha offered as she began filling three glasses from the beer keg.

'No single malt?'

'We do, but—'

'Single malt, then. Doubles.'

Martha finished pulling the pints and set them down on the bar. Then she turned to reach for the whisky. It wasn't alongside the other spirits within easy reach, but on a higher shelf – they didn't have much call for the more expensive brands – and she had to stand on tiptoe and stretch up to reach it. As she turned back she was uncomfortably aware of three pairs of eyes on her, appraising and somehow speculative.

'We haven't seen you in here before, have we?' she said conversationally, in an effort to hide her discomfort.

'No, but if it's as good as we've been told, you'll certainly be seeing us again.' That was the man who had requested the whisky, and as he spoke Martha was somewhat disconcerted to see him and the youngest of the three exchange a conspiratorial glance. 'You do a fine hotpot, I hear.'

'We do, but there's none left at the moment.' Somehow Martha managed to retain her composure. 'We shall be making fresh tomorrow, ready for the weekend.'

'Just as well we're not hungry tonight then.' The youngest man had an accent that suggested he might be a Londoner, and his eyes, so dark they were almost black, seemed to bore into Martha, making her more uncomfortable than ever.

'I'll get these.' The man who had ordered the beers felt in his pockets, exposing a silver watchchain that strained across his ample gut. The wallet he extracted was clearly the finest pigskin and it looked to contain more money than Martha had ever seen at one time in the whole of her life.

'And so you should, Percy, considering the way your luck was running today,' the small man remarked. 'You cleaned out the tote, if I'm not much mistaken.'

'Not luck, my friend – judgement. I know a good piece of horseflesh from a broken-down nag if you don't.'

They'd been to the races, Martha surmised. She'd heard there was a meeting at Salisbury this week and if they were on their way back to Bath it would explain them calling at a hostelry on the road home.

'And have one yourself.' Percy peeled off some notes from the wad in his wallet.

'Thanks, but I don't drink when I'm working.' Martha's discomfort made her unwilling to accept anything from these three strangers.

'Sensible girl, Martha.' She could have sworn the small man winked at her.

'How do you know my name?' she demanded, more disconcerted than ever.

'Oh – word travels. You'd be surprised,' the man said enigmatically, and he glanced again at the younger man, whose lips curled into an answering smile that was almost a sneer.

When they had taken their drinks to an unoccupied table, Martha carried on working, trying to ignore them. But even so she was aware that they were watching her through the smoke of the fat cigars they had lit, and suspected they were talking about her.

Who on earth were they? Perhaps their seeming interest in her was simply because she was the barmaid and they hoped she'd be up for a bit of sport. But how did they know her name?

After a while the fat man – Percy – caught her eye, lifted a finger and pointed to the now-empty glasses, summoning her for all the world as if she were a servant. Though she took food that had been ordered to the tables, it wasn't usual for her to do the same with drinks.

'Could you come to the bar please?' she asked politely.

Percy looked annoyed, but the youngest man got to his feet. 'It's all right, I'll go.'

Percy handed him some money and he approached the bar. 'Same again.'

She poured the drinks and took the money, but the man made no effort to return to his seat.

'You're a fine-looking woman, I must say, Martha.'

'Thank you.' She refused to meet his eyes.

'And I think you'll find we have a mutual friend . . .'

This time she did raise her gaze to his, surprised and puzzled. But he only smiled, wagged his head knowingly, and picked up the drinks. It was clear he had no intention at present of satisfying her curiosity.

By the time they left, the bottle of single malt was almost empty and the till contained far more than usual.

'We've done well tonight,' Seb remarked when he came in from working yet again on the skittle-alley and was bagging up the takings.

'We had three strangers in.' Martha was wiping down the bar. 'I don't know who they were, but they certainly seemed to have money to burn. They had a horse and carriage outside too. I think they'd been to the races – at Salisbury perhaps? – and stopped off on their way back to Bath. But what I can't understand is – they knew my name.'

'If they're into the horses perhaps they know Ticker Bendle,' Seb said. 'He might have recommended us. Anyway, whatever, let's hope they come again.'

'Mm.' Martha wasn't so sure. Their custom might be good for the Feathers, but she was almost certain Ticker Bendle was the local bookie who had set Joe on the path to ruin, and she had a bad feeling about the men.

Especially since they had seemed to take such an interest in her.

But to Martha's dismay, they were back a few days later, and twice again the following week. For some reason they seemed to have adopted the Feathers as a watering hole and she was puzzled as well as disconcerted. Salisbury races wouldn't be on again so soon; unless they had business in Wells, Shepton Mallet or Frome they must be making a special journey.

Apart from the one who was apparently called Percy she had no idea of their names, and tried to amuse herself by giving them nicknames. Fat Percy was Slug, the wiry little man she decided to call Spider, and the dark man who had claimed they had 'a mutual friend' she named Wolf.

'I don't like them at all,' she said to Seb. 'They say really odd things, and I feel they're watching me all the time. It makes my skin crawl.'

'I can tell them they're not welcome any more if you like,' Seb offered.

But uncomfortable as they made her, Martha couldn't allow him to do that. It was typical of Seb to look out for her, but the takings were always well up after they had visited and it would make for very bad business to turn them away.

'It's all right,' she said. 'I can handle them.'

'If you're sure.'

Seb had every confidence in Martha's ability to cope with difficult customers and so he accepted her assurance at face value.

It was an evening in August when the carriage pulled up outside the Feathers, but only two of the men walked into the bar: the slightly built man, Spider, and Martha's nemesis, Wolf. Martha groaned inwardly, but forced a smile as she greeted them.

'Good evening, gentlemen.'

Spider settled himself at a table and Wolf approached the bar.

'Your usual, is it?'

'To begin with.' As always, everything he said seemed to have a double meaning, and his mouth was twisted into an unpleasant smirk.

If only Seb weren't working on the skittle-alley again, Martha thought. When he was there, Wolf behaved himself, though he still watched her narrowly when Seb's back was turned. But Seb was anxious to get the alley ready for when the competitive season began in the autumn, and would only come in to help serve, at her request, if things got busy.

Well, at least the unwelcome customers had been later getting here this evening, she consoled herself. It was already half past nine; only an hour and a half until closing time, and in any case, when dusk fell Seb might decide to call it a day and come back to the bar.

This evening, however, he didn't and Martha guessed he must have taken a lamp with him so that he could continue for that extra hour or so. By a quarter to eleven most of the other customers had finished their drinks and left, and she was alone in the bar with Wolf and Spider.

'One for the road?' she asked them, hoping it might move them along.

'We're all right, thank you, darling.' It was Spider who answered her, but Wolf drained his whisky glass.

'I haven't finished yet.' Once again Martha had the strangest feeling that there was some hidden meaning in his words, and his eyes were on hers speculatively as he brought his glass to the bar.

She served him, then began collecting empty glasses from the other tables, wishing she could ring the bell to signify closing time, but not daring to. Opening hours were opening hours, and they had to be adhered to. But at least now Wolf had a fresh drink she didn't need to stay here and be stared at. She carried the empty glasses through into the kitchen, filled a pan with hot water from the copper and took it to the sink.

As she poured it, the door creaked, and she looked over her shoulder, expecting to see Seb, finished work on the skittle-alley for the night at last. Then her eyes widened and alarm twisted in the pit of her stomach. It wasn't Seb. It was Wolf.

'What . . . ?'

Boiling water splashed on to her wrist, but she scarcely noticed.

'I think it's time you and I had a chat, Martha.' He came closer, an unpleasant smile twisting his lips.

'You shouldn't be in here!' she managed.

He ignored her. 'About a mutual friend.'

It was the first time since that first evening that he'd mentioned a 'mutual friend', and she'd come around to thinking it was just part of his taunting.

'I don't think we have any mutual friends,' she said, as steadily as she could. 'Now if you would please go back to the bar . . .'

'Oh yes we do.' The unpleasant smile had become a snarl and his eyes were cold as the depths of a dark lake. 'Joe Hill? I'm sure you'll know that name.'

Martha stiffened. 'Joe?' she echoed, startled.

'Yes, Joe. He owes my boss a great deal of money, and he's anxious to contact him.'

An icy shiver prickled over Martha's skin and her stomach turned over. Could it be that either Spider or Slug was the loan shark Joe had fled to London to escape? And Wolf was one of his heavies? All of a rush she realised the reason why the men had begun coming to the Feathers and why they had taken such an interest in her, even known her name. Somehow they knew she was Joe's sweetheart; somehow they'd found her here.

'So,' Wolf said, his tone low and dangerous. 'Are you going to tell me where I can find him? Or do I have to make you?'

'I don't know where he is.' Though she was trembling inwardly, somehow Martha managed to keep her voice level. 'I haven't seen him for months.'

'I find that hard to believe. A nice-looking girl like you? Well, maybe you haven't seen him if he's lying low, but you know where he is all right.'

Martha stood her ground. 'Just get out of here. The landlord will be here in a minute . . .'

Wolf glanced swiftly over his shoulder and she thought she had him worried enough to back off. Instead, with one swift movement he grabbed her by the arms and propelled her towards the back door, and though she struggled as hard as she could she was no match for him. On the step she stumbled, but he jerked her upright and thrust her around the jut of the kitchen and into the passage between the house and the cottage. There he pushed her back against the wall, one hand firmly planted in her chest, whilst he grasped her chin between the thumb and fingers of the other, forcing it upwards so that her neck spasmed.

'Where is he, Martha?'

Terrified though she was, Martha was still determined not to betray Joe. 'I don't know,' she managed, spitting the words between her clenched jaws.

His hand slid down, tightening around her throat.

'You want to do this the hard way?'

Martha gulped for air, her legs like half-set jelly, panic rising in a choking tide.

But still she remained silent.

In the dim light, and with her eyes half-closed against the pressure on her throat, she had no way of seeing the look that had come into Wolf's eyes, had no idea of the excitement that had begun building in his gut. With this pretty girl completely and utterly at his mercy, it was no longer simply a job to be done – to discover the whereabouts of the man who had run out on his debt – but pure lust that was driving Wolf.

Maintaining the pressure around her throat he moved his hand from her chest to scrabble up her skirts. Martha struggled, ever more feebly, as she felt his body pressing into hers. But the darkness was closing in all around her and she knew no more.

For a moment as she regained consciousness, Martha felt nothing but utter confusion. Then, as she became aware of the ache in her throat, the pain between her legs, and her skirts, bunched up around her waist, panic flooded her once more and she sobbed, attempting to struggle to her feet and falling again before managing to scramble up and lean, shaking and weak, against the wall.

Wolf! Where was he? She looked from left to right, her head twisting jerkily and painfully, expecting to see him there in the shadows. But he was gone. She was in no doubt now what had happened – he'd half-strangled and raped her. But she hadn't told him where Joe was . . . had she? As some order returned to her disjointed and racing thoughts she felt sure she hadn't. But oh God, oh God, he'd raped her! Bile rose in Martha's sore throat and she vomited weakly on to the rough stones of the passageway, then wiped her mouth, straightened her clothing, and made her way out of the passage, still steadying herself against the wall.

Across the yard she could see a light still burning in the outhouse. Seb must still be working on the skittle-alley. That explained why he hadn't missed her and come to look for her. Oh, if only he'd come to look for her! But perhaps it was just as well he hadn't. He'd have gone for Wolf, and heaven only knew what might have happened. Seb was no weakling, but Wolf was powerfully built, and for all she knew a man like him might carry a knife . . . If he'd beaten Seb badly, or stabbed him . . . It was just too awful to contemplate.

She started towards the outhouse, then stopped. When he found out what had happened, Seb might still go after Wolf. It wouldn't be impossible to find him now that she knew who he was, even if she still didn't know his real name. Things could still go from bad to worse. And besides . . .

Martha pressed her hands against her cheeks, wet with tears she didn't even know she'd shed, as burning shame consumed her. She couldn't tell Seb what had happened. She simply couldn't bring herself to say the words. She'd die of shame. And in the end, when it came down to it, it was her own fault. All her fault . . .

Martha turned away from the outhouse and went instead to the kitchen, half-afraid Wolf might still be there. But he wasn't, and no sound came from the bar either. She peeped around the door; it was empty.

She was beginning to get her thoughts in order now, the practicality that was second nature to her coming to the fore. She crossed the bar and locked the door, collected the empty glasses from the table where Wolf and Spider had sat, and took them into the kitchen. She washed her face and hands with the still-warm water from the copper and tidied her hair in the little mirror that hung on the wall. Then she turned to the nightly chore of washing up, intent on making everything seem as normal as possible. And she could scarcely believe how calm she had become. The feeling of living a nightmare still thickened the air around her, her throat ached and her most private places burned, yet she went about her normal tasks like an automaton.

When Seb finally came in she managed to force a smile.

'You've been working late tonight.'

There was a slight croakiness to her voice, and he noticed it.

'Are you starting a cold?'

'I have got a bit of a sore throat. It's probably hayfever,' she lied.

'I've made you late, too,' Seb said. 'Would you like me to walk you home?'

'No. I'll be fine.'

It was the last thing Martha wanted. She needed to be alone; the thought of having to talk to Seb all the way back to Hillsbridge was unbearable, and what could be worse than what had just happened to her?

'Sure?'

'Quite sure. You must be tired too. But I will get off now if that's all right.'

'Course it is. I'll just cash up and the rest can wait till the morning. I'm guessing the takings are good again – I saw the men from Bath's carriage outside, didn't I?'

'Just two tonight. Not Slug,' Martha managed.

And fled.

Almost from the first Martha knew what the outcome of Wolf raping her would be. She tried to tell herself it wasn't likely that a virgin would fall pregnant the first and only time she'd been with a man, but some sixth sense was telling her different, and she felt sick with dread.

As her time of the month approached she could think of nothing else, dwelling on every deep-seated little ache or niggle, hoping desperately it meant that the first trickle of blood would soon follow. It didn't, and her anxiety grew into panic. She couldn't have that monster's baby! She couldn't! But what could she do? She didn't know of anyone who carried out abortions and she had no one she could ask about such things. Besides, abortions were dangerous as well as illegal. Martha took baths as hot as she could bear, swallowed copious amounts of laxatives, pushed and prodded her stomach and even tried jumping down flights of stairs, twisting an ankle in her efforts, but all to no avail. And when she felt the first stirring of her baby deep within her she knew; she couldn't abort this helpless new life that was growing inside her.

Somehow she managed to carry on as normal, hiding her expanding waistline beneath the loosest clothes she possessed while the secret she was keeping assumed ever greater proportions. The thought of the shame she'd bring on her family, as well as anxiety as to how she could manage to raise a bastard child alone, tormented her to such an extent that she thought she would go mad with the worry of it all.

There was only one thing for it, she decided: she'd have to go away. To London. To Joe. She dreaded the thought of telling him what had happened just as she had shrunk from telling Seb, but she could think of no other answer to her problem. Joe would be furious as well as devastated, and probably guilt-ridden, but he'd be there for her. Though it was several weeks now since she had heard from him, she had no doubt of that. As soon as she was unable to conceal her condition any longer she'd write and tell him she was coming, get on a train and leave this nightmare behind.

But then one day Seb came into the kitchen where she was making up a lunch snack for one of the customers and told her there was someone in the bar who wanted to speak to her.

'Who?' she asked, her knife poised over the block of Cheddar cheese and puzzled that Seb seemed not to know her visitor.

'He said his name is Wally Reed,' Seb said. 'I can finish making up that ploughman's, if you like.'

'I don't know any Wally Reed. He can wait while I finish this,' Martha said, dreading to think how much cheese Seb would put on the plate if it were up to him.

Though she hadn't recognised the name, when she carried the snack through and saw the young man sitting on the bar stool, his face looked familiar.

'You wanted to see me?' she said when she'd taken the plate of bread, cheese and pickles over to the customer.

The young man shifted uncomfortably on his stool, twisting his cap between his hands.

'Yeah. You are Martha, aren't you? Joe's girl?'

At once Martha realised why his face was familiar. He was an old school friend of Joe's, and she thought he was the one Joe had mentioned as already being in London when he'd dropped the bombshell on her that he was going to London too.

'Oh yes! Are you in touch with him?' she asked eagerly.

He nodded, but looked more uncomfortable than ever. 'I was, yes.'

Martha frowned, her hopes of getting news of Joe, and sending a message to him, fading. 'Not any more?'

Wally Reed bent his head, chewing on his lip and twisting his cap even more tightly between his hands. Then he looked up, meeting her eyes reluctantly.

'There's no easy way to say this, Martha. I'm sorry, but Joe's dead.'

'He can't be . . .'

For a split second Martha stared at him in disbelief, then her legs began to give way under her. She grasped the bar for support and lowered herself on to another bar stool, trembling. Dear God, she must have given away Joe's whereabouts that awful night! And Wolf and maybe some more of Spider's heavies had found him and . . .

'What happened?' she managed.

'He had a bad fall at work a couple of weeks ago. The ladder slipped. They took him to St Mary's, did their best for him, but he didn't make it. Died the day before yesterday. I come down to tell his mam and dad what's happened, let them know about the funeral, and they reckoned I ought to let you know as well.'

'Oh my God, I can't believe it. Oh my God – Joe . . .'

Martha was desperately trying to hold herself together but the shock was rushing through her like waves crashing on a beach.

'What's going on?'

She hadn't seen Seb come out of the kitchen; now he was there, just the other side of the bar, puzzled and anxious.

'Oh, Seb!' she cried. 'It's Joe! He's dead!' And as if speaking the words out loud made them real, the tears began, pouring down her cheeks.

Seb was out from behind the bar in an instant, his arm round Martha's shaking shoulders, and she buried her face in his broad chest.

'It's all right, love. I'll close the pub. You're all right.'

Martha covered her face with her hands, unaware of all the curious stares focused on her.

She didn't think she would ever be all right again.

Seb took her through into the living room – he knew his mother and father would be in bed in the cottage by now – and settled her in one of the easy chairs with a glass of brandy.

'Drink this. I'll just go and lock up and I'll be back.'

When he returned Martha was sitting exactly as he'd left her, staring into space, the brandy untouched on the occasional table beside her.

He put the glass into her hands. 'Have some of this. You've had a terrible shock.' Still she sat unmoving and he lifted the glass to her lips. 'Come on now – even if it's just a sip.'

Obediently she did as he said, but she gagged on the strong liquor and some trickled down her chin, mingling with the tears she had not bothered to wipe away.

He got out his handkerchief and wiped her face gently. 'I don't know what to say, Martha, except that . . . well, I'm really sorry . . . What happened? Did that chap say?'

For a long moment she said nothing, still staring into space. Then, just as he thought she wasn't going to reply, she took another sip of the brandy, swallowed it this time without gagging, and spoke.

'His ladder slipped and he fell . . . He was working as a window cleaner at some important place in London . . . I don't know any more than that . . .' Her face crumpled again. 'I can't believe he's dead! I can't believe I'll never see him again! And I don't know what I'm going to do now . . .'

'There's nothing you can do, love. You just have to carry on and . . .' He broke off. *Try and get over it*, he had been going to say, but that sounded crass and uncaring.

'You don't understand!' Martha cried harshly. 'I was going to go to London, to him, and now . . .'

'Martha . . .'

Though he'd been careful not to let his feelings for her show since the day he'd overstepped the mark and tried to kiss her, they hadn't changed one iota. If anything, he was more in love with her than ever and had decided the best way forward was to bide his time. It had been his guess that Joe had gone for good, and when Martha came to realise that he would be in with a chance. Now, hearing her say she'd been going to go to Joe in London was a thorn in his heart. And seeing her so distraught didn't bode well, either. She must really love him and would probably never forget him.

'I just don't know what I'm going to do!' she repeated. The tears were pouring down her cheeks again and she bent double, burying her face in her hands and rocking to and fro as if her grief was a physical pain.

Seb dropped to a crouch beside her, feeling totally helpless, and if he hadn't been so close he might not have heard her next words, which were no more than a whisper.

'I'm in such terrible trouble. And if Joe's dead, there's no way out . . .'

'What are you talking about, Martha?' Seb asked gently, half-wondering if shock had made her take leave of her senses.

'The mess I'm in,' she whispered. 'Oh, I know I shouldn't be thinking about that now, you'll think I'm heartless, that I didn't love him. I did – I did – and I can't bear that I'll never see him again. But it's not just that. It's everything else too . . .'

'But what, Martha?' Seb pressed her, puzzled. 'Tell me. If you're in trouble, I'll try to help. But I can't if I don't know what it is.'

For long moments Martha continued to rock, her face still buried in her hands. Then she looked up at him with eyes awash with tears.

'I'm going to have a baby.'

Seb stiffened with shock, and a sharp pain knifed through his heart. Whilst he'd been hoping she would forget about Joe, she'd been meeting up with him, making love to him. The very thought was anathema to him and he reacted with a surge of anger.

'You've been seeing Joe, then? Why have you been pretending you haven't?'

She shook her head violently.

'No – it's not Joe's! That's the whole trouble . . .'

'Not Joe's?' This was even worse. 'Then who . . . ?'

Martha sniffed, gulped, wiped her cheeks with her hands.

And told him.

Seb paced the floor. It was two in the morning. He'd seen Martha home, waited until the door closed after her, and walked back to the Feathers where he'd poured himself a stiff whisky. He was exhausted, but wired. There was no way he could go to bed, no way he'd sleep with this anger boiling inside him.

What Martha had told him was beyond belief, and yet he did believe her.

'Why didn't you say something? Why didn't you tell me?' he'd demanded.

'I couldn't,' she'd whispered. 'I was so ashamed.'

He'd wondered why the men from Bath had suddenly stopped frequenting the Feathers; wondered why they'd started coming there in the first place, if it came to that. Now he knew. He'd failed Martha. She'd said she didn't like them, didn't trust them, but he'd been so pleased with the extra revenue their visits were bringing in that he hadn't acted to protect her. And that night, when the man she'd nicknamed Wolf had raped her, he'd been so taken up with trying to get his skittle-alley finished for the season that he hadn't been back to the pub once to make sure she was all right.

And all for nothing, he thought bitterly. There was no way the skittle-alley would be ready this year.

Seb slammed his fist into the wall, grazing his knuckles and scarcely noticing the pain.

He was hurt that Martha hadn't felt able to confide in him, hurt that it had been Joe she had planned to go to. But now Joe was dead. And Seb could think of only one way he could help her with her terrible situation. By suggesting he made an honest woman of her. It wasn't the way he'd wanted to ask her to marry him, and she might not be agreeable, but at least he could put the offer on the table. And he'd do it tomorrow. If she came in to work he'd ask her then; if not he'd go to see her at her home. One way or the other this had to be resolved, and quickly.

His mind made up, Seb finally went into the house and up the stairs to bed.

'Why would you do that for me, Seb?' Martha asked. 'Why would you marry me?'

'Because I love you. I've loved you from the first moment I laid eyes on you.'

'And you'd take on another man's child? Because, whoever the father was, I can't abandon the baby.'

'If you want to keep it, then I'll be a father to the child.'

'Oh, Seb, I don't know how to thank you . . .'

'Then it's yes?'

She nodded. 'And not just because of the baby,' she said hesitantly. 'I think I love you too.'

Seb took her in his arms. 'That's all right then.'

Now, all those years later, Martha tossed and turned, as far from sleep as ever, while Seb snored gently beside her.

Theirs had been a good marriage. Though she had never forgotten Joe, she'd spoken the truth when she'd told Seb she loved him that long-ago night when he'd offered to marry her, take on the child she was carrying, and save her from the shame and disgrace she'd have faced. It was a love that had crept up on her, a love she'd tried to deny out of loyalty to Joe, and over the years it had continued to grow. As for Seb, there had never been anyone but Martha for him from the first moment he'd set eyes on her.

They'd gone on to have more children of their own, and Seb had been a loving father to all of them. But as Garth had grown and started to exhibit unwelcome traits, Martha had done her best to keep them hidden from Seb. She was very afraid they had been inherited from his natural father, and the last thing she wanted to do was to draw attention to the circumstances of his conception. Neither should Seb have to cope with the problem that was Garth. That was hers and hers alone.

But for all that she acknowledged that there was a great deal of his despicable father in him, he was her son too, and she loved him just as fiercely as she loved Conrad and Lewis, and was even more protective of him, sometimes, she knew, to the detriment of the other two boys.

Whatever happened, she would be there for him, fighting with all her might to set him on the right path and ensure he didn't follow in his father's footsteps. Whatever it cost her, she would never give up on him.

Worried as she was about what Ernie had come to tell her, and wholly undecided about what her next step should be, Martha's resolve was as strong as ever. She'd refused to abandon him as a baby and she wouldn't abandon him now.

Chapter Six

St Peter's Workhouse – June 1896

'Don't go, Ella – please don't leave me!'

Jeannie clutched at her sister's sleeve, gazing up at her with pleading, tear-filled eyes.

'It will only be for a couple of hours, Jeannie. And we wouldn't have been together in any case. You'll be in lessons with Miss Owen and I'd have been in another room with the rector. He wants me to go to the rectory today instead, that's all.'

'But why? Why does he want you to go there?'

'Because it's easier for him. All the books he needs to teach me are there,' Ella explained, repeating the reason the rector had given for wanting both her and Leo to begin having their extra tuition at the rectory rather than in the workhouse.

'But it's such a long way away!' Jeannie wailed.

'No, it's not. It's only just down the road.'

'It *is* a long way! I don't want you to go, Ella! Please don't go . . .'

'I have to if I'm to get an education to give us a better life,' Ella said patiently, though she was beginning to despair of her sister ever getting over her terrible insecurity.

It had been bad enough before Mammy had died; since then Jeannie couldn't bear for Ella to be out of her sight.

'I don't care about that! I just want Mammy . . . and you.'

'Jeannie . . .' Ella tried to prise herself free of her sister's clinging hands, close to tears herself. 'You're making me late – and Leo too.'

Miss Hopkins, who had agreed that Ella and Leo could take their lessons at the rectory – as she agreed to anything the rector suggested – had stipulated that the two of them must walk there and back together, though they would be taught in separate rooms. This had pleased Ella enormously – it meant that she and Leo would have a little time together without having to constantly be on the lookout for a master or mistress who would chastise them for fraternising. Now, however, knowing that Leo would be waiting for her only added to her helpless frustration.

Jeannie was crying in earnest now and Ella didn't know what to do, torn between the need to go and anxiety at leaving her sister while she was in such a state.

Fortunately, just at that moment, Miss Owen's head appeared round the half-open door.

'Whatever is going on?' she asked.

Jeannie was crying too hard to answer, but Ella explained, and Miss Owen crossed the room to touch Jeannie's shoulder.

'Come on, my dear. It's time for lessons.' Jeannie pouted, still clinging to Ella's sleeve. 'We're going to read a story,' Miss Owen went on. 'You'd like that, wouldn't you?'

Jeannie looked up at her uncertainly.

'*The Water Babies*. We started it yesterday, remember? Don't you want to find out what happened to Tom next?'

Slowly Jeannie nodded and at last relaxed her hold on Ella's sleeve. Miss Owen took her hand and eased her further away.

'Off you go, Ella,' she said. 'And don't worry about Jeannie.

She's going to be fine until you get back, I'll make sure of that.'

'Thank you,' Ella said, grateful for the schoolmistress's kindness in this horrible place where it was in such short supply.

In the doorway she paused, looking back. Miss Owen had crouched down to Jeannie's level and was wiping away the last of her tears.

Relieved, Ella ran along the corridor towards the entrance hall where she knew Leo would be waiting.

The rectory was a big square building constructed of Bath stone and set at the end of a drive that curved between vast lawns and a guard of honour of horse chestnut trees. In spring they were covered with dome-shaped blossoms of pink and white, in autumn the conkers would come tumbling down, a magnet for local children who made quick forays into the rectory grounds to collect a pocketful then racing out again before they could be caught. Now, however, in June, the drive was scattered with nothing but fading blooms.

Beside the front door hung a bell the size of a pig's bladder with a rope attached. Leo grasped the rope, jangling the bell enthusiastically, and taking delight in the racket it made, while Ella jiggled nervously from one foot to the other. The prospect of entering this imposing house was as daunting as the rector himself.

Just as Leo was about to jangle the bell again the door was opened by an elderly maid, smartly attired in a long black dress and frilly white cap and apron.

'All right, all right, there's no need for that,' she admonished him. 'I heard you the first time.'

Ella was on the point of apologising for Leo, who appeared quite unabashed, but before she could, he spoke for himself.

'The rector's expecting us.'

'Oh, is he indeed! Then I suppose you'd better come in.'

Leo strode in confidently and Ella followed him into an entrance hall, the floor of which was covered with bright Italian tiles, polished to a high sheen. It was dominated by a large painting of a sweet-faced Christ, arms outstretched in a gesture of welcome, but Ella thought there was nothing welcoming about the collection of voluminous black cloaks hanging on a hall stand – the ones that made the rector look like a giant raven – or the enormous black umbrellas in a rack beside the door. Almost eight weeks of private lessons had done nothing to make her more comfortable in his presence, and though he'd been nothing but kind something about his silky smooth manner turned her stomach in much the same way as the peculiar musty smell of him did.

'The rector is in his study,' the maid informed them. 'Wait here, and I'll see if he's ready for you.'

She bustled away into the depths of the house, reappearing a few moments later.

'This way,' she said brusquely, and Leo and Ella followed her stiff frame along a passageway hung with the Stations of the Cross.

'Your pupils, sir,' she announced, and stood aside for them to enter the room.

'Ella. Leo. Come in.'

A shadow blocked out the sun streaming in through bay windows. Rector Evans, clad as always all in black apart from the white dog collar showing at the neck of his cassock. Why did he wear that at home? Ella wondered. Didn't he ever change into something less formal? Or was the cassock intended to impress her and Leo with his position of authority?

'Miss Hopkins raised no objection to your coming here then.' It was a statement rather than a question.

'No, sir.'

'No, sir.'

They answered in unison.

'Good. So we'll begin.' He crossed to a bookcase and selected a leather-bound volume. 'I'd like you to begin reading this, Ella, while I set some work for Leo. I'll be back shortly.'

Ella chewed her lip. She'd known, of course, that she and Leo would be taught in different rooms, but now that the moment had come the thought of being separated from him in this strange house frightened her.

'Please take a seat, Ella,' the rector said, as if he'd noticed her nervousness and wished to put her at her ease. Then he ushered Leo out.

Left alone, Ella crossed to the big bay window, which looked out on to yet more lawns edged with rose bushes and a trellis with what looked like sweet peas twining their way up towards the light. A chintz-covered seat followed the curve of the window. Ella plumped down on to it, resting her back against the white-painted wooden panel that backed it and glanced down at the book the rector had given her.

The Water Babies by Charles Kingsley.

'Oh!' She was surprised, and a little disappointed. She knew the book well – Miss Owen had read it aloud when Ella was in her class just as she always did, just as she was reading it to Jeannie and the other little ones now. Ella had expected something a bit more grown-up, something by Charles Dickens, perhaps. But at least she'd be able to answer any questions the rector put to her about the content without getting flustered, tying herself into knots and making herself look stupid. She opened the book and flicked through the first familiar pages before her attention wandered and she looked around what was evidently to be her classroom.

As in the hall and corridor, the walls were hung with prints in wooden frames – Ella recognised 'Behold I Stand at the Door and Knock'. There were also some framed samplers which she imagined had been made for him by one of his lady parishioners. One, in large and intricate scarlet letters on an ecru ground, read: 'Suffer the little children to come unto me.' A big, slightly worn, leather armchair sported an embroidered cushion, anti-macassar and sleeves, stitched in similar style, and on the mantelshelf above a narrow fireplace a brass cross was flanked by china figurines wearing flowing robes – some of the saints, Ella supposed.

The rector's desk was placed against the wall on the far side of the room from the window, a captain's chair pushed into the well between pillars of drawers. How peculiar! Ella thought. If this were her room she'd have it where she could see out of the window and enjoy the view of the garden, not stuck away over there facing nothing but a blank wall and yet another sampler.

She wished she dared investigate the bookshelves to see if there was something she'd rather read than the familiar *Water Babies*, and even got up and took a tentative step towards them before her courage failed her and she sat down again. She didn't want to appear too forward on her very first visit here.

She was flicking through the pages of *The Water Babies* again when the rector returned.

'How have you been getting on?' he asked.

'Um . . . very well . . .' Ella faltered, and then, deciding honesty would be the best policy, she added: 'I do know it, actually. We read it with Miss Owen.'

'I see. Would you like to read it again, or would you prefer to try something different?'

'Something different,' Ella said, hoping she wasn't saying the wrong thing. But the rector seemed unfazed.

'I'll see what I can find for next time,' he said, with one of his smarmy smiles. 'You're a good reader, Ella, as is your dear little sister. Perhaps you'd like something more challenging.'

Ella nodded, wondering what she'd let herself in for, and wondering too how Rector Evans knew how well Jeannie could read. But then, he did seem to take a lot of interest in her – out of sympathy, she supposed.

'For today, however, I'd like you to read aloud for me from the book I chose, and then answer some questions about it.' He crossed to his desk and sat down in the captain's chair. 'Come and stand beside me.'

Obediently, Ella followed him.

'A little closer, if you please. I'm afraid my hearing is not as good as it once was.'

Reluctantly, Ella moved nearer, trying not to wrinkle her nose at the musty smell of the rector, stronger than ever when she was in such close proximity.

She was uncomfortable, too, with the way he was looking at her from beneath his hooded lids, and the way he was moistening his fleshy lips.

'Shall we begin?' There was something almost suggestive about the words, and Ella's discomfort grew stronger. But somehow she retained her composure and began to read aloud.

It was as she turned the second page that she felt his hand at the hem of her skirt. She stiffened, a trembling beginning deep in her stomach, but somehow she continued reading, stumbling over some of the words as his hand crept stealthily up her leg and shock and horror constricted her throat.

'Don't be afraid, my dear. You are doing very well.' His tone was silky, encouraging.

As his fingers reached her inner thigh Ella froze, and no more words would come.

'Good. I think that will do for today. We'll continue next time, perhaps with a different book,' he said, as if nothing untoward had happened at all. 'Now, I must go back and see how Leo is doing. I've set you some sums. Long division – we were doing it last week, if you remember. You can do them while I'm gone.'

He rose, reached across the desk for an exercise book and pencil and placed them directly in front of the captain's chair. 'Sit here, my dear.'

Then, without another word, he left the room.

Ella sank into the captain's chair. She didn't want to, didn't want to sit where *he* had sat, or be anywhere near it, but her legs were shaking so much they didn't feel up to supporting her. Yet at the same time she could hardly believe what had just happened.

He wouldn't really have put his hand up her skirt, would he? Could she have been mistaken, imagining it because she was so nervous? Or perhaps stroking her leg was his way of trying to set her at ease, though it had had quite the opposite effect. If it was that, he might be offended by her reaction to what he thought was a kind gesture, perhaps decide not to give her private tuition any more. Not that she wanted him to. She didn't want to be alone with him ever again. But without his help and support she'd never be able to better herself, never realise her dream of working as a classroom assistant, never be in a position to provide for Jeannie properly as she'd promised Mam she would.

The chaotic warring thoughts and feelings jumbled around inside her head and her stomach, making her feel sick and trapped. She had to forget what had happened – or what she *thought* had happened – and prove she was worth him investing his time in, or she and Jeannie would never have a decent life. And she had to begin now, with the sums he'd set her.

She picked up the pencil and bent over the exercise book, but the figures were swimming in front of her eyes and her brain refused to work properly. She'd managed only three of the long divisions out of the ten he'd set her by the time he came back, and she wasn't at all sure if she'd got them right or not. But to her surprise he didn't scold or criticise, only praised her.

'They were difficult calculations, Ella,' he said sympathetically. 'We'll look at them again next time.'

Next time. Ella felt sick again with dread. But she merely nodded. 'Yes, sir. I'm sorry, sir.'

He laid a hand on her shoulder and she tried not to shrink away.

'Don't worry about it, Ella. We all have to learn to walk before we can run.'

'Yes, sir.'

'Off you go then.'

With a feeling of utmost relief, Ella left the study and hurried along the passage past the Stations of the Cross to the entrance hall where Leo was waiting for her.

'That was good, wasn't it?' Leo said as they walked back down the drive between the horse chestnut trees. 'A comfy chair with a cushion to sit on instead of that hard bench at St Peter's that gives you a sore bum.'

Ella said nothing.

'What about you? Did you have a proper chair?' he asked.

She nodded.

'What's it like in his study, anyway? Does he have loads of Bibles and prayer books and stuff?'

'I didn't really notice.'

Leo half-turned, looking at her. 'What's the matter, Ella?'

'Nothing.'

'Something is. You're not usually backward in coming forward.'

'Nothing's wrong!' Ella snapped.

'Didn't you get on very well with the work he set you? If that's what it is I'll help you if I can.'

Ella grasped at the straw he was offering. 'It was long division. I don't like arithmetic, and especially not long division.'

'Well, there you are. Look, next time we're both on garden duty, I'll go over it with you if we get the chance. It's easy when you get the hang of it.'

'Thanks,' Ella said, thinking: If only it were that simple!

Leo took her hand, pulling her round to face him and looking at her intently. 'You know you can tell me anything, Ella,' he said unexpectedly. 'If there's something else . . .'

Ella's face burned, and as she felt tears gathering behind her eyes she turned her face away.

If only she *could* tell him! But she couldn't. If she did he might say or do something stupid that would get them both into trouble, and she wasn't even sure she hadn't misinterpreted the whole incident. And besides . . .

She couldn't bring herself to talk about what she thought had happened. She was too embarrassed, and too ashamed, as if it was all her fault. If she told Leo she'd never be able to face him again.

'There's nothing else. Really.' With an effort, she managed to keep her voice steady.

And then they were back at St Peter's, and if the chance to speak out had ever been there, it had gone again.

This was something she had to keep to herself. She couldn't tell Leo, and certainly couldn't tell anyone in authority. They'd never believe her, anyway. They'd think she was making it up.

Her chance to make a better life for herself and Jeannie would be lost, and all for nothing.

For the first time in her life Ella was glad to see the gates of the workhouse close behind her, shutting out the outside world and offering her some semblance of safety.

'Ella!' As she entered the common room, Jeannie ran towards her, throwing her arms round her sister's waist and holding on tight. 'Oh, I'm so glad you're back!'

'I told you I wouldn't be long.' Ella smoothed Jeannie's fair hair away from her face, a wave of tenderness washing over her. 'Did Miss Owen read *The Water Babies* to you?'

Jeannie nodded enthusiastically.

'It's really good! We've got to the bit where Tom meets Ellie – Ellie, that's almost you, isn't it? Ella – Ellie?'

'You'll never believe it, but I've been reading *The Water Babies* too,' Ella said. 'We might even have been reading it at the same time.'

Jeannie's eyes filled with wonder. 'Oh – I wish I'd known! I'd have felt better then. As if you were here with me.'

'Jeannie, you know I'll always be here for you.' Ella bent and kissed her sister's head.

'Always? Even when I'm grown up like you?'

'Always,' Ella said firmly – though she sometimes wondered if Jeannie would ever be properly grown up. Already she was young for her age, and though Ella thought some of her dependency was down to the traumatic events that had blighted her short life, she still worried that in some ways Jeannie would remain a child for ever.

'That's enough, you two!' Miss Hopkins materialised beside them. 'Ella – go and put your books away safely in your locker, and Jeannie, come with me. Your face is in need of a good wash and your hair could do with brushing.'

It was true – her face was very dirty, from rubbing her tears away with ink-stained fingers, Ella guessed, and her hair certainly needed tidying.

'Go on, Jeannie,' Ella encouraged her.

As she took the exercise books containing the homework Rector Evans had set her, sick dread overwhelmed her again. She didn't want to go back to the rectory, didn't want to have to struggle with long division, even if Leo helped her to understand it, didn't want to have to stand beside the rector as he marked her work or had her read to him. But she could see no way out of it if she was to make a better life for her and Jeannie.

Ella felt the jaws of the trap closing in around her, and was overwhelmed with despair.

Chapter Seven

Her worst fears were realised. Over the next few weeks the same horrible scenario was repeated each time Ella was alone with Rector Evans in his study. It never lasted long, but those few minutes seemed like an eternity to Ella, and left her sickened and traumatised. Yet somehow she managed to steel herself to remain motionless as the searching fingers crept ever upwards until they reached her tenderest and most secret places, stroking her gently. When it happened at the beginning of her lesson she was incapable of concentrating afterwards on the work he had set her; when it came later she spent most of the hour's tuition nauseous with dread. And still she dared not object, much less bring herself to tell anyone what was going on.

One afternoon, however, things came to a head with a terrifying inevitability. Once more they were working on her long division, still shaky in spite of Leo's efforts to help her, scarcely able to think straight because of her dread of what was to come. Ella knew she'd made a mess of the simplest calculations, and when the rector called her over to his desk her stomach was alive with butterflies of trepidation, both for his unwelcome attentions and for the verdict he would pass on her inability to master what he had been drumming into her over the past weeks.

'Oh, Ella.' The Rector shook his head regretfully, frowning at the almost indecipherable figures and the many crossings out. 'We are failing to make progress, wouldn't you agree?' Ella nodded miserably. 'I confess I am beginning to wonder if you are capable of what I had hoped we could achieve.'

He was going to tell her the private lessons were at an end, she thought, with a dizzying combination of relief and regret.

But he didn't. Instead she felt the familiar touch of his creeping fingers up beneath his skirts but this time they didn't stop between her thighs. A finger jabbed into her, and pain shot through her, so sharp that she almost cried out. But the rector did not withdraw his hand, simply moving it around inside her, and the look on his fleshy face terrified her. The hooded eyes were half closed, his moist lips parted and trembling, and a sheen of sweat had broken out on his domed forehead. With his free hand he lifted his cassock and drew her towards him. Beneath the heavy cassock he was stark naked.

Ella gasped again, a gasp that was almost a scream. She had never seen a man's body before, especially not one in a state of arousal, and she was revolted by what she saw now. As the rector attempted to pull her towards him, she struck out at him with both hands and sprang backwards so violently that his intruding finger scraped her painfully before she was out of his lascivious reach. She turned, heading mindlessly for the door, but before she could reach it she tripped on the edge of the Indian rug and he caught her by the arms, twisting her round to face him once more. His expression now was dark and angry, yet the words that came out of his mouth were regretful.

'Ella, you disappoint me. I thought we could be friends. I help you to achieve a worthwhile goal in life, and in return you do something for me. But it seems you are unwilling to render even this small favour.'

Beyond words, Ella simply gazed at him with terror in her eyes, her whole body shrinking from him.

The rector waited a long moment, then his fleshy lips curled. 'If I were to offer to tutor your dear little sister instead of you, I think I would find her much more amenable.'

As she took in the meaning of his words, Ella's blood turned to ice, and she found her voice. 'Don't you dare! Don't you dare touch Jeannie!'

'She's very young – and very pretty,' he taunted her. 'I'm sure she would be only too eager to respond to affection.'

'Just leave us alone!' Ella screamed at him, struggling to break free of his grasp. 'Leave us both alone!'

The rector's lip curled. 'I'm sorry you are taking this attitude, Ella. But think about what I have said. Is it to be you? Or your sister? The decision, my dear, is yours.'

'No!' Ella screamed again. 'Let me go! Let me go!'

Quite unexpectedly the rector loosened his grip on her arms, and straightened. To her surprise his expression had turned to one of dismay.

'What are *you* doing here?' he barked ferociously.

Ella swung round. In the doorway was Leo, wide-eyed with astonishment and concern.

She stopped for nothing. Without a moment's hesitation she made a dash for the door, pushed past Leo, and fled. Down the corridor. Past a startled maid in her black uniform and crisp white cap and apron. Across the entrance hall. For a moment she thought the heavy brass knob on the front door was not going to turn; her hands were so slippery with perspiration they slid round it uselessly. Then, somehow, she managed it, dragged the door open, and rushed out. She was halfway down the drive before her legs gave way beneath her and she sank to the ground beneath one of the horse chestnut trees.

* * *

It was there that Leo found her, shaking and crying. He dropped on to the grass beside her, putting his arm around her, but she pushed him away. She couldn't bear to be touched just now, not even by Leo.

'What is it, Ella?' he asked urgently. 'Why are you in such a state? I heard you screaming, and came to see what was the matter. The rector said you'd just had a funny turn, but . . .' He looked at her questioningly.

Ella simply buried her face in her hands and lowered her head to her knees.

'Come on, Ella. This isn't like you,' Leo said helplessly. 'You haven't been yourself for weeks now. Ever since we started coming here for our tuition. You've got to tell me what's wrong.'

'I can't.' Her voice was muffled by her hands and her skirts. 'Just leave me. Go back and finish your lessons.'

'I'm not going anywhere until you tell me,' Leo said decisively.

'I can't.'

'You can. You must. Whatever it is, you can't keep it to yourself any longer.' Still she was silent, and he went on: 'Is it the rector? Has he done something to upset you?'

After a moment Ella nodded, closing in on herself even more.

'The bastard!' Leo exploded. 'What?'

'I can't . . .' Ella began to sob again.

Leo put his arm around her tentatively. This time she didn't pull away, but leaned into him, her tears soaking his shirt. He waited until her sobs quietened, then tried again.

'What, Ella? What's he done?'

Ella snuffled, her face buried now in his shoulder.

'What?' he asked again. 'Tell me, or I swear I'll go back in there and beat it out of him.'

'No!' She raised her head, looking at him with desperation in her eyes, anguish written in every line of her face. 'You mustn't do that! You'd go to prison!'

'Then tell me what it is he's done.'

Her lip trembled. Then, in little more than a whisper, she said: 'Things I didn't like. Terrible things.' She hesitated, unsure how to go on, and Leo waited, struggling to keep his patience. At last she went on: 'He's been touching me. Under my clothes.'

'You mean . . . ?' Leo patted his own chest.

'No . . . up *there* . . . you know . . .'

'Dear God!' Leo muttered, but with such venom that Ella began to tremble again. 'The bloody bastard!'

'There's worse,' Ella whispered. 'Today . . .'

'What?'

'Today . . . Oh, Leo, you know we've wondered why he wears that cassock when he's at home?' Now she'd begun, the words came tumbling out. 'Well, today I found out. He hasn't got anything on underneath it, and . . .'

Leo stiffened, every muscle, every sinew, every tendon tensing.

'He didn't . . . ?'

'No, he tried to make me, but I didn't. And then he said . . .' She faltered again. 'He said if I wouldn't, Jeannie would . . . And I'm so scared, Leo! She's only little, and I promised Mammy I'd look after her, but I can't . . . I can't do *that*! I can't! And I don't know what to do . . .'

Shocked, horrified and furious as he was, Leo fought to keep his temper under control. All his instincts were screaming at him to return to the rectory and beat the hell out of the filthy old bastard. But he knew that could only end in disaster for all of them. His head spinning, he sought desperately to find an answer.

'You've got to tell someone, Ella.' It was the only thing he could come up with.

'I've thought of that, but it wouldn't do any good,' Ella said wretchedly. She was a little calmer now that she no longer felt so alone. 'He'd just deny it and nobody would take my word against his.'

'But if I backed you up? Said what I heard – and saw . . .'

'They still wouldn't believe us against him. He's the rector, Leo, and Miss Hopkins worships the ground he walks on. Besides, if you spoke out against him, he probably wouldn't help you any more to get that scholarship.'

Leo huffed disgustedly. 'I don't know that I want to see the filthy old toad ever again.'

'It's your future at stake here, Leo,' Ella said earnestly. 'You can't throw it all away for me. I won't let you.'

'And what about your future? Honest to God, Ella, you're all that matters to me.'

'Then help me think of a way to make sure he doesn't start teaching Jeannie . . . doing those awful things to her . . .'

Leo's fists clenched. 'I'll kill the bastard before I'd let that happen!'

'Don't say such things, Leo,' Ella begged. 'I'd like to see him dead, goodness knows, but you mustn't even think such things, let alone say them. What you've got to do is go back in there and say you couldn't find me. Pretend you don't know what he's been doing. Please! I couldn't bear to think you'd lost your chance of a good future because of me.'

Leo hesitated. He didn't want to leave Ella, didn't want to go back into the rectory, but she was so insistent and he didn't want to upset her any more than she already was either. And perhaps she was right. Biting his tongue, controlling his fists and continuing with his lessons meant he would still have a chance of a better life, even if Ella had lost hers. If he took it, made something of himself, he'd be able to look after her and Jeannie. Give them the sort of life they deserved.

'I'm not letting you go through this on your own, Ella,' he said, looking her straight in the eye. 'Just make sure you wait for me so we can talk some more, come up with a plan.'

'I'll be down on the road. Now – go, Leo, before he comes out looking for you.'

Reluctantly, and still seething with anger, Leo went.

Ella walked to the end of the drive and sat down with her back against the perimeter wall, hugging her knees to her chest for comfort. In spite of the warmth of the day she was shivering and her stomach was still turning over. Every time she thought of what had happened, bile rose in her throat and she thought she might be sick. But she had to calm down, had to try and think of a way out of this terrible predicament. Feeling sorry for herself would do no good. It was Jeannie she must think of now, and how to keep her safe.

Could it be, she wondered, that it was Jeannie he had lusted after all along? Had she been just a convenient way of getting her sister into his clutches? Ella found herself remembering the way he talked about her – 'Your dear little sister' – and how he was forever mentioning how pretty she was. He never missed an opportunity to take her hand, stroke her hair, pat her cheek. Once she'd even seen him take Jeannie on his lap and now, picturing the look on his horrible paunchy face as he'd held her there, Ella's blood ran cold. It was the same expression as the one he'd worn that first day when he'd slid his hand under her skirts.

Ella was in no doubt now but that he'd carry out his threat to get to Jeannie at the first opportunity. And somehow she had to ensure that never happened.

But how? How could she protect her vulnerable little sister from that evil man? She was just a child herself, while he was a respected figure in the workhouse, and the outside world too, hiding his debauchery beneath a mask of holy righteousness and fooling them all. Especially Miss Hopkins, who seemed to revere him and would do anything to curry favour with him.

No, there was no way of preventing him from having his wicked way with Jeannie whilst they were still incarcerated in the workhouse.

Which left only one alternative.

Escape.

She'd run away, Ella thought, and take Jeannie with her. How they would manage it, she didn't know, but she felt sure Leo would help her. They'd put their heads together and come up with something.

From out of the sky, and through the tracery of branches above her head, a tiny feather fluttered down, coming to rest in the folds of her skirt, still bunched up between her knees. A sudden feeling of wonder came over her and she gazed at the feather, breath catching in her throat. She uncurled her fingers and carefully picked it up. It was purest white, and soft to her touch – a fragment of down from a baby bird.

Or a message from the angels.

Ella looked up. Not a single bird was to be seen, and a sense of calm enveloped her.

'Mammy!' she breathed, and in the gentle whisper of the breeze in the leaves overhead she thought she heard Mammy's voice, sweet and loving.

'I'm with you, my love. I'm always with you.'

Leo was approaching down the drive. Ella thrust the feather deep into the pocket of her skirt, being sure to tuck it underneath her handkerchief so there was no danger of her losing it. But she didn't mention it to Leo. He'd probably think she was being silly and fanciful and she didn't want worldly wise words to break the spell.

She was, however, going to tell him what she planned, and ask for his help in putting it into action. But first . . .

'What did he say?' she asked.

'Just what he said before. That you'd had a funny fit for no reason he was aware of.'

'Well, he wasn't going to tell the truth, was he?'

'And he said . . .' Leo hesitated.

'What?'

'That he thought the lessons were proving too much for you, and that he's going to speak to Miss Hopkins and get them stopped.'

'He didn't say anything about Jeannie?' Ella asked anxiously.

'No, but I don't suppose he would – not to me.'

'He will to Miss Hopkins though.'

'Maybe not. It might have been just a spur of the moment threat to get you to do what he wanted.'

'You didn't see his face when he said it.' Ella shivered. 'He's obsessed with her, Leo. I think I was just a stepping stone. After all, she's much prettier than me – and younger. More easily led.'

'You're pretty too,' Leo said loyally.

Ella ignored the compliment. 'He's always asking after her, making a fuss of her when he has the chance. I hadn't thought anything of it, but now . . . He'll go after her, I know it. And I can't let that happen. I've got to get her away from here, somewhere he can't reach her.'

'But how?' Leo asked, perplexed.

'We'll run away, and you have to help us.'

'Run away?' he echoed. 'Where would you go?'

109

'We've got relations in Hillsbridge.' Ella's words came tumbling out now. 'Daddy's brother – Uncle Ted. He's a miner, like Daddy was. We'll go to him.'

'Would he take you in?' Leo asked doubtfully. 'Mightn't he send you straight back to the workhouse?'

Ella bit her lip, trying to stifle her own doubts. She didn't know Uncle Ted very well, nor his wife, Auntie Ethel. She thought the two brothers had fallen out over something, and though she had no idea why, she thought it had something to do with Auntie Ethel. She'd only been about four at the time, but she could well remember a shouting match between Daddy and Uncle Ted because it had frightened her so, and she recalled that Auntie Ethel's name had been mentioned – 'that bloody woman', Daddy had called her, and said she had Ted right under her thumb. Ella had wondered what that meant and pictured sour-faced Ethel with a hand on Uncle Ted's head, pressing with her thumb until he fell down. She knew what it meant now, of course – it meant that Ethel called the tune in their house, and she realised Leo might well be right. After all, they hadn't come to her and Jeannie's assistance when they were orphaned. If Ethel said they had to be sent back to the workhouse, then perhaps Uncle Ted would have no choice but to return them.

But she couldn't give up on her plan.

'We had really nice neighbours when we lived in the Ten Houses,' she said. 'They used to look after me and Jeannie sometimes when Daddy was at work and Mammy wasn't well. They wouldn't let us be sent back if they knew . . .'

'You hope,' Leo said.

'They wouldn't, I'm sure. And I've got to get Jeannie away from that wicked man. Please, Leo, help me.'

'I suppose.' Leo was torn between anxiety for both Ella and

Jeannie if they stayed at the workhouse, and fear of what would become of them in the dangerous world outside. 'I'll have a think about it. But for now, we'd better be getting back or we'll both be in trouble.'

'Don't take too long about it,' Ella pleaded. 'We've got to come up with a plan soon, or it'll be too late.'

In silence they hurried back along the road to the workhouse, both lost in their own chaotic thoughts.

It was Leo who came up with the plan.

'Look, I'm working in the garden down by the gate tomorrow. I've got to cut back all the ivy that's growing along the fence and dig out some sycamore saplings. If I can dig right under the fence and bend it up a bit, you could squeeze out underneath. I don't think anyone would notice – it's pretty overgrown down there. And if you and Jeannie managed to creep out after lights out you wouldn't be missed till morning.'

'Oh, Leo – yes!'

They were whispering to one another through the wire fence that divided the boys' and girls' exercise yards.

'Tomorrow night, then. I'll cover the hole up next day.'

'Make sure you do. I don't want you getting into trouble. And thank you, Leo. You're a real friend.'

'Just trying to help you out. But for God's sake, take care, Ella,' he said anxiously.

'You too.'

'I'll be all right. It's you I'm worried about. And . . . I'll miss you, Ella.'

'And I'll miss you.'

'Ella Martin! Come away from that fence!' Miss Hopkins' strident voice carried across the exercise yard.

For a moment longer the two friends looked at one another,

and Ella saw her own sadness at parting reflected in Leo's eyes. She raised her hand to the wire, he raised his, and their fingers touched.

'Ella Martin!' Miss Hopkins shouted again.

Ella tore her eyes from Leo's and moved away. On the far side of the yard she turned; he was still there watching her, his bright hair burnished by the sun, his hand still gripping the fence where their fingers had touched.

Tears stung her eyes. She hated the thought that she might never see him again, her best – her only – friend. But what choice did she have? At all costs she had to get Jeannie away from the evil rector. And she had to do it alone.

With the weight of the world on her shoulders, Ella turned and walked away.

'What . . . what are you doing, Ella?' Jeannie's voice was thick with sleep.

'Hush!' Ella whispered urgently, laying a hand over her sister's mouth. 'Get up and get dressed, and don't make a sound.'

'But why?'

'We're going on an adventure.'

Ella was already dressed herself and had packed her own and Jeannie's things into the carpet bag they had brought with them to the workhouse and which had been stored in the bottom of her locker. Now she crossed the dormitory, opened the door softly, and peeped out, keeping watch while she waited for her sister to get dressed. Jeannie, still half asleep, seemed to be taking for ever. Ella went back to her as she struggled to get her arms into the sleeves of her dress.

'Hurry up!' she whispered, pulling the dress down over Jeannie's slight form.

She stuffed Jeannie's pillow part way beneath the thin sheet – she'd already done the same with her own, hoping that from a distance and in the dim light it would look like a sleeping child. Unless there was a disturbance of some kind the mistresses rarely came right into the nursery. She made one last foray to the door to check that the coast was clear, hurried back, climbed on to her bed and pushed the small window she'd unlatched earlier fully open – fortunately the dormitory was on the ground floor. Then she grabbed the carpet bag and tossed it out.

Jeannie was watching, wide-eyed now, holding one of her boots in each hand. Ella took them from her and tossed them out too.

'Come on!' She took Jeannie's hand, pulling her on to the bed and hoisting her up towards the open window. 'Hold on to the frame and climb out.'

Jeannie cast a terrified glance at her sister. 'I can't!'

'Yes, you can.'

'I'll fall and hurt myself!'

'No, you won't. It's only a little way, and it's soft grass underneath. Go on, Jeannie! I can't hold you up for much longer.' Still Jeannie hesitated, and she went on: 'We're getting away from this place. Don't you want to?'

A small sob that might have been agreement, and to Ella's relief Jeannie crawled out. Ella followed, landing on the grass beside her sister with a soft plop.

'Good girl,' she whispered. 'Now, put your boots on quickly.'

While Jeannie did so, Ella tried in vain to close the window after them, but it was just out of her reach.

'Can you push it shut if I lift you up?' she asked her sister.

This time Jeannie didn't argue, perhaps realising the importance of not leaving any more evidence of their escape than they had to. Ella struggled to hoist her up, but in the end

113

she managed it, and Jeannie gave the window a shove so that it was almost closed.

It would have to do. Next, they had to cross the grounds without being seen and find the escape route Leo had promised to make. Supposing he hadn't been able to? Ella thought, experiencing a moment's panic. Supposing he'd been assigned a different duty today, or hadn't been able to dig deep enough? They'd be stranded, unable to get out, and unable to get back in.

But she wouldn't think of that now. She had to trust in Leo, and she did. It was her own ability to carry this through she was most worried about, and the awful consequences if she failed.

A nearly full moon in a clear sky made it almost as bright as day, increasing the danger of them being seen. A cloudy night would have been better. But at least it wasn't raining!

Ella made sure both she and Jeannie were tucked away in the shadow of the building while she looked all around, checking the coast was clear. Nothing moved, and all was quiet but for the occasional mournful hoot of an owl and a dog barking somewhere in the distance. She picked up the carpet bag.

'Follow me, and keep close to the wall,' she whispered to Jeannie.

They set off stealthily along the length of the wall and around the corner of the building, reaching it without mishap. Now they had no option but to break cover. Once again, Ella checked for any signs of life, then, her heart in her mouth, she grabbed Jeannie's hand.

'Now! Run for your life!'

As they covered the open ground, Ella kept expecting to hear a warning shout, but none came, and the two girls threw themselves into the shrubs at the far side and wormed their way into the long grass beyond, where they lay for a few moments, catching their breath and allowing their fast-beating hearts to slow a little. Then Ella instructed Jeannie to wait there while she looked for the passage Leo had promised to dig.

She found it easily enough, following a trail of uprooted sycamore saplings. Where it ended Leo had hidden his efforts under some debris, and when she pulled it aside she could see the pit in the freshly dug earth and the wire fencing bent up by a foot or so. She hurried back to where Jeannie was waiting.

'Come on. Hurry.'

Together they returned to the escape spot, and Ella helped Jeannie down into the hole. She was beginning to show signs of nervousness again and Ella gave her a little push.

'Go on. You've got plenty of room. When you're out, I'll push the bag under. Just get it out of the way so I can get through.'

Reluctantly Jeannie did as she'd been told, though she had some difficulty pulling the bag up out of the tunnel. Ella reached forward to help her, then scrambled under the fence herself. It was a tight squeeze and she caught the bodice of her dress on the sharp wire and had to tear it to free herself. Then she was through and the two of them were on the outside.

Brushing the dirt from her hands and knees, she looked down at the bent fence and the hole in the earth beyond. She wished she could do something to conceal it in case it was discovered after they were found to be missing and before Leo had the chance to fill it in again. She didn't want him getting into trouble for helping them, but she couldn't see that she could do anything about it. She'd just have to trust that he'd deal with it as soon as possible.

'Where now?' Jeannie asked.

'Down to the main road. But we have to hurry in case we're missed and they come looking for us.' Ella picked up the carpet bag, took Jeannie's hand and started off as fast as her little sister's legs could manage.

Free! They were free! But for how long?

At the junction with the main road into Bath, Ella turned left.

'Where are we going?' Jeannie asked again.

'Hillsbridge.'

'Hillsbridge?' Jeannie had no memories of the town.

'Home,' Ella said. 'We're going home.'

'How much further?' Jeannie whined.

'Not much,' Ella tried to reassure her, though she wasn't sure they were even halfway. They'd walked along a straight, flat road, passing the Fuller's Earth Works, down a winding hill into a valley, and now the road led upwards again, round bends, with open country on both sides. They'd passed only a few houses and a farm in the valley, and to Ella's relief there had been no traffic on the road with the exception of a man wobbling along on a bicycle. She'd pulled Jeannie into the shadow of the hedge, out of sight, but she suspected the man was too tipsy to be aware of anything beyond keeping the pedals turning and himself upright.

'But my legs hurt, Ella! And I'm tired!'

'I know. So am I. But we've got to keep going.'

'Can't you carry me?' Jeannie pleaded.

'No, my love, I can't.' Truth to tell, it was as much as Ella could do to keep going herself. There was no way she could carry Jeannie. If only Leo were here! she thought. He'd lift her sister up on to his shoulders without a moment's hesitation.

Somehow they struggled on up the hill. It wasn't steep, but it was relentless. As they rounded a curve in the road, a building on the right-hand side came into view.

'A house!' Jeannie gasped. 'Is that Hillsbridge?'

'No, we're still out in the country,' Ella said apologetically.

'Can't we stop there? Please!'

'We don't know the people who live there.'

'But couldn't we just have a rest?'

'I don't know. Perhaps if they're all in bed we could sit down in the garden, out of sight of the road.'

As they drew nearer, Ella could see it was more than just a house, though it was the shape of one, with a small cottage attached. By the light of the moon she could see an inn sign. 'The Three Feathers', it read, the words spread above and below a depiction of the Prince of Wales' feathers, painted in white on a red background.

'It's a pub,' she said.

There was a faint light showing between roughly drawn curtains at one of the upstairs windows, but the ground floor was in darkness.

'They must have closed for the night,' she said. 'Let's cross the road and have a look.'

They trudged across the road and along the side of the building – no lights showing there either – and came upon a collection of outbuildings at the rear, which were also in darkness. Perhaps they could have a rest here, she thought hopefully.

The first door she tried was locked, and so was the second, and her heart sank. But when she tried the door handle of the largest of the outbuildings it turned, and she was able to push the door open.

It was dim inside, lit only by moonlight filtering in through small, high-up windows, but as her eyes became accustomed to the gloom, Ella saw chairs arranged along two of the walls and some sort of wooden platform, about three feet in width, running the length of the wall opposite the door. Curious, she approached it. A sort of tunnel ran along the wall above the platform, and above the spot where it ended was a blackboard, mounted on nails, and covered with rows and columns of white-chalked figures. Jeannie had already collapsed on to one of the chairs, but Ella walked the length of the platform, and at the other end found a well where bottle-shaped wooden objects and some large, solid-looking balls lay higgledy-piggledy. She'd never seen anything quite like this before, but something else had claimed her attention.

Directly behind the well, hay bales were stacked one on top of the other, forming a low barrier. Realising the potential they offered refreshed her and she hurried back to where Jeannie sat, head already nodding on her chest.

'Jeannie, I've found the perfect bed!' She grabbed the carpet bag, pulling out their shawls that she'd made sure to pack. 'Come on!'

A sleepy Jeannie followed her, sucking on her thumb, and Ella spread one shawl over the top bale of hay and laid out the other to be used as a blanket. She helped Jeannie up, then climbed up herself, pulled the shawl over the two of them, and curled up beside her sister, who was almost instantly asleep.

They'd have to be up and gone before daybreak, Ella thought, but for the moment they could rest, if not sleep. This was the strangest bed she'd ever slept in, yet it felt far more comfortable than the hard mattress at the workhouse, and despite all her best efforts, within moments Ella was also fast asleep.

Chapter Eight

In the small front bedroom over the bar, Garth Packer was wide awake.

There'd been yet another confrontation with his mother about his wild ways, but he was used to that. It was water off a duck's back. If she wasn't accusing him of stealing, she was warning him about getting some girl in the family way. If she wasn't chastising him for drinking and smoking, she was complaining that the hours he kept were far too late when he had an early start at his uncle's farm in the morning.

Bloody farm! He hated it. Milking cows, cleaning up muck, working in the fields, shivering in winter, sweltering in summer. He wouldn't stick it for a moment longer than he had to, and he thought he might have a word with Ticker Bendle, the local bookmaker. Unbeknown to his mother and father he'd been a runner for Ticker when he was ten or eleven, and he was in hopes he could persuade the bookie to take him on as an assistant.

In the meantime there was nothing for it but to stick it out at the farm. The only alternative – a job in the coalmines – wasn't something he'd even consider.

Tonight, however, it wasn't any of these grievances that was keeping him awake. It was what he'd overheard after he'd come home late again and three sheets in the wind from all the rough scrumpy he'd consumed. He'd rolled into the kitchen and as he'd tried to get himself a drink of water he'd managed to knock over a whole tray of glasses that were on the cupboard by the sink. Every last one of them had smashed to smithereens on the tiled floor. Some were empty, but others contained dregs of beer and shorts – there must have been a good quarter pint left in one of them – so that the shattered glass swam about in a murky, smelly ocean.

Garth swore. Martha, coming in from the bar with yet more glasses, stopped short. She'd heard the crash, but hadn't anticipated quite such a disaster.

'Oh, for crying out loud, Garth!' she exclaimed.

'It wasn't my fault!' His tone was injured, but his words were a bit slurred. He grabbed a cloth from the sink, thinking that if he attempted to clear up the mess he might escape another tongue-lashing, but Martha swiftly intervened.

'No – not like that! You'll cut yourself, and then we'll have blood all over the place too. Get the long-handled brush and we'll sweep it all out the door and clean it up in the morning when the beer's drained away.'

Seb appeared in the doorway. 'What the dickens is going on?'

'It's our Garth – knocked over a whole load of glasses.' Martha had put down her own tray, pushing it well back on the counter out of harm's way, and was reaching for the broom Garth was holding out to her.

'Hmm,' Seb grunted, giving the boy a look that said more than any words.

'It wasn't my fault,' Garth repeated sullenly. 'She left it too close to the edge.'

Careful as he always was to avoid criticising or being the

one to dole out punishment, and slow to anger as he usually was, Seb's temper rose at the boy's insolence and for once he spoke up.

'*She?*' he echoed emphatically. 'Who's *she*? The cat's mother? It's time you started treating your mother with more respect, my lad. And from what I can see of it, you're tipsy again. At your age! Where did you get it? Who sold it to you? Or did you help yourself from my cellar?'

'No!' Garth said indignantly.

'I wouldn't put it past you.'

'If that's what you think of me, I will next time.'

'You cheeky little sod!' Seb was beside himself. 'There won't be a next time if I have anything to do with it. And if I catch you in that cellar, I'll tan your backside, big as you are. Get to bed before I do it right now.'

A bit shocked by Seb's uncharacteristic outburst, Garth went, muttering swear words under his breath. He'd reached his room when he realised he hadn't had the drink of water he'd been craving.

The confrontation had gone some way to sobering him, and now, burning with resentment, he decided he'd go back for it. The miserable old bastard wasn't going to deny him a glass of water in his own home!

He went back downstairs, holding on to the banister as he still felt a bit unsteady, and through the bar. Then, as he reached the kitchen door, which was ajar, he heard Seb and Martha's voices, and realised they were talking about him.

'I don't know what I'm going to do with him, I really don't. I'm at my wits' end.' Martha sounded despairing.

'He's a handful, sure enough. But I wish I hadn't lost my temper with him. It's not my place, is it? I don't have the right.' That was Seb.

'You've every right! And he's more than just a handful. To tell you the truth, I'm worried to death about him. And you don't know the half of it.'

Garth groaned inwardly. He didn't understand what his father had meant by 'having no right'. But never mind that. His mother had promised to say nothing to his father about what he'd been up to at the farm, but it sounded as if she was going to go back on that.

'There's a lot I haven't told you,' she was continuing. 'I've had our Ernie here, saying they've been missing money, and—'

'He's been stealing from them?' Seb sounded shocked.

'Well, Ernie had no proof, but I have to say there have been times when there's been less money in my purse than I thought there should be. I've spoken to Garth about it, and though he denied it, I'm hoping that'll be an end to it, for now, at any rate. And Ernie reckoned he's been carrying on with the dairymaid, too. Getting up to all sorts.'

'You should have told me!' Seb said. 'Why ever didn't you tell me?'

'You know very well why.'

'Because you're afraid he's taking after his father.'

'Well, there is that. But I'm in hopes he'll grow out of it. No, the truth is I haven't said anything because I didn't want you to think badly of him. And I didn't want to worry you with it either. You've been so good, bringing him up as your own, and when all's said and done, he's my responsibility. You shouldn't have to pay for my mistakes.'

'Oh, you silly woman!' Seb exclaimed. 'As I recall it wasn't your mistake – it was your misfortune. And as far as I'm concerned, he is my son. I've never treated him any differently to the others, and I never will. But you've got to let me in, Martha. You can't deal with all this on your own.'

Garth had heard enough – too much! His head was reeling again, and not, this time, from the cider. He backed away and collided with a bar stool. There was sudden silence from the kitchen. He turned and crossed the bar hastily, hurrying up the stairs to his room. With the door shut firmly behind him, he sank on to the bed, trying to make sense of what he'd overheard. In the space of just a few minutes his world had turned topsy-turvy.

'You're afraid he's taking after his father.'

'You've been so good, bringing him up as your own.'

'I've never treated him any differently to the others, and I never will.'

What did it all mean? There was only one conclusion to be reached. Seb wasn't his real father. Conrad and Lewis weren't his real brothers – not that he'd worry much about that. Conrad was a soft sissy and Lewis was a goody-goody who never took his nose out of a book.

And what was it his mother had called him? *A mistake.* And Seb had called him a misfortune. That hurt, and Garth wasn't used to being hurt. It made him angry. In a sudden rage, he beat his fists into the mattress beneath him, catching his knuckles on the iron bedstead so hard he thought his finger was broken, but the pain was so satisfying he did it again.

A tap at the bedroom door, and his mother's voice called softly: 'Garth?'

He didn't move, or answer. She must have guessed it had been him who had knocked over the bar stool, guessed he'd overheard what they had been saying, and come up to try to explain. Fifteen years too late. Well, let her whistle. Let her think he was asleep. Let her keep on wondering if he *had* heard, and worry about it. He didn't owe either of them anything, the lying toads . . .

Martha called his name softly again, but at least she didn't come in uninvited. He didn't know what he'd have done if she had. After a minute or so he heard the creak of the floorboards as she moved away and her footsteps going downstairs.

His mouth was so parched now that even his lips felt dry and swollen, but he wasn't going to risk going down for a drink until he was sure they'd gone to bed. He didn't want to see them again tonight; didn't actually want to see them again ever.

He got up from the bed, crossed to the window and pulled the curtains across roughly. Then he returned to the bed and lay down, still fully clothed, still angry, but with other questions now creeping in. If Seb – miserable bugger – wasn't his father, who was? Someone he knew? Or some stranger? Whichever, it meant only one thing. His mother, the sainted Martha, was a slag. She'd been with someone else, either before – or after – she'd married Seb. After, he supposed – he couldn't imagine any man taking in a woman who was carrying someone else's child. But then again, he was the eldest by four years, so maybe she had been single when she'd done . . . what she'd done. But that didn't make it any better. She was still a slag, easy. Maybe she'd had it away with so many lads even she didn't know who his father was.

Quite forgetting how ready he was to take advantage of any girl who took his fancy, Garth felt sick with disgust.

At last he heard Martha and Seb come upstairs, heard their bedroom door close behind them. He waited a few more minutes, just to be safe, then opened his door a crack and looked out. The coast seemed to be clear. He took his boots off and crept along the landing in his stockinged feet, then down the stairs, keeping to the side of the treads so as to lessen the risk of them creaking. Across the bar, back to the kitchen. The glass had all been swept up, but the floor was still wet enough to soak through his socks. But at last he could get that much needed drink of water. He filled a pint glass to the brim and downed it in one go, then refilled it and drank again more slowly.

He should go back to bed now, he supposed, but the anger was still burning in his veins, the unanswered questions still buzzing in his brain, and he knew he'd never sleep. The thought of tossing and turning was anathema to him. He needed something to vent his feelings on.

A game of darts? But he didn't trust himself not to take them upstairs and use his parents as a target instead of the board. Besides, the darts were light. It might take skill to aim them for the bull, but he didn't think his hand was steady enough, and where was the satisfaction in that?

Now – skittles! That would be more like it. At least the balls were good and heavy; if he set the pins up – something he was quite accustomed to doing when the team had a home match – he could hurl the balls down the alley with all the force he could muster and pretend Mam was the centre pin and Dad right behind her. Ye-es! He'd wipe them clean off the alley – and what about Uncle Ernie? Telling tales to Mam about what he got up to on the farm . . . Ernie was an old bastard too. He'd get the lot of 'em.

Garth lit a lamp; it would be dark in the alley. Then, aware that there would be broken glass outside the back door and he was wearing no shoes, he went back through the bar and unlatched the door that was directly across the yard from the skittle-alley.

Taking both the lamp and the remains of his glass of water with him, he crossed the yard, feeling quite satisfied suddenly. For tonight, pretending the skittles were his family would have to do, but he was going to find a way to get his own back on them if it was the last thing he did.

* * *

125

Quiet as Garth had tried to be, Martha had heard the click of his bedroom door opening and his footsteps on the stairs. She'd been as unlikely to go to sleep as he had been, worried as she was that her son had overheard what she and Seb had been saying.

When she'd heard the bar stool overturn she'd waded through the mess on the kitchen floor, but by the time she reached the bar, there was no one to be seen. Garth. It had to have been Garth. He was the only one of her three sons likely to have still been awake – Conrad and Lewis had gone to bed long ago.

'Oh – what have we done?' she'd asked Seb distractedly. 'How much do you think he overheard?'

'You don't know he heard anything.' Seb was his old, calm self.

'Why else would he have knocked over the stool and just disappeared?' she argued.

'He was drunk. He just blundered into it, I reckon.'

'But if he did hear . . . Oh, for him to find out like this! I should have told him years ago, in a nice way . . .'

'You know we agreed never to do that,' Seb said. 'There was no reason for him to ever find out.'

'But now he has. He has, Seb, I'm sure of it. I'm going to go up and make sure he's all right.'

'Just leave him be, Martha,' Seb advised.

'I can't.' She hurried out.

When there was no reply to her tap on Garth's bedroom door she thought perhaps Seb was right and she was worrying about nothing. Calm down, she told herself. But she couldn't. Garth was such a difficult boy at the best of times. If he had overheard the conversation goodness knows what it would do to him.

'Try and forget it, and get some rest,' Seb said when they'd finally cleared up the mess in the kitchen and gone to bed.

'Whatever needs to be said can wait until the morning.'

Typically, he was soon asleep and snoring while she lay fretting. And when she heard the sounds that told her Garth had gone downstairs she wondered what he was up to, and decided that this might be her chance to talk to him, while nobody else was about.

She slipped out of bed, careful not to disturb Seb, though it would have taken the Pines Express racing through the room to wake him normally. She pulled on her dressing gown, thrust her feet into her slippers, and went downstairs.

There was no sign of Garth in the bar or the kitchen. She checked the small living room; he wasn't there either. Where was he? And then she saw a faint light showing at the windows of the skittle-alley, a light moving slowly along it. The kind of light thrown by a lamp.

What in the world was he doing in the skittle-alley?

With some trepidation Martha went out and across the yard.

'What the hell . . . ?'

Whether it was the exclamation of surprise or the lamp light on her face that woke Ella, she would never know. She had been so soundly asleep that for a moment she had no idea where she was. Then, as she moved her arm and encountered scratchy hay, she remembered, and alarm pulsed through her. She turned her head on the folded shawl and looked up to see a figure standing beside the bales of hay.

She couldn't see a face, but from what she could see she knew it was a man. Tall, well-built, and the hand holding the lamp was much too big for a woman. Fear knotted her throat, froze her limbs. And then he spoke.

'Who the hell are you?' His voice was rough, but sounded quite young. Not an old man then, thank goodness! Not Rector

Evans come to drag them back to the workhouse. But of course it wasn't him! If it had been she'd have smelled that sickening odour of his. This man smelled too, but of something she thought might be strong drink. 'How did you get in here? And what'ya doing?'

Against her, Jeannie stirred. 'Ella . . . ?' she murmured.

'Blimey! There's two of you!' the rough voice exclaimed.

Jeannie began to whimper, and Ella wrapped her arm protectively around her sister.

'I'm sorry . . .' she said, finding her voice. 'We'll go.'

'Too right you will!'

Ella scrambled to a sitting position, pushing aside the covering shawl and swinging her legs over the edge of the bale of hay. 'Don't tell anyone we were here . . . please!'

Another lamp appeared at the far end of the skittle-alley.

'What in the world . . . ?' This time the voice was a woman's. She advanced the length of the alley.

'Garth? What's going on?'

'Don't ask me. There's two kids here, asleep. I just found them.'

'Two children? Garth, what have you been up to now?'

'Nothing to do with me. I just came in to have a game of skittles and found them here, like I said.'

For the moment she ignored the peculiarity of a game of solo skittles in the middle of the night and turned her attention to Ella and Jeannie.

'Who are you, then? What are you doing here?'

'Just having a rest. We were tired,' Ella said, still sounding frightened. 'I'm sorry. We'll go, like he told us to.'

'But where to? Where are you from?'

'Don't ask, please. And please, don't tell anyone we were here.' Ella repeated her plea to the man – or boy, perhaps. With a second lamp giving more light she could see that he was quite young, only a couple of years older than her.

Sizing up the two children, the woman seemed to come to a decision.

'You can't go anywhere at this time of night. Goodness knows what might happen to you. You'd better come into the house and we'll have a cup of tea. And perhaps you'll enlighten me as to what this is all about.'

They had no choice but to do as she said, Ella realised – and in any case, the thought of a cup of tea was a tempting one. She began folding the shawl they'd used as a coverlet.

'Leave that,' the woman said. 'We'll come back for that later.'

'But we might need it.' *If we're able to make a run for it*, Ella was thinking.

Stubborn to the last, she continued folding the shawl and placed it in the carpet bag, then went to lift Jeannie down from the hay bales.

'Garth!' the woman said sharply. 'You do that. This one's not big enough. She'll strain herself.'

As Garth made to do as his mother said, Jeannie let out a frightened wail and shrank back, almost toppling off the make-shift bed. He caught her just in time and lowered her to the floor, where she made a dive for Ella, clutching at her waist and burying her face in her sister's chest.

'It's all right, Jeannie,' Ella said comfortingly, though she wasn't at all sure that it was.

She grabbed the second shawl, stuffing it into the carpet bag without stopping to fold it.

'Come on then.' The woman turned away, then added over her shoulder: 'You too, Garth. You don't want to be out here playing skittles when you ought to be in bed.'

The little procession made its way down the skittle-alley, Ella carrying the carpet bag in one hand and holding on to Jeannie with the other, and the boy – Garth? – bringing up the rear. Across the yard they went, through what appeared to be a bar room, and into a kitchen. There the woman set water to boil on a gas ring and instructed Garth to fetch some chairs from the bar.

'If they don't sit down, they're going to fall down,' she said with a nod at the children.

Ella looked round, desperately searching for an escape route, but could see none.

As if reading her mind, the woman said sharply: 'Don't even think about it. You're going nowhere till I find out what this is all about.'

Ella lowered her eyes, then looked up again at her captors. The woman was quite tall, the boy – Garth – taller, and very good-looking with a head of unruly dark hair, a strong chin and dark eyes set beneath heavy brows which almost met over the bridge of his nose, the only jarring feature. The woman wore a wedding ring, Ella noticed, and another ring on the third finger of her right hand, silver, and set with a small, unostentatious light blue stone. An engagement ring, perhaps, but why didn't she wear it above the wedding band like most people did?

More importantly, though, she had a kind face. Even when she spoke sharply, whether to them or to the boy Ella assumed must be her son, there was nothing vicious in her eyes, and though they were surrounded by a myriad of tiny worry lines, they were compassionate rather than accusing.

'Right,' the woman said, handing Ella a cup of tea. 'Explain yourselves.'

Ella faltered. 'I can't.'

'Why not?'

'I just can't.'

'Well, it's clear enough to me you're running away.' The woman indicated the carpet bag, which Ella had placed very close to her feet. 'What I want to know is – where from – and why?'

Ella dropped her head so as to avoid those kind, searching eyes, and said nothing.

'All right. So what are you called?'

'I'm Ella and this is Jeannie,' Ella muttered, still looking at the floor.

'And I'm Mrs Packer, and this is my son, Garth. How old are you?'

Ella hesitated, but Jeannie, who seemed to have recovered from her fright and was less reluctant to talk than Ella, spoke up.

'I'm eight, and Ella is eleven. And please could I have a cup of tea too?'

'You only have to ask.' Mrs Packer poured another cup, and Jeannie released her hold from Ella's waist and took it. 'Would you like a biscuit?'

Jeannie nodded eagerly, and when Mrs Packer opened a tin and offered it to them she wasted no time in picking out a custard cream. Ella took one too. After their exertions, supper seemed a very long time ago.

'Garth.' Mrs Packer turned to her son. 'Why don't you go to bed? You've got an early start in the morning. And . . . we'll talk later, if you want to.'

The meaning of her last words was lost on Ella, but the boy knew what she was talking about all right.

His face changed, a sullen look disfiguring the handsome features. Without another word he left the kitchen.

Jeannie had finished her biscuit and was looking longingly at the tin.

'You'd like another one, I see.' Mrs Packer held the tin out to

131

her with a wry smile. 'Take a couple while you're about it.'

Jeannie did, but Ella shook her head, unwilling to put herself further in the woman's debt.

'Now.' Mrs Packer settled herself, leaning back against the sink, arms folded about her midriff. 'I want to know why you two were asleep in our skittle-alley.'

Neither girl said anything, and after waiting a minute or so she went on: 'I'm right in thinking you're runaways, aren't I? Where from, that's what I want to know.'

Still Ella remained silent, but Jeannie, who had warmed to this woman who had given her biscuits, piped up.

'The workhouse.'

Mrs Packer looked amazed. 'What workhouse? The one in Bath?'

Jeannie nodded. 'St Peter's.'

'You've never walked all that way!'

'That's why we were tired,' Ella said. Now that Jeannie had given the game away there was no more point in keeping quiet.

'What about your mother and father?' Mrs Packer asked. 'What are they going to think when they find you gone?'

'We don't have a mother or father,' Ella said. 'They're both dead.'

'Oh my Lord! You poor little things!' Mrs Packer's distress was obvious. 'Don't you have any family to take care of you?'

'We've got an uncle in Hillsbridge,' Ella said. 'That's where we're going.'

'But why didn't he come for you?' Ella didn't reply. 'Does he know you're on your way?'

'No,' Ella admitted. 'But if he won't let us stay with and him and Auntie Ethel we're going to where we used to live. We know a lot of people there.'

Mrs Packer shook her head, looking more worried than ever.

'You should have got it sorted it out first. Why did you just run away on the off-chance?'

'We had to,' Ella said shortly, staring down at her boots.

'Had to? Why? Were you treated unkindly?' Mrs Packer was clearly determined to get to the bottom of the matter.

For a long moment Ella said nothing. Then she looked up again, her eyes full of tears. 'Worse than that.'

'Worse how?'

A solitary tear rolled down Ella's cheek. 'I don't want to talk about it.'

'Well.' Sensing her distress, Mrs Packer seemed to come to a decision. 'You can't be going to Hillsbridge or anywhere else tonight. We don't have any bedrooms to spare, and I can't turn any of my boys out of theirs when they're fast asleep. But there's a couple of sofas in the sitting room. You can sleep on those for tonight. Then in the morning we'll decide what's to be done. Come on.'

Jeannie followed her happily enough; Ella hung back and picked up the carpet bag.

'Oh no, you don't, missy,' Mrs Packer said sharply. 'I'll take care of that. I don't want you running off again.'

She took possession of the bag, went to the back door, made sure the key was turned in the lock, and pocketed it. Then she showed them into a small, cluttered room which did indeed have two sofas squashed in on each side of a fireplace. The remaining space, for what it was worth, was taken up by a dining table and chairs, a chiffonier, and a glass-fronted cabinet filled with ornamental china.

'I'll fetch you some blankets, though I doubt you'll need them. It's a warm night. And you can use the cushions for pillows,' Mrs Packer said.

'I want to sleep with Ella,' Jeannie ventured.

'Well, you can't. There's no room for two on them.' Mrs Packer's tone implied she would stand no nonsense. 'Here.' She propped a cushion against the arm of one of the sofas. 'Make yourself comfortable. I'll be back in a minute.'

Jeannie took off her boots and plopped down on the chintzy sofa; after a moment Ella reluctantly followed suit.

Mrs Packer was soon back with an armful of flannelette sheets. She spread one over Ella and tucked the other around Jeannie.

'Try and get some sleep, my love,' she said kindly.

'Night night,' Jeannie murmured, just as she did to Ella. She sounded sleepy and almost content.

For a moment Mrs Packer hovered beside Ella. 'You too,' she said. 'Try not to worry. We'll sort everything out in the morning one way or another.' Then she went out, closing the door behind her.

'Night, Jeannie,' Ella said softly, but Jeannie was already asleep.

Well, it could have been worse, Ella thought. At least they had somewhere safe and comfortable for tonight, and the woman – Mrs Packer – hadn't called the police or the workhouse. But what would happen tomorrow? All very well for Mrs Packer to tell her not to worry – she couldn't help it. Would they manage to get to Hillsbridge? And would someone take them in if they did? Or would they be returned to the workhouse and the awful attentions of Rector Evans?

Determinedly, Ella settled her head against the cushion and closed her eyes. She really did need to get some sleep if she was to be able to cope with whatever tomorrow would bring.

Well, Martha thought as she climbed back into bed beside a still snoring Seb, at least she had something to think about now besides her concerns over Garth.

Those poor little girls! Thank the Lord Garth had gone out to the skittle-alley. Any other night and they wouldn't have been found, and goodness only knew what might have happened. And thinking of what *could* have happened to them on the lonely road from Bath made her shudder.

As for why they'd been desperate enough to run away . . . even without being told, she had her suspicions. She'd heard horror stories about how children were sometimes abused in institutions, preyed on by dirty old men in positions of responsibility. And these two were orphans, with no one to turn to.

Dear Lord, if some filthy bugger had been doing unspeakable things to them, and she ever found out who it was, she'd cut his pecker off! Bad enough what had happened to her, and she'd been a grown woman. These girls were so young, so vulnerable. The older one had some spirit, it was true, but the little one was just like a fairy, delicate, and trusting with it.

Well, she'd see to it they were safe now if it was the last thing she did.

With that intention firmly fixed in her mind, Martha eventually fell asleep.

Chapter Nine

In spite of her broken night's sleep, Martha was up bright and early next morning as usual. She liked to make a pot of tea and take a couple of cups over to the cottage so that Seb's parents could enjoy it in bed. Then she'd start cooking breakfast for all of them before the others came down.

This morning her first port of call was the sitting room to check on the two little girls, and was relieved to see they were both still fast asleep. They'd been tired out, the poor lambs! But at least they were safe now, and she was determined to make sure they stayed that way.

As she set the kettle to boil she wondered what would be the best way forward. Perhaps Seb could cycle over to Hillsbridge and look for the relatives the girls had mentioned, or failing that, their old neighbours, to make sure they had somewhere to go. If someone was willing to take them in, all well and good, but until she knew they were going to be properly cared for they were going nowhere. If they had to stay on here for a couple more nights, so be it. She'd get Lewis to move in with Conrad and they could have his room. As for Seb, she was sure that when she told him her awful suspicions as to what had happened to the girls at the workhouse, he would be in complete agreement with whatever she decided.

The tea made, she poured two cups and, one in each hand, headed for the adjoining cottage. Then she stopped short, tea slopping over from the cups into their saucers.

A uniformed policeman was standing at the cottage door, his hand raised to knock.

'Hello!' she called urgently. 'Can I help you?'

The policeman turned towards her, lowering his hand. She didn't recognise him as any of the constables from Hillsbridge and her heart came into her mouth as she realised he must have ridden out from Bath on the bicycle that rested against the wall beside him.

He approached her. 'D'you live here?' he asked abruptly.

'Yes. In the Feathers. I'm the landlady.' It wasn't strictly true, it was Seb's father, Algie, whose name was over the door. But it sounded good, and gave her some standing. 'What do you want?'

The policeman removed his helmet, tucking it under his arm. 'I'm making enquiries about some missing persons,' he said, rather officiously. 'Two inmates absconded from the workhouse last night.'

'Absconded?' Martha repeated, playing for time. 'I wasn't aware the workhouse was a prison.'

'They're minors, and in the care of the authorities, which makes it a very serious matter.' His chest puffed out with self-importance. 'Have you seen anything of them?'

'Certainly not!' Martha replied without hesitation. 'We don't allow minors on licensed premises, Constable.'

'You're sure of that?'

'Perfectly sure. We keep a respectable establishment here.'

The policeman jerked his head in the direction of the cottage. 'What about this place? Who lives in there?'

'My husband's parents occupy that cottage,' Martha said,

phrasing her words as formally as she could in an effort to assume the upper hand. 'They are quite elderly, and I'd be obliged if you would refrain from disturbing them.'

'I've been told to ask everybody,' the policeman returned stubbornly.

Martha felt panic flutter like butterflies in her stomach. She didn't want Algie and Maud to get to hear about the children she was hiding until she and Seb had managed to sort something out.

'When did these children "abscond" as you put it?' she asked, adopting a haughty tone.

'Last night, after they'd been put to bed, as I understand it.'

'In that case, you are certainly wasting your valuable time,' Martha said. 'Seb's parents always retire early, and would have been fast asleep by the time they could have got this far. In fact, I wouldn't have thought it likely two children could have managed it at all. You'd be better employed searching the hedges and ditches in the vicinity of the workhouse, I'd have thought. Now, if that's all, I have to take my parents-in-law their morning tea before it goes stone cold.'

As she spoke, a sound from the kitchen made Martha's heart miss a beat. If it was one or both of the children the cat would be well and truly out of the bag.

Somehow she retained her composure, saying in a voice loud enough to be heard in the kitchen: 'I assure you, Constable, there are no runaways here, nor have been. Thank you, and good day.'

'Just be sure if you should see hide or hair of them, you'll report it right away,' the constable told her in his officious way.

'Don't worry, we will.' Martha moved back into the doorway, heaving a sigh of relief as he returned reluctantly to his bicycle. Then she went in, closing the door firmly behind her.

She'd been right, there was someone in the kitchen, but it wasn't either of the girls. It was Conrad, pouring himself a cup of tea from the pot she'd made earlier.

'Who were you talking to?' he asked.

This was a fresh dilemma for Martha. She hadn't stopped to wonder what she would tell her two younger sons about the girls. How could she have been so stupid as not to think of it? Now, with every chance the children would wake up and come into the kitchen at any moment, she realised the boys had to be warned.

'It was a policeman,' she said. 'He's looking for two little girls who've run away from the workhouse in Bath.'

'Oh.' Conrad accepted it without question, and Martha was forced to continue.

'Look, Conrad, the thing is – they're here. Garth found them hiding in the skittle-alley last night and I've put them to bed in the sitting room.'

She had his full attention now.

'They're in our sitting room?' His eyes, the exact same hazel as Seb's, opened wide. 'Why didn't you tell the policeman?'

'Because if I had they'd be taken back to the workhouse. It's a dreadful place, Conrad. They've been treated very badly.'

'What . . . ? They're not going to stay here, are they?' he said, horrified at the very idea of his home being invaded by *girls*.

'Only until we can get in touch with their family and find them somewhere safe to go. But in the meantime, you mustn't breathe a word of it to anyone, and neither must Lewis. Do you understand?'

'I suppose, but . . .' Conrad looked worried. 'Won't you get in trouble if the police find out they were here all the time?'

'The police won't find out, as long as you and Lewis keep quiet about it,' Martha said reassuringly, though she felt a flicker of anxiety herself. There were laws against this sort of thing, she felt sure. But nothing on earth was going to make her allow those poor children to be sent back to the workhouse without her doing her best for them.

'What have we got to keep quiet about?' Lewis was in the doorway now, still in his nightshirt, and rubbing the sleep out of his eyes.

'There's two girls in our sitting room,' Conrad supplied before Martha could, and then she had to go through the whole thing again.

'Don't worry, we won't say anything,' Lewis said, serious as ever, when she had finished. And then: 'Is there any tea going?'

'I'll make a fresh pot,' Martha said. 'That one will be cold by now, and I haven't taken your granny and grampy theirs yet. Go up and get dressed for school, and you can have a cup when you come down again. But there won't be a cooked breakfast this morning, I'm afraid. You'll have to make do with bread and jam.'

As he drove the cows in from milking Garth had more or less forgotten about the children he had discovered asleep in the skittle-alley. It was the conversation he'd overheard between Martha and Seb that was occupying his mind.

The anger he'd felt last night at discovering he'd been deceived all his life had mutated into a deep burning resentment, but all the questions it raised were playing on his mind as insistently as ever.

If Seb wasn't his father, who was? Did his mother even know, or had she been such a slut that she couldn't be sure? In his experience girls who were easy didn't limit their favours to one chap. Would he ever be able to discover who he really was? Find out what Seb had meant when he'd said: 'Because you're afraid he's taking after his father?'

This was the one thing that gave Garth a bit of a thrill. He rather liked the idea that his father might well be a rogue. There was something appealing about the notion, and it explained his own wild ways. The satisfaction he derived from flying in the face of what was deemed acceptable, the urges to fight and steal, bed girls, smoke cigarettes, drink too much, the determination to get his own way and put one over on anyone who crossed him. Yes, he thought he would like his real father, who would be right behind him whatever he did, not a miserable old sod like Seb, who generally wanted nothing but a quiet life, and rarely took a stand on anything. Last night's outburst had been so unlike him it had really taken Garth by surprise. But his usual quiet acceptance just went to prove he wasn't Garth's real father.

Nor did he look anything like Seb. Until now he'd never stopped to question where his dark good looks and swarthy build came from. If he'd thought about it at all, he'd assumed they were from his mother, who was also dark haired. But Conrad and Lewis were much fairer skinned – Lewis even had a sprinkling of freckles – their hair mid-brown, their eyes hazel. They were more slightly built than he was too, and didn't look as though they'd grow as tall, but given their ages there was still time.

No, Garth wouldn't mind betting he took after his real father in appearance as well as nature, and that, too, gave him a fillip of satisfaction.

A sharp, rather high-pitched voice invaded his thoughts.

'Hoi! Get a move on, can't you? There's too much work to be done for you to be idling about with them bliddy cows.'

Uncle Ernie. Another miserable sod. Or was he really his uncle? Thinking about it, Garth supposed he must be, since he was Martha's brother. Darn it – he'd like to have been able to disown Ernie too, along with Seb.

Never mind. He'd get rid of the lot of them when he found his real father.

With that thought, Garth slapped the rump of the rearmost cow, causing a small stampede towards their field, and resigned himself to having to do whatever Ernie told him – for the time being, at any rate.

Conrad and Lewis both attended the school in the nearest village, half a mile away on the road to Hillsbridge. As they set off up the long hill they discussed the peculiar situation they'd woken up to.

'Who do you think they are?' Lewis asked.

'Well, Mam said they're called Jeannie and Ella,' Conrad supplied.

'Yes, but Jeannie and Ella what?' Lewis persisted. 'And where do they come from?'

'The workhouse. Don't you ever listen to a word Mam says?'

'The workhouse isn't a place you *come from*,' Lewis scoffed. 'It's where people *go to* when they haven't got a home or any money.'

'So?'

'Well, they must belong somewhere.'

'Perhaps they're orphans.'

Lewis considered. 'Perhaps they are, but if so, why aren't they in an orphanage?'

'I don't know. Perhaps there wasn't room for them.'

'And why would they run away?'

'I don't know that either. You ask too many questions,

142

Lewis. All I hope is that they're gone by the time we get home. I don't want you moving in with me. You and all your books.'

'I haven't got that many!' Lewis protested.

'You have. And you'll want to keep the light on to read them when I want to go to sleep. Besides, you don't want girls moving into your room, do you? They'll make it smell all girly!'

'I don't mind,' Lewis said truthfully. 'If they've got nowhere else to go.'

Conrad snorted. 'You're just a big softie, Lewis.'

They walked in silence for a bit, catching their breath from the steep climb. Then Lewis said: 'How did Garth come to find them in the skittle-alley anyway? What was he doing in there? There wasn't a match last night, was there?'

'Who knows with Garth? He's a nutter,' Conrad said.

'Yes, he is a bit,' Lewis agreed. 'But he's still Mam's favourite.'

Conrad looked at him sharply. 'No, he isn't.'

'He is,' Lewis said. 'He can get away with murder.'

Conrad considered. 'You're right there. We get it in the neck if we step out of line, but he does what he likes. Yet he's older than us. It doesn't mean he's Mam's favourite.'

'If you say so.' Lewis kicked a small stone along the footpath. 'At least he's not Dad's.'

'What d'you mean?' Conrad asked.

'Haven't you noticed the way Dad looks at him sometimes?' Lewis said.

'No. But then, your eyes are better than mine now you've got your glasses.'

Lewis self-consciously pushed his new spectacles up on his nose. He didn't like having to wear them, they made him feel conspicuous, and he'd been the object of a lot of teasing from the other boys in his class. But at least it meant he could read his beloved books more easily. He'd strained his eyes, Mam had said, and they'd start to get better now. Lewis hoped she was right. The sooner he could leave them off, the better.

They'd crested the hill now, and the road ran straight and level from here to the school, which they could see just beyond a row of houses and a few shops, with the playing fields on the opposite side of the road.

A policeman on a bicycle overtook them and wobbled to a stop just in front of them, one foot on the kerb, the other on the road. Conrad and Lewis looked at one another, scenting trouble.

'You two,' the policeman said when they reached him. 'You haven't seen any little girls wandering about, have you?'

Both boys shook their heads, and Lewis felt the colour rising in his neck beneath the collar of his shirt and hoped it wasn't going to rise into his cheeks. Fair as he was, he blushed far too easily.

Conrad, knowing his brother as he did, rushed to the rescue.

'There's lots of girls at school, though,' he said, hoping to draw the policeman's attention away from Lewis. 'They'll all be lined up in the playground in a minute.'

The ruse succeeded.

'I'm well aware of that, Sonny Jim.' The policeman's tone was authoritarian. 'This is a serious matter, so don't be so damn cheeky.'

'Sorry, sir, I just thought—'

'I know what you thought. You thought you were being clever. Well, you're not. I'll ask you again. Have you seen two girls you don't know on the road this morning?'

That made things easier!

'No, sir,' they both answered, perfectly truthfully. 'We haven't seen anyone.'

For a moment the policeman continued to eye them suspiciously, then he pushed himself and his bicycle away from the kerb and rode away. Conrad and Lewis heaved sighs of relief.

'I didn't like the way he looked at us,' Lewis said.

'I expect he looks like that at everyone,' Conrad said. 'He can't help it.'

They walked on, but by unspoken agreement the subject of the two girls who'd made such an unexpected appearance at the Feathers was not mentioned again.

Ella and Jeannie were awake. Martha had only just managed to tell a startled Seb of the situation when she heard them moving about and talking to one another in voices too low for her to be able to make out what they were saying.

Mindful of what she suspected they had been subjected to at the workhouse and thinking they might be frightened by coming face to face with a man, she indicated the back door with a sharp nod of her head.

'P'raps it would be best if you made yourself scarce for a bit. Let me get them something to eat, and we'll talk to them later,' she said softly, and added: 'And you'd better go and warn your mam and dad. They were still in their dressing gowns when I took them their breakfast, but I don't want one of them coming over and finding those girls without knowing they're here.'

Seb nodded silently and went out, and Martha went through to the living room.

Both girls, who had been sitting side by side and close together on one of the sofas, jumped up as the door opened. The blankets, Martha noticed, had been neatly folded and placed one on top of the other.

'It's all right,' she said reassuringly. 'Don't move on my

account. I just thought you might like a cup of tea and something to eat.'

For a moment neither girl answered her, and neither did they resume their seats. Then Ella said: 'Thank you, but I think we'd better get going.'

'I don't think that's a good idea,' Martha said. 'The police are out and about looking for you.'

The two girls exchanged frightened looks.

'Are they here?' Ella asked, her voice trembling.

'No, my dear, they're not. But they have been. Don't worry. I didn't tell them anything. You're safe as long as you stay here.'

'But—'

'Just for the time being, until we're sure you've got a place to go. Now, why don't we see about some breakfast? Do you like bacon and eggs?'

'I don't know,' Jeannie said doubtfully. She didn't remember ever having them, though the smell wafting in from the kitchen was very like the one that came from the staff table at the workhouse on Sunday mornings.

But Ella brightened, her fear forgotten momentarily. She remembered all right! And already her mouth was watering.

'Oh yes!' she said eagerly. 'And you will too, Jeannie.'

'That's all right then.'

They followed Martha into the kitchen, where she popped four rashers of bacon into the pan. As the delicious aroma intensified she cut two slices of bread from a loaf and added them to the pan, sliding them about to soak up the liquid fat.

'And fried bread?' she asked over her shoulder. 'I bet you do.'

Ella could scarcely believe it. She hadn't tasted fried bread since they'd been in the workhouse.

'Will I like that too?' Jeannie asked, and Martha's heart twisted suddenly.

Those poor little mites! On top of what they'd endured, they'd missed out on so much.

When the bacon and bread were done, Martha slid them on to a couple of plates she had ready, and cracked two eggs into the pan. One broke, the yolk running into the white, and she moved it to one side and cracked another, this time without breaking it. If these two hadn't had a good cooked breakfast in years, she wasn't going to serve them a broken egg.

'Right. Let's get you settled. You'd best eat in the sitting room, just in case . . .' She stopped, not wanting to mention the police again. She didn't think they'd be back, but better safe than sorry.

She poured two cups of tea and gave one to each of the girls, then, carrying the plates of food herself, she herded them into the sitting room. Once they had started on their breakfast she returned to the kitchen and opened the door to let Seb know the coast was clear.

'What did your mam and dad have to say about it all?' she asked, pouring yet more tea, this time for her and Seb.

'Well, as you can imagine, Mam wasn't best pleased.' Seb grinned wryly. 'But Dad's right behind us. If the police come knocking on the door again, he'll send them packing, and when it's opening time he'll keep an eye out to make sure they don't come barging into the bar.'

Martha frowned as realisation dawned. 'But the bar's right next to the living room. We can't have any of the regulars spotting them either. We're going to have to keep them well out of the way when the pub's open.'

'Unless we can find these relations of theirs first.'

'Let them have their breakfast in peace, Seb,' Martha said. 'Then we'll have to talk to them.'

He nodded. 'Sure thing. And when we know where to find their family, I'll get on my bike and ride over to Hillsbridge. The sooner we can sort them out the better.'

'But they're not going back to that workhouse. I won't have it.' Martha had never been more determined about anything.

'No, you're right.' Seb sipped his tea. 'Ah well, at least it's taken your mind off Garth.'

She snorted. 'For the moment.'

'He'll get over it,' Seb said placatingly. 'And at least now I know what's been going on, you're not having to cope with it all on your own.'

Martha sighed. 'I don't know what I'd do without you, Seb.'

'We're a team, love. Always have been, always will be. And don't you forget it.'

For a few minutes he was silent, deep in thought. Then he went on: 'As for these poor little girls, just remember I took on one child that wasn't my own. If needs be, I can always take on two more. We won't see them sent back to the workhouse. If I can't find their relations, don't worry.'

Gratitude flooded her veins and Martha reached across and covered his hand with hers. She was thinking that for all her worries about Garth and now the added problem of the two runaways, she must be the luckiest woman alive.

The two girls had enjoyed every mouthful of their breakfast.

'That was lovely!' Jeannie said, wiping egg from her lips with her finger and licking it so as not to waste even the tiniest bit.

'I told you you'd like it.'

'Ye-es! It was nicer than anything I've ever tasted before.' She paused, still savouring the flavour. 'Why have we got to go to Hillsbridge?'

Ella laid her knife and fork carefully on her plate the way Mammy had taught them. 'Because that's where Uncle Ted and Auntie Ethel live.'

'But I don't know them,' Jeannie objected. 'What are they like?'

'Uncle Ted's all right, I think. He's Daddy's brother, so he must be.' But she sounded a little uncertain, and Jeannie picked up on it.

'Has he got any children?'

'I think so.'

'And Auntie Ethel is his wife?'

'Yes.'

'Is she nice?'

Again, Ella hesitated. 'I hope so.'

'But if they are our auntie and uncle, why have they never been to see us?'

'It was too far, I expect.'

Jeannie sighed. 'I wish we could stay here! Then we could have bacon and eggs every day. She's nice, too – the lady.'

'Mrs Packer. Yes, she is. But she's just being kind. She wouldn't want us here all the time.'

'Why not? We wouldn't be any trouble. Can't we stay here, Ella?' Jeannie pleaded.

'No, Jeannie, we can't,' Ella said flatly. 'We've got to move on and make our own way in the world.'

Jeannie sighed again, a long, loud sigh. 'Well, I'm going to ask her anyway.'

Outside the door, Martha's heart felt fit to burst. She'd been on her way in to see how the children were getting on, and had stopped and listened to what they were saying. But she didn't want them to know she'd overheard what was essentially a very private conversation, so she took a few backward steps before bustling in.

'Well, that's two of the cleanest plates I've seen in a long time!' she said cheerfully. 'Would you like anything else? Some bread and jam perhaps? Or another cup of tea?'

'We're fine, thank you. It was lovely,' Ella said politely, but Jeannie had other things on her mind.

'What we'd really like is to stay here, wouldn't we, Ella? Oh please, can we stay here?'

Martha hesitated. 'We'll have to see.'

After what she'd just heard she was beginning to wonder if it was a bad idea for Seb to ride over to Hillsbridge to find the girls' family, or failing that, friends who would take them in. It didn't sound as if the aunt and uncle had ever had much to do with the children, and Jeannie had put into words what she wondered herself – why had they never visited them at the workhouse when they had been left alone in the world? Surely, even if they hadn't been in a position to take them in, they should have at least visited and made sure they were being properly cared for? Perhaps taken them for a day out occasionally? Let them know there was someone who cared? But they hadn't. If they'd been unwilling to look out for them when they were orphaned, why would they do so now? Once they knew the children had run away – if they didn't already – and also knew their whereabouts, the great danger was that they would notify the authorities. Even if they didn't, they might talk about it to friends, neighbours, anyone really, and the cat would be well and truly out of the bag. If the police or someone from the workhouse turned up at the door and took them away, Martha would never be able to forgive herself.

She went into the kitchen. Seb was already tucking his trousers into his bicycle clips.

'I don't think this is a good idea, Seb,' she said, and explained her doubts.

'P'raps you're right, love.' He rasped his fingers across his chin. 'What d'you reckon we ought to do, then?'

'I think the only thing for it is to let them stay here for the time being,' she said.

'Ah, I reckon you're right,' he said, nodding.

Chapter Ten

Three weeks later

Ella and Jeannie were still residing at the Feathers. What had begun as a roof over their heads for one night only had somehow mutated into something much more permanent.

The first days had been difficult for a number of reasons, chief amongst them the necessity for keeping their presence secret. Hiding two children in a normal family home might have proved something of a challenge, but on licensed premises it was ten times more difficult. Ella and Jeannie were banished upstairs during opening hours, and even when the door was shut and locked after the last customer, Martha kept a close watch to make sure they stayed well out of sight, even standing guard at the corner of the building when they crossed the yard to use the privy.

Keeping them indoors during the summery weather and long light evenings pained Martha, but she couldn't see she had any option, and at least they were allowed to play in the skittle-alley when there was no danger of them being seen or heard. The boys showed them how the game was played and Ella soon became adept at aiming the ball down the wooden alley, though

Jeannie could only manage to throw it a few feet and it invariably ended up in the gulley on one side or the other, causing her much frustration. She far preferred a game of marbles on the smooth surface.

Martha had looked out a couple of dolls which had been stowed away in a chest since Lily's death, as well as the remains of a dollies' tea set in pretty porcelain, but the children had to be sure they packed it all away and brought it into the house if there was to be a home skittles match. Boys didn't play with dolls and miniature china tea sets!

At least the police activity was no longer so much of a worry. When they'd combed the district and found neither hide nor hair of the children, they'd given up the search. Martha hoped the authorities at the workhouse had given up too. Surely, for them, it would just be two mouths fewer to feed. But it was too early yet to become complacent.

Another problem in the beginning had been Ella's unwillingness to remain at the Feathers. She was fiercely independent, Martha realised, and used to being the one to take care of her little sister. But in the face of Martha's persuasion and Jeannie's pleas she had eventually agreed, and began to become more relaxed as the enormous responsibility was lifted from her shoulders.

And although to begin with Conrad had objected to having to share his room with Lewis, and though there was still the occasional squabble, they seemed to have resigned themselves to the situation and decided it wasn't so bad after all. Actually – though they'd never admit it – they had come to quite like having the girls about the place. A game of cards or snakes and ladders was more fun with four, even if Jeannie was a bit slow and got upset when she invariably lost until, feeling sorry for her, the boys sometimes made sure they let her win.

As for Martha, she soon found she was enjoying having them there. She'd never got over the loss of her only daughter, and somehow it seemed to her as if these two little girls had been sent to help fill the gap in her heart and her life.

Especially Jeannie. Young for her age as she was, she reminded Martha of her own Lily. And she was such an affectionate child, with none of Ella's reserve. She would run to Martha as if she was her own mother, and always wanted to be tucked in at night with a bedtime kiss. Fond as she had grown of both of them, it was Jeannie who held a special place in her heart.

The thought of them leaving saddened her. She couldn't keep them hidden for ever, she knew. They were prisoners here just as they had been in the workhouse, safe from abuse, yes, but without friends and experience of life in the outside world. Martha had already decided that now that the long school summer holidays had begun she'd let them come out of hiding, and explain their presence away by saying they were the children of a cousin who had been taken ill or died and she and Seb were looking after them. She didn't think anyone in the village would doubt her word; local matters such as the fierce competition between friends and neighbours to win prizes at the local flower show and an argument that was raging about the upkeep of the churchyard would have claimed their attention, and they would have forgotten all about the police enquiries for two missing girls three weeks ago.

It wouldn't end there, of course. They would need to attend school when the new term began, and they really should be registered with a doctor. Martha could foresee problems with anything that needed proper identification. There were bound to be questions about who they were and where they'd come from, and a vague assertion that they were her cousin's children wouldn't stand up to scrutiny.

Remembering what Seb had said about his willingness to take them on, Martha wondered if there was any possibility they could adopt the children. Surely, if there was no one else willing to give them a home, there could be no objection?

She had no idea how they would go about such a thing, and she couldn't help worrying that she and Seb might face serious consequences for having lied to the police, and kept the children concealed for so long.

She wasn't going to let that spoil her enjoyment of having them around, though, and it wouldn't shake her determination to keep them safe. When she and Seb had had the chance to talk it over properly she'd seek advice, perhaps from the minister at the Baptist chapel, who was approachable and kindly, perhaps from a lawyer in town. She might even write to their Member of Parliament. She rather liked that idea.

But for the moment she had other things on her mind, problems she couldn't ignore. Chief amongst them was, of course, Garth.

So certain was she that Garth had overheard the conversation between her and Seb that Martha had taken the first opportunity to speak to him that presented itself. It had arisen when he'd arrived home from the farm just after five the day after the upset had happened. Conrad, Lewis and the girls were playing dominoes at the sitting room table, Seb was working in the garden, his parents were in their cottage and there was almost a clear hour until opening time.

Martha had the kettle on the boil and the pot warming, and when she heard Garth kicking off his muddy boots outside the back door she quickly made a cup of tea. She was going to need it, even if he didn't.

He came in with a scowl on his face and walked past her without speaking, making for the door to the bar.

'Garth – we need to talk.' Her voice was steady though her stomach was churning.

He stopped, half-turned. 'What about?' he asked bad-temperedly.

'I think you know very well. Something I should have told you a long time ago. I need to explain . . .'

'Well, I don't want to hear your explanations.' He turned to face her fully, glowering at her as only he could. 'I can make a good guess at why you never told me. You didn't want me knowing what a slag you are.'

The venom in his voice cut Martha to the quick. 'It wasn't like that.'

'No? I don't want to hear any more of your lies, Mam. There's only one thing I want to know. Who's my real father?'

It was the one question Martha had no intention of answering.

'You don't know him,' she said. 'Garth, please, let's sit down and have a cup of tea. Let me tell you why your dad and I decided it was best—'

'He's not my dad!' Garth interrupted her. 'He had no right to have any say in what I was told or what you were going to keep from me.'

Outrage at the unfairness of this sparked Martha's anger, and it momentarily took precedence over her desire to make things right with her eldest son.

'To all intents and purposes he *is* your father, Garth. He's brought you up as his own, paid for the food you eat and the roof over your head, always been there for you. That's what makes him your father – not that . . .' She broke off, stopping short of using the words she would have liked to describe the bastard who had raped her.

'If you say so.' Garth's tone was derisive. 'I've still got a right to know who I am. Where I came from. You have no right to deny me that.'

'Oh, Garth . . .' Martha floundered helplessly. She'd gone over this in the long dark sleepless hours of the night, but now that the moment had come the words failed her. How could she tell a fifteen-year-old boy the truth of what had happened? That his father was a scoundrel and a rogue and a rapist? Better that he thought badly of her than that.

'You don't know, do you?' he demanded scornfully.

'I don't know his name, no.' At least Martha could answer that. She knew him only by the nickname she'd given him – Wolf.

'And I don't suppose he even knows I exist, does he?'

'No, he doesn't, and it's best that way. Please, you must believe me. For your own sake.'

He snorted. 'For your sake, you mean. And *his*.' It was as if he was unable to even speak Seb's name. 'So the two of you can keep your dirty little secret. I don't suppose *he* wanted people to know what sort of a whore he'd married, any more than you did.'

'You young toad! How dare you speak to your mother like that? Apologise this minute!'

Seb had picked a basket of runner beans and was bringing them in; he opened the back door just in time to hear Garth's angry words.

Until last night Garth had never seen his father lose his temper and it had shaken him more than he cared to admit. But he met Seb's furious gaze with a defiant stare.

'Why should I?'

'Because she's your mother, that's why. She's put up with enough from you, and if I'd known the half of it I'd have had my say long before now. Well, I'm telling you now. If you don't mend your ways, you'll find yourself out on your ear, and without a job too, from what I can hear of it. Now – say you're sorry, or I swear I'll throw you and all your belongings out on the pavement.'

Garth hesitated. It wasn't in his nature to apologise, and he didn't see why he should have to. They were the ones who should be doing the apologising. It was them in the wrong, not him. But he didn't want to risk Seb carrying out his threat. Didn't want to end up sleeping rough, like those two kids he'd discovered in the skittle-alley.

'Sorry,' he mumbled.

Martha nodded an acknowledgement, though she was clearly upset.

He headed for the door, but just as he reached it, she called his name. 'Garth!'

He turned sullenly.

'I'm sorry too. We'll talk again, I promise.'

He sneered, made again to leave, but again she stopped him.

'There's something else you need to know. Those two little girls . . . they're still here. But you mustn't tell anyone. They ran away from the workhouse, and the police are looking for them. If they find out they're here, they'll be taken back, and that mustn't happen. You've got to keep it quiet, Garth. Do you understand?'

He shrugged, and the expression on his face made clear what he was thinking: *More lies.*

'D'you hear what your mother says?' Seb's voice was still hard. 'Just for once do as she says, unless you want to condemn them to a fate a darned sight worse than yours.'

When Garth had gone, Martha turned anxiously to Seb. 'You don't think he will tell anyone, do you?'

'I'm past knowing what he'll do,' Seb said despairingly.

'One thing I do know, I won't have him speaking to you like that.'

Upset as she was, Martha immediately flew to her son's defence. 'He's hurt, Seb. And angry. He didn't mean it. He wanted me to tell him who his real father is, and . . .'

'Did you?'

'I didn't tell him how it came about, no. I couldn't bring myself to. And I never knew the bastard's name, so I couldn't tell him that either.'

'You knew he came from Bath, though. And that he was a heavy for a loan shark.'

Martha looked up, meeting Seb's eyes directly. 'You think I should tell him? As much as I know? And what about Conrad and Lewis? Should we tell them?'

'Leave that to me. I'll have a quiet word with them when I get the chance. You've got enough on your plate as it is. As for Garth, well that's up to you, Martha. But you've got to bear in mind the sort of man he was; whether you want Garth going looking for him. Remember the mess your Joe got into mixing with that crowd. And what the consequences were for you.'

Martha twisted her hands in the folds of her skirt, sick with worry and indecision.

Seb gave her arm a squeeze. 'Put it out of your mind for now. Like I said before, it'll probably all blow over, and we've got other things to worry about, haven't we? Like what we're going to do about those two girls. Now, is that a pot of tea? I think we could both do with one. And then I must get washed and changed and ready to open up.'

For the time being, that had been the end of it.

Garth had eaten his tea in stony silence, gone out to meet some of his pals, and not returned until late. Martha had the additional worry that he might blab about the two girls, but there had been no dreaded knock on the door, no sign of a police uniform.

It was much the same in the days that followed. He hadn't raised the subject of his real father again, and Martha had begun to dare to hope that Seb was right, and he wasn't going to pursue it any further. But he was barely speaking to either of his parents, the scornful looks he gave Martha when she tried to talk to him the only real communication.

'He'll get over it,' Seb had said, back to his usual pragmatic self after the rare losses of self-control, and Martha could only hope he was right.

Worrying about it, however, was casting a long shadow over the pleasure she took in having the girls about, safe from the horrible place where they'd been forced to live and subjected to who-knew-what abuse. She couldn't decide how much she should tell him if he should ask her again, and part of her thought that perhaps he did deserve the truth. But she couldn't forget what Seb had said about the danger of him getting mixed up with a bad crowd if he set out to try and find his father. Garth was enough of a worry already without coming under their influence.

Martha tried to push her anxiety about her son to the back of her mind. He was at a funny age, neither a child nor a man. Hopefully he'd grow out of it soon, and forget all this nonsense about finding out who was his real father. In the meantime she could only do what felt right.

For the most part things had returned to normal at the work-house. The master, furious, and worried as to how the episode would reflect on his stewardship, had instigated an immediate investigation, and when the open dormitory window was established as the girls' way of escape from the building, poor

Miss Wilson, who had been on duty that night, had been disciplined and threatened with dismissal should she be found wanting again.

As to how they had managed to leave the grounds, that remained an unsolved mystery. While all the hullaballoo was going on inside the workhouse, Leo had slipped quietly away, to all intents and purposes to continue with the work he had been doing the previous day. He'd filled in the burrow, bent the wire back into place as best he could and hoped the long grass would hide it from anything other than close inspection.

Luck was with him. A wooden fence at the end of the vegetable garden was found to be broken, and it was wrongly assumed that was how the girls had made their escape. Leo thought wryly that he needn't have gone to all that trouble if he'd known about it. But the main thing was, his plan had worked. Ella and Jeannie had got away.

He couldn't help worrying about them, however. Had they managed to get to their uncle in Hillsbridge? Or were they still out there somewhere alone? Jeannie was such a fragile little thing, and though he had no doubt of Ella's resourcefulness, who knew what dangers they might have encountered? All day he fretted, wondering how they were faring and if they would be caught and brought back. He almost hoped they would be; at least then he'd know they were safe. Ella should have reported what had happened and if the girls were returned to the workhouse he'd make sure she did, and back her up. He'd lie, if necessary, and say the rector had attempted something similar with him.

But the days passed and Ella and Jeannie were still missing. He still thought of them constantly and missed Ella dreadfully, and as for his lessons, it was all he could do to continue with them. The very sight of the evil rector made his stomach churn, and he wished with all his heart that he could beat that smug face to a pulp. But the tuition was important for his future, and for Ella's. He'd meant what he'd said when he'd promised she'd be a part of it. Though for the moment he had no idea where she was, he'd find her one day and ensure that she and Jeannie never wanted for anything again.

It was this that kept him going through those dark weeks. This that made him work harder than ever at his lessons.

Rector Evans would get his comeuppance one day, but for the present he was a means to an end.

Unbeknown to Leo, or to anyone else, there was someone who already viewed Rector Evans with deep suspicion.

Miss Owen had never liked the man. There was something about him that raised the hairs on the back of her neck in the same way a cat's fur stands on end when it scents an enemy. Exactly what it was, she couldn't put her finger on. He was always perfectly pleasant and polite to her, and everyone else, as far as she was aware. But perhaps it was just that – he was *too* nice, wearing his bonhomie and smug holiness like he wore his cassock and cloak, an affectation that covered some unpleasant-ness deep within. Could it be that he was the cause of those two poor children running away? Miss Owen sincerely hoped not. But she had been raised as a strict Methodist, and she had distrusted priests ever since, as a young woman, she had read the scandalous *Awful Disclosures of Maria Monk*. The book was supposedly written by a young nun who was only one of many who were systematically abused by the monks in their convent and the bodies of the children born to them disposed of in lime and acid in the basement.

Rector Evans wasn't a monk or a Catholic priest, of course, but sometimes she thought he might as well have been, always creeping about in his long, black, flowing garments and living all alone in that great big rectory with only his elderly maid for company. And Ella and Jeannie weren't nubile young nuns, they were still children, but they were pretty little things, and utterly and completely defenceless, while the rector was held in high esteem by everyone at the workhouse.

Miss Owen made up her mind that she would keep a close eye on the rector. For the moment, it was all she could do.

'You're late home today.'

When Garth hadn't arrived home from work at his usual time, Martha had become anxious, checking the kitchen clock every five or ten minutes and wondering what could be keeping him. Now at least he was here, though she wasn't expecting a civil response to her perfectly natural remark.

To her surprise, however, Garth faced her looking pleased with himself instead of scowling and going straight upstairs to change with nothing more than a disgusted grunt.

'I had someone to see,' he said, sounding almost triumphant.

'Oh? Who was that then?' Martha asked.

Garth didn't answer directly. It looked as if he was enjoying himself. 'I've got myself a different job. I'm not going to work with Ernie any more.'

'What do you mean – you've got yourself a different job?' Martha was astounded.

'I hate that bloody farm. So I've found something a darn sight better.'

'But what? Where?'

'I'm going to work for Ticker Bendle.'

Martha's heart came into her mouth. 'Ticker Bendle? The bookie?'

A grin spread across Garth's good-looking face at her shocked reaction. 'Yeah. The bookie. You never knew, but I used to collect bets for him when I was a nipper. So I went to see him, asked him if he would take me on as an assistant. And what d'you know? He said he'd been thinking for some time he could do with some help, what with keeping the office open and going to the races when they're on as well. He's going to train me up. I start next week.'

All the colour had drained from Martha's face. It was through Ticker Bendle that Joe had got into gambling, become involved with that awful crowd that had included Spider, Slug and Wolf. She was sure it was Ticker who had told them she was a barmaid at the Feathers. And the horror of what had ensued had followed her down the years.

'Garth, you can't.'

'Why not?'

'Well . . . you can't let your Uncle Ernie down like that,' she floundered. 'What will he do without you?'

'Find some other mug to do the dirty work, I suppose. I don't know, and I don't much care.'

'At least it's a regular wage,' she argued desperately.

'I can make a whole lot more working for Ticker,' Garth asserted. 'You know the saying? The bookie always wins.'

'You can't do it, Garth!' Martha cried vehemently. 'I won't let you!'

Garth smirked. 'Just try to stop me.'

And with that he turned and headed for his room.

It was as he changed out of his dirty working clothes that the thought struck him.

He'd expected some opposition to what he planned to do. He knew his mother was against any form of gambling, which was why he'd kept it secret when he'd been acting as a runner for

Ticker in his youth. And he'd guessed she would object to him leaving Uncle Ernie in the lurch – he was her brother, after all. But he'd been startled by the violence of her reaction. Now, suddenly, something Ticker had said during the interview came back to him.

Until today, he'd had no contact with the bookie since he'd stopped collecting bets for him at the age of eleven. But as soon as he'd introduced himself, Ticker had shaken his head disbelievingly.

'Good Lord, lad, you've grown since I last saw you!'

'Well . . . yeah . . . I was just a nipper then . . .'

'I can't believe my eyes. You put me in mind of some-one . . .'

At the time, it hadn't registered with Garth. He's been too intent on the opportunity to talk Ticker into giving him a job. Now, though, he remembered every word.

Something like excitement rose in his chest and he crossed to the mirror that stood on top of his chest of drawers. He could only see himself from the waist up, but that was enough. Thick black hair. Black eyes. Swarthy skin. Broad shoulders, and muscles already well developed from his hard physical work on the farm.

Garth had already convinced himself that he must take after his real father in looks. In the last few years he'd grown from a scrawny kid to a man – well, almost a man. And the change in his appearance had taken Ticker by surprise. *You put me in mind of someone . . .*

Could it be that Ticker knew his real father? Was it poss-ible that fate had stirred him to ask the bookie for a job? Might it be that at last he was going to learn the answers to his questions?

Exhilarated, Garth pulled his shirt on over his head. He'd

still have Mam to contend with, and perhaps Seb – he'd stopped calling him Dad since he'd learned the truth – too. But he wouldn't be deterred. A new life lay ahead of him, and perhaps a new family as well. Garth couldn't wait.

Chapter Eleven

Martha had done all she could to prevent Garth from going to work for Ticker Bendle, but he'd defied her, and Seb had taken the view that it was best to let the matter drop.

'You'd have the devil's own job to stop him. Truth to tell I don't know how you could, short of locking him in his room. And then he'd most likely climb out the window. He's not a nipper any more, and he's got a mind of his own.'

'You can say that again,' Martha said despairingly. 'But he's only fifteen and he's still my son.'

'Just think what it would be like if you did find a way to stop him,' Seb argued. 'He'd only take it out on you. If you ask me it's better to let him do it if that's what he wants. Standing in his way would only make matters worse.'

Reluctantly, Martha had accepted that Seb might well be right, but that didn't stop her from feeling guilty that Garth was letting Ernie down, or worrying about how the move might affect Garth's future. She was ashamed but relieved when her brother seemed less than sorry that Garth would no longer be his responsibility, and mortified when he added: 'At least I'll be able to take on a lad I can trust. You know I only kept him on for your sake, our Martha.'

Now, however, her mind was made up. There was nothing

she could do to keep Garth away from the shady world that had set Joe on the path to disaster and indirectly cost him his life. All she could do was pray that her son didn't go the same way. And she determined to turn her attention to something she hoped she might have some control over – the fate of the two little girls who had entered her life so unexpectedly and stolen her heart.

She talked it over with Seb and they decided that it would be best to seek the advice of a solicitor. And so, one morning in August, she set out on the long walk to Hillsbridge.

Although it was still only just after ten o'clock the sun was already high in the sky and by the time she reached the out-skirts of Hillsbridge Martha was hot and sticky, her cotton blouse clinging wherever it touched, her feet swollen so that her boots felt tight, with the beginnings of a blister on her heel, and rivulets of perspiration running down her forehead and neck. As she walked down the long hill into town she dreaded the thought of having to climb it on the way home in this heat. But she pushed the thought aside. The important thing was to find out the lie of the land regarding the children, and get advice as to how she and Seb could set about making a permanent home for them.

The solicitor's office was above a row of shops in the main street. Martha knew this because there was a gleaming brass plate on the wall and a frosted glass panel in the door bearing the legend 'Willoughby and Clarence, Solicitors and Attorneys at Law'.

About to ring the bell, Martha paused for a moment to find the little bottle of eau-de-cologne that she kept in her bag, pour a few drops on to her handkerchief, and mop her forehead and neck. She was apprehensive enough about the forthcoming interview without having to worry about her personal hygiene!

Satisfied she'd done her best to make herself presentable, she rang the bell, opened the door, and started up the steep flight of stairs that faced her. She was startled when a figure materialised at the top of the stairs – a small man, stooped and balding, wearing a black jacket over a wing-collared shirt.

'Good morning. Can I be of assistance?' His voice was scratchy, like a pen that is running out of ink.

Martha stopped, holding on to the wooden handrail and peering up at him. 'Mr Willoughby?'

The little man gave a short laugh, every bit as crackly as his voice. 'No indeed. I am Mr Horler. I'm afraid Mr Willoughby is no longer with us.'

'Oh!' Martha was nonplussed. There was no mention of a Mr Horler on the brass plate, or the inscription on the door. And did he mean Mr Willoughby had retired, or had he died? 'I'm sorry to hear that,' she said, hedging her bets.

'A great loss,' Mr Horler said solemnly.

'Then perhaps you could help me?' Martha suggested.

'Oh dear me – I am not a solicitor.' The little man sounded almost offended. 'That is Mr Clarence.'

'Then can I see Mr Clarence?'

'You don't have an appointment, I presume?'

'No.' If I did I would hardly be asking for Mr Willoughby, Martha thought, annoyed. 'But I'd be much obliged if the solicitor could spare me a few minutes. I've come a long way to see him.'

'Very well, I'll enquire. Your name is . . . ?'

'Mrs Packer,' Martha supplied.

The clerk disappeared without another word, leaving Martha to wonder whether she was supposed to follow him. But whatever, she wasn't going to wait on the stairs. She climbed the last few and found herself in what had apparently once been a landing, but, judging by the two chairs placed along the wall with an occasional table separating them, now did service as a waiting room.

Voices came from behind one of the doors leading off – the clerk's scratchy tone, and one much richer, deep and plummy – but she was unable to make out what was being said. Then the door opened wider and the clerk emerged.

'Fortunately, Mr Clarence's next appointment is not due quite yet, and he's prepared to see you. But I must mention time is very limited.'

Martha didn't bother to reply. She'd had enough of this officious little man, and was wondering what to expect from the solicitor. But she was ready for him. She wasn't going to be fobbed off just because she was nothing more than a glorified barmaid.

The office she marched into was, to her surprise, not much larger than the makeshift 'waiting room'. It was dominated by a large, tooled-leather desk covered with manila folders tied with pink tape and more files piled on the floor beside it, whilst the walls were filled with shelves bearing what Martha assumed must be legal books. A portly gentleman whose face was dominated by side whiskers and a pair of owlish glasses rose from his chair behind the desk to greet her.

'Mrs Packer, I believe?' He offered her his hand, indicated that she should take the chair opposite his, and resumed his seat. 'How can I be of assistance?'

Martha hesitated, suddenly anxious that what she was about to say might lead to untold problems for having kept the children hidden for so long. 'This is in confidence, isn't it?'

Mr Clarence's eyes narrowed behind his thick glasses. 'Client confidentiality is assured, yes.'

Martha nodded, satisfied. 'It's about the two children who ran away from the workhouse in Bath.' She went on to explain what had happened, and her and Seb's part in it. 'We can't bear to think of them having to go back to that terrible place, and what they were suffering there,' she finished.

Mr Clarence removed his spectacles and rubbed his eyes. He looked shocked by Martha's story.

'Dreadful! Dreadful,' he muttered.

'The thing is, we want to give them a home,' Martha went on. 'Is there any way we could adopt them?'

Mr Clarence considered. 'There is no such thing as formal adoption, Mrs Packer. I very much hope that one day it may be recognised in law, but for the present . . .'

Martha's heart sank. 'You mean—'

She was interrupted by a tap on the door and the officious clerk's face appeared.

'Mr Benjamin is here, Mr Clarence.'

Martha's heart sank still further. Was the solicitor going to end her consultation before she had the answers she so desperately wanted? To her immense relief, however, he instructed the clerk to ask the client if he would be so good as to wait a few minutes.

'If that's your wish.' The clerk's disapproval was evident in his clipped tone, but he withdrew, and Mr Clarence turned his attention once more to Martha.

'It is possible to enter into a private arrangement, however,' he ventured.

'With the workhouse?' Martha quailed at the thought of having to deal with the very people who had allowed such atrocities. 'I wouldn't know where to begin. And I'm not sure the authorities would think us suitable, seeing as we lied to the police.'

'Added to which there is the question of the accommodation being on licensed premises.'

'I assure you we keep a very orderly house!' Martha responded hotly.

A faint smile lifted the corners of the solicitor's mouth. 'I have no doubt you do, Mrs Packer. However . . .' He paused, and Martha waited with bated breath.

'I think the best course of action would be for you to leave this with me,' he said at last.

'But what could you do?' Martha asked.

'I have a great many contacts, Mrs Packer, including some of the board of governors of the workhouse. I shall speak to at least one of them and plead your case. Now, I really mustn't keep my client waiting any longer, so if you will give your details to my clerk I will contact you when I have some news. In the meantime, I suggest you continue as you have been.'

'Oh, thank you!' The simple words seemed inadequate to express the gratitude Martha was feeling. 'Thank you so much! And the bill . . . will you send that to me too, or do I pay your clerk before I leave?'

'There will be no charge, Mrs Packer.' He rose, offering her his hand, and Martha rose too.

'But I've taken up your time,' she protested.

'Think of it as my contribution to your kindness to those two poor little ones,' he said with a smile. 'I have to say I am touched. It's good to know there are compassionate people in this world as well as wicked ones.'

A faint colour rose in Martha's cheeks as she took the solicitor's proffered hand. 'Thank you again.'

She left the office, waited while the objectionable clerk showed the gentleman who had arrived for his appointment into Mr Clarence's office, then faced down his obvious disapproval as she gave him her name and address and informed him the solicitor had said there would be no charge for the advice he'd given her. She no longer cared that his lips tightened into an even thinner line, was no longer worried about the long walk back in the hot sun, beginning with the steep climb.

There was light at the end of the tunnel, and she couldn't wait to tell Seb the good news.

There was good news too for Leo. He learned that he had been successful in obtaining a scholarship to Marlborough College and would start there as a boarder at the beginning of the new term. He knew he had Rector Evans to thank, both for the hours of private tuition that had prepared him for the examination, and for securing the place for him. The college had been founded back in the 1840s for the sons of clergymen, and Leo guessed that the rector had pulled some strings on his behalf. But it did nothing to diminish his hatred of the evil man. It had been all Leo could do to sit through his lessons when all he wanted to do was smash that bloated face to a pulp, and when the rector broke the news of his success, beaming, and clapping Leo on the back, he had drawn away, sick to his stomach that he'd let the old lecher get away with what he'd done to Ella, what he planned to do to Jeannie, and what he might do to some other poor girl.

There was money also from some fund or other to buy Leo's uniform and all the accoutrements he would need to take his place at such a prestigious school, and it was the hated rector who accompanied him to Bath on a glorified shopping trip. With all their purchases parcelled up and carefully wrapped, Rector Evans had treated him to tea at the Old Red House, but with the horrible man sitting opposite him he had little appetite for the toasted teacakes, oozing butter, or the ice cream served in little silver dishes.

At least when he was a boarder at Marlborough he would no longer have to endure the twice-weekly tuition sessions, he told himself, and his one regret was that he couldn't share his good fortune with Ella.

He missed her dreadfully and wondered and worried about her every day, wishing she had let him know what had happened, but guessing that even if she had written to him the letter would have probably been intercepted. He was relieved she and Jeannie hadn't been returned to the workhouse but he couldn't stop himself from thinking of a myriad of scenarios as to why this hadn't happened. Were they safe? Had they managed to get to their relatives in Hillsbridge? Or had some harm befallen them along the way? His stomach fell away at the thought of it and he tried to convince himself that if something dreadful had happened, he would have heard about it. The master at the workhouse would have made a point of warning all the other children what dangers they would face if they ever considered following in Ella and Jeannie's footsteps and making their escape.

And he was as determined as ever that when his education was completed he'd find Ella and Jeannie, ensure they were well and happy, and never, ever lose touch with them again.

Garth couldn't remember a time when he'd ever been happier. For the whole of his life he'd felt a misfit, as if he didn't belong anywhere. Not his family – he had nothing in common with his brothers, nor, come to that, his father. Not at school, where he'd forever been in one scrape or another. And certainly not on the bloody farm. Lately he'd enjoyed meeting up with his mates – he'd sought out lads as wild and rebellious as he was – but when he got home from spending time with them there was usually hell to pay for staying out late, smoking and drinking, which sent him straight back into one of his dark, resentful moods.

But the minute he'd stepped into Ticker Bendle's office, it

had felt right, just as it had when he'd acted as the bookie's runner as a nipper. That had been good too, hanging about outside the Hillsbridge pubs, keeping a sharp look out for the coppers, surreptitiously taking the betting slips and stake money from the punters who sought him out, racing back to Ticker's with them, and collecting his earnings at the end of the day – not exactly riches, but at least a bit of money of his own to spend as he liked. Best of all had been feeling he'd got one over on his mother and father. If they'd known what he was up to he'd probably have had a good hiding. Besides disapproving of gambling, they would have been horrified to think their son was breaking the law.

Ticker was a good sort, jovial and broad-minded, if not exactly generous – the wage he was paying wasn't much more than the pittance he'd earned on the farm. But he did stand Garth a drink when he'd had a particularly lucrative day, either at the pub just up the road, or from the bottle of Scotch he kept in his filing cabinet. And judging by the piddling little amounts he had to pay out, and the bulging money bag in the safe, at least Seb had been right about one thing – in the end, the bookie always won. One day, Garth thought, he'd follow in Ticker's footsteps and make a mint for himself.

Another advantage was that he could smoke freely in the office. It was always full of smoke anyway from the fat cigars Ticker enjoyed. And though he had hated lessons at school and never learned a great deal beyond the three Rs, the things Ticker was teaching him kept him interested, even enthusiastic. Arithmetic made sense when it meant money in the bank, lists of runners and riders made interesting reading, and there was satisfaction to be had in writing down results in a hand neat enough to be legible.

As for learning tic-tac, the sign language used by bookies at racetracks to communicate the odds of a horse to other bookies and officials, Garth was fascinated, and couldn't wait to be able to master it. He'd only just begun, of course – there was so much of it, and the names given to the odds, either rhyming or backslang, was as confusing as it was unfamiliar. Ticker had donned a pair of white gloves and found another pair for Garth – they were worn so as to make the hand signals clearer, he explained. He'd started with the simpler signs, and Garth was soon making the sign of 'evens', or 'Major Stevens', as Ticker called it – simply extending the forefingers on each hand and moving them up and downwards in opposite directions. The next was for 5/4 on – known as 'wrist' – and indicated by placing the right hand on the left wrist. And he'd also learned 9/4 on – 'top of the head'. That was easy – all he had to do was to place both hands on the top of his head. As other signs were added he began to become a little confused, but he persevered, and had even taken to practising in front of the mirror in his bedroom when he was sprucing up.

Only one thing had disappointed him since he'd come to work for the bookie. He was no closer to discovering who was his real father.

He'd raised the subject on his second or third day, saying as casually as he could: 'Who is it I put you in mind of, then?'

Ticker had looked up from the money he'd taken out of the cash drawer and was counting on to a small table, looking a bit puzzled. 'What's that?'

'When I came to see you about a job. You said I put you in mind of someone.'

'Oh. Yes.' He squinted at Garth's face from behind the smoke of his cigar. 'Yes, you do.'

'I wondered who it was, that's all. I didn't think there was another one of me.'

'Bit put out about that, were you?'

'No, just curious. Who's my double?'

Ticker shook his head. 'Search me. All the men I see – how can you expect me to remember that? Now look – you've made me forget where I was. I shall have to start this lot all over again.'

He returned to the piles of coins and Garth realised he was going to get no further. Today, at any rate. But there was something about the look on Ticker's face that might have been discomfort that made Garth wonder. The bookie's tone had been short and uncomfortable too. Was it just that he was annoyed at being interrupted when he was counting the money? Did he really not remember who it was Garth reminded him of? Or did he remember very well, and not want to say?

Garth made up his mind to try again another time. He'd keep a good lookout when he accompanied Ticker to the race tracks too. He was more convinced than ever that his real father had some connection to this world. It was the reason he felt so at home here. And sooner or later he was going to find the man whose blood flowed in his veins.

'Do you think . . .'

Jeannie dropped her gaze from Ella's and chewed on a finger.

'Do I think what?' Ella asked, guessing that whatever it was Jeannie wanted to know was going to have to be forced out of her.

For a long moment, Jeannie remained silent, then all of a sudden she burst out: 'I really, really want to marry Garth. Do you think he'll wait for me until I'm old enough?'

Ella suppressed a smile. She could hardly have failed to notice that her sister was besotted with the eldest Packer boy – ever since he'd been the one to find them in the skittle-alley she seemed to see him as her hero. When he was at home she followed him around like a puppy dog, and to be fair, he did nothing to discourage her. But Ella wasn't altogether happy with the situation. There was something dark and dangerous about him that Jeannie was oblivious to. Or perhaps it was that which attracted her to him.

'Oh, Jeannie! It's years and years before you need start thinking about getting married!' she said.

'But he's older than me. I'm afraid he might not wait . . .' Jeannie's small, elfin face was puckered with anxiety.

'Well, he's only fifteen, so it will be years and years before he starts thinking about it either,' Ella said.

'I suppose.' Jeannie still looked glum.

'Let's go and see if we can finish off that jigsaw puzzle,' Ella suggested.

'But it's so hard! There are so many pieces . . .'

'Perhaps when Garth gets home from work he'll help.' Ella would have much rather he didn't, but she'd say anything to put a smile back on her sister's face.

It worked. Jeannie brightened at once. 'Oh, do you think so?'

'Let's see if we can show him it's nearly finished.' Ella took her sister's hand and led her into the sitting room.

The letter from Mr Clarence arrived much more quickly than Martha had expected, or dared hope, with the afternoon post. She knew at once from the fancy copperplate writing on the manila envelope that it must be from the solicitor, and she hurried through into the bar where Seb was wiping down tables and sweeping up crumbs from the dinnertime trade.

'Seb – I've got a letter . . .' Her stomach was churning and she felt breathless from a potpourri of excitement and apprehension.

Seb straightened, cloth in hand. 'What does it say?'

'I don't know. I haven't opened it yet.'

'Well, go on then.'

She held it out to him. 'You do it.'

'Don't be so silly. My hands are all dirty. Go on, open it, do.'

Carefully, Martha tore the envelope open, extracted the letter and unfolded it. Her shriek of joy and relief as she read it brought a smile to Seb's face.

'Come on then. Don't keep it to yourself. Let's hear what he's got to say.'

'It's going to be all right. Just listen to this. "I have been in touch with the relevant authorities and they have no objection to you assuming the care of Ella and Jeannie Martin." Isn't that wonderful? And he says, "all documentation pertaining to the children will be forwarded to you in due course", whatever that means.'

'Identification papers, I suppose,' Seb said.

'I suppose. So we can register them with a doctor, and get them into school. Oh, Seb – I can't believe it! All this time we've been worrying ourselves for nothing!'

'We'd better tell them then, hadn't we?'

'Yes, we had!' She went to the door and called the children. 'Ella! Jeannie! Can you come down here a minute?'

The two girls appeared a few minutes later looking anxious and puzzled.

'Don't look so worried!' Martha said. 'I've got some wonderful news for you. How would you like to stay with us?'

'But we are . . .' Jeannie sounded confused.

'No, not just for now. Be part of the family. Properly. You won't have to hide away any more. You'll be able to go out to play, start school, come to market with me . . .'

'Oh! Yes!' Jeannie rushed to her, burying her head in

Martha's stomach, and Martha put an arm around her, holding her close.

'But how . . . ?' Ella asked.

'Don't worry your head about that. It's all been arranged. Are you pleased too?'

Ella simply nodded, but the broad smile that spread across her face told Martha all she needed to know.

She'd done it. The girls were safe. And the rush of love for them that filled her was as heartfelt as if they really had been her own children.

Chapter Twelve

1898

'Ella, you can't go! You can't leave me!'

The words were an echo of Jeannie's plea when Ella had been leaving the workhouse to go to the rectory for the first of her private lessons, but this time the circumstances were quite different. Ella, now thirteen, was going to take up her first job in the working world, as a nursery maid for the young family of one of the directors of a Bath foundry which manufactured cranes for docks all over the world.

For the last two years she and Jeannie had attended the same school as Conrad and Lewis, and they had arranged the placement for her. It wasn't quite the same as what Rector Evans had promised her – working as a classroom assistant – but it was the next best thing. She would have the care of two young children, and she couldn't wait to meet them. The only disadvantage was that she would have to live in, and that meant leaving Jeannie.

But Jeannie would be fine, she told herself. Martha was like a mother to her, and the boys were the brothers she never had. She'd be able to get home on her days off, at least once a week, and it was time Jeannie learned to stand on her own two feet, though in her heart of hearts she worried that that was never going to happen. Although Jeannie was now ten years old, she was as childlike as ever, and still needed a rock to cling to. Just as long as that rock wasn't Garth, Ella thought. She wouldn't trust him any further than she could throw him.

'Ella! They're here!' Martha called.

Her new employers were sending a carriage for her – a great luxury – and Martha had seen it arrive from the kitchen window.

'I have to go, Jeannie. I can't keep them waiting.' Ella picked up her carpet bag – the same one that she'd brought with her – and went to the door, Jeannie still hanging on to her arm.

'Come on, Jeannie.' Martha had followed them, and now she took the little girl's hand. 'Don't be silly, now. Bath's only six miles away, not the ends of the earth. And Ella will be back again to see you before you know it.'

'I will, I promise.' Ella bent down and kissed her sister. 'Just be a good girl for Martha. Can you do that for me?'

Jeannie nodded, but her lip was trembling and there were tears in her eyes. As Ella tugged herself free she turned to Martha, burying her head in her stomach.

'Aren't you going to wave goodbye to your sister?' Martha asked.

Jeannie shook her head, sobbing. As she climbed into the carriage, the last sight Ella had of her was the back of her head and shaking shoulders.

Well, there was nothing she could do about it. She would just have to trust that Martha could calm her down. Ella felt a stab of guilt as she realised she actually felt relieved, as if a burden had been lifted from her shoulders. She'd keep her promise to Mammy, of course she would. But the years of responsibility for her sister had weighed more heavily on her than she'd realised. Jeannie would be perfectly safe at the Feathers with Martha and Seb; there was no need to worry about her. For the first time she could recall, Ella was free to live her own life.

The house that the carriage drew up to was grander than any Ella had ever seen. It was one of a long, curved terrace that seemed to reach the sky, and sunshine glinted on the tall windows and turned the pale stone of which the crescent was built golden yellow. On the other side of the cobbled road vibrant green lawns stretched away, broad and wide as a meadow. The coachman climbed down and came around to help her out, but Ella refused to allow him to take her carpet bag from her.

As the coachman handed her out of the carriage, the white-painted front door of the house opened and a lady emerged, a small child in her arms. Ella's heart beat a little faster. She'd expected to be taken to a servant's entrance, and be greeted by a maid, but this lady must be her new employer, and the child in her arms one of Ella's new charges.

Suddenly overcome with shyness, she hesitated, then, gathering her courage, walked across the pathway towards the house, where the lady waited with a welcoming smile on her pretty face.

'You must be Ella,' she said by way of greeting. 'I am Mrs Henderson. Please, do come in.'

Ella stepped inside, overawed by the grandeur of the entrance hall.

'I expect you'd like some refreshment after your journey,' Mrs Henderson said. 'Do leave your bag in the hall. Evie will take it upstairs for you.'

'Oh, it's all right . . .' Ella was as determined as ever not to let it out of her possession if she could help it!

'As you please.' Mrs Henderson showed her into a vast drawing room, luxuriously furnished, and light and airy thanks to the tall sash windows. 'Do sit down.' She pulled on a bell rope. 'Evie will bring us tea.'

Ella looked around, half afraid to take a seat on any of the plush sofas, and settled on a spindle-legged chair with a round seat and carved arms, perching on it uncomfortably.

'Now, this is Angelina . . .' She set the toddler down on the Persian carpet, and as she did so, Ella noticed a thickening of her waist beneath her dress. So there was another baby on the way! She felt a little thrill of pleasure.

'Mama! Is she here?' A small boy came bursting into the room, his rosy face eager.

'And this . . .' Mrs Henderson said with a smile, 'is Eustace.'

Eustace had stopped short, grasping his mother's legs and gazing at Ella curiously.

'My, Eustace, what *have* you been up to? You look like a baby hedgehog! What will Ella think of you?' As she spoke, she reached out, smoothing down his hair as best she could with her fingers. It was the exact same rich chestnut as her own, Ella noticed.

The tea arrived, brought in on a silver tray by a maid Ella assumed must be Evie. Porcelain cups and saucers patterned with roses, a matching pot and milk jug, silver teaspoons, dainty lace-edged napkins, a plate of tiny macaroons . . . Once again Ella felt overwhelmed.

At least Mrs Henderson seemed pleasant and friendly, and the children were nothing short of adorable.

I'll get used to it, Ella thought. But it was still so different to anything she had ever known before that it was daunting, nonetheless.

* * *

Jeannie was playing a game of cards with Conrad and Lewis when Garth got home from work. Martha had instigated it, whispering to the boys that she 'needed to have her mind taken off Ella', but it hadn't entirely been a success. Jeannie was still moping, and not concentrating properly, and the boys were beginning to get annoyed. She'd dropped her hand several times as she tried to sort the cards into suits and then number order – they were playing Sevens – and she kept saying she didn't have a card to lay on the table when she did, or playing one that didn't run in sequence.

'For goodness' sake, Jeannie!' Lewis exclaimed. 'Don't you know that the jack comes after the ten, not the king?'

Jeannie pouted. 'They look the same to me.'

'They do not. You're just doing it to be a pest.'

As Garth's voice carried through from the kitchen, Jeannie threw her cards down on the table.

'I don't want to play any more. You're so mean!'

'Come on, don't be silly,' Lewis said swiftly, thinking he would catch the rough edge of his mother's tongue for upsetting Jeannie when they were supposed to be cheering her up. 'Let's start again. You can be dealer, if you like.'

But Jeannie was already heading in the direction of the kitchen. The two boys exchanged wry glances. They knew they couldn't hope to entice her back when Garth was on the scene.

'What's up, Jeannie?' Martha asked.

'The boys are being horrid. I don't want to play with them.'

'Oh dear,' Martha sighed. 'Ella's gone to Bath today,' she added, speaking to Garth. 'And Jeannie's not very happy about it.'

'You'll get over it, kid,' Garth said. He seemed a little preoccupied.

'Will you play with me, Garth? Please!' Jeannie turned to

her hero, her turquoise eyes sad as a lost puppy.

'Not today, Jeannie.' He was already making for the door. She trailed after him miserably, but Martha called her back.

'You can help me. Get out the cups and we'll make a pot of tea.'

Jeannie hung her head and stuffed her thumb in her mouth, yet another childish habit she had yet to grow out of.

'Buck up now,' Martha said briskly. 'If the wind turns while you've got that face on you'll get stuck with it.'

But there was no cheering Jeannie. Martha hoped this mood wouldn't last too long, but she wasn't holding her breath.

Ella, meanwhile, was feeling optimistic. She was delighted with her room, not up in the attics as she'd expected, but on the same floor as her new master and mistress and the children – so that she'd be on hand to see to them if they woke in the night, Mrs Henderson had said. It was quite small, but light and bright like the rest of the house, with a view over the extensive grounds at the back of the house. When Ella had pushed up the sash window and leaned out for a better look, she had seen a paved patio set with garden furniture directly below the window, and a lawn, rose beds, a weeping silver birch and what looked like a walled garden beyond. Inside, there was more than enough room for her few belongings, with a wardrobe, tallboy and dressing table, and a pretty floral jug and basin stood on a marble-topped washstand. There was a connecting door to the nursery, which Ella decided she would leave open at night so as to be sure she heard the children if either of them cried.

The food was delicious, fish in a parsley sauce with mashed potatoes for lunch, followed by tapioca pudding, and she had eaten with Mrs Henderson, Eustace and Angelina. It seemed she was to be treated more like a member of the family than a servant. Angelina still had a bottle of milk before being put down for her afternoon nap, and Ella gave it to her, along with a teaspoonful of Woodward's gripe water, and cradled the little girl on her lap until Angelina's eyes drooped and she fell asleep in her cot.

Eustace was also enjoying a nap, so Mrs Henderson and Ella were able to chat in peace and begin to get to know one another.

The new baby was due around Christmas, Mrs Henderson said, and it was the reason she and her husband had decided to employ a nursemaid. Until now she had cared for the children herself, but: 'I think three children under five might be a little too much!' she said, smiling ruefully. Ella couldn't help but think of all the poor families where the mother had to manage a whole string of children alone, but she was glad, nevertheless, that Mrs Henderson had opted for assistance, and that the school had put her forward for the post.

Mr Henderson had arrived home from his office at around five thirty. He was a small, rotund man who was fast losing his hair, and Ella couldn't help but wonder that Mrs Henderson had looked at him twice. She was so attractive, with her thick brown hair, green-flecked brown eyes and generous mouth. But Ella supposed there were no rules as to where you should love, and Mr Henderson – John, as Mrs Henderson called him – seemed a pleasant man, and just as ready as his wife to accept Ella into the family circle. Ella had also learned that Mrs Henderson's given name was Sylvia, but she couldn't imagine she'd ever have cause to use it. To her, her employer would always be 'Mrs Henderson'.

Now Ella was helping to prepare a nursery tea for the children, learning their likes and dislikes in readiness for when she would be expected to do it on her own. Boiled eggs and bread and butter soldiers were a favourite, it seemed, along with jelly and custard. But potted fish paste was to be avoided at all costs – Eustace had been violently sick after wolfing down Cook's concoction, it seemed.

Yes, all in all, Ella thought she had landed on her feet with this position. But as she buttered bread she couldn't help but think about Jeannie and hope that she wasn't in too dark a place.

On any other day Garth would have humoured Jeannie; her adoration flattered his ego. Today, however, although he no longer had to change out of filthy working clothes as he'd had to when he was working on the farm, he went straight upstairs to his room, where he stood in front of the mirror, looking at himself with a critical eye. Two years had matured his features and a dark shadow covered his cheeks and chin unless he shaved every morning – he rubbed his hand over it now and it rasped against his fingers, no longer the soft down of a boy, but the incipient beard of a man.

In the two years he'd been working for Ticker Bendle he'd often caught the bookie studying him when he thought he wasn't looking, and Garth was convinced Ticker knew very well who Garth reminded him of. But he hadn't asked again. He didn't want Ticker to know he was that interested. Better to keep his powder dry and wait until the right opportunity presented itself. And today something had happened that had convinced him he'd done the right thing.

They'd been at the races – Bath. As usual, Ticker had set up his stall and Garth, now adept at using the language of tic-tac, had donned his white gloves and been kept busy communicating the odds of the runners to the other bookies.

It was in a lull between races that the man approached Ticker's stall. He was small and wiry, with a heavily lined face and thinning grey hair barely covering a shiny pink scalp.

An expensive-looking coat was slung casually about his thin shoulders and he carried a top hat which had probably blown off in the stiff breeze that whistled across the exposed racecourse high above the city, and an ivory-topped cane.

'Ticker, you old devil!' he greeted the bookie. 'Fancy seeing you here!'

'Hardly a surprise, I'd have thought,' Ticker returned. 'I've got a living to make.'

He sounded less than pleased to see the man, Garth thought.

'But I thought you made it out in the sticks.' The man seemed oblivious to Ticker's cool tone. 'I thought you had an aversion to our lovely city.'

Ticker merely shrugged, raising one bushy eyebrow.

'You have an apprentice, I see.' The man turned to Garth, his eyes narrowed and piercing, his scrutiny so close that Garth shifted uncomfortably. 'And who might you be, my boy?'

Garth mumbled his name.

'And where do you come from, may I ask? Do you live in Hillsbridge like Ticker?'

'Well, just outside. Fossecombe.'

'Not at the Three Feathers public house, by any chance?' Garth nodded. 'Well, well, what a small world!'

The man's thin lips had twisted into what passed for a smile and sudden realisation made Garth's breath catch in his throat. The questions, that piercing gaze – this man, who was an acquaintance of Ticker's at the very least, had seen the likeness Ticker had seen in him. He knew, or had known, Garth's real father.

Faced with the chance he had awaited for so long, Garth was rendered speechless. All the questions he wanted to ask deserted him and he could only stare back at the man while his heart pounded in his chest.

'I have to say I'm impressed with your mastery of the art of tic-tac,' the man said.

It was a good five minutes since Garth had made his last signals; the man must have been watching him for some time, perhaps had even come across to the stall with the express purpose of seeing him at close quarters and even speaking to him.

'He's picked it up very well,' Ticker interposed. 'And now, if you don't mind, Elliot, he's got work to do and I've got punters to attend to.'

Again the man ignored the brush-off. 'I'm sure it's not his only talent. I'll bet you're pretty handy with your fists, too, eh, lad? He reached into the pocket of his coat, drew out a pigskin wallet, and extracted a calling card, holding it out to Garth.

'If ever you get tired of working for this bad-tempered old fart, this is where you can find me. I'd be only too happy to give you a job, and I'd certainly pay better wages. Don't forget, now – Garth, is it?' He turned to Ticker. 'Good to see you again, old friend. And I hope you won't stand in this lad's way if he wants to better himself.' With that he settled the topper back on his head and walked away, swinging his cane.

Garth found his voice. 'Who was that?'

'You don't want to know,' Ticker said shortly. 'And the best thing you can do with that . . .' he nodded in the direction of the calling card Garth was holding, 'is to drop it in the first rubbish bin you see. I'm telling you – he's bad news.'

'You know him, though.'

'Knew him. Back in the days when I was young enough and daft enough not to know better.'

'How?' Garth asked.

Ticker turned his back, clearly unwilling to answer, and Garth decided to let discretion be the better part of valour. He had the man's card. He would know where to find him. Before Ticker turned back and saw what he was doing, Garth pushed it deep into his pocket.

Now, in the privacy of his room, he took it out again, examined it, glowing with anticipation, and tucked it into the smallest dressing table drawer. He could scarcely believe that finding his real father was within his grasp. The man had recognised him, just as Ticker had. But unlike Ticker, if Garth was right, he was being offered an opportunity to meet the man. Maybe the offer of a job was a genuine one. Or maybe he was wrong about the whole thing. But there was only one way to find out, and all that remained was for him to work out the best way of going about it.

His name was Elliot Marsh, he was sixty-three years old and he came from a long line of criminals. One of his ancestors had been hanged at a crossroads as a highwayman, another family member had been deported to Australia. His grandfather had ploughed his ill-gotten gains into property in Bath, a city second only to London for its plethora of gaming houses, but by the time his father and uncle were young men, legislation had driven the wealthy back to their gentlemen's clubs, where their committees were able to claim that all gaming on the premises was purely of a private nature, and therefore outside the law.

The Marsh brothers, Elijah and Samson, as resourceful as their family had always been, had converted the basement of the house they owned on Pierrepont Street into a gambling den, or a 'copper hell', as such places catering for the working classes were known. The rich had their 'gold' or 'silver' 'hells', but Elliot's father and uncle had decided that if they set their sights lower they were more likely to be able to avoid the long arm of the law.

It was into this world that Elliot had been born. His father, Elijah, had made enough money that Elliot had the best of everything, from fine clothes and toys to an education at a top boys' school. But true to family form he had not used his education to go into one of the respectable professions. Instead he had joined the 'family firm' and by the time he was in his late twenties he had carved out a profitable niche for himself. Financed in the beginning by his father, he set himself up as a loan shark, and those who lost their shirts in the copper hell were referred to him. Elliot vetted them carefully, refusing to deal with any older man he thought would never be able to repay him and would most likely spend the advance on gambling to try and recoup his losses. That sort were of no use to him. Those that he believed had access to funds, however, were the recipients of his largesse. In general they were professional men whose addiction drew them back time and time again to the den – a bank employee, a solicitor who had access to his clients' accounts, the manager of a well-known and prosperous grocery store. Faced with ruin, and seeing their debt spiralling ever higher, they were prepared to risk all in an effort to save their reputations.

But it was the younger ones that interested Elliot most. Lads sowing their wild oats, with not a penny to their name. He was careful to let their debts increase until he was certain they had no chance of ever clearing it, and then moved in with threats of what would happen to them if they didn't find a way to repay him. That way, he explained to them, was to rob, burgle and mug, and bring their spoils to him.

Since he was a small man, and incapable of being taken seriously by a strapping lad, he employed an enforcer, a swarthy former seaman more than capable of putting the frighteners on any of his targets who proved unwilling to do his bidding, and, if that didn't work, roughing them up. When word spread there was less need of physical violence – the stories of injuries inflicted by Jack the Tar were enough to bring them into line.

He also cultivated acquaintances among the local constabulary, playing hail-fellow-well-met, inviting them into the hostelry that provided a front for the copper hell, offering them a nip of good brandy to warm them on a cold night and make the long hours plodding the streets pass more quickly. His father and uncle already had a senior officer or two in their pockets, and the goings-on in the basement room behind its padlocks and grilles was able to continue unchallenged.

By the mid-1870s the ground-level rooms of the tacky hostelry had been converted into a so-called 'gentlemen's club' which was intended as a front for the gaming and the money laundering, and Jack the Tar was ready to take life more easily. Elliot recruited a new man in his place. Aaron Walters had been scraping a living in bare-knuckle fighting, and with a travelling fair, and was unable to resist the offer Elliot made him. There was a whiff of danger about him, but Elliot liked that, and after they had been a team for a few months had almost come to think of him as the son he would have liked to have had. He had shelved any concerns he might have had about how far Aaron would go; a hard man was exactly what he needed, and he was a most effective bodyguard as well as an enforcer.

Elliot took him everywhere with him and the two men became friends. Besides making him feel safe – he had many enemies, he knew – he enjoyed introducing Aaron to a lifestyle he could only previously have dreamed of.

When his father and uncle were of an age that they were no longer able to run the club, Elliot had taken over. He had spent a great deal of money turning the upper rooms into a luxurious salon and bar where well-heeled punters could enjoy a drink and the company of a young lady before or after going down to the basement where the gaming still took place behind locked doors and barred windows. But that too had been smartened up to cater for the better-off, and there were now attractive female croupiers in low-cut gowns who might have stepped out of an old-style Western bar.

It had made him more money than he'd dared hope for, and he had run down the money-lending business and disbanded his gang of young thieves. Nowadays he was rich and successful and considered himself to be an almost-respectable businessman. Aaron had moved with him, acting as a bouncer at the club when a bouncer was needed and Elliot's minder when he was not.

Aaron hadn't been with him that day when he went to Bath races though. He'd cried off at the last minute – Elliot suspected a woman might be at the root of that. There was a hostess at the club he'd been showing a lot of interest in. Although he was married with a son, Kelvin, whom Elliot had taken on as a stable boy when he reached school-leaving age, women had always been Aaron's Achilles heel – that and a fondness for the bottle. Elliot supposed that went hand in hand with his aggressive masculinity and at one time he'd indulged his minder's peccadillos, but recently his arrogance and sense of entitlement had begun to rankle. Elliot had never married, and had no one to leave the club to in his will, and had once been foolish enough to mention that Aaron might well be his beneficiary in recognition of his friendship and long service. From that moment on, Aaron had begun acting as if the club was already his, behaving dictatorially with the staff, implementing subtle changes and adopting a familiarity with Elliot that went too far beyond the boundaries of their previous relationship for Elliot's liking.

He needed taking down a peg or two, Elliot thought, and that day at the races he thought he'd happened upon a way to do just that.

He'd left some of his friends in the racing fraternity in the beer tent and gone to answer a call of nature when he spotted Ticker Bendle across the green sward.

Once upon a time they'd been friendly, but for some reason the miserable old bugger had cut himself free and it was years now since he'd set eyes on him. But it wasn't Ticker who grabbed his attention now, however. It was the young man with him.

Elliot stopped, staring, the urgency of his call of nature forgotten. Good Lord, it could have been a young Aaron! The dark complexion, the coal-black hair, the dark eyes. His build was similar too, already muscular. In a few years he would have the same impressive physique.

Ticker hadn't seen him. Elliot continued on his way to the public conveniences deep in thought. He was in no doubt but that the young man was Aaron's son – who knew how many bastards he had fathered? But if he lived at the pub in Fossecombe, it was a safe bet his mother must be the young barmaid Aaron had taken a fancy to. It could be that he'd married the girl when she found herself in the family way.

Elliot cast his mind back to the last time he and Aaron had gone to the Three Feathers.

They'd taken to going there, he and his pals, for a reason. One of his debtors, Joe Hill, a young man he'd hoped to recruit to his army of thieves, had done a runner, and he'd learned from Ticker that Hill's sweetheart was a barmaid there. Aaron had hoped he would be able to discover the young man's whereabouts. That night – the night when the opportunity to get the barmaid on her own had finally presented itself – his friend Percy had cried off, so it was only him and Aaron.

When the bar had emptied but for the two of them and the barmaid, Martha, had gone through into a back room, Aaron had followed her. He hadn't found out where Joe Hill was; she didn't know anything, Aaron had said. But there was a scratch on his cheek that looked as if it could have been caused by fingernails, and his shirt wasn't tucked in properly, and Elliot had a pretty good idea what had happened. He hadn't mentioned his suspicions – best he didn't know what his heavy did to get the information he wanted – and Aaron hadn't said anything either. But now, all these years later, looking at this lad who was a dead ringer for a young Aaron, Elliot's curiosity was aroused.

On his way back to the beer tent he made sure to steer a course that would take him closer to Ticker's stall.

'Ticker, you old devil! Fancy seeing you here!' he exclaimed jovially.

But his eyes were on the lad. He hadn't been mistaken – the lad was the spitting image of Aaron.

When they'd chatted for a few minutes he waved his topper in the direction of the lad.

'You have an apprentice, I see,' he said, and proceeded to ask the questions that were burning his tongue.

The answers he received convinced him he was right. The young man's name – Garth Packer – meant nothing to him, of course. But the fact that he lived at the Three Feathers was proof enough. Aaron had had his way with the barmaid that night and this lad had come into the world as a result of it.

Elliot's devilish streak and his desire to put Aaron in his place surfaced then. He chuckled inwardly as he imagined his minder's reaction if he came face to face with a son he didn't know he had, one far more like him than Kelvin, and chuckled inwardly.

'If ever you get tired of working for this bad-tempered old fart, this is where you can find me,' he said, getting out a business card, and added: 'I'd be only too happy to give you a job, and I'd certainly pay better wages.'

It wasn't an idle offer, either. Aaron, like Jack the Tar before him, would soon be too old to act as an enforcer and protector. Who better to replace him than his own son, who already looked as if he was well able to take care of himself, and in a few years would be at least the man Aaron had been when Elliot had taken him on?

Elliot had left the racecourse that day well satisfied. He'd baited the trap, now all he could do was wait and see if Garth Packer took it.

Chapter Thirteen

Ella was not the only one to leave school and start work in the outside world. Conrad had also reached his thirteenth birthday and Martha had spotted an advertisement in the local paper for an assistant in the gents' outfitters in Hillsbridge. She'd told Conrad to put on his Sunday best suit, make sure he was clean behind the ears, and get to the shop before the position was filled, and she'd gone with him to make sure he didn't bunk off along the way. She remained outside the shop when he went in, trying to see what was going on inside through the window display of coats, shirts and neckerchiefs. Clarence Ford must have caught sight of her hovering, because when Conrad emerged he followed him and addressed Martha.

'You've a fine lad there, Mrs Packer,' he said, thrusting his thumbs into the pockets of his trousers. 'I'm confident I can train him up in the business and he will be an asset to it. He can begin on Monday, and he'll have Wednesday and Saturday afternoons off.'

'Oh – thank you,' Martha said, pleased.

'You can be proud of him,' Mr Ford said, and disappeared back inside the shop.

'Well done, Conrad.' Martha wished she could ruffle his hair as she used to when he was younger, but now he was as tall as she was, and in any case he wouldn't thank her for it in full view of passers-by. But a word of praise wouldn't go amiss. 'I am proud of you,' she added.

It was no more than the truth. He was a credit to her, polite and dependable, and she thought the job would suit him very well. She was proud of Lewis, too. He was doing very well at school, according to his teacher, and was going to be put forward to take a scholarship that would see him going to a good school in Wells if he was successful.

She only wished she could be as proud of Garth. Working for a bookie wasn't what she or Seb considered a respectable job and he was as moody and unpredictable as ever. He drank and smoked, she knew, and she wouldn't be surprised if he didn't indulge in betting and gaming too. To be truthful, she was only surprised he'd kept the job as long as he had. She'd thought he would have blotted his copybook long ago. But he and Ticker seemed as thick as thieves and she supposed she should be grateful for it. As for trying to get him to mend his ways, she'd more or less given up on it. All she could hope for now was that he'd grow out of the moodiness and learn the error of louche behaviour too as he got older; and she could be grateful that the subject of his real father was never now mentioned, and hadn't been since Seb had explained the situation to Conrad and Lewis.

'Well?' Seb enquired when they got home again. 'How did it go?'

Martha smiled at Conrad, indicating with a nod of her head that he should be the one to relay the good news to his father.

'Yeah, I got the job, Dad,' he said, straight-faced. 'I start on Monday.'

'Good for you!' Seb slapped him on the back and gave his

shoulder a squeeze. Then and only then did Conrad smile, a big Cheshire cat grin that spread from ear to ear.

'Yeah, it's all right, isn't it?'

The rapport between father and son was good to see, and Martha felt a glow of warmth that at least in Conrad – and Lewis, too – Seb had sons to be proud of.

Ella sat in the rocking chair in the nursery singing softly to little Angelina, who snuggled on her lap. The child was almost asleep, and Ella knew she should put her in her cot, but she was reluctant to relinquish the small firm body. As she came to the end of the song she buried her face in Angelina's silky-soft hair, breathing in the scent of soap and enjoying the warmth of the small body close to hers. She was happy, happier than she could ever remember being since the days when Jeannie had been just a baby and Mammy had still been the loving, caring mother of her childhood. The days when she'd felt secure, when she'd had not a care in the world. Living here in this wonderful house, with children to keep her occupied and employers who treated her as one of the family, was more than she'd ever dared dream of. And it wasn't as if she'd been dropped in at the deep end; Mrs Henderson was still there, teaching her all she needed to know about childcare, so that when the new baby arrived and she was preoccupied with him or her, Ella would be more than capable of coping on her own.

She still wished she hadn't had to leave Jeannie behind, of course, but she knew her sister was loved and well cared for, and the last time she'd gone home – for two years now the Feathers had felt like home – Jeannie had seemed happy enough, and although she'd been a bit clingy when the time had come for Ella to return to Bath, there hadn't been the tears that there had been the first time she'd left. And Mrs Henderson had promised

Ella's sister could come to visit once Ella was completely settled in. No, Jeannie would be fine, she reassured herself. Martha would make sure of that.

Ella had made some new friends too, other girls who worked as nannies. On sunny afternoons when they pushed their charges out they would often congregate in the park or the Parade Gardens, chatting while rocking the perambulators and keeping a close eye on their older charges who loved to play together.

Sometimes the girls talked about their families, of mothers who fussed over them when they went home on their days off, of proud fathers, pesky little brothers and sisters, or perhaps of a wedding in the family.

'What about you, Ella? Where do your mother and father live?' Though Amy Hawkins was two or three years older than Ella, the two had become especially friendly, and her question was asked out of interest, not nosiness.

'I don't have a mother, or a father,' Ella said, almost apologetically. 'They're both dead.'

'Oh, that's awful!' Amy reached over and squeezed Ella's hand, wishing she hadn't raised the subject. 'What happened? Was it an accident?'

'No, they both got ill . . .' Ella didn't want to say their deaths had occurred in the workhouse. Though she wasn't ashamed of her parents, there was a terrible stigma attached to being reduced to such circumstances. 'I have a little sister though – Jeannie,' she went on quickly. 'She's ten now, and she still lives with the family who adopted us. They keep the Three Feathers at Fossecombe.'

'A public house!' One of the other girls, Maria James, the daughter of a Methodist minister, sounded shocked. But as she caught the warning glare Amy flashed at her, she flushed and backtracked. 'Oh my goodness, how exciting!'

From that moment on Ella's mother and father had never

again been mentioned, though sometimes one or other of the girls would ask after Jeannie.

All in all, Ella was very happy with her lot, and her only regret was that she couldn't share her good fortune with Leo. She thought about him often, wondering if he had won a scholarship as Rector Evans had more or less promised him he would, and if so, where he was now and how he was getting on. Did he ever think of her? Or was he too busy with his studies and the new friends he would have made to spare her a thought? He would have no idea where she was, of course, and have no more idea where to find her than she had of finding him.

Sometimes, when out pushing the children, she passed a grand building with a broad drive set behind wrought-iron gates and a notice beside them announcing it was a boys' public school, and she wondered if it was possible Leo might be a pupil there. But although she'd seen quite a few of them either out in the grounds or leaving at the end of the day, she'd never caught so much as a glimpse of anyone with his flaming red hair.

Really, there was nothing for it but to try to forget him, though that was easier said than done. But she'd been lucky. So lucky. Now, sitting in the rocking chair in the nursery with little Angelina snuggling close to her, Ella closed her eyes and whispered a prayer of thanks.

'You're always there looking out for us, aren't you, Mammy? And I am so, so grateful.'

The peace she always felt when she spoke to Mammy washed over her, and the voice in her head spoke softly but clearly.

'I'm so proud of you, Ella. And yes, my love, I will always be here.'

Garth drew a pile of betting slips towards him, leafing through them and extracting the ones that he was pretty sure would be losers, then totalling up what the possible payout on the others was likely to be. Then he pulled out the cash drawer which sat beneath the counter in Ticker's office and counted out how much it contained before carefully replacing it. Yes, he reckoned there was plenty there to pay out the winners without having to raid the safe and enough left over for him to take a cut. If he scrapped a couple of the losing betting slips – and there were a couple already – and pocketed the stake money Ticker would never be any the wiser.

It was a trick he practised regularly when he was alone in the office, always cautious not to overdo it. He didn't want Ticker to become suspicious, and to be truthful it was the thrill of stealing and getting away with it that gave him the buzz of smug satisfaction. The amount he was able to pocket was the icing on the cake.

He'd be unceremoniously sacked if Ticker ever found out what he was doing, he knew, but since Elliot Marsh had more or less offered him a job he'd worried less about that. He hadn't been to see him yet, figuring that it might be best not to look too keen, but one of these days he was going to go to Bath, not so much to take Elliot up on his offer as to see if he could find his real father. The prospect dangled like a juicy plum just waiting to be picked.

He could be wrong, of course. Maybe he'd imagined the whole thing. But when he remembered the way Elliot had looked at him, the fact that as soon as Garth had said he lived just outside Fossecombe Elliot had mentioned the Three Feathers, his eagerness to give Garth his calling card and Ticker's obvious disapproval, it all added up to one thing.

Both Ticker and Elliot knew the man who had sired him, and they'd been alerted because of the family likeness.

The door of the betting office opened and a man came in. Garth recognised him as one of the few punters who'd struck lucky today and had a few bob in winnings to collect. That was all right. He'd already reckoned that into his calculations.

Garth smiled to himself as the man walked out again, looking pleased. He'd be back again tomorrow for sure. There was nothing like the sniff of a win to encourage a punter to risk more next time. Or a big loss. There were always the fools who chased their losses and having seen it happen too many times Garth was determined not to be tempted into gambling himself. Why would he when there were so many other ways of getting money?

He counted out some of the money from the cash drawer, pocketed it, screwed up the relevant betting slips and tucked them into his pocket too. He thought he might go to Bath on Sunday this week. And he hoped his lucky streak would hold and he would find his real father.

'I'm worried about your dad,' Martha said. 'I don't like the look of him at all.'

Algie had been poorly for a few weeks now. He'd come down with what had at first seemed like a cold but instead of getting better he seemed to be getting worse. The cough had gone to his chest and he was wheezy and breathless, he had lost a lot of weight, and although the weather was still quite warm he had dreadful fits of shivers which lasted a couple of hours at a time. Apart from treating his cough with thick linctus which seemed to do no good at all, the doctor only shook his head and looked anxious, in spite of his reassuring words.

This morning when she'd taken him and Maud their cups of tea he could barely speak for shivering, but when Martha put a hand on his forehead he seemed to be burning up.

'You've got a temperature, Algie,' she said. 'You don't want to be all wrapped up in that blanket.'

She tried to pull it down but Algie clung on to it, fighting her with all his strength.

'I'm cold!' he managed between chattering teeth.

'You're not. You're too hot. You've got to get that temperature down.' She tried again, and managed to wrest it from him, but the moment she let go he covered himself up again.

'I think we ought to get Dr Blackmore in to look at him again,' she said now. 'There's something radically wrong with him, if you ask me.'

'All right. If that's what you think I'll ride over and ask him to call.' Seb got up and reached for his cap.

'I do. We've got to get to the bottom of it, Seb.'

'That might be easier said than done,' Seb said grimly.

But he put on his bicycle clips and left anyway.

It was the middle of the day, and the Feathers had already opened by the time Dr Blackmore arrived. Martha was cutting off hunks of fresh bread to make a ploughman's for one of the regulars, and when she saw the pony and trap pull on to the courtyard she hurried into the bar.

'Can you finish off for me, Seb? The doctor's here.'

'I'll go, if you're in the middle of something,' Seb offered.

But Martha was insistent. She wanted to get to the bottom of what was wrong with Algie, and she didn't trust Seb to be forceful enough. If the customer had to wait for his bread and cheese that was just too bad.

She took off her apron and hurried across to the cottage. Maud, very frail herself, had let the doctor in, and he was in the tiny sitting room where Algie huddled in an armchair, a blanket still covering his knees for comfort though the shivering fit had stopped now.

Dr Blackmore opened his medical bag and took out a narrow

cylinder, about six inches in length and inscribed with the words 'Dr Clifford Allbutts's Clinical Thermometer'.

'Just pop this in your mouth,' he instructed Algie.

Algie did as he was told, and after a little while the doctor removed and inspected it.

'Your temperature is a little on the high side,' he remarked. 'I think we'll have a window open, and that blanket off.'

'I told him,' Martha said. 'Perhaps he'll listen to you, doctor.'

'Can you open your shirt for me, Mr Packer?' he asked. 'I'd like to listen to your chest.'

Martha and Maud waited anxiously.

When he'd used his stethoscope on both Algie's chest and back, and prodded his neck and under his arms, Dr Blackmore sat down in the other armchair looking serious.

'Is your cough productive?' he asked.

'What's that, doctor?' Algie managed, puzzled.

'He means are you coughing up any phlegm,' Martha said. 'You aren't, are you, Algie?'

'Hmm.' The doctor was thoughtful. 'All things considered, I think it would be best to get you into hospital, Mr Packer.' He turned to Maud. 'If you could get some things together for him, I'll take him now.'

'Oh my goodness . . . Hospital! Oh, I don't know about that . . .' A shocked Maud appeared incapable of thinking straight, let alone getting a bag together.

'It's all right, I'll do it,' Martha said.

As she headed for the stairs Maud called after her: 'Don't forget his Thermogene.'

'I don't think he'll be needing that,' Dr Blackmore said. 'As I said, his temperature is already high, and I'm coming round to the opinion that the cough isn't caused by phlegm, but fluid that's collected around his lungs. In any case I think we can trust the hospital to keep him as warm or as cool as necessary.'

When she'd packed a bag for Algie and whilst Maud was helping him put on his boots, Martha ran across the yard to tell Seb what was happening.

'I think I ought to go with him,' he said.

'I think so too,' Martha said. 'Your mam's not in any state to go, and that's a fact. But how will you get home?'

'I expect Blackmore will bring me, but if not, I'll just have to walk it. Can you manage here?' Seb was already putting on his cap and coat.

'Yes – you go. But I think I'll close early. I don't think your mam should be on her own.'

'Do that then.'

He hurried out, and Martha went through to the bar.

'Can you drink up, please?' she asked the customers. 'We've got a bit of a family crisis. Algie's being taken to hospital.'

That caused something of a stir. The regulars had all known Algie well, and they were concerned to hear the news, full of questions that Martha was unable to answer. She went out to the yard where Algie was already settled in Dr Blackmore's trap, his head slumped on to his chest, his thin arms wrapped around himself.

'Don't worry, he'll be home again in no time,' Martha consoled the distressed Maud. But she had a sickening feeling that Algie might never come home. He looked like a man with one foot already in the grave.

They stood together watching as Dr Blackmore turned out on to the road.

'Goodbye!' Maud called tremulously, and Martha wondered if she was thinking the same, that she might never see her husband alive again.

Martha put an arm around her mother-in-law's thin shoulders.

'Come on, come in with me, Mam,' she said. 'You don't want to be on your own.'

Surprisingly, Maud raised no objection, and Martha led her inside.

'I expect you could do with a nice cup of tea,' she said.

'I'd rather have a glass of milk stout,' Maud said, and that brought a faint smile to Martha's lips.

'You know what, Mam? I think I'll join you.'

Sadly, Martha's prediction was proved right. Just a few days later Algie was dead, and a pall fell over the household.

'He had a good life, and we must be thankful for that,' Martha said, stoic as ever, but it didn't truly reflect the sadness she felt, and although Seb agreed with her, he felt the loss of his father deeply.

Conrad and Lewis were subdued – death wasn't something they'd ever encountered before – and they crept about, solemn faced and quiet as mice. Life would never be the same again without Gramps.

For Ella, who had been allowed home from Bath on compassionate grounds, it brought back still-raw memories of her mother's death. The way she hadn't looked like Mammy at all when Ella had gone to see her in the morgue, and the icy coldness of her hand when she'd touched it; the horror of her coffin being lowered into the ground, the pitter-patter of the earth raining down on it, Jeannie's sobs as she fled from the grave, and her own grief and despair.

Perhaps Jeannie was reminded of it too, for she clung to Ella like a limpet, and reverted to her old childish habits of whimpering and sucking her thumb.

Only Garth seemed unmoved, going on with his life as if nothing had happened.

Maud, however, was inconsolable. Already frail, she seemed to be shrinking before their very eyes, and on the day of the funeral she was unable to get out of bed.

'I don't think she's fit to even think of going,' Martha said.

'What does she say?' Seb asked.

'Well, she wants to go, of course, and I've said to wait and see if she feels any better as the morning wears on. But we don't want her collapsing, do we? I think we should persuade her not to, and I'll stay here with her. I can make sure everything's ready for when you all get back, and if she's up to it she can come over and help, or at least feel a part of it.'

'I thought you had it all in hand,' Seb said.

'I have. But there's always something she can do, even if it's only putting the urn on for the tea.'

'I shall want something a bit stronger than tea,' Seb said grimly.

'The bar will be open for anybody as wants it.'

The Feathers had been closed as a mark of respect ever since Algie's death, but would reopen today for the wake. Martha had made piles of sandwiches, which she had covered with a damp cloth, and baked two big fruit cakes and a batch of scones. How many people would come back after the service she didn't know, but she was certain there would be a good turn-out for the service. Algie had been well-known and well-liked in the community.

In the event, Maud had to admit defeat. There was no way she was fit to attend the funeral, and Martha helped her over to the bar, where she sat, silent and all of a tremble while Martha set out the food on two tables she'd dragged together against the wall.

'Can I get you anything, Mam?' she asked when she'd done. 'How about a milk stout? That's what you like, and it does you good.'

Maud answered with a slight nod of her head; even that seemed to take an effort of will that was almost beyond her.

Martha opened a bottle, poured it into a glass, and took it to her. To her surprise, Maud looked up, her eyes milky and sunken in her pallid face.

'You're a good girl, Martha. You've been a good wife to my Seb and a good mother to those boys.'

Martha shrugged. 'I'm not so sure about that.'

'Well, you have, and I'm grateful. You'll be a good landlady too, now that Seb's name is going to be over the door. And it's no more than you both deserve.'

Martha was lost for words. In all the upset it hadn't occurred to her that Seb would now be the landlord of the Feathers, and she didn't think it had occurred to him either. It hadn't been mentioned, at any rate. And she knew that Algie's death was too high a price for either her or Seb to pay for it. They were happy enough as they were, running the pub without authentication. Nothing could make up for losing Algie.

But things had changed, nonetheless. Whether they wanted it or not, they were entering a whole new era. The next generation of Packers. Landlord and landlady of the Three Feathers.

Chapter Fourteen

Elliot Marsh was feeling frustrated. So far the young man who was the spitting image of Aaron Walters hadn't taken the bait and come to see him. Not only was he disappointed not to have the chance to see Aaron's reaction when he came face to face with the lad, he also had high hopes of taking him on as a bouncer at the club in readiness for the day when he could succeed Aaron as his bodyguard.

Well, if Mohammed wouldn't come to the mountain, the mountain would go to Mohammed.

One afternoon he instructed Kelvin, the stable lad who also acted as coachman, to prepare the barouche and drive him out to Hillsbridge. There were no local race meetings that day, and he guessed the young man he was interested in would leave Ticker's office at the end of the day's business.

There were two ways the lad could get home from his place of work, one cutting through the town, the other a circuitous route cross-country. Elliot told Kelvin to go to the place where the two routes met, far enough from Hillsbridge to avoid attracting attention and well before the hill leading down to the Feathers.

There they pulled into a spot that gave Elliot a view along both roads and he settled down to wait. When the young man came into sight, he'd have Kelvin accost him and bring him to the carriage.

They'd been there for an hour or more, the horses were getting restive and Elliot was beginning to give up hope, when he spied a bicycle heading towards them. As soon as the rider was close enough for him to be able to identify him, Elliot issued his instructions.

'That's the lad I want a word with,' he said. 'And when you've sent him over to me, make yourself scarce until I tell you different.'

Garth was surprised when he saw the fancy carriage pulled in at the junction on the other side of the road, a most uncommon sight. Yes, there were horse-drawn vehicles – carts, delivery wagons, farm trailers piled high with bales of hay, but not anything as grand as this one. And he was even more surprised when the driver jumped down and accosted him.

'Someone wants a word with you.'

Garth's first reaction was to try and ride off – he didn't know what he was wanted for, but he thought it might well mean trouble. But the young man, who looked to be about his own age, had taken hold of the handlebars of his bicycle and was standing right in his way; he was going nowhere.

'Who's that then?' he asked belligerently, hoping to brazen it out.

'Never you mind. Just get over there.'

Garth wasn't used to being bullied. He was usually the one doing the bullying. 'Not until you tell me who it is, and what they want me for.'

'The name's Mr Marsh. I don't know what he wants. I just do as I'm told, and you'd do well to do the same.'

Garth squinted into the sun, already low in the sky for

evening, raising a hand to shade his eyes, and his heart jolted, beating hard against his ribs. It was the man from Bath races who had given him his calling card. The one he felt sure knew his real father. And he realised why he had been putting off going to Bath. As long as he didn't know for sure he could dream. He'd be devastated if he was wrong. Or if he was right, and his father wasn't anything like he imagined. The moment of truth was within his grasp and he wasn't sure he was ready for it.

'Go on!' the coach driver urged him. 'Mr Marsh doesn't like to be kept waiting.'

Garth took a deep breath. This might be his one and only chance. His heart still beating so fast that it reverberated through his body, his mouth dry, he crossed the road.

The wiry little man – Mr Marsh – was watching him closely. As he reached the carriage the man moved across the seat to make room for him.

'Get in.' His tone was silky, but there was no mistaking the note of authority.

Without answering, Garth climbed up the step and sat down.

'You've disappointed me. I've been expecting you. Why haven't you been to see me?' The man's eyes were on him, hooded, but piercing. Garth shrugged, pretending nonchalance. 'I hoped you might take me up on my offer,' the man went on. 'Perhaps I didn't make it clear – I pay my employees very well. A great deal more than you are earning as Ticker's assistant, I dare say.'

'I get by.' Garth wasn't going to mention that he supplemented his meagre earnings by stealing from his employer. Or that he was afraid he was going to have to be more careful in future if he wanted to keep his job – he had a nasty feeling that Ticker was becoming suspicious.

'I'd say you are well capable of taking care of yourself,' the man said, 'and you're just the one to act as a doorman at my club. Whatever Ticker pays you, I'm prepared to double it, with accommodation thrown in. And good prospects for the future.'

Garth's jaw dropped. This all sounded too good to be true. What possible reason could this man have to drive all the way out from Bath to speak to him, let alone make him such a generous offer? He could think of only one reason: it had something to do with his real father.

'Well? What do you say?'

Garth hesitated, wondering if he dare ask for more. If this man was so anxious to reel him in, perhaps at his father's behest, he might well be able to squeeze him a bit further. But he didn't want to risk it, and what more could he want? Double his present wage, and better still to get away from the Feathers, and Seb, Martha and his annoying brothers – half-brothers, he reminded himself. To be able to do as he liked with no one to disapprove was a dream come true.

'All right,' he said.

Mr Marsh's thin lips twisted into a satisfied smile. 'Champion. Why don't you come with me now and have a look at where you'll be living and working?'

Again Garth hesitated. He was expected home; his tea would be on the table and Martha would wonder where he was. Or perhaps she wouldn't. The whole house had been upside down ever since the old man had died and now Maud was ill too and Martha was kept busy nursing her.

'What about my bike?' he asked.

'We'll find room for that.' Without waiting for Garth's affirmation he waved to the coachman, pointed towards Garth's bicycle and indicated that he should bring it across the road.

As soon as it was stowed they set off, the matched horses'

hooves clattering in unison. Along the road, through the village, down the long hill – as they passed the Feathers Garth saw Conrad and Lewis kicking a ball about on the path between the house and the cottage. But to Garth's relief they were too engrossed in their game to so much as spare a glance for the carriage, much less see their brother riding in state. He didn't want them running to Martha or Seb with the news before he had had the chance to think how he was going to play this.

Excitement was bubbling in his veins now, along with a certain amount of apprehension. Was he going to meet his real father at last? The smug look on Mr Marsh's thin face suggested to him that it was very likely indeed.

There was nothing on the outside to indicate the nature of the business that lay behind the white painted door, reached by three stone steps flanked by shiny black handrails finished off with golden globes. The coachman helped Mr Marsh down, but Garth quickly jumped down by himself. He wasn't about to accept assistance from a lad not much older than he was. The coachman resumed his position in the driver's seat and was about to pull away to take the carriage and horses to their stabling in a nearby mews, but Mr Marsh stopped him.

'You'll need to take my guest home, Walters. Wait here, if you please.'

'Sorry, sir. I thought he'd be riding his bike.' The lad sounded a bit fed up. He'd expected to have the rest of the evening free, Garth guessed, and smiled unpleasantly to himself. What a ponce, all done up in that fancy uniform and silly hat.

'We're not open yet, of course. That's why I thought it would be an ideal opportunity to show you around.' Elliot had mounted the steps and produced a bunch of keys, selecting one and opening the door.

An Italian tiled vestibule led into a large room, furnished with velvet-covered sofas and chairs, and dominated by an ornate chandelier of crystal teardrops. It was the artwork hanging on the walls that caught Garth's eye, however. He'd never before seen anything like it. The pictures in the Feathers were prints of rural scenes – a bluebell wood, a river with overhanging trees, a portrayal of the harvest, big shire horses and the corn golden beneath a blue sky. These were different enough to make Garth's eyes pop out of his head. He wasn't familiar with the word 'erotic' but the gambolling nymphs, the bare-breasted women and half-naked men caressing them left little to the imagination.

Cor! Garth thought. I wouldn't mind having some of that!

'This is the salon,' Elliot said, encompassing it with a sweeping gesture. 'My clients find it most relaxing.'

'Relaxing' was hardly the word Garth would use to describe it. He could feel the heat and stirring of his body and hastily removed his gaze from the tempting scenes.

'Would you care for something to drink? Cognac, perhaps? Or a good single malt? We have a fine selection.' Elliot indicated the bar, which occupied one corner.

'No, you're all right.' For all his underage drinking, Garth had never tasted anything but beer and cider, but he was sufficiently aware of the perils of hard liquor to know this was not the best time to start on something that might well render him incapable.

'As you wish. We will visit your living quarters in a moment, but first there is someone I'd like you to meet.' He crossed to the bar, and brought his hand down hard on a gilded bell that stood on the counter. 'Aaron Walters is my right-hand man. He's been with me for more than twenty years. Ah – Aaron . . .'

A gilded door opened and a man came into the room and

Garth froze, his heart seeming to stop beating until it started again with a thud that reverberated through his body. Except that he was at least twenty years older than Garth they might have been mirror images. It was his father. It had to be. He'd found him. Garth stood rooted to the spot, his breath coming fast and shallow, overcome by an emotion stronger than anything he'd ever felt before, seeing nothing but this older version of himself. And the man was staring at him too as if mesmerised. Neither he nor Garth were aware of Aaron's satisfied smirk until he spoke, his voice smooth as a cat's purr.

'This is Garth Packer. His home is the Three Feathers just this side of Fossecombe – you know it, don't you? I've offered him employment and accommodation and I'm happy to say he has accepted. He'll be joining us as soon as he's worked out his notice with Ticker Bendle the bookmaker. Garth would like to see the room that will be his – perhaps you could show it to him?'

Aaron's face, which had until then registered only shock and total bewilderment, contorted, ugly with sudden rage. His shoulders were rigid, his hands balled to fists.

'Bastard!' he ground out, then turned on his heel. As he reached the gilded door he kicked out at it and Garth heard the sound of splintering wood. Then he pulled it open and stormed out, slamming it after him.

'Oh dear. I'm afraid Aaron can be somewhat unpredictable. I'm sorry.' But Elliot didn't sound at all regretful. He sounded pleased with himself. 'Unfortunately, I will be unable to show you your quarters – my poor legs can no longer cope with so many stairs. Will you take it on trust that they will be entirely suitable?'

For a moment Garth was unable to make any response. That man, Aaron, was his father, he was sure of it. Even the outburst of rage was very like his own. But it didn't bode well. If he had known who Garth was – and the way he'd stared at him told Garth he had – then his reaction hadn't been at all what Garth had hoped for. Just what he had expected he wasn't sure. But certainly not this.

'I hope you haven't been deterred by Mr Walters,' Elliot continued. 'He'll come around, given time.'

Elliot knew. He'd known from the first time he'd set eyes on him, Garth was certain, and he'd engineered this meeting maybe simply for his own entertainment, judging by the pleasure he'd taken in dropping the bombshell. But it seemed he was still standing by his generous offer of employment and accommodation. That puzzled Garth, but it was too good to turn down just because his father hadn't welcomed him with open arms.

Garth felt a hardening in his gut. Perhaps Elliot was right and the man – Aaron – would come around when he'd had time to get over the initial shock. And if he didn't, well, too bad. He'd be here, a thorn in Aaron's side, a constant reminder of how he had made Martha pregnant and walked away, never acknowledged the son he had made.

'I'm not put off that easy,' he said.

'Good. Then in that case I'll expect you as soon as you've worked out your notice. I'll have the carriage take you home this evening, but I'm afraid you'll have to make your own way in future.'

'It's all right. I can ride my bike.' Garth thought it would give him time to think all this over before he had to tell his mother and Seb what he planned.

Elliot didn't argue. 'As you wish. Walters will be glad to be stood down, I imagine.'

Walters. Garth felt a jolt of shock all over again. Wasn't that what Elliot had called his father – Aaron *Walters*?

'Is he a relation of . . . ?' he broke off. He couldn't say 'my

218

father' just yet, but he didn't know what else to call him.

'Aaron?' The amusement was back in Elliot's voice. 'Yes. His son.'

Once again, Garth was lost for words. He'd barely taken any notice of the coachman and certainly hadn't been struck by any resemblance to himself. But then, his face had been half hidden by that stupid cap. And he'd definitely been shorter and slighter than Garth. The striking likeness between him and his father had certainly passed the coachman by. Now Garth regretted having said he'd cycle home. He'd have welcomed the chance to get a better look at the young man who might well be as much his brother as Conrad and Lewis, perhaps ask him a few questions. But it was too late to change his mind. He'd just have to contain his curiosity until he came to Bath to work for Elliot. And it was yet another reason why he needed the long ride home to process all he'd discovered.

'What the hell were you thinking!' Aaron Walters was still shaking with rage when he confronted Elliot in the bar.

Elliot, who was used to Aaron's bad-tempered outbursts, merely smiled.

'Calm down, man. You'll give yourself a heart attack or a stroke. When I met young Garth I realised at once he is just the man to take your place now that you're approaching the time when you'll be too old to function as a bouncer or minder.'

Naturally, his words only inflamed Aaron further.

'I've plenty of good years in me yet. That's not why you brought him here.'

'Really?' Elliot raised an eyebrow. 'Then what would you say was my motive?'

'You know very well. There's no mistaking who he is. And you were there that night.'

'You're admitting it, then? That you took advantage of that poor barmaid when what you were supposed to be doing was finding out the whereabouts of Joe Hill?'

'I'm admitting nothing.'

'Really, Aaron, you scarcely need to. I knew at once you'd done more than exert a little pressure on the girl. It was written all over you. And if that wasn't enough, you refused to go back there, even though you hadn't elicited the information I wanted that evening.'

'So?' Aaron challenged him.

'You knew there was a good chance you'd given that poor girl a bastard. But I thought that after all this time you'd like the chance to meet your son.'

'And why would I want that? I have a son. Kelvin.'

'But Kelvin takes after his mother – in looks, anyway. This one is so like you. I thought you'd be pleased.'

'You thought nothing of the sort. You were making mischief, as usual. I know you, Elliot. I haven't been with you all these years for nothing.'

Elliot smiled and raised his hands in submission. 'Ah, there you have me, Aaron. But what's done is done. The boy will be working for me alongside you and Kelvin. And I'm afraid you'll have to either like it or lump it.'

'Sod you, Elliot.' Still scowling, Aaron stumped off.

But Elliot wasn't concerned. Aaron wouldn't walk out on him, he knew. They'd been together for so long, and Aaron had too much to lose. Elliot had no children of his own, nor any close relatives left living, and Aaron was well aware that he meant to leave everything to him, or, should Aaron predecease him – not so unlikely, given his line of work – to Kelvin. Elliot had him over a barrel and he knew it.

The little man smiled to himself as he imagined how much

more mischief he could make with Garth on the scene. If he proved himself, Elliot might even write him into his will too. That would set the cat among the pigeons and no mistake. Yes, he was very glad indeed that he'd gone to Bath races that day. What he'd discovered would provide him with amusement for a long time to come.

Late summer turned to autumn, the leaves a blaze of fiery shades against a brilliant azure sky and falling in drifts to carpet the ground beneath the trees. Maud was still clinging to life, her tiny shrunken body seeming to grow smaller and more fragile by the day until she was little more than skin and bone. On some days Martha was able to get her up to sit in a chair where she could watch the world going on around her – a world without her beloved Algie; on others she stayed in bed, sleeping most of the time.

The clear weather was replaced by overcast days and misty nights when the fog hung in a clammy blanket and the once bright carpet of leaves turned dull and sodden. And one morning when Martha went to take Maud her first cup of tea she was unable to rouse her. At first Martha thought she had gone, slipped away peacefully in her sleep, but the wrinkled skin on the backs of her hands was still warm, and when Martha fetched a mirror and held it to her lips it misted over, slowly but surely.

Conrad was sent to fetch Dr Blackmore; he'd then go straight on to work at the gents' outfitters. When the doctor arrived, an hour or so later, he confirmed she was in a coma, and had possibly suffered a stroke, though he couldn't be sure.

'It may just be that she's had enough and her body is shutting down,' he said. 'There's really nothing to be done but wait and see. The next few days will tell.'

The same suffocating atmosphere that had prevailed following Algie's death descended on the house; it was as if every stick and stone was holding its breath.

'It's a blessing in disguise,' Martha's sister, Ivy, said when she came to visit, and privately Martha agreed with her – Maud's life had become nothing but a trial to her and death would be a happy release. But she'd kept her thoughts to herself. Maud was Seb's mother, when all was said and done, and he'd never have another.

Each morning she sponged Maud down, marvelling that a heart could continue to beat in that scrawny chest, washed her face and combed her hair. Then she managed to get some thin gruel into her using a pap boat that she'd sometimes used for her children and which she'd found at the back of one of the kitchen cupboards. Every couple of hours she turned her mother-in-law in an effort to avoid the dreaded bed sores, though she couldn't see that this could go on long enough for her to be afflicted by them.

The day before she'd fallen into the coma Maud had said: 'Do you know, it's a funny thing, but a bit ago I thought I saw my mother. Standing in the doorway, just like you are. And every bit as real.'

'I expect you'd been to sleep, and dreaming,' Martha had said, but Maud, though puzzled, was insistent it hadn't been a dream.

'I can't understand it,' she had said. 'What in the world was she doing here?'

'It was just fancy, Mam.' But Martha hadn't liked it. She'd heard before of folk seeing long-dead relatives when their own time was near and now she was more convinced than ever that this time Maud would be gone before long.

Once again she was right, just as she had been with Algie.

On the fifth day Maud's breathing changed, and minutes later she was dead.

On the day of the funeral it poured with rain, falling relentlessly from a leaden sky. But that wasn't the only reason there were far fewer mourners filling the pews of the little church than there had been to see Algie laid to rest, Martha knew. Where Algie had been an enthusiastic landlord, and everybody's friend, Maud had very much kept herself to herself. It was one of the reasons she missed Algie so much, Martha thought. He had been her world, her companion and friend as well as her husband.

The funeral was over, Granny Packer had been laid to rest in the double grave where Algie waited for her, and they were back at the Feathers where Martha had once again laid out a spread. When Algie's wake had been held the food had disappeared as fast as if it had been devoured by a pack of hungry wolves; this time she had made more 'to be on the safe side'. When those who had come back to pay their respects had left, the serving platters were still piled high with sandwiches cut into neat triangles that Maud would have dismissed as 'too much fuss and bother', sausage rolls and slices of slab cake.

'We'll be eating this up for days,' Martha fretted.

'They'll go dry,' Lewis objected.

'So tuck in now. We can't let good food go to waste.' It was Martha's mantra.

Conrad, who had had the afternoon off from the gents' outfitters, took two sandwiches, opened one up, peeled off the cheese and put it in the other to make a double filling. The empty bits of bread he managed to conceal beneath the feathery fronds of a parlour palm. Martha would find it there when she cleaned the bar tomorrow, but she wouldn't be able to prove who put it there, and Conrad would deny all knowledge. In fact, he might risk it with another two sandwiches if he could do it without Martha seeing. The extra cheese made them much more palatable.

Ella too had once again been given time off to attend the funeral. Mr Henderson had brought her out from Bath in his pony and trap, and would collect her again tomorrow.

'They really are very good to you,' Martha had said, and Ella could do nothing but agree. She had certainly struck lucky when the Hendersons had employed her.

Now, Jeannie was tugging at her arm.

'Why isn't Garth here?' Her disappointment at not seeing him was written all over her face.

'I expect he's working,' Ella said.

'So should you be, and Conrad, but you're both here. And he would only have had to come from Bath like you. You come home every week to see us anyway, but Garth never does.'

Privately, Ella was glad Garth hadn't come to the funeral, and glad Jeannie saw little of him nowadays. She was clearly still obsessed by him, and Ella didn't like it. Didn't like Garth. Didn't trust him. But saying so to Jeannie would only upset her.

'You must realise Garth has his own life to lead now, though I'm sure he'll come home when he can,' she said gently. 'But Conrad and Lewis are here, and they're much more your age.'

'You've got to learn to be a bit more independent, Jeannie,' Martha chimed in as she cleared away used cups, saucers and glasses. 'Ella isn't going to want to come home so often now she's made some friends in Bath, will you, Ella?'

Jeannie pouted and chewed her lip, the ready tears starting to her eyes.

'Don't worry, my love, I'll still come out every week to see you,' she reassured Jeannie.

Her last promise to Mammy to look after her little sister would never be forgotten, and come what may she intended to keep it.

Things were about to become a bit more difficult, however. Just a few days later Mrs Henderson went into labour, and by nightfall the new baby had arrived, a few weeks early.

'I'm so sorry, Ella,' Mr Henderson said, 'but I'm afraid we are going to have to ask you to forfeit your days off for a little while, at least until Mrs Henderson is up and about again. The doctor has said she's not so much as to set foot to the ground for three weeks and we wouldn't be able to manage without you.'

'It's all right, I don't mind,' Ella said swiftly. She had, after all, been employed as a nursemaid, and the Hendersons had been so good to her, giving her time off for the two funerals, and in every other way too, that she could hardly refuse.

Jeannie would be upset, of course, and Ella wondered if she dared ask if her sister could come to stay for a few days as Mrs Henderson had suggested when she'd first taken up her post. But all things considered, that was probably a bad idea just now. She'd have her hands full, and Jeannie could be very demanding. Best to wait until things settled into a new routine and who knew? She might be allowed a few days off at Christmas. Until then, as Martha had said, Jeannie would have to grow up a bit and become more independent. It might be the making of her. Ella certainly hoped so.

'Oi! You! We could do with some help here!'

Garth was halfway down the stairs that led from his living quarters to the entrance hall of Marsh's club when the front door opened and Aaron yelled at him.

'What?' Garth shot back sullenly.

Things had not improved between him and his father in the few months he had been here. Far from accepting him, Aaron was perpetually cold and resentful. He had no interest in forming a relationship with the young man he supposed must be his son. He was a constant reminder of past follies, and a thorn in Aaron's side.

'We've got the Christmas tree here to get in and put up. Come on, look lively.'

'Sorry.' Garth sounded anything but. 'I'm dressed and ready to go out with Mr Marsh.'

If anything was guaranteed to infuriate Aaron it was this. Kelvin, his legitimate son, was nothing more than a stable lad and coachman, while this upstart accompanied Elliot Marsh everywhere just as he had once done himself.

'I'm training him up to take your place when you're no longer fit for the job,' Elliot had said dismissively when he'd tackled him about it yet again.

And once again Aaron had bridled. 'I'm good for another twenty years.'

Elliot had eyed him up and down sceptically and Aaron knew what he was thinking. He might still be big enough to be intimidating, with hands like hams, but he was running to seed. His muscles were softer than they used to be, a beer gut overhung the waistband of his trousers, and his face was mottled purple. He'd taken his looks and his prowess for granted and over-indulged himself on beer, whisky and brandy, not to mention the steaks and suet puddings, and it had taken its toll.

'If you say so,' Elliot had said offhandedly. 'I shall feel a good deal safer when I have a bodyguard as young and fit as you once were.'

If Aaron had been ill-disposed towards Garth before, this

was the final nail in his coffin. He largely ignored Garth, and snarled unpleasantly at him when he could not, just as he was doing now.

'Frightened of dirtying your fine clothes? Or just bone idle? Move your arse and get out here and give us a hand before I have to bloody well make you.'

Garth faced him out. He was disappointed at his father's rejection of him, but it didn't hurt nearly as much as he'd thought it would, and he certainly wasn't afraid of him. The animosity between them was like the rivalry of the old alpha male and the young upstart in a pride of lions.

'I'd like to see you try,' he said between gritted teeth.

Aaron took a step towards him, his face dark with fury, his big hands balled to fists. 'You arrogant little bugger . . .'

'What's going on here?' Fortunately, Elliot chose that moment to emerge from the bar.

'We've got to get in that great Christmas tree you ordered, and this little sod is refusing to help,' Aaron said.

'He's not dressed for it,' Elliot returned mildly. 'He's ready to accompany me to the Prince Albert club and he can't do that if he's covered in pine needles. Surely you and Kelvin can manage it between you?'

'Looks like we're going to have to,' Aaron grumbled. Furious as he was, he knew better than to argue with the man who was not only his employer, but held his future and Kelvin's in the palm of his hand.

'Let's go then, Garth.' Elliot moved to the door, and Aaron stood aside to let him pass. Garth followed close on his heels, smirking as he felt the fury in Aaron's gaze follow him. On the road Kelvin was struggling to unload an enormous Christmas tree from a trailer.

'Sorry, mate,' he muttered as they passed close by him.

He had nothing against Kelvin. In the beginning he'd thought him a milksop, no better than Conrad or Lewis, but since they were close in age he'd decided to give him a chance, and discovered that what Kelvin lacked in muscle he made up for with cunning. The two of them had formed something of an alliance – Aaron, disappointed in his legitimate son in spite of his determination to give him a secure future, often spoke to him in the same scathing tones as he did to Garth, and it gave them a common understanding. Sometimes, when he wasn't working, Garth would go down to the mews and the two of them would share a smoke leaning against the pale stone wall or sitting on upturned pails.

Garth hadn't told him of their relationship, however. When Kelvin had remarked that Garth looked more like Aaron than he did, Garth had laughed it off. If Aaron didn't want to acknowledge him, fair enough. He wasn't going to bring it into the open. He'd just bide his time and see what happened.

In the beginning, Garth had been afraid Elliot would change his mind about employing him, given Aaron's animosity towards him. He'd worked for Elliot for at least the best part of twenty years, by Garth's reckoning. But he was sharp enough to quickly realise that Elliot was enjoying the friction between the two of them. Elliot was behaving as if he and not Aaron was Garth's father, favouring him, kitting him out with smart clothes, taking him along to meetings, talking to him man to man.

From the conversations they had Garth was able to glean from Elliot some information about his father and the life he'd led.

Kelvin's mother, it seemed, had worked as a maid for Elijah Marsh. According to Elliot she'd been swept off her feet by the young Aaron, and Garth had no doubt it was true. After all, hadn't the man got Garth's own mother in the family way? And from his own experience he knew how easy it was to get a girl with the sort of looks and physique he and his father shared. But when she'd fallen pregnant Elijah had insisted Aaron marry her. For all his racy lifestyle he wasn't going to allow the young buck to get away with it.

It hadn't been a happy marriage, Elliot had said. Aaron had felt trapped, and so had his wife, Bonnie. Eventually, despairing of his continual liaisons with other women, she'd run away with a wealthy sometime patron of the club and left Kelvin with Aaron, who had installed a series of 'aunties' to care for the child.

'For all his faults, he's been my right hand for longer than I care to remember, but he's getting past it,' Elliot had said. 'And you, young shaver, are just the right one to take over. Unlike poor Kelvin, you're your father's son, right enough.'

His praise had made Garth swell with pride. It seemed that Elliot valued him for all the traits Seb and Martha had condemned.

And now as he walked down the street with Elliot he thought he had certainly landed on his feet. More money than he'd ever had in his life, good prospects, and the promise of his pick of the girls who worked as hostesses in the club – for free. Best of all, he was getting his own back on the father who'd abandoned him and still refused to acknowledge him or even treat him civilly.

Oh yes, this was the life! And he was going to make the most of it.

Chapter Fifteen

1905–1906

During the last years of the old century and the first of the new, the papers seemed to offer nothing but doom and gloom. A major epidemic of influenza in the cities killed people in their droves, and gravediggers were forced to work night and day, but fortunately that had not spread to the Somerset countryside.

In Liverpool and Manchester, thousands of gallons of beer had to be poured into the sewers when it was discovered they contained arsenic, which had killed at least four people and made several thousands more ill with a paralysis of the feet and legs. Apparently, the cause was sulphuric acid, supplied by a Liverpool company for the brewing of beer. 'Thank the Lord we don't get our beer from that brewery!' Martha remarked when Seb read it out to her.

The Boer War that had begun in 1899 raged on for more than two years – the siege of Ladysmith had lasted for a hundred and eighteen days, and it was seven months before Mafeking was relieved. None of the Packer family knew anyone unfortunate enough to be serving there, and though they were pleased when the Boers declared a truce in the May of 1902, it really didn't affect them. But in the January of 1901 they were all suitably shocked by the death of the Queen. She had been on the throne so long that she was an institution, and it was rumoured that the Prince of Wales, who had now become Edward VII, was in poor health himself.

Then, in the May, a terrible explosion in a pit near Caerphilly killed at least seventy-eight men, and that too hit home in the mining community. 'Whatever are we going to hear next?' Martha asked. 'Can't we have some cheerful news for a change?'

'At least they've changed the law so lads can't go underground to work now until they're thirteen,' Seb said. 'That's got to be a good thing.'

'Well, yes, but it's still too young. I can't understand the parents. I'd never let any of my boys go pulling putts of coal like human donkeys.'

'We're lucky. Some folk don't have the choice,' Seb stated mildly.

The next year, 1903, seemed to start better. Scott, Shackleton and Wilson set a new record travelling further towards the South Pole than any other explorer had done, but even that was tainted with sadness – they had been forced to pull their own sleds as their dogs had all died. And then the news grew darker again. Though it was half a world away, no one could help but be shocked when the King and Queen of Serbia were shot dead by disaffected army officers who had found them hiding in a cupboard in their bedroom.

In the December the Wright brothers made sensational news when they managed the first ever heavier-than-air flight on a beach in America, and in the February of the following year towns on the south coast were hit by a tidal wave that swept six cottages into the sea at Hallsands in Devon. High winds ripped the roof off one of the outhouses at the Feathers, and torrential rain soaked everything stored inside. Alarming news came in the October – two trawlers out of Hull had been sunk in the North Sea by the Russians. 'Whatever next!' Martha exclaimed, and Seb pointed out it was proof of one of his favourite sayings in times of trouble – 'Worse things happen at sea.'

There was cause for celebration when Lewis gained a place as a pupil teacher at a good school in Wells. Part of the time would be spent on his own lessons, and the rest teaching the younger boys. It meant he had to live in accommodation provided for him there and Martha was sad to see him leave the nest at such a young age, but grateful that his future seemed assured.

In the May of 1905 Mrs Henderson, who had taken a great interest in the forming of the suffragette movement back in 1903, was enraged when a women's franchise bill brought before Parliament was 'talked out of time' and one MP had the temerity to state that 'women had no sense of proportion' and that giving them the vote 'would be unsafe'. Worse still, six months later, Mrs Pankhurst's daughter, Christabel, and Annie Kenney were actually thrown into prison for assaulting police at a meeting in Manchester where Sir Edward Grey, a prominent Liberal politician, was speaking.

'I only wish they could make their point without resorting to violence,' she said, resting her hands on her rounded stomach and shifting in her chair – another baby was on the way, and she was suffering more discomfort than she ever had before. 'And that it should happen in front of Sir Edward Grey!'

Ella was in two minds about the suffragette movement. Yes, it was annoying to be classed as a second-class citizen, but she couldn't help feeling women had enough on their plates without getting involved in politics too.

She wondered what Mr Henderson thought about it. He

was a member of the Liberal party – the reason Mrs Henderson was so affronted that the kerfuffle with the suffragettes should have happened in front of Sir Edward Grey. From conversations she'd overheard, Ella thought that Mr Henderson was likely to be selected to stand as a candidate when a seat became available, and she wondered too what it would mean for her position if he was successful and the family moved away from Bath.

In the event she was soon to find out.

The ruling Conservative party had been falling into disarray since Joseph Chamberlain had resigned in 1903 to campaign for tariff reforms, and posters put up by his opponents warned of rises in food prices. 'Don't Be Deceived by Tory Tricks', they warned, and they, along with widespread poverty, talk of concentration camps in South Africa during the Boer War, and denominational schools being integrated into the state system, fuelled the party's unpopularity. Now, at the beginning of December, Arthur Balfour, the Prime Minister, resigned, and a general election was called for the middle of January.

As expected, Mr Henderson was selected to contest, a house was rented for him in Lewisham, and when it was decided the family would go with him Mrs Henderson raised the subject with Ella.

To begin with Ella was uncertain what she should do. She was happy with the Hendersons, loved her job, and had formed close bonds with the children. And with yet another baby almost ready to make its appearance into the world she knew Mrs Henderson would need her more than ever. But she couldn't help worrying about being so far from Jeannie.

Given a day off to go home, she talked it over with Martha who was of the opinion that she should go, at least for now.

'You have to stop worrying about Jeannie and think of

yourself for a change,' she said. 'She's almost eighteen, and you can't mollycoddle her for ever.'

'I suppose,' Ella had said, still not entirely convinced.

'In any case,' Martha had continued, 'at the moment, it's only up until the election, isn't it? If Mr Henderson doesn't win, he'll be coming back to Bath, won't he? You don't want to give up a good job like that for something that might never happen. And if it does, well, you can still think again.'

Jeannie, however, had been inconsolable.

'How can you?' she'd wept. 'What will I do without you?'

'You'll be fine, Jeannie,' Ella had cajoled. 'It might not be for long, and you've got Martha. And you love your job, don't you?'

When she'd reached school-leaving age, Martha had found Jeannie a position as an apprentice in the drapery shop in Hillsbridge, and she was thrilled to be working with silky fabrics and ribbons, hats and gloves. Besides which, as her opening and closing times were similar to the gents' outfitters where Conrad worked, they were able to go to and from Hillsbridge together, a great advantage given Jeannie's nervous and highly strung disposition. But with the threat of Ella being so far away, Jeannie reverted to the same childlike behaviour as when she was much younger.

'You can't go and leave me!' she'd protested. 'You promised Mammy! If you go, I'll never forgive you!'

For a moment Ella had almost given in. Then she'd hardened her heart. It wasn't as if she was abandoning Jeannie. She had a good home with a loving family. She would be perfectly fine, and well looked after.

'I'll write to you, Jeannie, and I'll come home to see you as often as I can. And it might only be for a little while. If Mr Henderson doesn't win the seat I'll be back in Bath.'

'And if he does?'

'We'll cross that bridge when we get to it,' Ella had said.

And so, when the Hendersons moved to London, Ella went with them.

One chilly morning in December, Seb cycled into Hillsbridge to post a package Jeannie wanted to send to Ella. It was a handkerchief Lilah, her beloved mother, had embroidered with Ella's name, which Jeannie had found among her own hankies, and a bracelet and necklace she herself had made for her sister by stringing beads on a length of ribbon. Letters were usually posted in the nearest postbox in the village, but wrapped in tissue and brown paper and string, and sealed with a blob of red sealing wax, it was quite bulky, and Martha was afraid it would cost more to send than the usual halfpenny stamp. As both Jeannie and Conrad were at work during the post office opening hours, Seb volunteered to cycle over and send the package off.

'I could do with getting a spare inner tube for my bike anyway,' he said. 'If I get a bad puncture I'd be stuck.'

It was almost midday by the time he got to Hillsbridge. Conrad was standing in the doorway of the gents' outfitters as his father rode past and they waved to one another. Conrad watched him until he turned the corner and was just about to go back into the shop when he heard a commotion. Shouts. The whinny of a frightened horse. A woman's scream. What sounded like the clang of metal and splintering wood. Alarmed, Conrad turned back just as a horse and cart rounded the bend at breakneck pace. There was no one in the driving seat, and milk churns were jolting and rocking in the cart so that one after the other rolled out on to the road.

A runaway horse. Something must have frightened it. A couple of men had emerged from the cycle repair shop on the opposite side of the street, and were making a dash to try to stop it, but Conrad automatically drew back into the shop, watching in horror as one man got hold of the horse's bridle and was dragged along the road before the other man managed to hang on too and slow the horse to a walking pace. One smoothed the horse's muzzle, murmuring something that he hoped would pacify it, while the other continued to hold on to the bridle with both hands.

Conrad breathed a sigh of relief. An out-of-control horse was a terrifying sight, especially to one not used to dealing with them. But as he stood there, adrenalin still coursing through his veins, a woman he recognised as Mrs Love, the police sergeant's wife, came running along the road.

'Conrad! For goodness' sake come quick! It's your father! He's been knocked down and he's hurt pretty bad!'

Stopping only to call over his shoulder to Mr Ford that he had to go, Conrad raced along the street in the direction from which Mrs Love had come. A small crowd had gathered beside the entrance to the post office, which occupied the corner where the road broadened out into the town square, obscuring Conrad's view, but as Sergeant Love moved them back he saw his father, lying motionless beside his bicycle. At the very same moment Dr Blackmore appeared, hurrying to the scene as fast as his ageing legs could carry him. He must have still been seeing patients in his surgery when someone had run to fetch him and stopped only to grab his medical bag, which thudded against his sturdy thighs.

Conrad pushed through the little crowd of onlookers, only to be stopped by Sergeant Love.

'Stay back, son.' He laid a heavy hand on Conrad's shoulder.

'But that's my dad!' Conrad gasped.

'I know. But best give him some air, and the doctor some room.'

'Let me go! I've got to see him!' Conrad was struggling frantically.

'You don't want to do that,' one of the women in the crowd warned him. 'He's not a pretty sight.'

Conrad ignored her and managed to slip free of Sergeant Love's grasp. Before he could be stopped again he dashed across the square to where Dr Blackmore knelt beside Seb's prone body and only then did he realise why the sergeant had been so intent on stopping him.

One of Seb's arms had been nearly torn off, blood gushing out to pool on the road, and his legs were twisted at unnatural angles with more blood pumping from one of them. As for his face, the mangled mess that the horse's hooves and the wheels of the cart had made of it rendered him almost unrecognisable.

'Dad!' Conrad gasped, shocked and horrified. He dropped to his knees beside his father, reaching for the hand that was relatively uninjured. 'Dad!'

There was no response beyond the merest flutter of Seb's fingers and a spasmodic gurgle of hard-won breath.

'Help him! You've got to help him!' Conrad turned to the doctor, his voice rising in anguish. 'He will be all right, won't he? He's got to be all right!'

Dr Blackmore turned, meeting Conrad's gaze with solemn eyes, and gave a small slow shake of his head.

'I'm sorry, lad. There's nothing I can do.'

'But he's alive!'

Dr Blackmore simply shook his head again, and Conrad seemed to hear the unspoken words loud in his head. *Not for long.*

'Dad!' Desperation flooded through Conrad's veins and he leaned forward so that his lips brushed Seb's ear. 'Hang on in there, Dad.' And then, as an afterthought because expressions of affection didn't come naturally to the men who lived in the rough, tough world of a mining town, he whispered, 'I love you, Dad.'

Whether Seb heard him or not, he didn't know. Gradually the laboured gurgles of breath turned to low rumbling rattles, Seb's fingers ceased to move beneath Conrad's and with one last gasp he was still. For a moment neither the doctor nor Conrad moved or spoke, then Dr Blackmore patted Conrad's hand and gently removed it from his father's.

'He's gone. I'm so sorry, lad. But there was nothing to be done.'

Still Conrad remained where he was, shaking now from head to foot and too stunned to be able to process what had happened.

'No! No!' The word echoed and re-echoed in his head, and he was only dimly aware of Sergeant Love helping him to his feet. But through the swirling mists one thought crystallised: Jeannie.

If someone went into the drapery shop and passed on the news of what had happened Jeannie would be distraught.

'My sister,' he said. It was how he always thought of her now. 'I've got to tell her before anyone else does . . .'

'Don't worry, my son. We'll see to it. And then we'll get both of you home.'

'I've got to get back to work . . .'

'Not today you haven't.'

Sergeant Love had taken charge of the situation, and Conrad could only be grateful for it.

As always, when faced with a crisis, Martha went into coping mode. While the rest of the family reeled in shock and grief she attended the inquest, held in the town hall, and made the necessary arrangements for the funeral. The true awful finality would hit her later when everything that had to be done had been done and life had settled back into what would be the new normality.

On the day Seb was laid to rest she took charge of the catering for the wake just as she had done for his mother and father, making mounds of sandwiches with the help of her sister Ivy, who had come to stay with Martha as soon as she received the news of Seb's death, and a tearful Jeannie. In church and at the graveside she stood tall and dry-eyed, head held high. Pride would not allow her to cry in public; it was her armour against the turmoil of emotion that boiled and bubbled beneath the stoic appearance she presented to the world, the emptiness she knew would overwhelm her if she allowed herself to contemplate a future without the man who had been her rock in good times and bad, the man she had depended on more than life itself.

Lewis had come home from Wells, but Ella was unable to attend the funeral. Mrs Henderson had not yet fully recovered from the birth of little Teddy, the new baby, and Mr Henderson was out every day from dawn till dusk and sometimes later, canvassing door-to-door and speaking at countless meetings ahead of the imminent election. There was no way Ella could be spared. By way of making it up to her Mr Henderson had wired a generous sum to a Bath florist on her behalf, so that at least there would be a beautiful wreath with her name on it to be laid on the grave of the man who had taken her and Jeannie in and treated them with such compassion and kindness.

Jeannie, who had scarcely stopped weeping since Conrad had come to the drapers' with Sergeant Love to break the awful news, was in fresh floods of tears when she learned Ella would not be coming home. But she was somewhat pacified to discover, to her surprise, that Garth would be attending.

From the minute he walked through the door, smartly

dressed, wearing a pristine white shirt and black tie knotted around the wing collar and a black armband on his coat sleeve just above the elbow, she attached herself to him like a limpet and Martha marvelled at his patience with her. Much as she loved Jeannie, her clinginess could be wearing, and Martha was grateful that she wouldn't have to cope alone with the girl all day. But she couldn't help wondering if the reason Garth was so kind to Jeannie was his way of underlining his disdain for her and his brothers. It had always been thus, even before he had discovered Seb was not his real father, and certainly since.

She was comforted that he was here, though. Perhaps, deep down, he realised how good Seb had been taking on the responsibility of a baby who was not his own and raising him as if he were. She hoped so. For all his faults, for all that she had so often despaired of him, he was still her son and her love for him had never diminished. Neither had the way she was always ready to make excuses for him, nor her optimism that one day he would learn the error of his ways and make something of himself.

Little as she had approved of him going to Bath and living and working in a gambling club, she thought now that maybe it had been the right thing for him after all. He was a grown man now, and by all appearances he was doing well for himself. Perhaps she had been wrong to try and steer him away from a life that was in his blood.

But now there was something she needed to speak to him about, something that might well have a bearing on his future.

As the wake came to an end and the last stragglers who had come to pay their respects had left, she gave Conrad the wink to distract Jeannie, who was still clinging on to Garth, and drew him aside.

'Garth – we have to go and see the solicitor tomorrow, and

you should be there too,' she said when they were finally alone.

Garth's mouth twisted into the all-too-familiar sneer. 'To hear the will read, I suppose? I don't see why I need to go. He won't have left anything to me.'

'You might be in for a surprise.' Martha gave him a straight look.

Garth frowned. 'You know what's in it?'

'Your father wouldn't have made such an important decision without talking to me about it,' Martha said.

'*Seb*, you mean.' Garth's tone was bitter. 'Well? What did I inherit? The mouse droppings in the skittle-alley?'

'Don't be disrespectful, Garth,' Martha said sharply. 'And it's not for me to say. That's up to the solicitor. So – will you be there? Or would you prefer Mr Clarence to notify you by letter?'

Garth's eyes narrowed; Martha could almost hear the wheels grinding like the workings of a clock inside his head.

'All right,' he said at last, and she wondered if the reason he had come to the funeral today was that, despite his sarcastic remarks, he had been hoping that he might have been left something.

'Can I stay the night?' he asked. 'It would save me making the journey twice.'

'Of course you can,' Martha assured him. 'This is still your home.'

At that moment, Jeannie, quickly bored of any company but Garth's, came back into the bar and the time for private conversations was over. Martha fervently hoped that Garth wouldn't be disappointed when he learned the provisions of the will.

As Jeannie slipped her hand into the crook of his arm Garth turned his attention to her once more, hot with the desire that had consumed him ever since he'd arrived for the funeral.

Since he'd seen her last Jeannie had grown into a very beautiful girl. She'd always been a pretty child, of course, but now she was quite stunning. While Ella's fair hair had darkened to light brown as she grew, Jeannie's was still the colour of spun gold, curling in long ringlets around her sweet face, and her eyes sparkled like aquamarines. They were fringed with long and surprisingly dark lashes and her skin was clear and creamy. Her frame was still delicate, her waist small enough to be spanned by a man's hands, her breasts small but rounded. And there was something very appealing about her trusting and childlike manner. Garth had been flattered by the way she still gazed at him with the same adoring eyes as she always had, but now there was something of the come-hither in them that had lighted a fire in his blood. He wanted her. And what – and who – Garth wanted, he almost always got.

But how to get her on her own? Even when the mourners had left the family would still be here. Since he was going to be staying overnight there was always the option of creeping into her room when the rest of the family were in bed and asleep, but the floorboards on the landing were notoriously creaky. If they didn't give him away, if he startled Jeannie awake she might cry out and wake someone. The only place he could think of where they would have some privacy was the skittle-alley. The dartboard would still be there, he guessed, and Jeannie had always enjoyed the game even if she was no good at it. Not that that was what he had in mind.

'Fancy a game of darts, for old times' sake?' He unbuttoned the collar of his shirt and unknotted his black tie to let it hang loose. 'I bet you can beat me now.'

'I *did* used to beat you sometimes,' she said, the coquettish note back in her voice and her turquoise eyes sparkling with mischief. 'But I think that was only when you let me win.'

'Never!' He picked up a lighted lamp from the window sill, then took her hand and led her out and across the yard. 'Remember when I found you here the night you ran away from the workhouse?'

She nodded, a shadow crossing her face, then her smile returned. 'I'll never forget it, as long as I live. At first I was really frightened of you.'

'You're not frightened of me now?'

'Maybe just a little bit,' she said coyly.

With only the light of the one oil lamp it was dim and shadowy in the skittle-alley.

'It's too dark to see the dartboard,' Jeannie pouted.

'It'll have to be skittles, then. Come and help me set them up.'

'It'll be too dark to see the skittles too.'

'Just throw straight and hope for the best.' He led her to the end of the alley, set the lamp down on a small table and picking up a couple of wooden pins, placed them on the white-painted markers. Then he straightened, climbed back over the edge of the alley, and patted the bales of straw stacked at the end to stop both balls and skittles.

'I wonder if these are the same ones you went to sleep on? Let's see if you still fit on there.'

With a swift lithe movement he caught her by the waist, hoisting her up on to the straw barrier.

'Garth!' She was giggling now. 'Get me down!'

'Give me a kiss, then.' He leaned against the bales, pulling her towards him and holding her fast.

'No! You're wicked!' But he knew she was only playing the coquette again, and when he lifted her chin with one hand she made no further protest.

Beneath his mouth her lips were soft and yielding. She wound her arms round his neck and he caught the tumble of golden ringlets, twisting his fingers between them and tucking them behind her ear. He kissed her again, tasting the sweet sherry she'd been drinking at the wake, breathing in the scent of her skin. He slid his hand to her small firm breast, felt the beat of her heart, rapid and strong, and the whisper of breath against his chin as she moaned softly.

Then, just as he rucked up her skirts, she stiffened in his arms and for a moment he thought she was going to go cold on him. But she wasn't trying to wriggle free, instead she was staring over his shoulder and instinctively he turned his head to see what she was looking at.

There was another lighted lamp at the far end of the skittle-alley, a figure holding it high, and an angry voice echoed in the dim silence.

'What the hell do you think you're doing?'

It was Conrad.

'For Christ's sake!' Garth ground out. 'Get out of here and leave us alone.'

'Not on your life.' Conrad put down the lamp and stormed down the alley. 'Jeannie? Are you all right? What's he done to you?'

Though he was half Garth's size he grabbed his brother by the hair and his shirt collar and hauled him away from Jeannie. Taken by surprise, Garth stumbled and fell over his own feet, knocking into the table where he had left oil lamp as he did so, and it rolled perilously close to the bales of straw.

'Christ!' Garth was on his feet again in an instant, tearing off his coat and throwing it over the lamp and the flames that were already licking along the spilled oil. Conrad followed suit, and between them they managed to extinguish the fire and stop it spreading. Jeannie, meanwhile, had jumped down from the straw bales and was standing well back, her hands covering her mouth, tears of fright welling in her eyes.

'Stupid bugger! You trying to burn us all to death?' Garth yelled at Conrad when the danger was over.

'You know why I did it.' Though Conrad wanted nothing more than to punch his brother full in the face, he knew he would be no match for him if it came to fisticuffs. If it hadn't been for the overturned lamp Garth would have beaten the living daylights out of him when he was back on his feet, and still would given half a chance. 'Just leave Jeannie alone, all right?'

'I'll do what I like,' Garth retorted. But the moment for what he had had in mind had come and gone. The brush with impending disaster had shaken him so that he was no longer in the mood for it, and clearly neither was Jeannie. She was creeping closer, her hands still covering her face and her eyes wide and glistening with tears above them.

'Are you sure it's out?' she asked in a trembling voice.

'Don't worry, Jeannie, we'll make sure it is,' Conrad said. 'I'll go and get a mop and a pail and we'll clear it all up. Why don't you come with me?'

Jeannie caught at his sleeve. 'Don't tell Martha, please! I don't want her to know . . .'

'So how are we going to explain our ruined coats?'

'Can't you say we were all having a game of skittles? And I threw the ball wide?'

'Garth?' Conrad looked at his brother.

Garth shrugged. 'Makes no odds to me.'

But for all that his plans had been thwarted for the moment, he felt curiously satisfied. He could have had Jeannie if Conrad hadn't come barging in when he did. She'd been willing, most likely wanted it as much as he did. Next time he'd make sure they were somewhere where they wouldn't be interrupted. And the added frisson of pleasure came from what he'd learned from the episode.

Conrad wasn't just being chivalrous. His blind fury had proved that. He fancied Jeannie himself. Perhaps was in love with her even. It was for her sake that he was prepared to lie about what had been going on in the skittle-alley. To protect her. And that gave Garth the advantage over his brother. He was the one she clung to, the one she wanted, and he could torment Conrad with it any time he chose.

Next morning, no mention was made of the events of the previous evening. Martha, Garth and Lewis walked to Hillsbridge, arriving at the solicitor's office ten minutes before the allotted time of eleven. Conrad, who had returned to work today, was already waiting outside the door with the brass plaque bearing the legend 'Willoughby and Clarence' – Mr Ford had given him an hour off to attend the reading of the will.

The four of them waited together on the pavement until the hands of the market clock had almost reached the hour, then went in and up the steep narrow staircase to the minute waiting room. They were greeted by a young man with heavily macassared hair and wearing a coat the sleeves of which were several inches too short, revealing thin, bony wrists. Mr Horler, the wizened little man Martha had seen when she'd visited Mr Clarence to ask his advice about adopting Ella and Jeannie, must have retired, and this young man, whom she later discovered was an articled clerk learning his trade, had taken his place as doorkeeper and greeter.

As he ushered them into Mr Clarence's office the great man himself stood, reaching across his desk to shake each of them by the hand, then waving them to be seated on the row of four chairs facing him. No wonder the waiting room had looked bare, Martha thought. Extra chairs had been brought in from there especially to accommodate them.

'I am very sorry for your loss.' Mr Clarence resumed his own seat. 'A tragedy. A tragedy indeed.'

It was the first time Martha had seen the solicitor since that long-ago day when he had advised her on the lack of formal adoption procedures, and she thought he had aged considerably. The side whiskers, though still luxuriant, were now shot through with grey, as was the remaining hair on his head, combed over carefully in an effort to conceal the extent to which it had receded, and his face appeared to have dropped, so that heavy jowls hung over the starched wing tips of his collar. His eyes were still sharp, however, behind the owlish spectacles.

'Thank you,' Martha said quietly, settling her bag with its tortoiseshell handle in the folds of her skirt.

'Now, it falls to me to inform you of Mr Packer's last wishes.' The solicitor turned the first page of a cream vellum document that lay on the table in front of him. 'It's a simple enough will, so rather than blinding you with all the legalese, perhaps you would prefer I summarise?'

'By all means,' Martha said. 'Conrad has to get back to work, so we'd be glad to get to the point.'

'Of course, I'll be happy to answer any questions you may have when I've done.' Mr Clarence glanced at each of them in turn over the top of his spectacles, then pushed them up again on to the bridge of his hawk-like nose.

'To begin. As I say, Mr Packer's wishes are, in one respect, very simple. All liquid assets – that is, any cash in hand or at bank – he leaves to Mrs Packer.' He inclined his head towards Martha. 'That should set your mind at rest, I think. As regards the remainder of his estate – namely the Three Feathers public house – this is to be shared equally between his three sons, Garth, Conrad and Lewis.'

Martha heard Lewis's sharp intake of breath and: 'What? He's left the pub to us?' Conrad said, disbelieving his own ears,

'To the three of you, yes,' Mr Clarence said. 'However – this is where some complication arises. As you are aware, both you, Conrad, and you, Lewis, have not yet reached the age of majority, meaning neither of you can inherit until you do. Garth, however, has passed that milestone and would therefore qualify immediately if it were not for a clause which Mr Packer agreed to on my advice, although naturally he hoped such a situation as this would never arise. This clause states that until the youngest of you reaches the age of twenty-one the bequest is to be held in trust, the sole trustee being you, Mrs Packer. I believe you are aware of this and agreed to it?'

He lowered his spectacles again, looking at Martha over the top of them.

'I am,' Martha confirmed.

'And you are happy to take on that responsibility?'

Martha nodded. 'Of course, I never thought it would come to this any more than Seb did. But yes, I'm prepared to look after things until Lewis is of age.'

'There is one additional clause,' Mr Clarence continued. 'And that is that Mrs Packer be allowed to live at the Three Feathers as long as she so desires. She is not, under any circumstances, to be deprived of her home.'

'We'd never think of turning her out!' Conrad said swiftly.

'It goes without saying,' Lewis echoed him.

Martha smiled her gratitude. But at the same time she couldn't help noticing Garth's expression. His old sullen look was back and Martha knew that if she looked into his eyes she would see not only disappointment, but anger. To the last Seb had ensured he treated all three boys equally, but still Garth wasn't satisfied. He'd no doubt been hoping to come into some money immediately, and he didn't want to have to wait three years until Lewis was twenty-one to get his hands on his inheritance, and even then share it with his brothers.

Garth hadn't changed one bit, she thought, and her heart sank at the realisation.

Chapter Sixteen

Martha was right – Garth had indeed hoped to be left something for himself in Seb's will. Until Martha had asked him to attend the reading it hadn't occurred to him except as wishful thinking – he wasn't Seb's son, after all, and there had been bad blood between them even before he'd discovered it. But when she'd said 'You might be in for a surprise' his hopes had been raised. Only to be cruelly dashed when he'd learned what it was he'd been bequeathed.

A disgruntled Garth set out for Bath, and the journey did nothing to lighten his mood. Damn Seb to hell. And damn Martha, Conrad and Lewis as well.

It was midday before he arrived back at Marsh's club, and when he rang the bell at the entrance it was Aaron who answered it.

When he saw Garth he scowled. 'Where the devil have you been? You were supposed to be back last night.'

'I don't have to answer to you,' Garth retorted.

'Maybe not, but you do have to answer to Mr Marsh. He wants to see you, so you'd better have a good excuse ready. He's in his office.'

Garth shrugged, concealing his apprehension. Elliot wasn't a man to be trifled with.

He went through the salon, empty at this time of day, to the small room at the back of the building that was Elliot's office, and knocked on the door.

'Come!'

Elliot was seated behind his desk, with a sheaf of papers and a ledger in front of him.

'Garth.' He took off his spectacles and gave Garth a straight look. 'We were expecting you back yesterday.'

'Yeah. I'm sorry. I had to stay over to go to the reading of the will with my mother.'

'Really?' Elliot arched an eyebrow. 'Why you? I'd have thought . . .'

He let his voice trail away, but Garth knew what he was thinking. Elliot was very well aware Seb wasn't his real father.

'Me too,' he said. 'But my mother was insistent. She knew I'd been included.'

'Well, well! So you've come to tell me you no longer need to work for your living?'

'Hardly,' Garth said bitterly. 'I've been left a third share in the Feathers along with my brothers. And I don't even get that until the youngest of them is twenty-one. And that's not for another three bloody years.'

'Oh dear. Well, never mind. Time is on your side. You're still a young man.'

'And what would I do with a third share of a pub in the middle of nowhere anyway?' Garth said, expressing his frustration.

'Sell it? Perhaps your brothers will buy you out?'

'They couldn't afford it. The pub does well, yes, but it's scarcely a gold mine.'

'Some third party then? A brewery, maybe? They might well be prepared to take it on, but they would no doubt want total control.'

'That's another snag. There's a clause in the will that says my mother can continue to live there as long as she wants.'

'Hmm.' Elliot considered. 'That could well be a problem, I agree. A sitting tenant is never a good inducement to a purchaser.'

'Is such a thing even allowed?' Garth asked.

'Is it legal, do you mean? I'm no lawyer, Garth, but I could ask the question of my solicitor if you'd like me to.'

'Yes,' Garth said. 'If you could find out for me how I stand in all this, I'd be very much obliged.'

Elliot smiled. He sensed an opportunity for making mischief that was not to be missed.

'Certainly – I'll make some enquiries. Now. It's dinner time if I'm not much mistaken. I think a beefsteak and oyster pie washed down by some good ale might be in order. Would you like to accompany me, my boy?'

Garth didn't need asking twice. He was hungry after the long morning and besides, seeing his father's face when he and Elliot left together would be an extra bonus.

There were important decisions to be made about the running of the Feathers, and they wouldn't wait. Conrad would be able to help behind the bar in the evenings and Jeannie could help with washing glasses if they were busy, and Ivy had offered to lend a hand with preparing food during the day. But she'd long since settled down, and with a husband and four children, her life was so busy Martha was unwilling to take advantage of her sister's good nature. They held a family conference round the sitting room table, and it was decided that Conrad would give up his job at the gents' outfitters and work full time in the pub.

'It would make sense,' Martha said. 'After all, it's going to be yours one day.'

'Mine, Garth's and Lewis's,' Conrad pointed out.

'But Lewis is training to be a teacher, and as for Garth . . . I can't see him wanting to come home now he's living the high life in Bath.'

She didn't add that she'd be hard put to it to trust him with the takings or the stock either.

'We ought to give him the chance, though.' Despite he and Garth never having really got on, Conrad was nothing if not fair minded.

'Maybe,' Martha said noncommittally.

'It's only fair he should do some of the work if he's going to get a share of the profits,' Ivy pointed out.

'Conrad will be paid a wage on top of his share.' Martha had already given the matter some thought. 'The only other alternative is for me to advertise for a barman or barmaid. But I have to say I'd prefer to keep it in the family.'

'If it's all right by Garth, it's all right by me,' Conrad said. Truth to tell, he quite fancied becoming the landlord.

'That's settled then.' Martha got up from the table. 'Now, would anybody like a cup of tea?'

'I wouldn't say no,' Ivy said, and Martha smiled wryly.

'When did you ever?'

It was something of a private joke between the sisters, the meaning of which was quite lost on the younger generation. In her day Ivy had been something of a flirt, and since everything had turned out well, with Seb rescuing Martha, Ivy had teased that she'd always thought she'd be the one who'd 'have to get married'.

'Don't forget,' Ivy said now. 'I can always come over and lend a hand if I'm needed. Don't be afraid to ask.'

'You're a brick, Ivy.' Martha patted her sister on the shoulder and disappeared into the kitchen.

* * *

Sad though she was not to have been able to attend Seb's funeral, and guilty as she felt at not being with Jeannie at Christmas, Ella was enjoying life in London. Whereas in Bath it had been only Mrs Henderson, the children and herself in the house most of the time, here in London there were constant comings and goings, conferences between Mr Henderson and his agent, Walter Robinson, party workers filling envelopes with propaganda, others collecting leaflets to distribute door to door. There was so little time to prepare for the election which was to be held over several weeks from mid-January! Fortunately, the Lewisham polling day was set for the beginning of February so they had a little leeway. Nevertheless, the house seemed always to be bursting with energy, creating a buzz that was as uplifting as it was infectious. Sometimes, when Mrs Henderson was well enough to keep an eye on the children, Ella was detailed to help with the leafleting. Folding an endless supply of sheets of paper extolling Mr Henderson's virtues and promises for the future might have been mind-numbingly boring, but working alongside the enthusiastic party activists made it almost a social occasion.

As the days raced by and the mood became ever more urgent, Ella was asked to help out with the delivering of yet more fliers to constituents' doors.

'Don't worry, we'll pair you with someone who knows the area well,' Mr Robinson reassured her, and Ella was pleased to think she would be able to begin to get to know her way around without fear of getting lost. The streets all looked so similar, with their tall, elegant houses, and the crescents encircling small parks where she could walk out with the children on fine days.

She'd imagined she would be sent out with one of the ladies, whom she thought of as 'posh', and although she had been perfectly happy to fill envelopes when she was just one of a crowd, Ella couldn't help feeling shy at the thought of being alone with one of them. She was all too aware of her humble origins, and the way she spoke, with a Somerset burr that was so different to their refined accents – 'they talk as if they've got a plum in their mouths,' Martha would have said.

To her surprise, however, it was a young man she hadn't seen before that Walter Robinson introduced her to, telling her his name was Monty. Tall, slimly built, with fair hair that flopped over one eye, and a small goatee beard, he took her hand and brushed it lightly with his lips.

'Glad to make your acquaintance, Miss Martin.' His voice was every bit as posh as the ladies'.

'Likewise,' Ella said, because she felt it was expected of her, but felt herself blushing as, with a wicked twinkle, he said: 'Leafleting today will be a great deal more pleasant than usual, I think.'

'Just behave yourself, Monty,' Mr Robinson said sternly. 'I'm trusting you to look after our young lady.'

'Don't worry, I will,' he replied cheerfully.

Out on the streets, he was the perfect gentleman, ushering her to the inside of the pavement so he was between her and the road, and resting a helping hand beneath her elbow where the paving stones were uneven.

'I don't suppose you're very used to city life yet,' he said and Ella bridled a little.

'Bath's a city,' she informed him.

He smiled apologetically. 'Of course. And a very fine one too. But London is something else. Perhaps you'd allow me to show you some of the sights when this business is done and dusted and John Henderson is our Honourable Member.'

Ella scarcely knew what to say. Was he asking her to walk out? But they'd only met ten minutes or so ago! Perhaps it was usual here in the capital, Ella wouldn't know. Though she was now almost twenty-one years old she had never walked out with a boy. The opportunity had never presented itself, and she hadn't wanted it to. Her fond memories of Leo were enough for her.

'Mr Henderson might not win and we shall be going back to Bath,' she hedged.

Monty laughed, supremely confident.

'Oh, he'll win. The Liberals are on the up-and-up. I guarantee you we'll be sharing a glass of champagne when the result comes in.'

'Well, we'll see about that,' Ella said primly.

They had reached a parade of grand houses.

'Time to start work.' Monty took a sheaf of leaflets from the leather bag he wore paper-boy style over his smart coat and handed them to her. 'We'll take alternate numbers – I'll do the odd and you can do the even, so I won't be far away if anyone bothers you.'

'I don't need nursemaiding!' Ella retorted. 'Why don't you start at the far end, I'll start here, and we'll meet in the middle.'

'You'd make me walk all that way twice? I'd have to retrace my steps to get to the next street we're supposed to be targeting. And besides, I promised Walter I'd look after you, and I like to keep my promises.'

For some reason, Ella felt the colour rising again in her cheeks, already rosy from the cold, and she turned away hastily, climbing the broad stone steps to the first house and pushing one of her leaflets through the gleaming brass letter box.

By the time they had covered the whole parade she was feeling more comfortable. As they'd passed one another on their allotted houses Monty had made various remarks that she would normally have considered cheeky, but the airy way in which he carried them off seemed somehow to make it all right. It was just his way, she thought. He didn't mean anything by it. But when the leather bag was empty and they were making their way back to the Hendersons' rented house he glanced at her and his eyes held hers.

'I hope I'll see you again, Ella,' he said, and this time the teasing tone was absent from his voice.

'It all depends if Mrs Henderson can spare me,' she replied, blushing yet again.

'She'd better, is all I can say, or she'll have me to reckon with.' Monty pulled a mock-threatening face, back to his easy manner and throwaway banter, and Ella found herself thinking that he really was quite nice, and certainly rather handsome. But she wasn't going to start getting ideas. He probably said the same sort of thing to all the girls.

Back at the house she thanked him politely for showing her the ropes, and went inside in search of her charges.

They were in the sitting room, playing with their building bricks and watched over by Mrs Henderson, who was nursing little Teddy. In recent weeks she had recovered much of her strength, and she greeted Ella with a smile.

'So – how did you get on with the Honourable Montague Lascelles?'

'You mean Monty?' Ella assumed her employer was poking fun at his foppish appearance and plummy voice. 'He seems nice.'

'I think he is, in spite of being born with a silver spoon in his mouth.'

Ella frowned. 'You *weren't* joking?'

'Of course not. His father is a baronet. And from what I could see of it he's certainly taken a shine to you.'

'But . . .' Ella was reeling in shock. She'd had no idea of Monty's standing in society. He had certainly been flirting with her but she couldn't imagine for a moment that it might be anything more than that, given that she was just a lowly nursemaid.

'I expect he was just being kind,' she said. 'Or it's his way, and he can't help himself.'

'Perhaps.' But there was a twinkle in Mrs Henderson's eye and a little curve to her lips that seemed to say she was not so sure about that. She knew all too well that Monty rather liked girls beneath him in class, and thought it was his way of infuriating the family who had very different ideas as to where his future lay.

Desperate to find a distraction from this embarrassing conversation, Ella sank to the floor beside Eustace and Angelina.

'This is wonderful work,' she said, nodding at the pile of bricks precariously balanced on one another in what appeared to be a tower.

'It's a castle,' Eustace said.

At that moment Angelina shifted position and managed to kick into the bricks, which came tumbling down in a cascade of red, blue and yellow.

'Now look what you've done!' Eustace cried.

Angelina looked at him with wide eyes that threatened tears and a thumb stuffed into her mouth, and in that moment Ella was reminded of Jeannie.

'We can build it again. I'll help you.'

She took one of the fallen bricks and settled it in the middle of the rug. Thankfully, Mrs Henderson did not mention Monty again.

Garth was in his room training his shoulder muscles with the dumb-bells he'd acquired to maintain his strong physique when the door opened and a voice cooed softly to him, 'Hey, handsome! Would you like to play?'

It was the standard invitation the salon girls used when attracting customers for their extracurricular activities, but the club was not yet open and Garth knew he was not expected to pay for their favours. After the men who frequented the club – mostly elderly and either portly or skinny – pleasuring him was a welcome treat for them.

Belle, the woman peeping coquettishly round the door now, was not one of Garth's favourites. She was older than the other hostesses; too much powder and rouge sat in the lines and wrinkles that were forming between nose and mouth and around her eyes, and although tightly corseted, her once glorious figure was beginning to thicken and droop.

'Not just now, Belle,' he said, concentrating on lifting the dumb-bells.

'O-oh,' she wheedled, and the babyish lilt in her voice was almost grotesque coming from someone of her age. 'You don't need to do that! You're perfect just as you are.'

As she spoke she shimmied across to him, swaying her hips provocatively, and ran her fingers over his muscles, rippling as he lifted the heavy weight.

'Belle . . . get out of the way or I'll drop this on your toes,' he said through gritted teeth.

She took a hasty step backwards, pouting. 'Don't be like that, Garth . . .'

A tap on the door – to Belle's frustration and Garth's relief – interrupted the attempt at seduction. It was Kelvin Walters, and the scene that met his eyes provoked an expression of envy. Belle might not be the most desirable of the salon girls, but none of them ever sought him out to bestow their favours.

'Mr Marsh is looking for you, Garth.' His tone was sulky.

'Okey-doke. Tell him I'm coming.' Garth lowered the dumb-bells and reached for his shirt.

'Perhaps we can meet up later?' Belle said hopefully.

'Not today, Belle.'

He left the room, went down the stairs and into the salon, where Elliot was waiting, seated on one of the plush chaises longues, swirling brandy in a balloon.

'Garth. Good. I hope I'm not inconveniencing you by sending for you during your leisure time.'

'Not at all. In fact you saved my bacon. Belle was just about to leap on me.'

'Ah, Belle.' Elliot shook his head sadly. 'That one is well past her prime. It's time for me to let her go and find someone a good deal younger – and prettier. But we don't want to talk about her. I have some news for you. Pour yourself a drink and come and sit down.'

Curious, Garth did as he was bid. The invitation to share Elliot's fine cognac was a sign that this was a congenial meeting and he wondered what could be coming. He didn't have long to wait. As soon as he was seated Elliot set his glass on a side table and began.

'You remember I promised to take advice on Seb Packer's will? Well, I've been to see my solicitor this morning, and I thought you'd like to know what he had to say.'

'Well?' Garth raised the brandy balloon to his lips, looking steadily at Elliot over the rim.

'It's impossible for him to be sure without seeing a copy of the will, of course, but if the legacy is left in trust, that is legally binding, and it is incumbent on the trustee to manage the estate until the terms are fulfilled.'

Garth snorted in disgust. 'There's nothing to be done but wait then.'

'It would seem so. Fortunately for you, you will only have to wait until your youngest brother – Lewis, is it? – turns twenty-one. Many legacies are not inherited until the age of twenty-five, which would mean you would have had much longer to wait.'

'That's something I suppose.'

'There is also the likelihood that the will is written so that should either you or one of your brothers be unfortunate enough to meet their maker before the youngest reaches the stipulated age his share would be divided equally between the two surviving siblings. Suppose, say, something should happen to Lewis, then you and Conrad would receive equal shares when he reaches the age of twenty-one, which is fairly soon, I believe.'

'In February. But it's not likely anything will happen to Lewis, more's the pity. He scarcely takes his nose out of his books. And there's still the problem of Martha. Who'd want to buy my share with her allowed to live there for the rest of her life?'

'My solicitor thinks there may be a way to get around that. There is a self-contained cottage on the premises, if I remember rightly. If she were to move into it, it would fulfil the terms of the will and free up the licensed premises to be sold.'

'I never thought of that!' Garth felt his spirits lift a little. 'The old folk moved over there when they retired. Martha could do the same.'

'And of course, by law you can demand your share even if you are unable to sell to a partner.'

'Conrad and Lewis would never be able to afford to buy me out,' Garth said.

'Then I believe they would be obliged to sell the Feathers in order that you receive your dues.' He smiled at Garth's astonished delight. 'I think that calls for a toast, don't you? Get yourself another drink and refresh mine, and we'll drink to your future.'

As he raised his glass, however, Elliot was thinking of

Aaron's reaction when he learned of his illegitimate son's inheritance, and in time have it paraded under his very nose.

Close as he had once been to his former minder, nowadays Elliot liked nothing better than to rile the man who had taken his friendship for granted, assumed far too much, behaved disgracefully towards the Feathers barmaid all those years ago, and now treated his son with such disdain. Aaron Walters deserved to be taken down a peg or two, and Elliot was just the man to do it.

Chapter Seventeen

Ella had never experienced quite as much excitement as she did when the polling day for Mr Henderson's constituency finally arrived. News had come in of Liberal victories in other constituencies where voting had already taken place, and party activists here in Lewisham were optimistic they would fare just as well.

The whole family were up with the lark, groomed and dressed, and the atmosphere around the breakfast table was electric. Even the children seemed to catch the mood, and nobody was able to eat very much of the spread a maid had prepared for them. They walked to their polling station so as to be there when it opened, and the two women remained outside with the children while Mr Henderson went in to cast his vote.

Monty, wearing an enormous yellow rosette, was amongst the party activists flanking the doors. He gave Ella a wave, but was much too busy with a pen and clipboard to come over and speak to her. She'd seen little of him in the last hectic days, but when they had chanced to meet he'd treated her with the same flattery and flirtatiousness as before, and Ella had begun to enjoy it.

When Mr Henderson appeared again he was immediately surrounded by party workers and it was clear he would not be coming home with them. A grand motor was waiting at the kerb to take him around the constituency in a last ditch effort to rally support, and even to convey to a polling station those who would otherwise be unable to get there. Reasonably confident though they might be, nothing was to be left to chance.

Back at the house the same frenetic atmosphere persisted. It had, after all, been the hub of Mr Henderson's campaign along with the official committee rooms. But the latter were a gentlemen-only zone, and so some of the ladies with the plummy voices had congregated here. They were chattering excitedly, nerves and anticipation making them even louder than usual. Ella was detailed to keep the children out from under their feet while Mrs Henderson attended to little Teddy but it was difficult to keep them under control with so much going on.

Since it was a fine, crisp day Ella decided the best thing to do would be to take them out to the park where they could play without disturbing anyone. But even there it was impossible to get away from the fact that it was polling day. Billboards and placards bearing pictures of the candidates seemed to be everywhere, on lamp-posts, on fences, even in the windows of the houses, and a noisy crowd of Labour supporters were singing a ditty – 'Vote, vote, vote for Thomas Bradley! He is sure to win the day . . .' Ella gave them a wide berth just in case she or the children were recognised and set upon. These things did happen, she had heard, though they seemed good natured enough, and it was too early in the day for them to be inebriated.

It was, in all, a crazy day such as Ella had never before experienced. And that evening, when Mrs Henderson broke the news that she had employed a babysitter for the children so that Ella could accompany her employers to the count, she could scarcely believe it.

'But I haven't got anything suitable to wear!' she said.

Fortunately, Mrs Henderson had the answer – a beautiful promenade dress with a pleated skirt and velvet ribbons.

'I can't get into it any more,' she said ruefully. 'I'm afraid four babies have ruined my waistline.'

'Oh . . . I couldn't!' Ella protested.

'Of course you could. Try it on.'

Ella had never seen anything so fine, and when she slipped it on and looked at herself in the full-length mirror in Mrs Henderson's room she could scarcely believe her eyes. Not only was it a perfect fit, but also the golden-brown wool fabric suited her beautifully, complementing her fair hair and complexion.

'And here is the cape I always wore with it.' Mrs Henderson produced a woollen cape in moss green. 'And a hat and muff. I shall want those back, I'm afraid, but you're welcome to borrow them.'

'Thank you so much!' Ella said. Now she was dressed for it, she realised just how much she wanted to go to the count. She'd been so involved in the campaigning, and besides, Monty would be there. A little thrill of excitement tingled in her stomach as she thought of him seeing her looking like a lady.

Sure enough, his eyes lit up when she and the Hendersons entered the room and he made his way through the throng to her side.

'I'm so pleased you could come, Ella!'

'The Hendersons wanted me to,' she said, a little shyly.

'And quite right too. You've worked as hard as anyone. You should be here.'

The room was abuzz with activity, tellers sitting at a long trestle with piles of voting papers laid out in front of them, supporters of all the candidates talking animatedly in their groups and occasionally joshing with their opponents, and boys running in and out with fresh boxes of ballot papers collected from the polling stations. They reminded Ella a little of the boys who acted as bookies' runners, except that the large boxes were nothing like the scraps of paper the runners carried concealed in their pockets to avoid detection.

As the night wore on the atmosphere grew steadily more electric. Monty had taken Ella into a side room for a much needed cup of tea when the buzz of anticipation reached fever pitch and someone ran in and announced that the result was about to be announced.

Ella's heart was hammering so hard she thought it would burst as she and Monty hurried back into the main hall. Mr Henderson and the other candidates were now standing in a row on the stage at the rear of the room and an officious-looking man with a mayoral chain draped around his portly chest had taken up his position in front of them. A hush fell over the hall as he prepared to read out the number of votes cast for each candidate. Without thinking what she was doing, Ella clasped Monty's hand, hardly daring to breathe, and so giddy she couldn't make head or tail of the figures. It was only when a cheer went up from Mr Henderson's supporters, and Monty clasped her about the waist and twirled her round and round that she realised.

He'd won! Mr Henderson had won!

The other candidates were clapping him on the back and shaking him by the hand and he stepped forward, beaming, to make his acceptance speech, thanking all those who had worked tirelessly on his behalf and promising to faithfully represent the borough in Parliament.

Then, before she knew it, Monty was pressing a glass of champagne into her hand.

'What did I tell you?' he said delightedly. 'Didn't I say we'd be sharing a glass of champagne tonight? And better still, you'll be staying in London. No running back to Bath for you!'

He raised his glass, clinking it with hers.

'To Mr Henderson.'

'Mr Henderson,' Ella echoed.

'And to us.'

Ella sipped the champagne – the first she had ever tasted – and as the bubbles tickled on her tongue she felt a rush of disbelief. How had she come to this? Nursery maid to an MP, drinking champagne with a baronet's son, dressed in finery more elegant and expensive than she could ever have imagined . . . It was like a dream. A dream from which she never wanted to wake up.

Over the rim of the sparkling glass her eyes met Monty's and excitement rose in her stomach like the bubbles in the champagne. She'd never felt this way about anyone but Leo, never wanted to. But she didn't suppose they'd ever meet again. Her life was here now. And perhaps the future was with Monty.

'So – you're going to be a pub landlord, I hear.'

Though there was the suggestion of a sneer in Aaron's voice, his tone was, for once, almost civil. Since Elliot had told him about Garth's inheritance he was optimistic that his usurper would leave Marsh's and return to the Feathers, and that with him out of the way Aaron would be reinstated as Elliot's minder, companion and heir. It was, after all, only since Garth had come on the scene that he'd been pushed out, and he felt sure it was only because he knew that Garth was his illegitimate son that he favoured him so. Aaron had known Elliot for long enough to understand the workings of his mind; the devilish streak that made him unable to resist making mischief.

'Not yet,' Garth muttered, trying to push his way past his father.

Aaron frowned. 'What d'you mean?'

Garth glowered. 'Didn't Elliot tell you I've got to wait another three years until bloody Lewis comes of age? He seems to have told you everything else.'

'Lewis?' Aaron queried. 'Who's he?'

'Seb's youngest son. All three of us have got to be twenty-one before any of us can touch the inheritance. It's in trust, whatever that means. And Martha gets to go on running the pub till then.'

'Oh, that's bad luck.' *For me as well as you*, Aaron was thinking.

'Yeah. My only chance of getting my hands on it sooner is if he snuffs it. And that's no more likely than a blue moon.'

Garth was walking away, but Aaron, whose sharp mind was working overtime, called after him.

'Hang on. Are you saying if this Lewis were to die you and your other brother – what's his name? – would get the pub straight away?'

'Yeah. Well, a whole lot sooner. Conrad will be twenty-one this month. But it's not going to happen, worse luck.'

'Come back here, son, and listen to me.' It was the first time Aaron had ever acknowledged Garth as his progeny and it stopped him in his tracks.

'What?'

'I'm not going to shout. Come here.'

Puzzled, and more affected by being called 'son' than he could ever have imagined, Garth retraced his steps.

Aaron's eyes were narrowed; Garth looked straight into them, coal-black mirror images of his own.

'What?' he asked again.

'These things can be arranged. You know what I'm saying?' Aaron's voice was low and hard.

Garth frowned. 'You mean . . . ?'

'Some sort of accident. Nobody need ever be any the wiser. It still gets dark early. Just tell me where he can be found, and I'll see to it for you. Does he still live at home?'

'Not in the week. He lives in at the school where he's a pupil/teacher . . .'

'Where's that?'

'Wells – but hold on. I don't know about this . . .' Garth was shocked by Aaron's casual offer to get Lewis out of the way, and almost as shocked by his own initial reaction – one of revulsion at the very idea of agreeing to the murder of his half-brother. He hadn't known he had a conscience. Hadn't known that there were certain things he would draw the line at even if they would benefit him.

'The pub – yours, this month? A half share in it instead of only a third? Come on, son, this is your opportunity to make something of yourself.'

Son. He'd used that word again. But this time it didn't have any effect on Garth. He didn't know why Aaron was suddenly acknowledging him, or what he had to gain from his suggestion, but whatever it was, he didn't like it.

'I'll think about it,' he said.

'Don't take too long.'

Left alone, Aaron smiled to himself. If Garth took after him, it wouldn't take long for him to come around to realising this was an answer to all his frustration. And if he didn't . . . Aaron thought he could find out exactly where he could find Lewis Packer without too much trouble. And hasten the departure of Garth from the world where he, Aaron, had once been Crown Prince. And would be again. All it would take was the cunning to see the plan carried through to its conclusion.

* * *

269

Garth was thinking about Jeannie. Truth to tell he'd thought of little else since Conrad had interrupted his intended seduction and his desire for her was stronger than ever. He had to have her, and Elliot's decision to get rid of Belle and take on a new girl had given him an idea. Jeannie would make a perfect replacement for the aging hostess. The customers would love her, and if they were under the same roof he would have her exactly where he wanted her. All he had to do was convince Elliot what an asset she would be, and then extricate her from Martha's apron strings, but he wasn't particularly worried on either account. Elliot would be delighted with her and with the whole new clientele she was certain to attract, and as for Martha . . . she could rage all she liked, but in the end he was positive Jeannie would choose to come with him and Martha wouldn't be able to do a thing about it.

He'd talk to Elliot right away, he decided, before he had the chance to interview other prospective hostesses. Pulling on his jacket, he went in search of his employer.

'Well, I have to say, if she's a patch on how you describe her, this Jeannie sounds perfect.' Elliot puffed on his cigar.

'I promise you won't be disappointed,' Garth said.

'In that case, we can do no worse than give her a try-out. She can have Belle's room, unless of course you . . . ?' He raised an eyebrow at Garth, his unspoken meaning quite clear.

'No. I think it would be best if she had a room of her own, for the time being at any rate.' The last thing Garth wanted to do was frighten Jeannie off. Though she clearly adored him, her nervous disposition meant that it would be imperative to take things slowly. 'And I don't think it would be wise to expect her to perform *all* a hostess's duties just yet, if you take my meaning.'

Elliot smiled. 'She needs to be broken like a temperamental

filly. Well, I'm sure I can trust you to do that, Garth. Judging by the effect you seem to have on the gentle sex.'

'Trust me, Mr Marsh, it will be a pleasure. So when . . . ?'

'Well, clearly I have to get rid of Belle first. I can hardly tip her and her belongings out on to the pavement. She's been with us for a very long time and been a good worker, though admittedly she's past her best. I'll give her a week's notice and a month's wages to keep her going until she can find some other employment. And perhaps in the meantime you would like to speak to your young lady and make sure she is agreeable to what you suggest. Tomorrow, perhaps?'

Garth nodded, though he had no intention of forewarning Martha and perhaps giving her the chance to spirit Jeannie away somewhere where he would not find her. Better to wait until Belle's room was unoccupied and he could bring her straight back to Bath with him.

'Good. Now . . .' He glanced at his pocket watch. 'It's time we opened the doors and let our eager clients in. Will you do that, please, Garth?'

'Yes, sir.'

Garth left the salon to do as he was bid, feeling pleased with himself. Only a week to wait. He'd face Martha's fury, and Conrad's too, when he tried to take Jeannie away, he knew. But Garth was quite used to confrontation. He'd never shied away from a good scrap and he wasn't going to start now.

Especially when such a prize was dangling before him.

Ella was seeing a great deal of Monty, with Mrs Henderson's obvious approval. She had always treated Ella as if she were one of the family, not simply a hired help, and now she seemed only too delighted that Ella had a beau, even someone like Monty. In fact, Ella suspected she was secretly enjoying the relationship which would almost certainly be frowned upon by his family. She even loaned Ella a fur tippet and muff to protect her from the cold when Monty took her out in his motor, which was open to the elements. Ella enjoyed these jaunts enormously as she was treated to the sights of London. She saw Buckingham Palace and Horse Guards Parade, Nelson's column in Trafalgar Square and Eros in Piccadilly. They drove along the Thames when it was shrouded in fog, and when icy weather threatened to freeze it over, and the surface of the water shimmered under the stars.

Most exciting of all, he was going to take her to see a musical show at the new Gaiety theatre, built three years ago at the corner of Aldwych and the Strand to replace the old one which had been demolished so that the road could be widened.

When he told her the name of the show – *Two Naughty Boys* – Ella wasn't sure it would be suitable entertainment. She'd heard there were all kinds of 'naughty' in the music halls and theatres and she feared that Monty might be leading her into bad ways. But Mrs Henderson was quick to reassure her. The 'naughty boys' just got up to mischief and played tricks on people, she said, and, reassured, Ella looked forward to her first ever theatre visit.

She could scarcely believe the turn her life had taken – a workhouse orphan riding out in a grand motor with the son of a baronet at the wheel – and she was still nervous that she might let herself down in some way, even though she'd learned many of the ways of the gentry from the Hendersons. She felt guilty too that she was out so often living the high life while Mrs Henderson was at home with the children. Now that Mr Henderson had taken his seat in Parliament he was out much of the time, and sittings in the House meant it was often late before he returned. But Mrs Henderson was insistent. Ella was not to worry about it.

With typical generosity, when the day came for the visit to the Gaiety she loaned Ella yet another cape of saxe-blue wool and a little hat that sat jauntily on her upswept hair, and when Monty came in to collect her he beamed with pride.

'I shall be the envy of every man in the theatre,' he proclaimed.

Ella rarely blushed now at the things he said, but she blushed then, both for the compliment and for the way he took her arm, assisting her down the steps and handing her up into the motor.

When they arrived at the Gaiety Ella was astonished at the sheer size and grandeur of it. Standing between Aldwych and the Strand it extended along both streets, and the frontage, on the corner between, was topped by turrets and a great dome. Inside, all was sparkling chandeliers and plum-coloured plush, underfoot the carpeting was so deep Ella's feet seemed to sink into it. There was an orchestra in the pit beneath the stage, and tiers of circular seating rose above the stalls. But to Ella's amazement it was to a stage-side box that the usherette led them, with gilt spindle-legged chairs upholstered in the same plum-coloured plush, and a little table, on which stood a bottle of champagne in a wine cooler and two long-stemmed glasses.

'Monty!' she gasped, lost for words.

'Nothing but the best for you, my sweet,' he replied with a smile.

Even before she had taken her first sip of champagne, Ella felt quite intoxicated, gazing around at the fashionably dressed ladies and immaculate gentlemen, some even wearing tail coats. And as the plum velvet curtains rippled and the smell of the greasepaint floated out into the auditorium, she thought she would burst with excitement.

The show was everything she'd dreamed it would be, and more. There was laugh-out-loud comedy as the 'naughty boys' played their tricks on hapless stooges, there were songs and music and dancing, and there were spectacular scenes that left her breathless. Then, in the interval, when the flares illuminating the stage were dimmed and the chandelier that hung over the auditorium bathed the theatre in soft yellowish-white light, Monty refilled their glasses with sparkling champagne and took her hand.

'Ella, I have something to ask you.'

She turned to him, puzzled.

'We haven't known one another very long, and you may think it is far too soon. But I've known from the first moment I set eyes on you that you are the woman I want to spend my life with. Dearest, darling Ella, will you do me the honour of becoming my wife?'

Ella's jaw dropped. Surely, this must be a joke of some kind? He couldn't really be asking her to marry him? Not only was it barely two months since they had met, their kisses had been tender and chaste, he'd always been the perfect gentleman and she'd been grateful for it. After her childhood experiences with Rector Evans she wasn't at all sure how she would react if he was to try and take things further. Nevertheless, she simply couldn't believe he was actually proposing marriage when she'd never so much as glimpsed the sort of passion she imagined a man would feel for his intended. And besides . . .

'But I'm not in your class, Monty,' she said hesitantly, still half expecting him to laugh and make one of his flattering, but flippant, remarks.

Instead he drew a small box out of his pocket and opened it. Inside she saw a ring – a huge sparkling diamond set in gold – and her stomach fell away. He wasn't joking – unless this was nothing but paste. And it looked genuine enough, as if it had cost a small fortune.

'I don't care who you once were, or where you come from,' Monty said. 'I don't care if my family disown me! You are worth fifty of the pampered princesses that belong in the circles I move in. Give me your hand, Ella. And please, my darling, say you will marry me.'

Frozen with shock, Ella felt him slipping the ring on to her finger. And in that moment, all she could think of was that she wanted it to be Leo sitting beside her, asking her to marry him, slipping a ring on to her finger. It was ten years since she'd seen him, ten years since they'd whispered their last goodbyes, but he was still there in her heart. How could anyone ever take his place? Especially this man she scarcely knew, who had been born with a silver spoon in his mouth, and who possessed such a sense of entitlement that he expected her to accept his offer of marriage without hesitation.

'Monty . . . I'm sorry—' she began, but he pressed his fingers to her lips, stopping her words.

'Don't say anything just now, my darling. I've shocked you, and for that I'm sorry. Take your time to get used to the idea of the wonderful life we can share.' Now his fingers closed over the ring which she had been trying to take from her finger. 'Keep it. It's yours, whatever you may decide. If you refuse me I shall have no further use for it. I shall either take my own life, or live as a monk. I want no one but you, Ella.'

He was so serious and earnest Ella couldn't bring herself to turn him down flat, and in any case, if she did she might live to regret it. He was kind, generous, funny, she liked him a great deal, and she'd never have another offer that would give her the sort of life Monty could. She'd want for nothing. Nothing but Leo . . . But she had no idea of Leo's whereabouts,

275

and doubted they'd ever meet again.

'Can I think about it?' she asked hesitantly.

'Of course you can. Just as long as in the end your answer is yes.'

The house lights were dimming, the curtain rising again, but for Ella all the enjoyment had gone out of the evening. She felt trapped, frightened. She lifted the champagne glass to her lips with a hand that trembled, and this time, instead of the bubbles bursting sweetly on her tongue, she was left with an aftertaste that was bitter as gall.

Monty left her at the door of the house the Hendersons were renting with his usual chaste kiss, which Ella returned reluctantly. She went into the house, taking off her gloves and hat, and fully expecting Mrs Henderson to bombard her with a thousand questions. Ella didn't know what she was going to say to her, how much she was going to tell her. She wished she could simply slip up the stairs to her room, but she knew she couldn't do that – Mrs Henderson would be very hurt. And in any case, as she reached the parlour door, her employer appeared. But instead of an eager greeting, Mrs Henderson looked worried, and rather than asking how the evening had been, she took Ella's arm, leading her into the parlour.

'Sit down, my dear. Something has happened.'

Alarm coursed through Ella. 'The children?' she asked quickly, her first thought for her little charges.

'No, no.' Mrs Henderson waved a hand as if it were a fan. 'Nothing like that. There was a telephone call for you.'

'For me?' Ella was startled. She couldn't imagine who would call her, apart from Monty. And she had been with him the whole evening.

'Now, I don't want to alarm you, but it was your mother.'

'Martha? But they don't have a telephone.'

'Well, she must have gone to someone who has and used theirs.'

'But why?' Ella felt sick with dread now, as all manner of dreadful scenarios flashed before her eyes like pictures in a magic lantern show.

'It seems your sister has run off with someone called Garth, and your mother begged me to give you a few days off so that you can go home and try to sort things out.'

Ella shook her head, relieved that at least no one was dead, but also totally bewildered. Jeannie – and Garth? It made no sense. Yes, she knew Jeannie had always been besotted with him, but he hadn't lived at home for years, and as far as she knew was still working at the club in Bath.

'I don't understand . . .'

'Well, I promised your mother – Martha – that we would put you on a train first thing tomorrow, and when you see her I'm sure she'll make everything clear.'

As always, Ella's sense of duty came to the fore.

'But what about you and the children?'

'Don't worry about us. We'll manage,' Mrs Henderson said briskly. 'We have Myra now and she can help me out where necessary.' Myra was a maid the Hendersons had taken on just a few weeks ago. 'In any case, if your family need you, your place is with them. Now, why don't you have an early night so you'll be fresh to travel in the morning? I'll have Myra bring you a cup of warm milk.'

Ella wasn't at all sure she would be able to drink it. Her stomach was churning, whether from the champagne, Monty's unwelcome proposal, or the startling news that Jeannie had run off with Garth she didn't know. But she just nodded.

'Thank you.'

'I must ask you – how did your evening go?' Mrs Henderson had followed her to the door.

'Oh – it was . . . amazing,' Ella said, and made her escape up the stairs.

In her room, she took off the diamond ring Monty had given her, hid it in her handkerchief sachet and laid a pile of undergarments on top of it, immediately feeling that particular load lightening a little. She didn't want to look at the ring, and she certainly wasn't going to wear it if she was going home to Somerset tomorrow.

What a day! she thought as she climbed into bed and pulled the covers up to her chin against the chill of the night air. Her thoughts were racing in wild circles; she honestly didn't know which to think about first. And she couldn't imagine she would sleep a wink.

The only consolation in this whole mess was that at least if she was in Somerset, she wouldn't have to see Monty. With that thought, and the cup of warm milk, to comfort her, she did, at last, slip into sleep.

Chapter Eighteen

To Ella's surprise Martha was waiting on the platform when the train pulled into the main Bath station, standing at the top of the steps where she could not miss Ella as she left and anxiously scanning the passengers as they alighted.

'Oh, Ella, thank goodness you're here,' she said, enveloping her in a bear hug. 'I've been worried to death.'

'So what's happened?' Ella asked.

Martha straightened her tippet and took Ella's arm. 'Let's go and get a cup of tea and I'll tell you.'

They went down the stairs to the barrier where Martha handed her platform ticket to the railway employee who was manning the gate, and Ella rummaged in her bag for her own ticket. Once outside, Martha pointed out a tea stall. There was a wooden bench against the wall beside it and they sat down, cradling their mugs of steaming tea.

'I'm so sorry to have to drag you back from London, but I couldn't think what else to do,' Martha began. 'Did your Mrs Henderson tell you what's happened?'

'She said something about Jeannie running away.' Ella had been puzzling over Martha's message all the way to Bath, and wanted the full story.

'Yes. With Garth. You know she's always been sweet on him. The silly girl would do anything he told her to. He turned up one day out of the blue and told her he'd got a job for her and the first thing I knew of it was when she packed her bags and said she was going with him.'

'A job?' Ella said. 'What sort of a job?'

'Hostess at that club where he works. And you can guess just like I did what that means.'

'Oh my goodness.' Ella was horrified. When Mrs Henderson had told her Jeannie had run off with Garth she'd imagined they were going to get married. She hadn't been very pleased about that – she didn't like Garth, and had never trusted him – but this was far worse than anything she could have imagined. Her beautiful, naive sister a 'hostess'. Yes, Ella could guess what that entailed; being pawed at by a lot of dirty old men. And with her inexperience of the big wide world she would have no idea of what that could lead to.

'Exactly,' Martha said grimly. 'I tried to tell her, but she wouldn't listen to me, and you were the only one I could think of who might be able to make her see sense.'

'Where is she now?' Ella asked.

'At that club, I suppose,' Martha huffed. 'That's why I came to Bath to meet you. I thought we could go straight there. I don't want her in that place another day if I can help it.'

Ella couldn't have agreed more. 'Do you know where it is?' she asked.

'I've got a pretty good idea. It's not far. Just up there.' She nodded her head in the direction of a street that ran at right angles to the station approach.

'Will it be open at this time of day?' According to the clock set into the station façade it was just after eleven.

'I don't know, but all the better if it's not. We don't want to make a scene in front of a whole lot of customers. Somebody will let us in, I shouldn't wonder.'

They finished their tea, took the mugs back to the tea stall and set off in the direction Martha had indicated.

These days the frontage of the building – tall, and built of Bath stone – was a far cry from its days as a low-class betting den. The door was freshly painted, the bell and the tastefully engraved brass plate proclaiming 'Marsh's' gleamed and the doorsteps had clearly been recently scrubbed. The curtain nets at the front windows made it impossible to see inside, but they were sparkling white, not grey from coal dust or brown from cigarette smoke as so many such hangings were. Martha tugged on the bell and a few moments later the sound of footsteps in the hallway could be heard. She gave Ella a satisfied nod, then squared her shoulders and drew herself up to her full height.

The young man who opened the door was slightly built, his face pockmarked from ancient acne scars.

'We're here to see Jeannie Martin,' Martha announced without preamble.

'Oh!' The young man seemed taken aback, and when he hesitated, Martha put a booted foot in the door.

'Come on, my lad, look lively.'

'But who . . . ?' The young man still looked uncertain and confused. Not the sharpest knife in the box, Martha thought.

'This is her sister, and I'm her mother,' she said, not relinquishing an inch. 'Please fetch her, or I'll have your tonsils on toast.'

As he retreated, Martha nodded in satisfaction, and when he disappeared up the stairs she pushed the door fully open and stepped into the vestibule, nodding at Ella to follow her. She had not the slightest intention of being turned away without first talking to Jeannie.

The door leading into the salon was open. Ella stepped aside, peering in, and was horrified at the artwork adorning the walls. The naked satyrs and nymphs gambolling in the large, gilt-framed pictures left her in no doubt as to what went on behind closed doors in this establishment.

'Ella?' Jeannie was on the stairs. 'What are you doing here?'

'Jeannie!'

Ella hurried across the vestibule and opened her arms, expecting her sister to run into them as she always did. But Jeannie stopped, standing perfectly still, her turquoise eyes wide and confused. To Ella's relief she was at least decently clothed in a ruffled blouse and long dark skirt that she had never seen before, though of course that was no indicator of what her sister changed into when the club opened its doors. She was alarmed, too, by Jeannie's vacant expression. Was it possible she'd been given laudanum?

'I just want to talk to you, Jeannie,' she said gently. 'Come down, please. It's so long since we saw one another.'

For a long moment Jeannie hesitated, then she came down the last few stairs slowly, as if in a trance. Ella reached out and took her hand. 'Why don't we go home?'

Instantly, Jeannie snatched her hand away. 'This is my home now.'

'It's not, Jeannie,' Ella said. 'This is no place for you.'

Jeannie pouted. 'It's Garth's home, so it's mine. He's going to look after me.'

'Jeannie – he's not—' Ella broke off, uncertain as to how to tell her that Garth was the last person she should trust, and at that very moment a door at the end of the passage opened.

'What the hell is going on here?' It was Garth, his voice aggressive, his muscles tense.

'We've come to take Jeannie home,' Martha said.

'I don't think so.' Garth advanced along the passage. 'Didn't she make it clear to you the other day? She wants to be here, with me, don't you, angel?'

'Yes.' Jeannie pushed past Ella and Martha and ran to him, clutching his arm as she had once clutched Ella's sleeve, and staring defiantly at her sister. 'You went and left me. You didn't even come home for Seb's funeral. I needed you, Ella, and you weren't there. But Garth was. And he always will be.'

Ella recoiled as if her sister had struck her. 'Oh, Jeannie, I'm so sorry,' she said, all the guilt and desperation she was feeling apparent in her urgent, desperate tone. 'Please, my love, don't do this. I'll give notice to the Hendersons and come home. I'll never leave you again, I promise.'

'Too late,' Garth said harshly.

'At least let's talk about it,' Ella said, ignoring him.

But Jeannie only turned her face into Garth's broad chest.

Holding on to her with one arm he backed towards the door he had come in through and pushed it open with the other.

'Mr Marsh!' he called, and a moment later the club owner appeared.

'What's wrong?'

'These people are trying to talk Jeannie into leaving. Tell them to get out, or so help me, I'll make 'em.'

'Garth!' Martha exploded. 'I'm not "these people". I am your mother! And Ella is Jeannie's sister.'

'Good gracious!' Elliot's tone was silky. 'Of course! It's been twenty years and more, but you've hardly changed at all. You're still a fine-looking woman.'

Martha stared at him, recognition dawning. It was the man who had been at the Feathers with Aaron the night he'd raped her. The one she'd called 'Spider'. The man to whom Joe had owed money. The man Aaron had said was his employer. He'd

283

aged, of course, but he was still dapper, well-dressed and upright. Still the same smooth operator. Aaron must still work for him. And Garth had brought Jeannie into this den of iniquity, under the same roof as the men who might well have ruined her life if it hadn't been for Seb.

'I remember you,' she said with heavy deliberation. 'As if I could ever forget. Well, I won't leave Jeannie here to suffer the same fate as I did. I'm taking her home, where she belongs.'

'Martha.' He even remembered her name, though she supposed it was likely Garth had talked about her when he'd come to work for him. 'Jeannie is happy here, and I am very happy to have her. She's a beautiful girl, and a great favourite with my clients. In fact, I'd be very sorry to lose her.'

'This is no place for a young innocent girl,' Martha said staunchly. 'You should know that as well as I do.'

Elliot smiled, an oily, self-satisfied smile. 'She's perfectly safe here. Despite what you might think I keep an orderly and reputable establishment – some of the members are the most influential citizens of Bath. Why, even the mayor—'

Martha snorted. 'High office doesn't guarantee high morals.'

'Possibly not, but I give you my word I will personally ensure Jeannie comes to no harm.' He turned to Jeannie, whose head was still buried in Garth's shirt front. 'You don't want to leave, do you, my dear?'

Jeannie shook her head violently. 'No.' Although her voice was muffled, there could be no mistaking her reply.

'So.' Elliot spread his hands as if to emphasise how right he was. 'Shall we agree to leave things as they are, for the time being, at any rate?'

Martha, and Ella too, knew they were beaten. They could hardly drag Jeannie away by force, and it was clear she had no intention of going with them of her own free will.

'Just mind you do take good care of her, or you'll have me to answer to,' Martha said, and Ella echoed her.

'Me too.'

In the doorway she looked back one last time at her sister, but afterwards the thing she remembered most was the satisfied smirk on Garth's face over the top of Jeannie's head.

'It's all right, they've gone,' Garth said, gently easing Jeannie away from him.

'Really?'

'Really.' He turned to Elliot. 'Thanks, Mr Marsh. They weren't going to take any notice of me.'

Elliot smiled thinly. 'I have to protect my assets.'

'Of course you do. And so do I. I'm going to take Jeannie up to her room. All this has upset her.' He took her by the hand and led her upstairs.

Although she had only occupied the room for less than a week, Jeannie had already made it her own. Her toiletries were laid out on the dressing table and marble-topped washstand, her lace-trimmed, heart-shaped nightgown case propped against the pillow alongside a rag doll. Garth moved them to the bedside chair, sat her down on the bed, and sat beside her.

'Come on, Jeannie. There's nothing to be afraid of now.'

She didn't reply, reaching out to retrieve the rag doll and hugging it to her.

Gently, he eased it away from her. 'You don't need that. You've got me.'

He put an arm around her, pulling her close, and she melted into him, her head buried in his shoulder. He stroked her hair away from her face and ran a finger around her ear, tugging at the lobe from which dangled a long ear-bob, and around her jawline. As she shifted her head slightly towards him he touched

285

her lips too, and felt them part beneath his probing finger.

He lifted her head and lowered his own, kissing her tenderly and only inserting his tongue where his finger had been when he felt her responding.

It wasn't in Garth's nature to take time with preliminaries, but he knew he couldn't rush Jeannie. Though he burned with desire for her he had so far done nothing more than kiss her. Fragile as she was, she had to be led, not taken by force. She saw him as her protector, and that was the way it had to remain or she would most likely panic and maybe even turn against him. Garth didn't want that to happen. Jeannie was a prize he intended to win. What was more, she was a bargaining chip should he need one with Elliot. The club owner saw her as a huge asset to his establishment, though it would take time before she realised her full potential. For the moment her greatest attraction, besides her stunning looks, was her innocent naivety. That needed to be preserved as far as was possible and the combination of it with the tricks and skills he would teach her would be irresistible. But the introduction would have to be made slowly and carefully, so that she came to enjoy, not fear, the experience.

For long minutes he kissed and caressed her before tentatively moving his hand to the fastening of her blouse and to his relief she did not protest. Small tremors ran through her as he found her nipple and teased it until it stood upright within its rosy areola. Satisfied that it was safe to go further he rucked up her skirt and ran his fingers up her thigh until they reached her most secret places and a small moan escaped her as a sharp pain that, if it had been a sound, might have been the scrape of chalk on a blackboard, shot deep inside her. And still she did not pull herself away.

So, as he had suspected, she was a virgin. He thought that if he wanted to he could take her now and she would not be unwilling, but he restrained himself. He had gone far enough for today. But as he whispered endearments into the soft skin of her throat he was already looking forward to what would inevitably follow as the 'lessons' progressed. He'd have her all to himself for as long as it took to prepare for what would eventually become Jeannie's stock in trade.

Martha and Ella said their goodbyes at the station entrance. Desperately worried about Jeannie and also Martha, who was visibly upset, Ella had wanted to go home with her to the Feathers, but Martha had insisted she take the train back to London.

'There's nothing you can do here, and you don't want to upset the Hendersons. It's a good job, Ella. You can't afford to lose it.'

'But what about you?' Ella had asked. 'Are you all right to go home on your own?'

'Course I am,' Martha huffed. 'Don't you worry about me. I can take care of myself.'

'If you're sure . . . I suppose I ought to get back. Mrs Henderson will have her hands full with only the one maid to help her look after the children.'

But she was unwilling to leave, all the same. She felt as if she was abandoning the sister she'd sworn to protect, and also Martha who had been like a mother to both of them.

'I might give it another go in a week or so,' Martha said. 'The gilt might have worn off the gingerbread by then. And I'll let you know, of course, what happens. Now, you'd better get up those stairs if you don't want to miss the train, and I'd better be getting back to Fossecombe. Ivy promised to come over to the Feathers and help Conrad out in case anyone wants feeding at dinner time, but she won't want to stay any longer than she has to.' She hugged Ella. 'Just you take care of yourself, my girl.'

Ella hugged her back. 'You too.'

She could feel tears threatening, and with a little wave she turned and walked into the station.

'Oh, Mammy, I'm so sorry,' she whispered silently as she climbed the stairs to the platform. 'I've failed Jeannie, and now I'm turning my back on her. But what else can I do?'

For once there was no answering voice inside her head to comfort her as there so often was when she talked to Mammy, and Ella felt as if her heart would break.

Lewis emerged from the school in Wells where he was a pupil teacher. Part of his time was spent taking lessons from Mr Fellowes, the headmaster, and part in taking classes himself. That was what he had been doing this morning: attempting to teach twenty small boys their times tables. They'd progressed to the six-times, and he'd written it on the blackboard and listened to the young voices chanting their way through it. He only hoped they'd remember what they'd learned tomorrow when Mr Fellowes came to test them on it.

It was dinner break now, though. Lewis had eaten with some of the boys at one of the long trestle tables set out in the school hall – beef stew, followed by spotted dick. He wasn't on playground duty today, and with a half-hour or so to himself he'd decided to take a short walk and get some fresh air.

A man was leaning against the low wall on the other side of the road smoking a cigarette, but Lewis barely noticed him. He walked down the road, past the cathedral, and on to the Bishop's Palace. He often spent his free time walking in the beautiful grounds, and watching the swans in the moat who had been taught to pull on a rope attached to a bell when they wanted feeding. It was only as he turned away from the moat that he saw what looked like the same man lurking in the shrubbery. Lewis frowned. Strange. As he left the grounds, walking back up the road towards the school, he glanced over his shoulder. He saw the man was also on the pavement, though some way behind him, but when he crossed the road and looked again there was no sign of him. Nevertheless, Lewis still felt inexplicably uncomfortable. There'd been a rough-looking character in Vicar's Close, the ancient cobbled lane where he had lodgings, yesterday. Lewis had assumed he was a workman, there to make repairs to one of the centuries-old houses, or perhaps even a beggar or a tramp. But now he wondered.

Was it possible the man was following him? On the face of it, it seemed highly unlikely. For what reason would he do such a thing? It couldn't be that the man intended to rob him – it would be clear to anyone that Lewis had nothing worth stealing.

No, it must simply be coincidence, Lewis thought. But he decided to keep an eye out in future, and if he saw him again he might report it to Mr Fellowes. Garth, of course, would have walked straight up to him and demanded to know what he was doing, Lewis thought with a wry smile. Not him. If there was anything fishy about the man he'd leave it to someone else to deal with it.

Like Lewis, Conrad wasn't one to invite trouble, but unlike his brother he wasn't afraid to meet it head on if the occasion arose or if he was roused to anger. That seldom happened – he had inherited Seb's philosophical approach to most situations. But he had also inherited the furious temper Seb could be driven to when he was finally roused. And just now, Conrad was steaming with fury.

'I'm going to Bath myself!' he declared when Martha got

home, distressed and despondent. 'I should have gone before, but I thought if anyone could persuade Jeannie to come home it was Ella.'

'So did I. But it didn't work, and she wouldn't listen to you either. Garth's got her exactly where he wants her.'

'We'll see about that.' He reached for his coat, hanging on a peg behind the door, and shrugged into it. 'We can't leave her there any longer, Mam. You know what she can be like. She never sees danger, or bad in anybody.'

Martha caught at Conrad's sleeve. 'Don't do it, Conrad. You'll only make things worse.'

'How could they be worse than they are now?' Conrad shook her off.

'You won't change her mind, and goodness knows what sort of reception you'll get. You wouldn't stand a chance against Garth, never mind Aaron Walters.'

'Sorry, Mam, but I can't just sit back and do nothing. If harm comes to Jeannie I'd never forgive myself.'

With that Conrad stormed out, leaving Martha more worried than ever.

Darkness had fallen and Conrad had still not returned.

'Something's happened to him, I know it,' Martha said to Ivy, who had stayed on to help her despite her need to get home. At times like this the family had always stood together. 'I warned him, but he wouldn't listen. Trouble is, he's always been sweet on Jeannie, and she's always been sweet on Garth.'

'Well, I can't argue with that.' Ivy had seen it, just as her sister had, and she'd often thought it was a shame it wasn't Ella Conrad had taken a fancy to. She was hard-working and level-headed, loyal and warm-hearted. But there was something about Jeannie besides her good looks that seemed to draw men like bees to a honeypot, and Conrad was no exception.

'I suppose I'd better go and open up,' Martha said. It was the last thing she wanted to do, but she couldn't have customers waiting outside the door. They wouldn't like it, and neither would Sergeant Love if he happened to pass by.

She went through the bar, unlocked the front door and opened it for a quick look out. As she did so it rammed back into her, almost knocking her off balance, as if someone was pushing on it from the other side. There didn't appear to be anyone there, but when she managed to get it open she was horrified to see a body slumped against the door.

'Oh my Lord, Conrad!' she exclaimed, dropping to her knees beside him. 'Oh, whatever . . . ?'

'Sorry, Mam.' His words were slurred.

Her first thought was that he had been drinking, but by the light shining out from the bar she could see that his hair was matted with blood and his hands, struggling to get a purchase on the doorframe and pull himself up, were crusted with it too.

'Ivy! Can you come and help me?' Martha called. She knew that if Conrad couldn't get up she'd never be able to manage to get him inside on her own.

Luckily, at that moment Howard Clark, one of their regulars, appeared out of the night. He was a farm labourer, big and strong, with muscles that bulged beneath his jacket.

'It's all right, Ivy, Mr Clark can do it,' she called over her shoulder.

Howard hoisted Conrad to his feet and half-carried him into the bar. 'What in the world have you been up to, lad?' he asked, sitting him down on a chair.

'Had a bit of a scrap, I think,' Martha said flatly. 'Could you get him in the kitchen, do you think? He can't be in here when the bar's open.'

The last thing Martha wanted was for anyone else to see Conrad in this state, and she certainly didn't want her family affairs aired in public. Doubtless Howard would be full of it when his drinking companions arrived, and the least said in front of him the better.

'Ivy, can you get Mr Clark a drink on the house and look after the bar for a bit?' she asked her sister when Conrad was installed in the kitchen.

'Yeah, course I can.'

'And thanks for your help, Mr Clark.'

Left alone with Conrad, Martha shook her head in horror at the state of him. His face was a bloody mess, one eye closed, a cut above it trickling scarlet on to the already discoloured swelling. His lip was swollen and cut too, and there was a nasty gash on his head. He groaned and clutched his ribs whenever he tried to move, and Martha wondered if one or more or them was broken. Certainly his breathing was shallow, as if trying to breathe deeply was painful.

She fetched the old tea caddy that contained lint, gauze and cotton wool along with a bottle of disinfectant, and filled a basin with warm water, chuntering all the while.

'I told you not to go there. I knew what would happen if you did. But would you listen? No. You knew best. Now look at the state of you! You won't be able to show your face in the bar for a week at least. And how did you get home? You never walked!'

'They brought me,' Conrad mumbled through his thick lips.

'Who? Who brought you? Not our Garth?'

'No.' Conrad winced as his mother dabbed at the cut on his head with cotton wool soaked in warm water and disinfectant. 'Some young chap – Kelvin, I think they called him.'

'Well, at least they had the decency to bring you home after they'd given you a hiding.' Martha rinsed the cotton wool and began dabbing at the cut above his eye.

'They wouldn't have, I don't suppose, if I wasn't passed out on the steps in front of the club,' Conrad said. 'They left me there till it was time to open up. They didn't want their fancy punters having to pass that.'

'Oh, Conrad.' Martha's anger had been the product of her hours of anxiety. Now, tending to her son's wounds, it died away as quickly as it had come, leaving her upset and wretched. 'I don't suppose you even got to see Jeannie, did you?'

He shook his head. 'No. The minute I asked for her they just laid into me.'

'I told you, Conrad. For the minute there's nothing we can do. We've just got to bide our time and hope she comes to her senses.'

'Let's hope that's not too late.'

'Amen to that,' Martha said. 'And now, when you're up to it, let's get you to bed.'

Chapter Nineteen

'You're not wearing your ring, my love.' Monty took Ella's hand in his, stroking her bare knuckle and looking at her reproachfully.

'No. Because I haven't given you my answer yet,' Ella said, her tone short. So worried was she about Jeannie she could think of nothing else. The last thing she wanted was to be drawn into another conversation about Monty's proposal but that, it seemed, was inevitable.

They were seated in Monty's car outside a grand restaurant where he had reserved a table. Given the choice, she wouldn't have been here at all, but Monty had made the arrangements with Mrs Henderson in her absence, and she hadn't been able to think of a way to get out of it.

'It would mean so much to me to see it on your finger,' he wheedled. 'I want the world to know you're mine.'

Ella felt a stab of irritation. Until now she'd allowed herself to be swept along, flattered that someone like him should be interested in her, and entranced by the glittering world he was introducing her to. Now, suddenly, he struck her as a little pathetic. A spoiled rich boy who thought he was entitled to have everything he wanted and on his terms.

'I'm not yours, Monty,' she said. 'Not yet, anyway, and perhaps never.'

'Don't say that, my sweet! Don't torture this poor lovelorn man!' He looked to be on the verge of tears, which only made her more impatient.

'I'm sorry,' she said. 'I don't mean to torture you, but I have to be sure it's the right thing before I can agree to anything, and I have a lot of other things on my mind at the moment.'

'What things? Tell me!' he demanded.

Ella bit her lip.

When she'd returned from Bath she'd confided what had happened to Mrs Henderson, who had been sympathetic and kind, even offering Ella extended leave of absence from her position so that she could go home and try once more to sort things out – an offer Ella had refused since she couldn't see that it would do any good and she didn't want to leave her employer in the lurch. But her pride wouldn't let her tell Monty. It wasn't so much that she was actually ashamed, more that she didn't want to divulge her family's private problems.

'I don't want to talk about it,' she said, not looking at him.

'Ella, darling, how can I help you if you won't talk to me?' He was wheedling again.

'It's private.'

'But if we are to be married there should be no secrets between us.'

Suddenly, Ella had had enough. She didn't love this man and at the moment she wasn't sure she even liked him. And it wasn't as if there was any passion between them. There wasn't. She was beginning to think there was something wrong with him. Those chaste kisses that he never tried to take further – it just wasn't natural. All he seemed to want was to treat her like a precious and delicate china doll, and to have her adore him in return.

'Please, Monty, take me home,' she said.

'But . . . my sweet . . . a table is reserved for us . . .' He gestured helplessly towards the building where soft lights glowed at the windows.

'I don't care.' Ella was adamant. 'Take me home or I'll get out and walk.'

To her relief he got out and started the motor without another word and they drove back to the Hendersons' in silence. Whether he was just sulking, or whether he was fighting a losing battle with the tears she'd thought were threatening, she didn't know. She didn't look at him to find out.

When they drew up outside the house he turned to her, wheedling again.

'I'll call you tomorrow, my love. Perhaps you'll be feeling more yourself by then.'

'Please don't,' Ella said. She got out of the motor without waiting for him to help her, and fled up the steps to the front door.

'Ella! What on earth is wrong? I thought you were going out to dinner.'

Mrs Henderson was just coming down the stairs – from the nursery, Ella supposed – and met her in the hallway.

'I wasn't hungry,' Ella said truthfully. Since coming back from Somerset she'd had no appetite at all. 'And I've told Monty I don't want to see him again,' she added.

'Oh my dear! But I thought . . .'

'So did he. But it just doesn't feel right.'

'Let's go and sit down, have a nice cup of hot chocolate – or perhaps a small sherry if you'd like one? All this trouble with your sister has upset you and it's bound to colour the way you feel about everything.'

'Perhaps,' Ella acknowledged.

'I meant it when I said that if you want to go home again it's perfectly fine with me.'

'I know. And it's really kind of you. But I honestly don't think there's anything more I can do at the moment. Better that I keep busy.'

'Well, if you're sure . . . come along.' She steered Ella into the parlour, poured sherry from the crystal decanter into two matching glasses that normally surrounded it on its silver platter, and handed Ella one.

'Drink this. There's nothing like a sherry to cheer one up, I find.'

Ella sipped, the sweet dark liquid warming her throat as it slipped effortlessly down.

'I hope Monty hasn't behaved inappropriately towards you,' Mrs Henderson said, taking her usual chair.

Ella shook her head. *Quite the opposite*, she thought, but merely said: 'No. He's always the perfect gentleman. It's just that . . . well, the truth of the matter is, I think, that I'm in love with someone else.'

'Oh, I see.' Mrs Henderson's eyes opened wide in surprise. 'I didn't know . . .'

'It's no use,' Ella said. 'It's idiotic of me, I know. Nothing can ever come of it. But . . .' Her voice trailed away.

'Do you want to talk about it?' Mrs Henderson asked.

Thinking that perhaps it was the sherry that had loosened her tongue, Ella told her.

Conrad was nursing more than painful cuts, bruises and a cracked rib. In fact, he would have willingly endured all the punishment he had taken and more if only he had been able to bring Jeannie home, and the pain in his heart was far worse than any of his other injuries.

Looking back, he couldn't be sure exactly when he'd discovered he had feelings for Jeannie. For a long time she'd simply been the little girl his mother had taken in. He'd always felt protective of her, she was so small and delicate; while Ella seemed well able to take care of herself, he'd known instinctively how vulnerable Jeannie was. But somehow he'd never been needed as her knight in shining armour. If she was bullied at school, Ella was always there to fly to her defence; at home she followed Garth around like a puppy dog and he was surprisingly tolerant of her, given his wild and belligerent nature. Now, however, all that had changed.

He'd opened his eyes one day and the pretty little girl had grown into a stunningly beautiful young woman, yet still every bit as vulnerable as she had ever been. There was an other-worldliness about her that reawakened the old urge to protect her, and sparked a magnetic attraction that had turned affection into a raging fire. He'd walked out with a few other girls – still did until his father's death had tied him to the Feathers – but none of them could hold a candle to her. Yet he'd done nothing about it. Though they'd become quite close walking together to Hillsbridge to work and home again, he knew she was still besotted with Garth, and he was afraid their relationship would be totally ruined if he let her know his true feelings. He'd taken her hand sometimes as they walked along the road between the fields of open farmland but her innocent trust in him was enough to stop him from trying to take things further. Somehow, despite her undeniably womanly curves, inside she was still a child.

And so when Garth had appeared on the scene and whisked her off to Bath, Conrad was not only furious but horrified. He had no illusions about the life his half-brother intended introducing her into. Along with Martha he'd done his best to stop her from going with him, but to no avail. She was as blind as ever where Garth was concerned; she'd have followed wherever he led, as if he were the Pied Piper and she was one of the children of Hamelin. And like them she was surely heading towards disaster.

When Martha had told him Ella was coming to Bath to try to talk some sense into her sister he'd been in high hopes that she would be successful. If anyone could make Jeannie listen it was Ella. Perhaps she'd even be able to explain to Jeannie just what it was that she would, in all likelihood, be expected to do. He'd tried, but she had only looked puzzled and he hadn't been able to find the words to enlighten her. When Martha had returned, dreadfully upset that their mission had been unsuccessful, he'd seen red and gone straight to Bath himself. And all he'd got for his trouble was an unholy beating. He'd been no match for Garth and his father; they'd humiliated him and dumped him unceremoniously outside the club, where he'd collapsed on the step, but not before he'd caught a glimpse of the decadent room that led off the hallway that confirmed all his worst suspicions about the place.

Now, Conrad burned with shame that he had been helpless to do anything to rescue Jeannie from that pit of iniquity, a shame that ran in a deep vein beneath the outward manifestation of fury. What sort of a man was he? No wonder it was Garth Jeannie was in love with. Garth, who was more than capable of looking after her. And equally capable of ruining her.

Despairing, Conrad buried his bruised and bloodied face in his hands. He hadn't cried since he was a little boy, and not often then. He'd always been scornful of Lewis's ready tears. Now his throat ached and his eyes burned and he knew it would take all his will power not to weep now. But what good would that do?

And what good would trying again do? If Jeannie was

determined to stay in that awful place there was nothing he could do, and if he tried he might well make things worse. All he could hope for was that she would come to her senses before long. Before it was too late.

Martha, too, was wracked with guilt that she was unable to protect the girl she thought of as her own daughter, a reincarnation almost of her beloved little Lily, and also that she had failed Garth. She'd tried so hard with him, to steer him away from the traits she had always feared had been inherited from his father, to make him feel secure and loved, to teach him decency and respect. She'd been too soft with him, she acknowledged that now, making excuses for him, hiding the worst of his misdemeanours from Seb. Would he have turned out differently if she had been more strict, less forgiving? She'd never know now. But she suspected not. The apple never fell far from the tree, as the saying went. Bad blood ran in Garth's veins and nothing she could have done would have prevented him turning out the way he had. And yet still she felt guilty. Sad, too, that his birthright had been such a toxic one. And angry that he could behave as he had. He'd cheated. Stolen. Beaten his brother to a pulp. And he was prepared to use Jeannie for his own ends. Of all the things he had done, it was that which hurt the most.

For the first time in her life Martha wished she could curl up in a ball like a hibernating hedgehog and retreat from the world. But she couldn't. She still had her responsibilities and it wasn't in her nature to give up on them. But all the same . . .

Oh, Seb! Martha moaned silently. Why did you have to leave me?

He had been her rock, and now he was gone.

Somehow she had to face all the trials and tribulations alone. She didn't know how she was going to manage it.

* * *

Garth eased himself out of Jeannie's embrace and turned his head to look at her. Her golden hair had fanned out on the pillow, her long black lashes lay on her faintly flushed cheeks like butterfly wings. Sleeping, she looked softer, younger, and even more beautiful.

No wonder Elliot was delighted with having her as a hostess and his clientele impatient to have her do more than bring them their drinks and listen to their chit-chat. But not yet, Garth thought. She was learning well, but he didn't think she was ready yet, and he didn't want her to be. He was enjoying teaching her, and enjoying having her all to himself. He didn't want to share her with anyone, especially the well-to-do lechers who made up the club membership. It couldn't last for ever, but he was going to stretch it out as long as possible.

It wasn't only the punters he was wary of though – he'd seen the way his father looked at her too and he didn't like it one bit. So far she'd been safe – Aaron would know only too well how furious Elliot would be if he jumped the gun, frightened her, and undid all the good work he, Garth, had done, and Aaron couldn't afford to upset Elliot. But afterwards, when she became available to anyone whose fancy she took, it would be a different story and the thought of his father having his way with her was anathema to him.

He loathed Aaron. He'd been so eager to meet his real father, but the way Aaron had treated him had turned him completely. He might have changed his tune since he'd found out Garth was to inherit a share in the Feathers and tried to worm his way in, but it was too late and Garth felt only contempt for him.

Now, as he looked at the sleeping Jeannie and felt the warmth of her body through her thin shift as she curled against him,

Garth experienced a very different emotion, one that was completely foreign to him. Tenderness.

You bloody fool, he berated himself. You don't go soft on any woman. You can't trust them any more than you can trust a man – there's only one person you can trust in this world, and that's yourself. And you'd do well to remember the other reason you brought her here. A bargaining chip to keep Elliot sweet.

With an effort he hardened his heart, turned his back on her and closed his eyes. But the sweet haunting smell of her was still in his nostrils, and Garth wondered what the hell was the matter with him.

In a dark alley just a few hundred yards from Marsh's club, Aaron was meeting with a man he knew as 'Pounds'. His nickname arose from the fact that he'd once been a policeman, pounding the beat, one of those who'd turned a blind eye to the gaming and whoring that went on behind closed doors. But he'd blotted his copy book and been dismissed from the force in disgrace. Nowadays he earned his living on the wrong side of the law.

'So. What news have you got for me about the Packer kid?'

'Not as much as I'd hoped for.' Pounds drew on a cigarette held in his cupped hand. 'For a start, I had to be sure which one was him. There's a lot of boys more or less his age at that school. I had a word with one of the groundsmen – an old pal of mine – and he pointed him out to me. But I've only seen him the once on his own, and that was in broad daylight with a lot of people about. He went down to the Bishop's Palace, walked round the moat, then went back to the school again. And he's usually with a couple of other chaps on his way to and from his lodgings.'

'Not good enough, Pounds,' Aaron said grimly.

'I don't know what you expect me to do about it,' the former policeman grumbled. 'I'm not going to do for him with witnesses around, am I?'

'How you do it is up to you. That's what I'm paying you for. But if you don't come up with the goods soon this nice little earner won't be paying for your beer and whisky chasers any more. Understand?' He dropped the cigarette he had been smoking on to the ground and stubbed it out with the toe of his boot.

Pounds shrugged. 'Better to call it off than finish up doing a stretch – or being a dead weight on the end of the hangman's noose.'

'A long stretch behind bars is exactly what you'll be looking at if you don't do what I want,' Aaron threatened. 'If I told what I knew about what you've been up to since you left the force your feet wouldn't touch the ground. So – can I count on you?'

'I'll do my best,' Pounds said dispiritedly.

'Right then. Make sure you do.'

Aaron walked back down the street to the club and wondered if this plan of his was worth pursuing. He wasn't getting very far with Garth, the young man was still hostile towards him in spite of his best efforts and he'd intimated that he intended to sell his share of the Feathers rather than going back there and running it. Aaron wondered if he should go after Pounds and call the whole thing off. But when he looked round there was no sign of the former policeman.

Chapter Twenty

A week later Conrad celebrated his twenty-first birthday. His ribs were still painful, especially if he had to lift a heavy barrel of beer, his lip still swollen, and the bruise beneath his eye still clearly visible though it had faded from ugly purple to a mixture of green, yellow and grey. When the regulars had first seen it it had caused quite a stir, but by now the jokes came less frequently and curiosity as to how he had sustained his injuries had died down.

Though neither of their hearts were in it, he and Martha had shared a celebratory glass of cider before the lunchtime opening, and when customers began arriving Martha told them their first drink was on the house.

'What's this in aid of? What be we celebrating?' Joey Miller, an old miner who was very hard of hearing, asked in the booming voice that had got louder and louder as he became more and more deaf.

'Conrad's twenty-one today.' Ben Chivers shouted his reply and gesticulated for good measure. 'He's just got the key to the door.'

'But not to the pub.'

Garth stood in the doorway, Jeannie beside him and clinging to his arm.

'Not till Lewis is twenty-one too. Where is the little bugger? Conrad, I mean. The birthday boy.'

His tone was jovial, and perhaps Martha was the only one who recognised the bitterness that lay behind it.

'He's just gone across the yard,' she said, mouthing 'the lav' before changing the subject. 'Well, Garth, this is a nice surprise. We didn't expect to see you today. Or Jeannie.'

'Couldn't let my brother's big day pass by and not pay him a visit, could I? I've even got him a present.' He held up a package tied with a ribbon which Martha knew must have been wrapped by Jeannie.

At that moment Conrad appeared, his jaw dropping when he saw his brother and Jeannie. Garth pushed his way between the tables, slapping him on the back.

'So, congratulations are in order. Not a kid any more. Now we just have to wait for Lewis, and I can get my hands on my share.' He winked at Conrad.

The customers were exchanging surprised and curious glances, all except Joey who asked loudly: 'What be goin' on?' None of them knew the contents of Seb's will, and Martha was not best pleased that they should find out like this.

'What d'you want to drink, Garth?' she asked, hoping it would keep him quiet. 'And what about you, Jeannie love? My, it's good to see you.'

'I'll have a pint, and Jeannie will have a half of shandy.'

'Why don't you and Conrad go through to the sitting room?' Martha suggested. 'I'll bring your drinks through.'

'What for?' Garth asked. He turned to Conrad. 'Though I don't suppose you're keen on showing your face out here. Not a pretty sight.'

'Thanks to your father,' Conrad growled.

Martha had had enough of this washing of dirty linen in

public. 'Go on, both of you. And try to be civil to one another.' She ushered them unceremoniously into the sitting room.

Jeannie gave her a quick, guilty smile, then scuttled after Garth, clutching at his coat tail. She was embarrassed, Martha guessed, and not only by the scene the brothers had caused. She was probably ashamed by the abrupt way she had left for Bath, the way Martha and Ella had been treated when they'd followed her, and the terrible beating Conrad had been given.

She only hoped leaving them alone together wouldn't lead to more fisticuffs, but at least if it did it would be out of sight of the customers.

'Look, I'm sorry about what happened to you, but you asked for it,' Garth said when the door was closed after them. 'You got no business trying to force Jeannie to come back here against her will. She'll visit when she wants to. She's here now, isn't she?'

Conrad lowered his eyes, glaring at Garth's highly polished boots and burning with fury. He knew very well why Garth had brought her with him. It wasn't enough that she knew Conrad was no match for him and Aaron, that he'd beaten him to a pulp and left him on the steps of the club. No, he had to parade her obvious devotion to him, glory in his triumph over his brother, sneer at his humiliation. And there was not a thing he could do about it. But worse was to come.

'Oh – we got you a birthday present,' Garth went on, holding out the parcel.

'I don't want your presents,' Conrad muttered.

'Course you do.' When Conrad made no move to take the parcel, Garth pulled off the ribbon, letting it drift to the floor, and tore open the wrapping paper to reveal a pair of boxing gloves which he thrust at Conrad with a smirk. 'Here you are. We thought they might come in useful.'

As if the so-called present wasn't bad enough, the 'we' was the last straw – Garth was intimating that Jeannie was in agreement with the cruel jibe. Conrad hurled the gloves across the room, almost knocking over a glass jug that stood on the sideboard.

'Get out.' He strode to the door, throwing it open. 'Just get out, you bastard.'

Smirking, Garth took Jeannie's arm. 'Come on, love. We know where we aren't wanted.' In the doorway he stopped, looking back at Conrad.

'Just one more thing. I ought to warn you, when Lewis comes of age and we get our inheritance, I've no intention of moving back here to run this place. I shall want my third share in cash. I don't much care how you get it, but if you have to sell, just don't include the cottage. I'm reliably informed Martha can live there and it will be within the terms of the will. Right, Jeannie. Let's get out of here.'

Conrad didn't tell Martha about the boxing gloves. He took them out and stuffed them deep into the rubbish bin, and he didn't tell her about Conrad's parting shot. He didn't think she would have heard above the chatter in the bar, and he didn't want to upset her. The Feathers had been in the Packer family for generations and Seb had left it to his three sons in the expectation that they would keep it going for those to come. Besides which, it was her home. He couldn't imagine she'd want to live in the cottage if the pub was under new ownership. But eventually she wormed it out of him and she was as horrified as he was.

'He wants to sell the Feathers?'

'Well, he made it pretty clear he wants his share when the time comes and I can't see how we could afford to buy him out.'

'Oh Garth,' Martha groaned, burying her face in her hands. 'What have you done to us?'

'Same as he always has,' Conrad said bitterly.

Martha could only shake her head in despair. It was what *she* had done to the family that upset her most. Seb had promised her all those years ago that he would treat Garth as his own, and he'd kept his word. But Garth had never shown the slightest gratitude, and now he was tearing their world apart. Jeannie . . . gone to who-knew-what sort of life. The Feathers . . . gone. Or would be when Lewis reached maturity. Burdened down by grief and guilt, Martha felt she had reached her lowest ebb.

Two weeks later

Pounds had decided he had to have one last try at getting to Lewis Packer. He hadn't seen Aaron since the night he'd met him in the alley, and he was short on other work that brought him enough to live on. He was still very dubious about the job, but his wife was beginning to complain that her housekeeping was running short – certainly not enough to keep her in the gin she enjoyed of an evening, and she hadn't had anything new to wear in a very long time. When his wife was unhappy, she made sure Pounds was unhappy too, and set about making his life a misery. So, determining he was going to take no unnecessary risks, Pounds went back to Wells.

To begin with it had seemed the same hopeless quest. Lewis was rarely alone, and when he was the circumstances were such that it would have been reckless to attack him. What was more, the days were beginning to draw out and when he left the school in the late afternoons it was mostly still daylight. And then one day the opportunity presented itself.

The school day was over and most of the boys and masters had left, but a light was still burning at one window, and when Pounds crept up to it, climbing on to a handy bench to peer inside, he saw Lewis still at the teacher's desk at the front of the classroom working on a pile of exercise books. Pounds watched for a few minutes. Lewis was marking the class's work, he supposed, and there appeared to be quite a lot of it.

Pounds withdrew into the shadows; he didn't want to be apprehended as a Peeping Tom. He wondered if he might be able to get into the school and the classroom without being seen. But he didn't want to take the risk of running into someone who might still be elsewhere on the premises. Instead, he hid in the bushes that lined the path to the main door and waited.

When he'd been sacked from the force he'd managed to keep hold of his truncheon by saying he'd lost it and it had come in handy on more than one occasion in his new career. Now he drew it out, rolling the thick wooden handle in the palm of his hand. He was almost ready to give up when the light in the classroom went off and the school was in darkness. Pounds felt a rush of adrenalin as he firmed up his grip on his truncheon and watched the door.

There was a gas lamp beside it; when it opened Pounds was able to see that it was indeed Lewis who was coming out, carrying a satchel. Pounds waited until Lewis was past him, then moved with a silent speed that those who didn't know him well would have been hard pressed to credit him with. He raised his truncheon, ready to bring it down hard on the young man's head, but at the last moment conscience got the better of him. He'd done some pretty dirty work for Aaron in his time, but never murder. Somehow he managed to divert his blow so that it landed on the lad's shoulder, but that was enough to make him stumble and fall headlong with a cry of pain, and at that very moment the figure of a man appeared at the far end of the path. Pounds dived for the cover of the bushes, forced his way through them and ran, into the darkness beyond. When he stopped to catch his breath there was no sign of any pursuer. As he approached the road he slowed his pace, not wanting to attract attention to himself by undue haste.

His pulses were racing in time with the thump-thump of his heart. Bloody hell, but that had been a close one! There and then Pounds made up his mind. This had to be the last time he undertook anything like this. The wife could moan all she liked and he'd have to put up with it as he always did, though there'd been little love lost between them for years. Even that miserable existence was better than spending the rest of his life in jail, or, worse, swinging on the end of a rope. Let Aaron Walters do his own dirty work in future.

From now on Pounds was going to stick to jobs that carried much lighter sentences if he was unlucky enough to get caught.

Martha was about to open the pub when there was a knock on the door.

'All right, all right,' she called. 'It's only just seven.'

'Police!' came the reply.

'Oh my Lord, what now!' Martha turned the key and opened the door.

She didn't recognise the policeman on the doorstep, nor the motor drawn up outside with the engine still running. There were few motors in Hillsbridge and she was sure the local police didn't own one.

'Mrs Packer?' the policeman enquired.

'Yes. That's me.'

'And Lewis Packer is your son?' Martha nodded, and he went on: 'I'm sorry to be the bearer of bad news, but he's been assaulted.'

Martha's hand flew to her mouth. 'You mean he's hurt?'

'I'm afraid so, yes. He's been taken to hospital and the doctor lent me his motor so I could come and fetch you.'

Although her heart had plummeted like a stone and her blood turned to ice, as always in times of crisis Martha collected herself swiftly.

'Let me just get my coat.' Leaving the policeman on the doorstep she hurried inside.

'Conrad!' she called up the stairs.

Conrad, who had been in a lot of pain after working until the Feathers closed at two, had gone to his room to rest. Now, in his stockinged feet, he came to the top of the stairs.

'What?'

'Lewis has met with some sort of accident. He's in hospital in Wells and there's a policeman come to take me down there.'

'Oh blimey. You want me to come with you? Or open the pub?'

'Neither,' Martha said firmly. 'You're in no fit state. Just put a notice on the door saying we're closed due to unforeseen circumstances, lock up and go back to bed. I'll take a key.'

'But . . . how will you get back?'

'Don't worry about that. They might bring me back, you never know. If not I expect I can get a cab. There's sure to be somebody in Wells with one. But I don't know what time that will be. I might have to stay till the morning.'

'Are you sure you don't want me to come with you?'

'No. Just rest and try to get fit. You might be needed in the next few days. Now, I must go.'

She grabbed her coat and bag and hurried out to the waiting motor.

* * *

'I think it's about time Jeannie began earning her keep. We've kept Alderman Bagshaw waiting quite long enough.'

Elliot had called Garth into his office, where he sat behind his desk, a tumbler of whisky within easy reach. Today, however, he didn't suggest Garth join him, a sign that this interview was strictly business.

Garth shuddered inwardly at the thought of the paunchy, elderly alderman with his moist palms and slobbering lips having Jeannie. His Jeannie, as he'd come to think of her.

'I'm not sure she's ready,' he said.

'Tommyrot. You've had her to yourself for quite long enough. If she's not ready by now she never will be.' He took a pull of his whisky. 'Haven't you told her yet what's expected of her?'

Garth didn't reply.

'Well, you'd better have a word in her ear pretty damn quick,' Elliot went on. 'I've promised Bagshaw, tonight's the night. I want her down here in her lowest-cut dress by eight at the latest. And she'd better be nice to him, or I'll hold you responsible.'

Garth lowered his eyes and nodded that he understood. Elliot was the boss. There was no arguing with him.

'Off you go then. And remember – eight sharp. No later.'

Knowing he had been dismissed, Garth went in search of Jeannie.

'Ready, love?'

Somehow, Garth kept his voice even. He had never seen Jeannie look more beautiful. The scarlet satin dress with its off-the-shoulder neckline was a perfect foil for her creamy skin, and a black sash tied tightly showed off her tiny waist. She'd blackened her long lashes and brushed her cheeks with a little rouge, just enough to give her a faint blush. And her turquoise eyes sparkled with her pleasure at having been chosen to entertain such an important man.

Garth didn't think she knew, though, what that entertainment was meant to be. He hadn't been able to bring himself to tell her. He'd simply said the alderman had requested her company. 'If you are agreeable to him you'll be well rewarded,' was the closest he had come to telling her the truth, and, to his shame, he'd added: 'Will you do this for me?'

She'd nodded, slipping her hand trustingly into his, and he'd had to remind himself that this was the reason he'd brought her here to the club in the first place. He just hadn't realised how much he would mind when the time came for her to fulfil her purpose. He'd thought he'd be able to let her go as easily as he did all his women. *You're going soft, you fool*, he told himself, and led her down the stairs to the salon.

The alderman was there, seated on one of the velvet chaises, and Elliot was with him. He smiled approvingly as Garth and Jeannie entered, and the alderman's eyes lit up.

'Beautiful, my dear!' he murmured, taking her hand and raising it to his lips. 'I'm sure you and I are going to get along very well indeed.'

'Good. I'll leave you now, and Garth can show you to the boudoir.' Elliot glanced at Garth, smirking, and Garth knew he was enjoying this. Like his father before him he had come to realise how happy mischief-making made Elliot.

Reluctantly, Garth led them to a small anteroom, one of several that was furnished especially for the purpose of gentlemen taking their pleasure with the hostesses. Here the decor was also red velvet – a banquette and drapes – and a chandelier with ten candles cast a soft light.

Jeannie whirled around, alarm in her eyes. Perhaps she had

313

heard from the other girls what went on in these anterooms, perhaps she had suddenly realised it for herself.

'Garth?'

He hardened his heart. 'You'll be all right, Jeannie. Just be nice to the gentleman and everything will be fine.'

Then there was nothing for it but to leave and close the door behind him.

There were some clients at the front door; Garth had to go and let them in. When he had taken their coats and escorted them either to the salon or the gaming rooms he went back into the passageway, glancing at the closed door. All seemed to be quiet, though he knew any sounds coming from behind it would be muffled by the heavy drapes and possibly drowned by the chamber music that was playing on the gramophone in the salon.

Then suddenly all hell broke loose. The door flew open and Jeannie came rushing out. She was sobbing, her hair had come loose from its pins and her dress sagged where it had been torn from her shoulder. Behind her in the doorway stood the alderman, red in the face and similarly dishevelled.

'Jeannie!' Garth tried to catch her, but she pushed him away.

'No! Don't touch me! Let me go . . .'

Before he could stop her she had fled for the stairs. Garth spread his hands helplessly in the direction of the disappointed alderman, and ran after her.

She had reached her room before he could catch her and was trying to close the door in his face. He was able to push it open easily – even hysterical as she was she had no chance of holding it closed against Garth. As he tried to take her in his arms she beat at his chest with both hands.

'No! No! Don't! Leave me alone!'

Garth realised that by delivering her to the alderman he had, in her eyes, become the enemy. Part of what had happened to her in that room.

'Jeannie, I won't hurt you. I love you.' Even as he said it he knew it was no more than the truth. But, in the grip of hysteria, she was beyond understanding him.

Again he tried to comfort her, again she pushed him away, sobbing, and he knew what he had to do.

He caught her firmly by both arms, forcing them behind her back, and looked down into her tear-stained face.

'It's going to be all right, Jeannie, I promise. Just calm down, and I'll take you home.'

She was still struggling as he propelled her down the stairs and out of the door. The motor was at the kerb outside and somehow he got her into it where she subsided against the leather seat, still whimpering, but at least no longer sobbing or fighting him.

'Stay here. I'm taking you home,' he said again. 'Do you understand?'

Her gaze was still unfocused and she didn't respond, and Garth had no choice but to trust she'd remain where she was while he started the motor, and to his relief, she did. He climbed up into the driver's seat, let off the brakes, and pulled away, heading for the road that would take them to the Feathers.

The hospital was in almost complete darkness, with just dim lights showing at some of the windows. Only the reception area was well lit. The policeman rang a bell on the counter and a nurse came bustling out.

'This is Mrs Packer,' the policeman said. 'Her son, Lewis, was brought in earlier and Dr Jordan lent me his car to go and fetch her.'

'How is he?' Martha asked urgently. She'd asked the policeman on the drive to Wells what had happened, and how badly hurt Lewis was, but he had been unable to supply her with any answers.

'All I know is he's been assaulted,' he had said. 'He was already on his way to hospital when I was informed, and I haven't had the chance to speak to him yet. And Dr Jordan was too busy attending to him to say anything besides that I should take his car and come for you.'

Now she got no answer from the nurse either. 'I'll fetch the doctor,' was all she said.

Martha felt sick with trepidation. In her experience it was usually a doctor who delivered bad news, and when he finally appeared, she braced herself, clasping her bag tightly to her chest as if to ward off what she was terribly afraid was coming.

Dr Jordan was a man of about her own age, tall, thin and slightly stooped, and with a long, lugubrious face, and she couldn't decide if it was his normal expression or if he had adopted it because of the news he had to impart.

'Doctor . . . ?' She couldn't bring herself to ask the question yet again.

'Mrs Packer. Thank you for coming.' His voice was doleful too.

'Well, thank *you* for getting me here,' she said. 'But . . . look, I'm worried to death. Can I see my boy?'

'All in good time, Mrs Packer. I have to confess when I sent for you I was seriously concerned about your son. His shoulder is shattered, but that wasn't my greatest concern. He was concussed, from striking the ground with his head when he fell, I imagine, and a bleed on the brain would be a very serious matter. However, he has now regained consciousness, and although he's still a little confused I'm satisfied he should make a full recovery.'

'Thank the Lord for that!'

'We'll have to keep him in for a few days at least, of course, until we're sure there are no complications, and to deal with his shoulder injury. But at least you'll know he's in good hands. And now – I expect you'd like to see him.' Martha nodded vigorously. 'Come with me, then. If you can talk to him, and he hears a familiar voice, it may well help him to regain his senses.'

Martha followed him along a corridor to a side ward that was also brightly lit. It must be at the rear of the building, the reason the light hadn't been visible from the approach. Lewis was lying in the bed, his head heavily bandaged so he resembled a one-eyed Egyptian mummy, and his right arm was suspended in a sling. He seemed to be asleep.

Martha moved across to the bedside, then quickly sat down on a chair beside him when her legs felt suddenly as if they would no longer support her. She took his good hand in hers and leaned towards him.

'Lewis? It's me. Mam.'

He opened his visible eye and moved his head on the pillow to look at her with a puzzled expression. But at least he recognised her even without his spectacles, which had been broken in the fall.

'Mam? What are you doing here?'

'You've had a bit of an accident. That's why I'm here. And it's no good asking me what happened because I don't know. I wasn't there.'

'I don't know either. I'd finished marking some exercise books, and I was going home, and I don't remember anything after that until I woke up here . . .'

'Never mind. I expect it will all come back to you. Just rest now. I'll stay with you for a bit, make sure those nurses look after you, and you don't play them up.'

A faint smile played on Lewis's lips. 'There's one I quite fancy playing up. She's a corker and no mistake. Trouble is, I've done something to my shoulder. It hurts like billy-o. But you don't need to stay if you don't want to. I'm all right, and you ought to be getting home. How did you get here anyway?' he asked as an afterthought.

'A policeman brought me, in the doctor's car. But I can't expect him to take me home again. I'll have to call a cab.'

'You'll do nothing of the sort.' Dr Jordan spoke from the doorway. 'PC Lomax will be only too happy to take the opportunity to drive my motor again, I'm sure. He's still here, having a cup of tea, but I've told him I don't want him interviewing Lewis tonight.'

'I would be grateful,' Martha said. Now she knew Lewis was all right, and in good hands, she was anxious to get home. She'd come back tomorrow. It would be a long day and exhaustion was beginning to take its toll on her.

Besides which she was worried about Conrad. She could scarcely believe that both her boys had been subjected to attack, and she couldn't understand why when neither of them were troublemakers.

She stayed at Lewis's bedside until the constable appeared and asked if she was ready to go, then kissed Lewis, and followed him out to the car.

The Feathers was all in darkness, but as Martha walked across the forecourt she was surprised to see a light flickering behind the net curtains at the cottage window. Had Conrad gone over there for some reason? But what? As she drew nearer she could see the door was ajar. Suspicious now, she wondered if some tramp had broken in to find a place to sleep.

Before investigating, she went into the Feathers and found

her umbrella in the stand by the door. Then she crossed the yard again and pushed the cottage door wide open.

'Who's there?' she called, brandishing the umbrella.

There was no reply. Cautiously, she stepped inside. The door opened directly into the little living room and by the light of the oil lamp which always stood on the dresser, and which was now alight, she saw a figure huddling against the far wall.

'Jeannie?' she said, disbelieving. 'Jeannie, is that you?'

No reply, but somehow Martha knew it was her, unlikely as it seemed. She picked up the oil lamp and its soft glow illuminated a dark shape in the middle of the floor. What in the world . . . ? She lowered the lamp to investigate and gasped in horror.

A body lay sprawled on the flagged floor, surrounded by a pool of something dark and sticky. A big body, tall and broad, and motionless, clad in a dark evening suit. Coal-black hair gleamed in the light thrown by the oil lamp.

'Garth?' Without seeing his face, she knew it was him. All the blood seemed to leave her body in a rush and her legs threatened to give way beneath her. She looked up again and held the lamp high so that it shone on the cowering figure.

She'd been right. It was Jeannie. And in her bloodstained hands she held one of Granny Packer's kitchen knives.

Somehow, she found her voice. 'It's all right, Jeannie. It's me – Martha.' Slowly she moved towards the shivering girl, who wore nothing but a scarlet satin gown, which hung loosely down over one arm so that her breast was almost exposed. 'What's happened, Jeannie?'

But she thought she knew. Why the two of them were here in the cottage was a mystery, but the reason for the knife, the bloodied body on the floor and the traumatised girl came to her in a flash as she relived the night Aaron Walters had raped her.

Like father, like son.

She'd taken in Jeannie and Ella to save them from abuse in the form of the disgusting Rector Evans, but the danger had been here too. In that moment Martha's mind was made up. She couldn't let Jeannie take the blame for this. Whatever it cost her she'd ensure the girl didn't suffer for what she'd done to protect herself.

'Give me the knife, Jeannie,' she said.

Still Jeannie remained motionless and silent, and Martha wrested it from the girl's cold, trembling hand. Then she took her across the yard and into the Feathers, stirred the fire to life and sat her down in front of it, wrapping a blanket round Jeannie's bare shoulders and washing her bloody hands in a bowl of hot water. Then she made her a cup of warm milk and held it to her lips. After a while, the trembling lessened, but still Jeannie said not a word.

Martha went upstairs and woke a sleeping Conrad.

'Something terrible has happened,' she said. 'Jeannie's here and she's in a dreadful state. Will you come down and look after her? I have to go out.'

'What . . . ?' Bleary from sleep, Conrad could make no sense of what his mother was saying. But the mention of Jeannie's name was enough to get him out of bed.

'You'll find out soon enough. Just don't let Jeannie go anywhere near the cottage.'

With that Martha left and started the long walk into Hillsbridge and the police station.

Chapter Twenty-One

Horror-stricken, Ella stared at the contents of the telegram that had just been delivered to the Hendersons' home.

'This can't be true! There must be some mistake!'

'What is it, my dear?' Mrs Henderson, who had been feeding Teddy, looked up, alarmed.

'It's from Conrad. He says Garth is dead, and Martha has confessed to killing him. Garth's her son! She'd never harm him! Never, in a million years!'

'Let me see.' Mrs Henderson held out her hand and Ella passed her the telegram. She read it, and shook her head.

'That's what it says, certainly. But that is just terrible.'

'It must be a mistake surely? I just can't believe it. Is it some sort of awful prank?'

'I'd hardly think so.' Mrs Henderson eased Teddy, who was almost asleep, off her breast, and cradled him in her lap. 'But there's only one way to find out. You must go home at once. No!' She raised a hand to brook any protest. 'No arguments this time, Ella. You absolutely must.'

Ella nodded. Since she had left Somerset it seemed everything about her old life had fallen apart. Seb, dead. Jeannie hightailing it to Bath to what Ella very much feared would be her ruination. And now this.

'I think you're right. I can believe Garth has got himself murdered. He's always been a wild one, and now he's involved with some awful people. But Martha . . . never! She hasn't a violent bone in her body, and she loves Garth so much. If she's been arrested they've got it all wrong somehow.'

'Go and pack a bag. I'll call a cab – or perhaps Monty would take you?'

'No, not Monty,' Ella said quickly. She knew Mrs Henderson was hoping that she would come around and make up with Monty, but he was the last person she wanted around just now.

As she stuffed a change of clothes and toiletries into her carpet bag, Ella thought of the ring he had given her, still hidden in her handkerchief sachet. She'd have to return it to him soon, but it would have to wait for the present. By the time she was ready, a cab was waiting at the kerb. She kissed the children, hugged Mrs Henderson, and hurried out to it.

'Paddington, please,' she said. And was on her way.

Fossecombe, and Hillsbridge too, were awash with gossip and rumour. Miners on their way to work in the Hillsbridge pits had seen a lone constable stationed outside the Feathers, a farmhand going in the opposite direction reported what looked like a mortuary wagon on the forecourt, and mothers taking their children to school were passed by a motor driven by a moustached gentlemen with Sergeant Love and another man as passengers. Later, the motor was seen parked outside the pub, but Sergeant Love and the two gentlemen were nowhere to be seen.

When Alice Love, the sergeant's wife, went out for a loaf of bread and a jug of milk, she told the shop assistant that her husband had been woken up in the middle of the night by Martha Packer.

'I don't know what was going on, Will didn't tell me,' she said, somewhat miffed, 'but a motor turned up a bit later. Will and Martha Packer went off in it – I know because when I heard it I looked out the bedroom window – and Will still hasn't come home.'

Back at the police station, she cooked some breakfast for herself and Will in the hope that he wouldn't be too much longer, but she'd eaten hers and his was keeping warm in the fireside oven before she heard him come in.

'Whatever is going on that's kept you all this time?' she asked.

'A bad business, Alice.' The sergeant sighed, taking off his helmet and putting it down on the kitchen table. 'Is that bacon I can smell?'

'Yes. I'll do you an egg now you're here.' She cracked one into the pan, poured him a cup of tea from the pot which was sitting on the hob. 'Well, are you going to tell me or not?'

He loosened his collar and took a sip of tea. 'There's been a murder.'

'What?' Her eyes widened. 'Not at the Feathers?'

'Yes. Well, in the cottage. Garth Packer – you know, the one that's been nothing but a worry to Martha since he was a nipper.'

Alice's hand went to her throat. 'He's killed somebody?'

'No, he's the one that's been killed. Stabbed, with a kitchen knife.'

'What . . . one of his cronies?' The egg was cooked now; Alice slid it on to the plate alongside the bacon and set it down in front of her husband,

'No. I could understand it if it was.' Sergeant Love picked up his fork, speared a piece of bacon and dipped it into the egg yolk. But suddenly he was no longer hungry. 'According to what she told me, it was Martha. She reckons she killed her own son.'

* * *

Conrad was at the sitting room table, his fingers pressed to his temples as if they could somehow steady his churning thoughts. Opposite him sat a thick-set, red-faced man with a handlebar moustache and bushy eyebrows who had introduced himself as Inspector Turner.

'There's nothing I can tell you. I was in bed and asleep. I didn't even know Garth and Jeannie were here, and I don't know why. They both live and work at a club called Marsh's in Bath.'

The policeman made a note on his pad. 'Marsh's. Go on.'

'All I can tell you is the first I knew that anything was wrong was when Mam woke me up and said she had to go out.'

'And she didn't tell you why?'

'No. She had to go to Wells earlier on – my brother Lewis had been attacked and taken to hospital. But she didn't say why she was going out again, and I was half-asleep and didn't ask,' Conrad said, implying that he had thought it had something to do with Lewis. It was a close approximation of the truth, but he didn't mention that she had asked him to look after Jeannie, and not let her go near the cottage. If possible, he wanted to keep her out of it. She was in a terrible state, catatonic almost, and Conrad's every instinct was to protect her.

Unfortunately, however, at that moment a board creaked overhead, and the inspector looked up sharply from the notes he was making.

'Is there someone else in the house?'

'No . . .' Lies didn't come naturally to Conrad, and in any case the board creaked again.

'The truth, please, Mr Packer.'

Conrad flushed with guilt. 'It's only Jeannie. My adopted sister. She doesn't know anything either.'

'I'd like to speak to her all the same.'

'She's in no fit state,' Conrad said.

'And why is that?'

Conrad brought his fists down hard on the table. 'Garth is dead. Mam's been arrested. Isn't that enough?'

'It's possible your sister witnessed what happened. Please fetch her.'

Reluctantly Conrad rose and went through the bar and up the stairs. He wasn't going to simply call her down. He needed to prepare her. But he had an awful suspicion the inspector might well be right.

Jeannie was on the landing, huddled in a corner. Her arms, clutching a crocheted shawl, were wrapped around herself and she seemed to be staring into space. She was dressed now in one of her old woollen skirts and a high-necked blouse that he had laid out for her. Through her open bedroom door he could see the scarlet satin gown lying in a heap on the floor.

He went to her, putting an arm around her shoulders. 'Jeannie, there's nothing to be afraid of, but the policeman wants to ask you some questions.' She shrank away. 'Come on, my love,' he urged her. 'I'll be right there beside you.'

He felt her body go rigid beneath his arm, a tremor running through her petite frame. Then suddenly she went limp and would have fallen if he had not been supporting her. He half-carried her into her bedroom and sat her down on the edge of the bed, then stuffed the crimson gown into her wardrobe out of sight and went back downstairs.

'It's no use. I can't get her down here. If you want to speak to her you'll have to come up.'

The inspector sighed deeply but he rose and made for the stairs. Conrad followed. There was no way he was going to leave her alone with the policeman.

Jennie Felton

As he went into Jeannie's room he noticed that the wardrobe door had come partially open as it sometimes did if it wasn't fastened securely. But thankfully the inspector's eyes were on Jeannie. Conrad crossed to the wardrobe, leaned against the door to close it, and then surreptitiously turned the little key in the lock.

Jeannie had shuffled back against the bedhead and was gazing at the inspector like a frightened fawn facing a predator. He went to her, sat down on the bed and took her hand.

'I'm here, Jeannie. I'm here.'

The inspector gave him a stern look. 'If I allow you to stay, I won't expect you to interrupt or prompt the young lady in any way.' He turned to Jeannie, and when he spoke he adopted a softer tone.

'So you are Jeannie Packer?'

Jeannie inched a little further away, but didn't correct him.

'Her name's Martin,' Conrad said. 'Jeannie Martin.'

The inspector shot him a look, then returned his gaze to Jeannie. 'I want to ask you about last night. Where were you when it happened?'

Still Jeannie made no reply.

'Did you see Garth Packer at all?'

Jeannie's lip trembled. She balled up her fist and stuck her thumb in her mouth as she had done as a child, but remained silent.

The inspector persisted, but his every question elicited the same response, and eventually Conrad could stay silent no longer.

'Can't you see this is getting you nowhere?' he demanded. 'Like I told you, she's in no fit state, and you're only upsetting her more. She needs a doctor, that's what she needs, not to be bullied like this.'

The inspector huffed with frustration and annoyance. 'Well, get her a doctor then. But her behaviour suggests she knows a good deal about what led to Mr Packer's death and I can assure you that when she's come to her senses I shall want to speak to her again. At Bath police station.' He rose from the bedside chair on which he had been sitting. 'Make no mistake of it, you will tell me what you know or you'll be charged with obstructing justice and will likely get a prison sentence.'

With that parting shot he headed for the stairs and after a concerned backward look at Jeannie, Conrad followed him.

'Can't you see she knows nothing about this?' he said when they were back in the sitting room.

'Frankly, no. She's putting on an act to conceal something, and so, I believe, are you. I suggest you think very carefully about your response, and advise Miss Martin to do the same. In the meantime I am going back to Bath. Effectively, this crime is solved. We have a confession from the perpetrator. But that doesn't mean I don't intend to make it watertight, and neither does it mean I'm not looking for accomplices. Be warned, Mr Packer.'

When the policeman had left, Conrad fetched himself a stiff drink from the bar. This was a living nightmare. He only hoped Ella had received the wire he'd sent and would be able to get home soon.

Thank God, he thought, for Sergeant Love. After he'd delivered Martha to Bath police station in the company of the officer who had been sent to collect them, they'd brought him back, along with a constable to secure the scene until investigations could begin, and the police surgeon on call. When the doctor had done all he needed to do, Sergeant Love had overseen the removal of Garth's body and stayed for a cup of tea and a glass of whisky. And before he left he'd promised Conrad that he would visit the post office and send a telegram to Ella, telling her what had happened, and asking her to come home.

He hadn't disturbed Jeannie, whom Conrad had put to bed. He hadn't speculated or cast aspersions. He simply looked very sad, as if he accepted that Garth had somehow eventually driven Martha beyond the limits of reason. Or attacked her, and she'd acted in self-defence.

What story was she telling? Conrad wondered. If he knew he might be able to back it up. Clearly the inspector didn't believe he knew nothing, and the same went for Jeannie. With good reason, Conrad thought. He didn't know if shock had caused her to lose her memory or if she remembered only too well and had retreated deep into herself to escape it. But sooner or later the inspector was going to want to question her and there was always the danger that he'd get something out of her that could tip the balance of the case.

Was Mam guilty – or innocent? Garth was dead. No disputing that. And he hadn't killed himself.

Murder – or manslaughter? Such a fine line to make the difference between a prison sentence and the death penalty.

Conrad drained his glass and poured himself another. Drinking the profits, Mam would call it. But he thought he was going to need it, and more, before this was over.

As the train pulled into Bath station, Ella found herself remembering the last time she had made this journey to try and talk Jeannie into coming home.

Was it possible Martha had come to Bath to try again and there had been some sort of altercation? The telegram hadn't said where Garth had been killed, or how, but after what had happened that day she couldn't imagine he would have gone to the Feathers. That it had happened here, in Bath, was the only explanation that made any sense. But she still couldn't believe Martha would have done such a thing. However angry she might be about Garth, however worried about Jeannie, she just didn't have it in her.

A few cabs were waiting outside the station. Ella approached one of them and was soon on her way to Fossecombe. As they passed the end of the road where the workhouse was situated she glanced towards it and shuddered, wondering if conditions there were still as bad and pitying the poor folk who had no other home. Then, as they emerged into open countryside, she thought of the seemingly endless walk she and Jeannie had set out on the night they had run away. How on earth had they managed it, two little girls all alone? And how lucky they had been to find refuge at the Feathers! How kind and generous Martha had been! No, whatever the provocation, Ella simply couldn't see that Martha could have been responsible for Garth's death.

As the cab drew up outside the Feathers Ella's heart came into her mouth. She'd given up on the vague hope that there was some awful mistake but she had no idea what she was going to have to face and she just didn't feel ready for it. But somehow she had to. She paid the cabbie and walked up to the main door.

The notice Conrad had pinned to it was still there, and still just about readable though a storm of rain during the night had made some of the letters run. 'Closed Due to Unforeseen Circumstances'. Well, that was one way to describe it, Ella thought, not knowing that it referred to Martha going to Wells Hospital to see Lewis and Conrad was unfit to look after the bar because he, too, had been injured. But she should have guessed the pub would be all locked up, and went around to the kitchen door instead, rapping on it loudly.

At first there was no answer and she knocked again. A face appeared at the window. Conrad. But Ella gasped at the state of him, the bruises and the swelling that had still not subsided. What on earth had happened? Had he somehow been involved in Garth's death?

Recognising her, Conrad came to the door and opened it.

'Oh, Ella, thank God you're here.' Besides his injuries, he looked like a man at the end of his tether. 'You got my wire, then?'

Ella nodded. 'I don't understand any of it though, Conrad. Let's go in, and you can tell me what's happened.'

She went into the kitchen and Conrad shut the door and locked it.

'Let me get you something to drink first. The kettle's on the boil.'

Ella saw the bottle of whisky and tumbler on the counter and thought she could do with something stronger herself.

'We've got some sherry, I presume?'

'Course.' He went through to the bar and returned with a bottle of Harvey's Bristol Cream, the very brand she'd come to like through sharing a drink with Mrs Henderson.

Ella poured herself a generous measure and sipped it, grateful for the warmth that spread through her like a comfort blanket.

'So. Tell me. I'm guessing from the state of your face that you and Garth got in a fight.'

Conrad touched his face gingerly. 'Well, yes, though it was his father, Aaron, who caused most of the damage. And that was a couple of weeks ago. I went to Bath to try and fetch Jeannie home, and the bastard gave me a beating for my trouble.'

'Oh, Conrad. And you didn't have any success with Jeannie, I suppose?'

'No. But let me start at the beginning. The night before last a policeman came to take Mam to Wells. Lewis had been assaulted, and was in hospital.'

'What!' This just got worse and worse. '*Lewis?* Don't tell me he's mixed up in this too?'

'Not as far as I know. Mam never got the chance to tell me about it.'

'Is he still in hospital?'

'They're keeping him in for a couple of days but he's what they call "comfortable", or at least that's what Dr Blackmore said – he was here just now . . .' He broke off, not wanting to tell Ella about Jeannie for the moment. 'Anyway, I'd shut the pub and gone to bed – I wasn't feeling too good – and the next thing I knew Mam was back and calling up the stairs saying she had to go out. I didn't know what the hell was going on. She was gone some time – she must have walked all the way to Hillsbridge – and when she came back Sergeant Love and another policeman were with her. And she said she'd killed Garth, over in the cottage.'

'The cottage? I thought it must have happened in Bath! What was he doing out here? And why were they in the cottage?'

'Search me. But . . .' The moment had come. He couldn't put it off any longer. 'All I can tell you is Jeannie was with them.'

Ella's eyes widened. 'Jeannie?' It seemed unbelievable that Jeannie should have come home of her own free will. 'Well . . . didn't she say what happened? Is she here now?'

She half-rose from her chair. Conrad laid a hand on her arm.

'She's in her room, resting. She's terribly upset, and Dr Blackmore gave her something to help her sleep.'

Ella shook herself free of Conrad's grasp. 'I must go to her.'

'Leave her for a bit. I don't think she's slept at all since . . . well, whatever happened. If she can get some rest she might be more like herself when she wakes up.'

331

'I won't disturb her if she's asleep,' Ella said. 'But I must see her.'

Again, Conrad took hold of her arm. 'There's something you need to know, Ella. It's not only that she hasn't slept. She hasn't spoken either.'

Ella swung round to face him. 'What do you mean, she hasn't spoken?'

'I can't get a word out of her, and nor could Dr Blackmore or the detective. It's like she's locked up inside herself. Dr Blackmore thinks it's because she's in shock. That's why I'm so glad you're here. I don't know what to do with her, but if she'll talk to anybody, it's you.'

Ella nodded, a thousand thoughts and emotions making her head spin. Whatever had happened must have been terrible; Jeannie had always been so vulnerable, and she hadn't been here for her. Once again she had failed to keep her promise to Mammy.

Without another word she left the kitchen, went through the bar, which smelled strongly of stale smoke and beer, and up the stairs.

Jeannie was asleep. Clearly whatever Dr Blackmore had given her had worked. With her face bare of rouge and her hair spread out across the pillow she looked younger than ever, almost no older than the little sister Ella had spirited away from the workhouse. But there was a little frown crinkling her forehead and as Ella took the chair beside the bed she whimpered and turned her head from side to side as if trying to escape a bad dream.

'It's all right, Jeannie. I'm here.' Ella took her hand, gently stroking it with her thumb, and after a moment or two Jeannie's face cleared and she was still again.

For ten minutes or so Ella sat there, her head full of unanswered questions, watching her sister sleep and wondering what could have happened. Why had Garth been here? What had he been doing in the cottage? And Jeannie – had he brought her with him, or had she run away from Bath and he had followed her? Most pertinent of all, was it possible that Martha *had* been responsible for Garth's death – or was she claiming she was to protect someone else? Jeannie, perhaps, or Conrad? Not Jeannie, surely! She was too small and slender to be able to inflict fatal wounds on a strapping young man like Garth. He'd have been able to overpower her with no more harm done than a few minor cuts. And in any case, she adored Garth, always had. Ella just couldn't see it.

As for Conrad, he'd been in bed and asleep – or so he claimed. But had he been? Ella knew how he felt about Jeannie. Perhaps he'd been so enraged to see his brother here with her that he'd taken leave of his senses, his anger fuelled too by the beating he'd received at the club just a couple of weeks ago. But surely Conrad wouldn't sit back and let his mother take the blame? Unless, of course, she'd persuaded him that she would receive a far more lenient sentence, whilst he would very likely go to the gallows.

Ella massaged her forehead with her free hand – she could feel the beginnings of a headache throbbing in her temple and behind her eyes. This was a living nightmare and for the moment she didn't know what she could do to make it go away.

Perhaps, as Conrad had suggested, she would be able to get Jeannie to talk, draw out something at least in the way of explanation. And, if she was allowed, she would try to see Martha. Having reached a decision made her feel a little better.

Jeannie was still sleeping, more peacefully now. Ella released her hand, got up and crept down the stairs, not wanting to wake her sister yet. She'd take the opportunity to talk things over with Conrad again. Perhaps between them they could come up with something.

In one of the small bare interview rooms at Bath police station Martha sat facing a frustrated Inspector Turner and his sergeant across a table. She was pale and drawn, but also dogged and determined.

'I've told you, over and over. It was me that killed my son. Why isn't that enough for you?'

'Because there's more to it than that.' The inspector pointed his pen at her, making jabbing motions as if it were the knife that had taken Garth's life. 'Your other son and your daughter admit to being on the premises, and I don't believe for one moment they weren't involved. You'd be wise to make a full and frank confession here and now, otherwise the charge will be murder.'

Martha returned his stare defiantly. 'When my husband died he left the Feathers to his three sons. It's held in trust until the youngest, Lewis, comes of age. Garth's the oldest, and he's impatient to get his hands on his share. He's always been a worry to me, and truth to tell it wouldn't surprise me if he was behind the attack on Lewis in Wells, where he's a pupil teacher.'

'Really? Where was this attack, and when?' It was the first Inspector Turner had heard of it.

'That same afternoon – well, evening. In Wells, where he's a pupil teacher. Somebody hit him so hard with a heavy object his shoulder was broken and he hit his head on the ground when he fell. A policeman from Wells came, took me to the hospital to see him, and brought me home again. And when I got back, Garth was here.'

'So you're saying you took a knife to him because you

thought he was responsible for the attack on his brother?'

'I was pretty mad with him, yes. But it was the last straw when he had the bare-faced cheek to tell me that when they inherited he wanted his share in cash, and if the Feathers had to be sold to raise it, then so be it. That pub's been in the family for generations, and it's my boys' home. And mine, if it comes to that. We got into an argument, and I . . . well, you could say I lost it. I got the kitchen knife and stabbed him with it. And that's all there is to it.'

'Not quite,' the inspector said. 'The body was found in the cottage next door, which, as I understand it, is unoccupied. Why were you there, and not in the house?'

'Because the house was all locked up.' That, at least, was the truth.

'Don't you have a key?'

'Course I do. But I didn't want to wake Conrad up if there was going to be shouting. Nor Jeannie,' she added quickly.

'And the cottage was open?'

'Yes. Whoever went over there last must have forgotten to lock up after themselves.'

'All right. If the cottage was unoccupied, where did the knife come from?'

'Seb's mother and father lived there until they died. We've never got round to clearing out their stuff. They kept the knives in the dresser drawer.'

Inspector Turner realised he was hitting his head against a brick wall. He'd had both the cottage and the pub kitchen searched to see which one was missing a carving knife, but there was one in each. The only explanation was that one household or the other had possessed a spare. He'd send an officer back to see if there was an odd carving fork that matched the murder weapon – if it had been taken from the pub kitchen it would prove the door had not been locked, as Martha claimed. And if the quarrel had started in the pub, then it would add weight to his suspicion that one or the other family members who had supposedly been asleep and heard nothing were, in fact, involved.

'I shall be questioning both your daughter and your other son again, and believe you me, I will get the truth out of one or the other of them,' he said grimly, and motioned to a uniformed policeman who had been standing behind Martha. 'Take her back to her cell.'

As soon as he had finished with Martha, Inspector Turner paid a visit to Marsh's club, where he was shown into Elliot's office, and proceeded to break the news of Garth's murder and Martha's arrest.

'Dear God, this is shocking!' Elliot had turned as white as his hair. 'I need a stiff drink.' He rose and crossed to the cabinet. 'Can I offer you one, Inspector?'

'Not while I'm on duty, thank you all the same.' He waited until Elliot was back in his seat before asking: 'Garth Packer worked for you, I understand?'

'Yes. He helped me keep things in order. He was well able to take care of himself, if you get my meaning. Not at all the sort of fellow to get himself stabbed. In an argument I'd expect the other chap to get the worst of it.'

'When did you last see him?' the inspector asked.

'It would have been early yesterday evening. I was out myself, at a meeting, and I didn't run into him when I got back, at about eleven. I did think it peculiar that there was no sign of him or Jeannie Martin this morning – Jeannie is one of my hostesses – and I hoped they hadn't run off together. They were very much in love, you see. Where is Jeannie now? She'll be in a dreadful way about this.'

'She is. I've spoken to her – or tried to – but got nowhere. She couldn't – or wouldn't – say a word. The shock seems to have struck her dumb, or caused her to lose her memory, or both.'

'Would you like to have a look around their rooms?' Elliot offered.

'I don't think that will be necessary since we have a confession.' Inspector Turner felt he'd already wasted too much time on what was an open and shut case.

'Might I just mention that as his mother is to be charged with his murder and his father –' Elliot had no intention of telling the policeman that Garth's real father was very much alive, and living under this very roof – 'his father is dead, I would like to be entrusted with the funeral arrangements when the body is released. He was like a son to me.'

'That's very kind of you, sir,' the inspector said. 'Would you like your intention conveyed to the family?'

'Of course. And my condolences too. Especially to poor Jeannie.'

The inspector nodded his agreement. 'I'll call the local sergeant and get a message to them as soon as I get back to the station,' he promised.

When the inspector had left, Elliot refreshed his whisky and set the bottle and another tumbler on the desk before sending for Aaron. He had no idea how Garth's real father would take the news, but he was certainly in need of the alcohol himself, and although there was little love lost between the two of them he guessed Aaron would be able to use one too.

In the event, Aaron seemed totally unmoved.

'He brought it on himself, I wouldn't wonder,' he said harshly.

337

'Don't you want to know the details?' Elliot was a little shocked, in spite of the fact that he was under no illusions about Aaron's nature.

'Not really. But you might as well tell me, I suppose.'

'Well, the fact is that his mother has confessed and is in custody. She'll be appearing in court tomorrow. I intend to attend the hearing. Would you like to come with me?'

'No.' Blunt and to the point. 'What about the girl? What's she got to say about it?'

'Nothing.' Elliot was beginning to feel disgust. 'She's been struck dumb by the shock of it, and lost her mind, from what I'm told. That's all for the moment, Aaron.'

When Aaron had left the room he returned the tumbler he had set out for him to the cabinet. In the event he hadn't felt like offering the heartless sod a drink. And what in God's name was he doing still employing him? Any affection he'd ever felt for the man had long since dissipated. He'd look around for a replacement for him and for that useless son of his and then they'd both be out on their ears.

That left only one problem; now that Garth was dead who was he going to leave his estate to? And could it be that he would be the only one to mourn the young man he had, as he'd said to the inspector, truly looked on as a son?

Elliot filled his own glass yet again, drank, and stared unseeingly into the bottom of it.

Chapter Twenty-Two

'I think we need to get your mam a solicitor,' Ella said.

She'd cobbled together a scratch meal of bread, cheese and pickles, which neither of them felt like eating, but they'd taken it through to the living room from where Ella thought she would be able to hear Jeannie if she woke.

'Perhaps you're right,' Conrad said doubtfully. If Martha was insisting she had been responsible for Garth's death he didn't see what use a solicitor would be, and taking such a step felt like admitting the seriousness of the situation. But it *was* serious, and a solicitor might make all the difference to the sentence that was passed.

'I could ride over to Hillsbridge and have a word with Mr Clarence, now you're here to look after Jeannie,' he suggested.

Ella nodded. 'Why don't you do that? He knows Martha well, and he'll be on her side, I'm sure.'

'He'll charge, though,' he said. 'Can we afford it?'

'Whatever it is, we'll find it. We have to do the best we can by Martha.' Ella speared a pickled onion so forcefully that it flew off her plate and rolled on to the floor. 'I could kill Garth if he wasn't already dead. He's caused nothing but trouble for this family as long as I've known him. Upset Martha time and again, done God knows what to Jeannie, got you beaten up, and perhaps Lewis too . . .' A thought struck her. 'Perhaps while you're in Hillsbridge you could go to the doctor's and see if he knows how Lewis is and when he's likely to be able to come home.'

'Yeah, I'll do that. But what will he be coming home to?'

'I wonder if Martha told him she'd visit again today? Perhaps the doctor could also tell the hospital she can't make it, in case he's expecting her. Not what's happened, though. It would only set him back again.' Ella put down her fork and pushed away her plate with the copious remains of the meal still on it. 'But I still don't think Martha has it in her to do what she says she did, however much he provoked her. There's more to this than meets the eye. And I'm not going to rest until I find out what it is.'

It was mid-afternoon before Jeannie woke. Ella had gone upstairs to check on her several times before she found her stirring and sat beside her bed holding her hand while she came through the muzzy layers of sleep. There was a little more colour in her cheeks now, but when she opened her eyes she stared at Ella with such a confused look that Ella thought she had not recognised her.

'Jeannie? It's me! Ella!' she said softly.

Jeannie's lips moved as if she was going to speak and relief coursed through Ella's veins. But no words came.

'Darling Jeannie.' Ella smoothed the damp curls away from her sister's face. 'You've had such a lovely long sleep. I expect you're hungry – and thirsty too. Would you like a drink of water, or a cup of tea?'

Still Jeannie said nothing, but she looked at the glass of water on the table beside her bed. Ella helped her raise herself on the pillow and lifted the glass to her lips. Jeannie drank, and when she pushed the glass away Ella took out her handkerchief and wiped away a trickle of water from Jeannie's chin.

As she did so, Jeannie clutched convulsively at her hand. So she did recognise her, Ella thought.

'What do you say we go downstairs?' she suggested. 'It's cold up here, and there's a nice fire going in the sitting room. We can have a good chat in comfort.'

Jeannie nodded silently, pushed the blanket aside and swung her legs over the edge of the bed. Ella wound a thick shawl around her shoulders and eased her to her feet. At least Jeannie didn't seem to have any physical injuries that she could see. The sickness was all in her mind. But she preceded Jeannie down the stairs anyway just in case she should stumble.

In the living room, Ella settled her sister in a fireside chair.

'I'm just going to make us a cup of tea,' she said. 'Will you stay here?'

She hurried through the bar to the kitchen, but even before the kettle had come to the boil Jeannie was there in the doorway behind her, obviously reluctant to let Ella out of her sight. She came closer, clinging to Ella as she had done when she was a child.

'I've come all the way from London to look after you,' she said, spooning tea into the pot. 'What do you think of that? And Conrad will be back soon too. He's just gone into Hillsbridge on an errand.'

She didn't mention what the errand was, nor give any explanation for Martha's absence. The last thing she wanted was to upset her sister any more than she already was.

The tea made, Ella took it into the sitting room and settled Jeannie in the fireside chair once more. For a little while, as they drank their tea, she chattered on about life in London. It seemed the safest topic of conversation and it required no effort on her part.

After a while she wondered if she dared to try and find out from Jeannie exactly what had sent her into this self-imposed silence.

She leaned forward, taking Jeannie's hand again. 'Can you tell me what's wrong, darling?'

As before, though Jeannie's lips began to move silently, no words came. But her eyes were full of anguish and desperation, as if she longed to share her private hell, and a tear rolled down her cheek.

'Can't you speak, Jeannie?' she asked. 'Do try, my love, please. For me.'

Again Jeannie's lips moved soundlessly, then she bent her head to her chest, the tears falling faster now and splashing on to her sister's hand.

Somehow, Ella thought, she had to find a way to get her sister to open up, and an idea occurred to her.

'I won't be a moment.'

She hurried out into the bar and fetched the pad and pencil Conrad used to keep a note of what drinks he'd served, and tot up any big rounds. Arithmetic wasn't his strong point and he wasn't able to do the sums in his head as Martha did. She took them back into the sitting room along with a tray, which she settled on Jeannie's lap.

'Can you write it down for me? Or draw a picture?'

For a long moment, Jeannie hesitated, then she picked up the pencil, letting it hover over the paper before beginning to scribble, drawing first a matchstick man, such as a child might draw, not standing upright, but lying flat. Next she scored an outline around the 'body' that looked like a fluffy cloud. What on earth did it mean? Was she trying to portray Garth, floating up to heaven? But even as Ella wondered Jeannie gripped the pencil hard between her fingers and thumb and began to fill in the cloud, scribbling over and over it until it stood out, stark and black, and the lead of the pencil snapped beneath the pressure she was exerting on it.

Blood. Garth lying in a pool of blood. Ella's throat closed, and for a moment she was as speechless as Jeannie. She must have seen him, lying there. Ella had no regard for Garth. If she felt anything for him it was hatred, and she could not be sorry that he was dead. But Jeannie had idolised him. No wonder she was traumatised. Anyone would be. But for someone as fragile emotionally as Jeannie . . .

'Darling – what happened?' she asked urgently.

Jeannie raised her anguished eyes to Ella's and shook her head.

'You don't know? Or you don't remember?'

Another shake of her head, and the tears began streaming down her cheeks once more.

Ella realised she couldn't push her sister any further. She was still none the wiser as to what had happened, but one thing was clear. Jeannie had either witnessed Garth's murder or come upon the body. But the information she could provide was locked inside her and there was no hope of finding out what it was any time soon.

The sisters were both still in the sitting room when Conrad returned, but Jeannie had fallen asleep again, her head resting against the wing of the fireside chair, her hands, clutching the blanket, spasming occasionally as some bad image invaded her dreams.

'How did you get on?' Ella asked, keeping one eye on Jeannie to make sure she didn't wake and be upset again by talk of the desperate situation.

'Mr Clarence can't help us,' Conrad said, throwing himself

343

down in the other fireside chair. 'He says he's no expert in criminal law.'

'Criminal!' Ella repeated, shocked. 'Martha's no criminal!'

'Well, maybe you and I know that, but it's a crime she'll be charged with, and Mr Clarence thinks we'd do better to get someone experienced in these things to represent her. We've got to do the very best we can for her, Ella.'

Something in the way he said it gave Ella pause for thought, and again the question she really didn't want to know the answer to niggled at her. Of course it was only natural for Conrad to want to do his best for his mother, but was that because he knew she was innocent? Knew, for a fact, not just because of blind faith in the impossibility of her being capable of killing her own son? Was it imperative for him to secure her release in order to salve his own conscience? Ella no longer knew what to believe or who to trust. She only knew she couldn't rest until she had found out the truth of what had happened, and done what she could for the woman who had saved her and Jeannie so long ago.

'So what does Mr Clarence suggest?' she asked.

Conrad pulled a piece of paper torn from a legal pad from his pocket. 'He's given me the name and address of a firm of solicitors in Bath who handle this sort of thing,' he said. 'But it's a lot more urgent than we thought. Mr Clarence telephoned the police station while I was there and they expect Mam to be charged tonight, and remanded to appear in front of the magistrates tomorrow.'

'Oh my life!' Ella's hand went to her throat. She hadn't realised the wheels of justice would turn so quickly.

'Exactly,' Conrad said, grim-faced. 'Anyway, as I say, Mr Clarence came up trumps. He got straight on the telephone to these solicitors, filled them in on the case and gave our family a glowing reference while he was about it, and they've agreed to represent Mam, for the time being at least. Someone will go and see her this afternoon, get her side of the story, and go to the court tomorrow to try for bail.'

'One of us ought to be there,' Ella said.

'Don't you think it's best to leave it to the solicitor?' Conrad said, and again the worm of suspicion twisted in Ella's gut. Conrad looked uncomfortable, not a doubt of it. Perhaps he didn't want to see his mother handcuffed and brought low. Or perhaps . . . She tried to push the thought away. Conrad might be one of the few people Martha would lie to protect, but surely – surely – he wouldn't remain silent and let her do it?

Ella made up her mind. 'If you'll stay here and look after Jeannie, I'll go,' she said. 'Martha needs to see at least one friendly face when she has to stand in the dock. I might even be able to have a word with her. And it will give me the chance to speak to the solicitor.'

Conrad looked relieved. 'Course I'll look after Jeannie. But how are you going to get there? Mr Clarence said court starts at ten, though he doesn't know what time Mam's case will come up.'

'I'll set out early and get the train. There's bound to be at least one for people who work in Bath.' Ella's mind was made up.

'You'd better have this.' Conrad passed her the sheet of paper bearing details of the solicitors, and Ella read it. They were called Churchill and Deane, and their office was in Queen Square.

'Churchill,' she said. 'Isn't that the name of a Liberal MP?' She was sure she'd heard Mr Henderson mention him.

But Conrad wasn't listening. He was staring at the bar pad on which Jeannie had drawn her depiction of Garth's bloody body.

'What's this?'

'Jeannie drew it. I was trying to find out if she knew anything about what happened. She still couldn't – or wouldn't – speak, but she drew this. She must have seen Garth lying there, even if she didn't see him killed. Either way, it's no wonder she's in such a state. It shook me up, I can tell you, when I saw it.'

Distressed, he reached over to stroke Jeannie's hand and as he did so she stirred.

'Not a word!' Ella said softly, putting her finger to her lips.

Conrad nodded impatiently – of course he wouldn't. But his full attention now was on the young woman he'd fallen in love with.

'I'll make a pot of tea,' Ella said, and left them alone.

Martha was charged at six o'clock that evening. She listened in silence as the charge was read out to her by Inspector Turner.

'Is there anything you'd like to say?' he asked.

She shook her head. 'Nothing more than I already have.'

'Then you will be returned to your cell and appear in front of the magistrates tomorrow.'

Martha only nodded stiffly, though inwardly her stomach was turning over. She was dreading a sleepless night spent on a hard bunk with a thin pillow and only a rough blanket felted from washing to keep her warm, and even more she dreaded the court appearance which would almost certainly mean more sleepless nights on similar hard beds, how many she dared not think. But her resolve was as strong as ever. She'd had her life, and a good one.

Now it was up to her to make sure the younger generation enjoyed the same good fortune.

The man who walked into Wells hospital dressed in a smart coat and trousers with a tie knotted neatly at the neck of his shirt was almost unrecognisable as the ruffian who had stalked and attacked Lewis.

Ever since the attack he had been plagued by anxiety that he might have injured the lad severely, as well as wondering whether either he or the man who had happened on the scene might have seen his face and given the police a description, even able to pick him out of an identification parade if it came to that. There wasn't much he could do about that, but he could at least find out what damage he'd caused to the lad.

Why the hell had he ever got mixed up with Aaron Walters? he asked himself. The trouble was he was in too deep now to get out. Walters knew too much that would land Pounds in deep trouble if he chose to share it with Pounds' former colleagues.

Now he approached the reception desk, where a young nurse was writing up case notes.

'I'm enquiring about young Lewis Packer.'

'And you are . . . ?'

'His uncle,' Pounds lied. 'His mother doesn't live in Wells, and doesn't have any way of finding out how he's doing, and when he's likely to be able to go home.'

'I'll find out for you,' the nurse said, and disappeared into the depths of the hospital.

A few minutes later she was back.

'He's as comfortable as can be expected, but he'll be kept in for a few days yet,' she said. 'You can go in and see him if you like. It's visiting time until half past seven.'

'Right. Thanks.'

Pounds had no intention of showing his face on the ward. Even if he didn't recognise him, Lewis would ask who the dickens he was, and deny he was his uncle. But neither did he want to appear to be reluctant to see Lewis.

He stepped away from the desk and made a show of checking

his pockets as if he was looking for something. The minute the nurse's back was turned, checking files in a cabinet, he hurried out, then looked back through the glass panel in the door to make sure she hadn't seen him go. No, she was still engrossed in her task. He was safe for now. But for how long?

Cursing Aaron Walters in the choicest language he could summon up, Pounds left the hospital.

Next morning, Ella was up with the lark. She put out everything Conrad would need to make breakfast for himself and Jeannie, wrapped up a slice of bread and a chunk of cheese to take with her, drank a quick cup of tea, and left for the long walk to Hillsbridge. To her relief a few people were waiting on the platform, a sure sign a train was due shortly, and, right enough, before long, the signals clanked, the gates to the level crossing closed, and it came into view with a puff of steam. Ella climbed into a third-class carriage and settled herself into a corner seat.

'Nice day,' a man sitting in the opposite corner commented.

'Yes.' Ella didn't want to be drawn into conversation. She had too much on her mind. She fastened her gaze on a poster above the seat next to him proclaiming the charms of Weston-super-Mare as a holiday destination, hoping he would get the message. At the next stop a cheery woman with a basket of eggs entered the carriage, and to Ella's relief she and the man were soon engrossed in small talk.

When the train eventually pulled into Queen Square station, Ella bought herself a cup of tea at the tea stall and took it to a nearby bench to drink it and eat her bread and cheese as quickly as she could. Though she knew she was early, with an hour and more to spare, she wanted to be sure to be there in good time, and she had no idea where the petty sessions court was situated.

When she returned her cup to the tea stall she asked the vendor for directions but she was soon lost in the maze of streets and had to ask a passer-by and a policeman before she found it.

The imposing building almost unnerved Ella but she gathered her courage, climbed the steps and found herself in a vast tiled lobby with no idea which way to go. Yet again she was forced to ask, and following the directions she was given found herself in a courtroom with a raised platform at the far end which she imagined was where the judge or the magistrates would sit, a wooden structure that must be the dock and another for witnesses. At the moment all were empty but there was some activity in the central area with clerks laying out papers on the desks and a couple of men who looked like solicitors leafing through them. There were also a few people sitting on benches that encircled the room and which Ella guessed were for the general public. None of them looked very reputable – a woman with untidy grey hair escaping from beneath a battered straw hat, a couple of men who might well be tramps judging by the bundles tied to sticks that were propped up beside them, and a gaggle of girls who looked like streetwalkers. Ella tentatively took a seat as far as possible from them.

She heard the door behind her open and an elderly man, wiry, slightly stooped, and carrying a cane made his way down the aisle to the bench in front of her. An expensive-looking coat was draped over his narrow shoulders. Ella wondered why a man of his standing was here, and also why there was something vaguely familiar about him. Had he come to the Hendersons' house when they were still living in Bath, perhaps one of her employer's friends in the Liberal party? But she quickly forgot about him as her thoughts returned to Martha.

Where was she now? How must she be feeling? If Ella was overawed, how much worse must it be for Martha? And why was she putting herself through this ordeal if, as Ella believed, she was innocent?

The courtroom was filling up now as more people filled the benches. Did they all have an interest in one of the cases to be heard? Ella wondered. Or did some of them come to the petty sessions regularly? Judging by the way they settled themselves comfortably and talked between themselves she thought it likely they did, especially when she saw one woman get out her knitting, settle the ball of wool in her lap, and set the needles clacking. That was what the old women used to do watching the aristocracy go to the guillotine in the French Revolution, she'd heard, and the thought made her feel sick.

The area where the legal representatives had their desks was becoming busier too with smartly dressed men taking their places, skimming through the papers laid out in front of them and occasionally crossing the floor to talk earnestly with others. Some had come in through the main entrance, and appeared to be accompanying their clients – a trashily dressed woman who looked as if she might well be a friend of the streetwalkers, a gangly lad with an acne-scarred face, and a slouching, ill-tempered-looking lout – but several had emerged from a door at the far end of the courtroom which Ella guessed was where those charged with more serious offences were being held. In all probability they'd been talking with their clients and taking their instructions. Ella hoped one of them was either Mr Churchill or Mr Deane – she couldn't help worrying that the solicitor Mr Clarence had spoken to might not turn up at all.

Two more men emerged from the inner sanctum and crossed the floor to one of the desks. The older one, white haired and bespectacled, had the florid face and paunch of one a little too fond of the bottle. But it was the sight of the younger one that made a steely fist clamp around Ella's already pounding heart.

Tall, athletically built, solemn faced. But it was his hair she could not tear her eyes away from. In a shaft of sunlight streaming in through the courtroom window it glowed golden red, just as Leo's had. In all the long years since she'd last seen him she'd never set eyes on anyone whose hair was the colour his had been.

It couldn't be, of course. And yet . . .

At the time he'd helped her and Jeannie to escape from the workhouse, Rector Evans – she still felt sick even thinking the name of the evil man – had been tutoring Leo to assist in getting him a scholarship to a 'good school'. Leo had enormous potential, he'd said. Was it possible he'd fulfilled his promise? Gone on to be articled to a firm of Bath solicitors? Supposing, just supposing, that that firm was Churchill and Deane!

Ella had caught only a glimpse of the young man's face as he'd come into the court, and she couldn't see it now, as his back was turned towards her. But her thoughts were churning, the awesome possibility that this might be Leo adding an extra layer of emotion to the anxiety that consumed her both for Martha's fate and the emotional well-being of her sister.

'All rise!'

Ella stumbled to her feet as two stern-looking men, one with a hawkish hooked nose, the other wearing a clerical collar, entered and took up their places at what she had imagined correctly was the bench.

The hearings were about to begin.

Chapter Twenty-Three

It seemed that the less serious cases were being dealt with first – the girl charged with soliciting was fined, warned that the next time she was up before the bench she would be dealt with more severely, and sent on her way. As they left the court the young women who looked as if they might well be her friends left too, noisily enough that the court steward began approaching them threateningly and they flounced out, giggling. Next up was the gangly lad, charged with affray – he didn't look as if he could knock the skin off a rice pudding, Ella thought, and it seemed the magistrates were in agreement with her. He too was fined and warned and he shuffled out, his chin resting on his chest. Then came the lout – a petty thief, it seemed. He received a prison sentence of a month to be followed by three years in a reformatory school, and as he was led away in handcuffs Ella began to tremble with apprehension. Was this what would happen to Martha? The crime she was admitting to was far more serious than the theft of a few shillings. Ella didn't think she could bear to see Martha treated this way.

There were fewer solicitors in the well of the court now, but the young man with a head of hair the exact same colour as Leo's was still there, sitting beside the older man whom Ella supposed was his senior. Again she wondered if they were from

Churchill and Deane and if they were there to represent Martha. Clutching her hands tightly together in the folds of her skirt she tried to tell herself that if they were it was a good omen. Leo had saved her and Jeannie; perhaps it was a sign that a young man with hair that flamed like his would save Martha. But she couldn't see how that could come about with things as they were.

A moment later the door beside the bench opened again and Ella's heart pounded – it was Martha who entered the court. Thank goodness she wasn't manacled, but a police officer held her firmly by the arm. She stood as tall and upright as ever, chin jutting fiercely, lips clamped together in a show of defiance. Ella didn't know if Martha had seen her or not; she hoped she had, but dared not do anything to draw attention to herself in case it breached some rule and got her thrown out.

The clerk of the court rose, asked Martha her name, and when she had given it, read out the charge and asked her intentions as to her plea.

'Guilty.' Her voice, firm and unwavering, rang through the courtroom.

'Mr Wainwright?'

A clean-shaven smartly dressed man, clearly either a barrister or a solicitor, rose and began to speak, outlining the 'brutal and bloody murder' of Garth Packer as admitted by the defendant, his mother.

Both JPs assumed shocked expressions, their gazes moving from the prosecuting counsel to Martha and back again.

'Do you wish to call any witnesses?' the JP wearing a clerical collar asked.

'Not at this time, Your Worship. It would seem the defendant and the victim were alone at the time. Of the two persons who were also present at the Feathers that night one was asleep until woken by Packer, by which time the victim was dead, and the other appears to have either been struck dumb by the shock of what occurred, or be suffering from trauma-induced amnesia. Either way, she is able to add nothing to Packer's version of events, which is, in any case, a full and frank confession of guilt.

'It is my submission the defendant should be remanded to quarter sessions and in view of the seriousness of the offence the prosecution will oppose any application for bail,' he finished, and took his seat with a flourish.

'Thank you, Mr Wainwright.' The magistrate shuffled some papers on the desk in front of him and looked up, stony-faced. 'Mr Deane. I believe you are here to represent Mrs Packer?'

Ella caught her breath. So the solicitor Mr Clarence had contacted had been as good as his word. He was here.

And it was the older man, flanked by the young red-haired one, who was rising to his feet.

'I am, Your Worship.'

'Since your client has confessed, I assume you have very little to say?'

Ella was taking a hearty dislike to this magistrate. Man of the cloth he might be, but he didn't seem to possess an ounce of compassion.

'On the contrary, Your Worship. In spite of her confession, I am convinced Mrs Packer is innocent of any crime. She is assuredly of good character, with not a single stain on her reputation as a kind, caring, law-abiding citizen.'

'Yet you have no witnesses to attest to that?'

'I was only appointed to represent Mrs Packer late yesterday afternoon, and so have had no opportunity to speak to any potential—'

'So your answer is no?'

'Sadly, at this point in time, it has to be. But—'

Impulsively, Ella leapt to her feet.

'I'll speak for her!'

All heads turned towards her and the JP in the clerical collar turned to the bailiff.

'Have this person removed immediately.'

'No.' It was the first time the hooked-nose JP had spoken apart from the whispered conversations with his colleague. 'I'd like to hear what the young lady has to say. She may approach.'

Trembling from head to toe, Ella squeezed past the man sitting next to her – a newspaper reporter, she had assumed, from the way he was scribbling indecipherable notes on an octavo-sized pad, and walked down the aisle between the forms.

'Take the stand, my dear.'

Ella crossed to the witness box, placed her hand on the Bible, and took the oath that was written on a card in copperplate and lay on the ledge in front of her. As she finished, she glanced up at Martha, who was shaking her head and mouthing the word 'No!' Ella swallowed hard at the lump of nervousness constricting her throat.

'Martha Packer is a wonderful woman,' she began, holding Martha's gaze. 'She had three children of her own but she took pity on me and my sister – two little orphans – when we ran away from the workhouse. We were desperate. I'd . . . I'd been taken advantage of by a wicked man, and the authorities would have done nothing because he was held in high regard. I'd managed to get my little sister away so that she wouldn't suffer the same fate, but we had nowhere to go and if we'd been picked up we'd have been returned to that . . . that hell-hole. Martha gave us a home, a family, and a lovely life. She was like a mother to us. Please, I beg you, don't send her to prison.'

Still gazing at Martha, she saw her adoptive mother's chin

tremble before she bit her lip and regained her defiant expression. She might have been touched by Ella's defence of her, but there was no way she was going to be budged on this. Was it possible she *had* been the one to stab Garth? Goodness knows, he'd caused her enough trouble over the years and perhaps the way he'd lured Jeannie into ruination had been the last straw.

'Do you have any questions for your witness?' The JP asked Mr Deane.

'No, Your Worship. I think she has already said all she needs to by way of a character reference. And I am sure no one could fail to be moved by her story.'

'I have questions, however.' The prosecuting counsel was quickly on his feet, and the JP nodded his acquiescence. 'Were you at the Feathers on the night of the slaying, Miss, er . . .'

'Martin,' Ella supplied. 'Ella Martin. And no, I wasn't at the Feathers that night. I am employed by a Member of Parliament as a nursemaid for his children and now live in London.'

A ripple ran round the court. In the employ of an MP! No wonder the young woman hadn't been afraid to take the stand. Mr Wainwright, however, was less impressed.

'Very laudable, I'm sure, Miss Martin. But if you now live in London I fail to understand how you can possibly know what Mrs Packer's state of mind was when she, by her own admission, plunged a kitchen knife into her son's body with such determined force that he lost his life.'

'I know her well enough to know she would never do such a thing, whatever she might say,' Ella said stoutly.

The beak-nosed magistrate had heard enough.

'Anything further, Mr Wainwright? No? Good.' He turned to Ella. 'Thank you for testifying Miss, er . . . Martin. You may resume your seat.'

As she climbed down from the witness stand Ella looked

directly at Martha, giving her a wan smile, but Martha merely gave a small shake of her head, impassive as ever.

Overcome suddenly by emotion, Ella's eyes filled with tears, and as she walked back to her seat she kept them firmly fixed on a point at the back of the court. She was still shaking from head to toe and for the moment she had forgotten all about the young, red-headed man. All she could think of was regaining her place on the wooden form before her legs gave way beneath her.

Through a loud buzzing in her ears she heard the announcement that the case was to go forward to be heard at the next quarter sessions in Bristol, heard Mr Deane ask for bail until that date, saw Mr Wainwright leap to his feet again to raise his objection.

'This is a dangerous woman! What more serious crime could she be charged with than murder? She should be kept in a place of safety.'

'If, as she claims, she did indeed cause Garth Packer's death, it was because she has been severely tried over many years and eventually lost her senses,' Mr Deane argued. 'I will personally guarantee that she will not abscond and will report to the police station on a regular basis. This woman, of whose kindness and generosity you have heard testified, will be in the bosom of her family and of no danger to anyone.'

'Tommyrot!' the prosecutor barked, earning a stern look from the magistrates. 'Surely Packer's family are the ones most in need of protection given that it was her own son she murdered.'

Mr Deane looked ready to argue again, but the magistrate in the clerical collar raised a hand to stop him.

'Thank you, gentlemen. We have heard your arguments and will consider the matter.'

They bent their heads together, apparently having a whispered argument, and Ella scarcely dared breathe as they deliberated. Then the vicar-cum-magistrate resumed his upright pose and glared at Martha.

'Bail is denied. You will be conveyed to Culversham Prison where you will remain until the next quarter sessions.'

Ella gasped audibly and covered her face with her hands as Martha was led away.

'No! No!' Tears were streaming down her cheeks now and she fumbled in her bag for a handkerchief, not seeing the two men making their way towards her from their desk in the well of the court.

'Miss Martin. I am so sorry I was unable to secure bail for your adoptive mother.' Mr Deane's voice. Ella mopped her eyes hastily. She didn't want the solicitor to see her crying.

'Ella.'

She looked up sharply. Not at Mr Deane, but at the other speaker, the young man whose hair was the exact same colour as Leo's. Into a well-loved face, no longer that of a boy, yet instantly recognisable. She gasped again in disbelief and her voice came out on a sob.

'Leo!'

'So you two know each other.' Mr Deane's voice broke the spell.

'We were friends in the workhouse,' Leo said. Mr Churchill and Mr Deane both knew his background; they'd been happy for him to serve his articles with them and he was now a junior solicitor in the firm. 'But I never expected to see you again, Ella. Especially not under these circumstances.'

He couldn't take his eyes off her. Tears were coursing down her cheeks again and all he wanted to do was take her in his arms and comfort her. But this was not the time or the place, and in any case the intervening years, in which so much had changed, lay between them.

'I think your reunion should take a back seat for the moment.' Mr Deane was all business again. 'I am going to ask to be allowed to speak to my client before she is taken to prison. Culversham, as you may or may not know, is in Wiltshire, a goodly distance away. It won't be easy to get to see her there, and I have a lot of questions to ask her. We spoke only briefly before the hearing.'

'Thank you so much for representing her,' Ella said huskily.

'I don't quite know how I came to be in this position,' Mr Deane said testily. 'I don't like losing my cases, Miss Martin, and to be honest, as long as Mrs Packer continues to assert her guilt there isn't a great deal I can do, apart from plead for leniency.'

'But we'll do our very best,' Leo promised. He looked at the senior solicitor. 'Would it be all right for Ella to see Mrs Packer too before she's taken away? If anyone can persuade her to give us something more to go on, it's Ella.'

'Oh yes – please! Could I see her?' Ella began mopping at her face again with her handkerchief, which was now a sodden ball, and Leo handed her his own, freshly laundered and neatly pressed.

'Here . . . use mine. You don't want Mrs Packer seeing you looking like that, do you?'

Ella shook her head and attempted a weak smile.

'Come along then,' Mr Deane said impatiently, and led the small procession to the door leading to the cells at the rear of the court.

This was beyond belief, Leo thought as he followed Mr Deane and Ella, weaving their way between the forms and the desks and chairs. He was still reeling from the shock that had all but paralysed him when Ella had taken the stand. Until she'd called out, he hadn't noticed the young woman in the public gallery, just one of many, and it was only when she'd stepped into the witness box that the first glimmer of recognition had caused him to sit up and take notice. He must be mistaken, he'd told himself. He'd thought about Ella so often over the many years since he'd helped her and Jeannie escape, and wondered where she was and how things had turned out for her, that he was somehow transposing the characteristics he remembered so well on to the face and body of a stranger.

And then she'd given her name as Ella Martin and he'd realised with a heart-wrenching jolt that he wasn't mistaken at all. It was Ella. And now that he knew it, he could see the eleven-year-old girl in the young woman in the witness box. The light brown hair might now be drawn back with combs and topped with a small, fashionable hat, but he knew exactly how, unpinned, it would fall around her face. He wasn't close enough to see the colour of her brown-flecked eyes, but he could picture them and the tip-tilt nose and generous mouth. She was alive and well, she hadn't been abducted by a dangerous stranger, or driven on to the streets, as he had always feared. She and Jeannie had been taken in by, and lived happily, it seemed, with the woman in the dock. So happily that she had been prepared to risk her dignity to defend her adoptive mother. Pride and admiration welled in his chest. Ella was the same girl he'd known, brave and principled. The same girl who had been prepared to risk everything to save her little sister from the evil intentions of Rector Evans, and somehow succeeded.

What had happened to her in the intervening years? he wondered. Since she had given her maiden name he assumed she hadn't married, but ironically, since she now lived in

London, they were both back here in Bath. When he'd finished school with exemplary grades in his final exams he'd had several offers from solicitors to train for the profession as an articled clerk and he'd never properly explained to himself why he'd chosen Churchill and Deane. He had no ties to the city and few happy memories. For him, as for all the others who had called the workhouse home, life had been hard and cruel. But deep down he knew the reason. He'd hoped he would find Ella again. He'd never forgotten her. She had been the one bright spot in an otherwise dark world. He'd have done anything for her, and he had. He'd risked terrible punishment to help her and Jeannie get away but fortunately his part in their escape had never been discovered. He'd done it because he cared deeply for her, and in so doing the sunshine had gone out of his life.

Now here she was seeking his help again – well, Mr Deane's really, but it came to the same thing. And Leo would do everything in his power to try to make things right for her.

Martha was handcuffed now. She sat erect on a hard chair in a dim room where the only light filtered through a small window high in the wall. The other chair in the room was in a far corner, so Ella dropped to her knees on the floor beside her adoptive mother, reaching for her manacled hands which lay in her lap.

'Don't touch the prisoner!' a policeman barked.

Defiantly, Ella planted a kiss on Martha's fingers before getting to her feet.

'I'm warning you, miss!'

'Best not,' Leo said softly. Ella nodded; she understood. If she breached the rules she'd be sent away before she had so much as spoken to Martha.

Mr Deane had dragged the other chair across the floor to sit facing his client.

'I'm very sorry I was unsuccessful in getting you bail,' he apologised, much as he had to Ella.

Martha shrugged. 'I expect I shall have to get used to prison.'

Like her face, her voice was flat and expressionless.

'You're not helping yourself, Mrs Packer,' Mr Deane pointed out.

Another shrug. 'I killed Garth. That's all there is to it.'

'But if you would only talk about the circumstances I can appeal for clemency.'

'He drove me to it, that's all I can say. He's a bad boy, always was, only I tried not to see it. Stood up for him. It's my fault he's . . . was . . . the way he was. My fault he did what he did. Now I've got to pay for it.'

'What did he do to make you so angry?' Mr Deane asked. He glanced at Leo, who was making notes on a legal pad, and nodded, satisfied that there would be some record of this conversation.

'Seduced my other adopted daughter. Introduced her to a way of life . . . well, depraved is the only word for it. Do you know Marsh's club? And what goes on there behind closed doors? I'm not talking just about the gambling. That's what he wanted her for. To turn her into a . . .' She broke off, unable to say the word, and looked at Ella. 'How is Jeannie?' she asked. 'And what about Lewis? Is he out of hospital yet?'

'Lewis is doing well. He'll be allowed home soon, they say.'

'Lewis?' Mr Deane interposed sharply.

'My youngest son. He's in hospital in Wells where he's a pupil teacher.' Martha turned impatiently to Ella. 'And what about Jeannie?' she asked again, even more urgently.

Ella hesitated, unsure whether it was wise to tell Martha how ill her sister was.

'She's very upset,' she said tentatively, and Mr Deane put in: 'So upset, in fact, that I'm told she either can't or won't say what happened.'

Martha's taut features seemed to relax a little but when she replied her tone was brittle. 'It's hardly surprising she's in a state, is it? She'd completely lost her head over my son. Fancied herself in love with him. That's why I had to do something. I couldn't stand by and see him ruin Jeannie.'

'I see. So you are adamant it was you who was responsible for killing your son? And you can't give me any more details as to what happened?' Mr Deane was looking very grim.

Martha shook her head, saying nothing more.

'Well, at least we have a motive,' Mr Deane said. 'I just hope I can get more in your defence before you come to trial.'

'So if you've got no more questions . . . ?' The policeman was becoming impatient.

Ella's mind had been working overtime since Martha had mentioned Marsh's club. Her memory had been triggered – she knew where she'd seen the elderly man with the cane before. The man who'd got up and left as soon as Martha's case had been heard. She leaned forward urgently. 'Did those awful men have anything to do with it? The ones we saw when we went to the club to try and bring Jeannie home?'

Martha was silent, avoiding Ella's questioning gaze. After waiting a moment, Ella went on: 'I think there's a lot more to this than you're saying, Martha, and I intend to find out what it is.'

Martha's eyes blazed suddenly and before the policeman could stop her she had reached out and grabbed Ella's arm with one of her manacled hands.

'Just leave it alone, Ella,' she said, her voice low and urgent. 'Leave it alone, or you'll be sorry.'

'That's enough now,' the policeman said sharply. 'I warned you. No touching.' He turned to Mr Deane. 'Right. You've seen your client. The prison wagon will be here soon and they won't want to be kept waiting. This interview is at an end.'

Tears were filling Ella's eyes again.

'Oh, Martha,' she whispered. 'I'll come and see you, don't worry. And whatever you say, we're going to do our best for you. You don't deserve this, any of it.'

And then there was nothing else for them to do but leave the small airless room. Leave Martha. Ella thought that her heart would break.

Chapter Twenty-Four

As they left the court Ella looked around for the man she had recognised as the one who had spoken to them and calmed the situation when she and Martha had visited Marsh's, but he was nowhere to be seen.

'Thank you, Miss Martin, for speaking up for Mrs Packer – for all the good it did. Would you be prepared to do the same again when the case comes to quarter sessions? It might hold some sway with the jury.'

'Of course,' Ella said, though inwardly she trembled at the thought of an even more imposing court than this one. A bewigged judge and barristers, a jury of twelve men, more officials, more police. But she'd do it. She'd do anything if it would help Martha's case.

Suddenly she caught a glimpse of the man she'd been looking for, emerging from the rear of the court building rather than the main entrance.

'That man . . . !' she said urgently. 'He's Mr Marsh, the owner of the club where Garth worked – the one where he took Jeannie. I'm going to have a word with him. See if he can shed any light on why they came out to the Feathers, because it's a mystery to me.'

'I don't think that's wise, Miss Martin.' It was more of an order than a warning.

'Why not?'

'You'll only muddy the waters and get nothing out of him.'

'But he may know something important! And if he knows nothing, why is he here?' she persisted.

'Because Garth Packer was employed by him, I imagine. And even if he did possess any knowledge we do not, I doubt it would be of any use whilst Mrs Packer continues to assert her guilt,' the solicitor said smoothly. 'Just leave him to me. I'll speak to him myself if I deem it necessary. And it's likely the barrister we engage will want to speak to him too, as well as the other witnesses – you do realise we will need a barrister to represent Mrs Packer at quarter sessions?'

'Oh, really?' Ella's heart sank. A barrister would be even more expensive than Mr Deane, she imagined. But whatever it cost, Martha must have the best representation possible.

'I don't think there's much more we can achieve today,' he went on. 'We'll find a cab to take you home.'

'I don't have enough money for a cab,' Ella said, embarrassed to have to admit it. 'I've only got enough for my train fare.'

'You shouldn't be bothering with trains. I'll pay the cabbie.'

'I can't let you do that!' Ella protested.

'Don't worry, I'll put it on my bill,' Mr Deane said easily.

'Oh . . . yes, of course,' Ella said faintly. His bill. How much was all this going to cost? A big-shot Bath solicitor's charges would no doubt be far higher than Mr Clarence's, and the barrister's even more.

'I could drive her if you don't mind me taking the motor,' Leo said. 'And I could talk to the rest of the family and have a look at the scene of the crime while I'm about it.'

Mr Deane thought for a moment, then nodded. 'Very well. I

trust you'll take care with it. Any dents or scratches and your pay will be docked to pay for the repairs.'

'Of course, Mr Deane. Let's go, Ella.'

The motor was almost as impressive as Monty's, pillar-box red with brass headlamps and an interior of red leather.

'This is really kind,' Ella said. She was feeling a little self-conscious and awkward. Strange, really, considering what good friends they had been, but in those days her heart hadn't fluttered when she was with him the way it was fluttering now.

'My pleasure!' he said, and as a flush crept up her cheeks he went on: 'I never pass up a chance to get to drive this big beast. I suppose you get to ride in them all the time in London.'

'Sometimes . . .'

As Leo cranked the engine to life she glanced back over her shoulder towards the court, thinking of Martha who was probably locked in a cell now, awaiting the arrival of the transport that would take her to prison. But she was surprised and pleased to see Martha's legal representative had approached Elliot Marsh and the two were now talking together. Perhaps some good would come from it.

'Is Mr Deane a good solicitor?' she asked.

'As he said, he doesn't like to lose his cases. He'll go for the best defence barrister, you can be sure of that.' Leo pulled away from the kerb.

'It's unbelievable that you work for the very practice our solicitor in Hillsbridge put us in touch with,' Ella said. 'How did it come about?'

Leo explained how his education had led to him becoming first an articled clerk, and then a junior solicitor.

'I'd seen life in the underclasses at first hand, how nobody gives a monkey's cuss to get them justice, and I made up my mind long ago that what I wanted to do was fight for them when they came up against the law for one reason or another. But enough about me, Ella. I've wondered so often what became of you. Worried about you, actually.'

'We were very lucky,' Ella said. 'But it was all thanks to you. If it hadn't been for your help we'd never have managed to get away. And *I* was worried about *you* – that you'd be found out and sent to that terrible punishment room.'

'Well I wasn't.' Leo shifted gear as they began the climb out of the valley bowl in which the city was set. 'We caused quite an upset between us, though. Everyone was blaming everyone else, the police were called . . .'

'I know. They came to the Feathers. Martha lied to them, and kept us hidden until the hue and cry died down. She saved our bacon, Leo. Took us in and treated us like her own. That's why I can't stand by and see her sent to prison for the rest of her life. Or worse.' She broke off, shivering, at the terrible thought that Martha might even go to the gallows, and she reached across impulsively, covering Leo's hand on the steering wheel with her own. 'Please, Leo, you've got to make sure that doesn't happen.'

'Of course I'll do all I can. I take it you think she's claiming responsibility to protect someone? That she's wholly innocent?'

The professionalism in the way he answered made Ella suddenly aware that this Leo was no longer the boy who worked in the workhouse garden, but a lawyer. Embarrassed by the intimacy of the contact with a friend she hadn't seen in ten years and really didn't know any more, Ella removed her hand from his and tried to frame an honest answer.

'That's what I thought to begin with,' she said. 'Now I can't help wondering. Martha thinks the world of Jeannie. She was beside herself when Garth lured her to Bath to live with him and work in that club – you can guess what goes on there. The so-called hostesses are no more than high-class prostitutes. Martha sent for me to come down from London and we went there to try and talk some sense into Jeannie. It was useless. We were more or less thrown out – and so was Martha's son, Conrad, when he did the same. He was badly beaten, by Garth and . . .' She broke off. She had been going to say 'his father', but she didn't think this was the time to get caught up in the details of Garth's origins, though she would tell him later. Instead she simply said: '. . . another man who works there. If Martha was desperate enough, and the chance arose . . .'

She broke off, anxiously waiting for Leo's reaction. When he said nothing, concentrating on manoeuvring the motor around the bends as the road passed between a parade of shops and climbed again past impressive dwellings, she went on: 'Anything like that incensed her, always has. It's the reason she hid us, I think. When I told her about Rector Evans she was so angry and disgusted, I think she'd have killed *him* if she'd had the chance.'

Leo spoke at last. 'That wouldn't have been necessary. He wasn't around much longer. He went to meet his maker before he had the chance to molest anyone else.'

'He died?' Ella said, startled.

'Took his own life. They found him in the Rectory hanging from the bannisters. He'd used that stole thing he used to drape around his neck when he was taking services. From what I found out later, he'd been called before the board of governors – they'd had a complaint about his behaviour.' He frowned, thinking. 'I have a feeling it was a Hillsbridge solicitor who reported him. Is it possible . . . ?'

'A solicitor helped Martha when she wanted to adopt us,' Ella said. 'Do you think she told him what had been going on and he . . .'

'Could well be. But as I understand it, the claim was also

backed up by one of the mistresses at the workhouse. Whatever. I suppose he decided hanging himself was preferable to facing the music. Miss Hopkins mourned him, of course, but I think she was the only one.'

Ella shuddered. She didn't want to hear any more. The very thought of the rector still turned her stomach. And in any case there were far more important subjects to discuss.

'What I can't understand is why Jeannie and Garth were at the Feathers. It makes no sense, unless Garth had fallen out with Mr Marsh for some reason, or Martha had forced a showdown. But Garth is dead, and Jeannie can't, or won't, say a single word. That's why I'm hoping Elliot Marsh may be able to shed some light on it. Do you remember I saw him leaving the court? Does Mr Deane know him?'

'I couldn't say. He may well do. He's a member of a lot of societies – Bath history, the photographic club, the Freemasons – you name it.'

'I can't somehow see someone like Mr Marsh being in any of those. Unless he goes along to drum up interest in his club by distributing indecent photographs of his hostesses,' she added as an afterthought.

Leo raised an eyebrow. 'Is it that bad?'

'Worse.' She couldn't forget the erotic pictures she'd glimpsed on the walls of the club salon.

They drove in silence for a few minutes, then Leo asked: 'Did you and Jeannie really walk all this way?'

'We did. We only stopped at the Feathers because Jeannie was too tired to go any further. The door to the skittle-alley was unlocked and we went in there for a rest and fell asleep.' She paused, remembering. 'It was Garth who found us. I think Jeannie's infatuation with him started from there. She was always following him around like a puppy dog, even when she was little.'

'And did he fall for her too?'

'Not then, certainly. He's seven years older than her. She was only eight, and he'd already left school and was working on his uncle's farm. Later? To be honest, I don't think Garth was capable of love in any shape or form. He chased the girls, yes, but just so that he could have his fun. Jeannie would be no more than another scalp on his belt. He really wasn't a nice person, Leo. And he treated his mother and Seb appallingly, especially after he found out . . .'

'Found out what?'

'That Seb wasn't his real father. Aaron someone was. I never did know what happened between them, only that Seb married Martha to save her from the shame and disgrace of being an unmarried mother.'

Leo listened quietly, his brow furrowed. 'So his real father works for Mr Marsh too?' he said when she finished.

'Yes. But according to Conrad they were at loggerheads. Aaron didn't want anything to do with him, and Garth hated him for it.'

They reached the bottom of the winding hill that led up to the Feathers, and as they rounded the last bend Ella pointed it out, up ahead.

'That's it.' Leo steered the motor across the road and on to the forecourt. 'And that's the cottage where Garth's body was found. You'll want to look round it later, I expect. But first come and see Jeannie, meet Conrad, and have a nice cup of tea.'

Conrad must have seen their arrival from the window as by the time Ella and Leo had climbed down from the motor he had the kitchen door open and was on his way out to meet them.

'Conrad – this is Leo, one of Martha's solicitors,' Ella said, seeing his puzzled frown. 'He's an old friend – we were in the workhouse together, would you believe. It was him who helped us escape. And Leo – this is Conrad, my brother.'

The two men shook hands.

'Pleased to meet you,' Leo said, but Conrad appeared to be a little wary of the suited and booted solicitor.

'Yeah,' he grunted, uncharacteristically ignoring Leo's outstretched hand. 'How did it go anyway?'

'Let's go inside,' Ella said. 'I've promised Leo a cup of tea before we get down to business.'

'Kettle's on the hob. But be careful what you say. Jeannie's in there.'

'I know you don't want her upset, but she has to know what's going on,' Ella said quietly. 'Perhaps it will shock her into remembering what happened. Or into telling us, if she remembers only too well, and just can't bring herself to talk about it.'

'A word, Ella.' Conrad signalled to her with his eyes that he wanted it to be in private.

'Do go inside and remember yourself to Jeannie,' she said to Leo. 'Conrad and I will only be a minute.'

Looking a little puzzled, Leo went into the house.

'What?' Ella asked Conrad shortly.

'We don't want Jeannie talking in front of the solicitor until we know what she's going to say,' Conrad said urgently. 'I think it's her Mam is lying to protect.'

'What?' Ella was staggered. 'But Jeannie would never harm Garth! She worshipped him! And besides, she wouldn't be strong enough.'

'If the carving knife was very sharp – and it probably was, knowing Grandma – and if she was desperate enough . . . perhaps he was trying to force himself on her . . . You know how childlike she is. She wouldn't stop to think of the consequences.'

Ella was silent for a moment, trying to digest what Conrad

372

was suggesting. She'd wondered if it was possible Martha was lying to protect Conrad, but she'd never considered it might be Jeannie. Her sister was so small and fragile she couldn't imagine her having the strength to inflict a fatal wound on strong, muscled Garth no matter how sharp the knife.

'Look, I've been over and over it,' Conrad said. 'The way Mam was that night . . . well, it wasn't like she'd just murdered her own son in a fit of madness. She was calm, controlled, the way she always is in a crisis. I think when she got home from Wells she found Garth's body and Jeannie in the state she is now and she decided to get her off the hook.'

'Surely Jeannie would have been covered in blood if she was responsible?' Ella argued.

'As would Mam if it was her. But somebody had washed in the kitchen. There were splashes of water all over the floor. And it was Jeannie's dress that had wet patches on the bodice and skirt. If it had been Mam washing herself, why was Jeannie the one with a wet dress?'

'Oh dear God,' Ella whispered.

It was certainly possible now that she came to think of it that it was *Jeannie* Martha was covering for. She loved the girl like her own daughter; she'd even confided to Ella once that she had in some way taken the place of Lily, the little girl she had lost. And she had blamed herself for Garth seducing Jeannie into going with him to Marsh's club. It would be Martha all over to sacrifice herself for Jeannie . . .

Ella shook her head vigorously. 'If that's the case we can't let her take the blame, Conrad. It could be that she's telling the truth – that she came home to find Garth taking advantage of Jeannie in the cottage and flew to her defence without any thought for the consequences. Or perhaps it was neither of them – it could have been a tramp, a convict on the run, even a burglary gone wrong – and Martha *thought* Jeannie was responsible because Jeannie couldn't tell her any different. We must get Jeannie to talk somehow.'

'But not right now. Not in front of a stranger.'

'Leo's not a stranger,' Ella argued. 'And he's one of the solicitors who will be putting Martha's case together.'

'All the more reason for him not to be there if we do manage to get something out of Jeannie. If she does admit responsibility, Martha won't thank us for exposing her. You know what would happen to her, don't you? She'd most likely be sent to a lunatic asylum and never released. Never.'

Ella winced at the terrible thought.

'Martha's charge might very well be reduced to manslaughter. That's what Mr Clarence said. If she claims it was in self-defence – and maybe it was! – and a jury believe her, she'd get off far more lightly. But not Jeannie. The way she is they'd call her mad.'

'But she's not!'

'You and I know that,' Conrad said. 'We know that it's just that she's never really grown up. But it wouldn't surprise me if a doctor declared otherwise.' He glanced towards the kitchen. 'We'd better go in. We don't want that solicitor chap upsetting her.'

'Leo won't upset her,' Ella said. 'She's known him since she was a little girl.'

'But will she recognise him?' Conrad had already started towards the house, but Ella stood for a moment gathering her racing thoughts.

Conrad was in love with Jeannie, not a doubt of it. He'd do anything, say anything, to save her, even see his own mother go to jail for a crime she didn't commit. In a way it was an adoration as blind as Jeannie's for Garth. And every bit as dangerous.

She followed Conrad into the house, where Leo was sitting beside Jeannie, talking to her in low, comforting tones. Though she was still not contributing anything, at least her eyes were focused on Leo's face and she appeared to be listening to every word he said.

Clearly, somewhere in her confused mind, she remembered him.

As Ella and Conrad entered the kitchen Leo rose to his feet.

'I think I should be getting back to Bath.'

'What about your cup of tea? And having a look around the cottage?' Ella asked, reluctant to see him go.

'Another time. I'll come back tomorrow perhaps? Jeannie and I have enjoyed seeing one another, haven't we, Jeannie?'

He smiled at her, and to Ella's astonishment, she returned his smile and actually nodded.

Ella followed Leo out to the motor. The things Conrad had suggested had shaken her to the core. Was it possible he was right, and Martha was lying to protect Jeannie? She didn't want to believe it, but neither could she deny it could be the truth. Should she tell Leo? If he was part of the team who would be representing Martha she supposed she should, whatever Conrad said. But she couldn't bear to think what would happen if Jeannie was arrested, or even questioned as a suspect. In her fragile state of mind she would be totally destroyed. And Ella was still clinging to the hope that this could somehow be resolved without bringing Jeannie into it.

'Do you think someone else entirely might be the killer?' she asked, harking back to the suggestion she'd made to Conrad. 'A thief, caught in the act, perhaps? It's very quiet out here, especially since the pub has been shut up, and we are on the main road to and from Bath. A criminal might well think they'd have easy pickings, only to be caught red-handed by Garth and Jeannie.'

'It's possible, I suppose, but I imagine the police will have thought of that, and looked for any evidence of a break-in.'

'Not necessarily, if they already had Martha's confession,' Ella argued.

'But Garth was killed in the cottage,' Leo said. 'I wouldn't have thought a burglar would think there was anything worth stealing in there. They'd have broken into the bar, surely, where the spirits and cigarettes are, and the till.'

'Maybe they tried and couldn't get in, so they thought they'd see if there was anything worth taking in the cottage.' She was grasping at straws, she knew.

'What if it was a vagrant looking for somewhere to sleep?' she suggested.

'It doesn't hold water,' Leo said. 'Why would Martha confess?'

'Because she didn't know that. If she came home to find Garth dead and Jeannie in a state of shock, perhaps she thought Jeannie was responsible. She wasn't, I'm sure,' she added hastily, 'but if neither of them could tell her different . . .'

'There's still the unanswered question as to why they were here at all, and what they were doing in the cottage,' Leo said.

'Oh, I don't know!' Overwhelmed suddenly by it all, Ella covered her face with her hands.

'Don't get upset, Ella,' Leo pleaded. 'I'm playing devil's advocate, that's all.'

'Well I don't want you to!' Ella sobbed. 'I want you to tell me that everything is going to be all right.'

Leo sighed. 'I wish I could.' He reached out, brushing a strand of hair that had come loose behind her ear and stroking the bit of her cheek that wasn't hidden by her hands. 'Don't cry, Ella, please.'

'You made things right before.' Her voice was muffled.

'This is different. You must know that.'

'Yes. You can't dig a trench to get Martha out of jail . . .' Her little strangled half-laugh became a sob. 'Oh, Leo . . .'

He did what he'd been wanting to do ever since he'd set eyes on her this morning. He took her in his arms and let her weep into his shoulder, and she clung to him like a drowning man to a life raft. For seemingly endless minutes she sobbed while he smoothed the nape of her neck with one hand and held her tightly with the other. At last her sobs quietened to soft snuffles and she raised her tear-wet face.

'I'm sorry. It's just all so hopeless . . . I don't know what to believe any more, and even if I did, it wouldn't make any difference. Martha took us in. Was a mother to us. And how have we repaid her? By destroying her family. And I just can't stand it any more, Leo.'

'Don't talk like that.' He wiped some of the tears from her cheeks with his thumb. 'You're strong, Ella. You always were.'

She shook her head. 'No, I'm not. I'm useless. I promised Mammy, when she lay dead, that I'd look after my little sister, and I've let them both down. I should have been here for Jeannie, not cavorting off to London. I'd never have gone if I'd thought for a moment . . .' she gulped, 'but I did. And look what's happened because I wasn't here for her.'

The tears began to flow again, her face upturned this time, close, so close to his. 'Ella . . .' he murmured, distressed for her agony. He kissed the tears from her cheeks, hot and salty, and then his mouth was on hers. She gave a little gasp, a quick intake of breath and instinctively moulded her lips to his. All the longing of the intervening years was poured into that kiss; all her wretched confusion at the desperate situation she had found herself in, powerless to help those she loved so much. Leo was her saviour, her rock. He always had been. With him beside her she *would* be strong. For Jeannie. For Martha.

But suddenly, to her shock and bewilderment, he pulled back, holding her at arm's length.

'I'm sorry, Ella.' He sounded regretful, ashamed almost.

'Why?' she asked, perplexed.

'Because . . . I shouldn't have done that. I don't want to give you the wrong idea.'

'What idea?'

'You know very well. I think the world of you, Ella. You know that. But . . .' He hesitated. 'The truth of the matter is I'm engaged to someone else.'

'Oh!' She closed in on herself as his words engulfed her in an icy flood. Her cheeks flamed – she was the one who was ashamed now. How could she have imagined for one moment . . . ?

'You never said.'

'The subject hasn't arisen.'

'Who . . . who is she?'

'Her name is Marigold. Marigold Deane. She's . . .'

'Your boss's daughter. I understand, Leo. And I'm really sorry for putting you in this position.'

'Don't be silly, Ella. It's not your fault. Besides, I kissed you first and I shouldn't have. I'm the one to blame. Forgive me.'

Ella swallowed hard, fought the sinking feeling that had hollowed out her stomach, pierced her heart. Summoning all her reserves of defiance, she tossed her head.

'It's all right. What's a kiss between old friends? And in any case . . .' She thought of Monty's proposal, and the ring hidden in her handkerchief sachet in London. 'I'm engaged too. To the son of a baronet, actually. An "Honourable" himself.'

'Well, I can't compete with that!' Leo actually sounded relieved and her heart sank still further.

'Look, I'd better be getting back to Jeannie,' she said. 'And if you do come back tomorrow to try to get her to talk – this never happened.'

'Agreed. And I promise we'll do our level best to sort this whole awful business out,' Leo said.

He went around to the front of the motor, bending down to crank it into life, and was lost from Ella's view. She turned back towards the house, but instead of going into the kitchen she rounded the corner, out of sight. Then she buried her face in her hands once more and sobbed as if her heart would break.

Leo pressed his foot down hard on the accelerator pedal as he shot away from the forecourt of the Feathers, only to have to brake sharply when the first bend in the steep hill he was descending loomed. The last thing he needed was to run Mr Deane's motor into a ditch. Only one thing would be worse – if his employer knew that his daughter's fiancé had kissed another woman.

What the dickens had he been thinking? Except, of course, that he hadn't been thinking at all. He was engaged to a charming, if rather spoiled, young lady, who had led innumerable suitors a merry chase, much to her doting father's despair, before setting her cap at him. He found her attractive and entertaining – she had a wicked sense of humour and loved nothing more than to behave outrageously on occasion – and, he had to admit, he was flattered that she should have singled him out of the pack for her attentions. By marrying Marigold, his future in the firm of solicitors where he had served his articles was assured.

Why in the world would he risk all that? He and Ella had been childhood friends, nothing more. It was ten years since he'd helped her and Jeannie escape the workhouse and he'd never expected to see her again. What was more, she was engaged to be married too, and to a titled gentleman at that. But in that moment when she had sobbed in his arms it was as if the years had rolled away and they were back in the rectory garden and he was comforting Ella when she'd told him of the way that old goat Rector Evans had been behaving towards her. Except that now they were no longer children but a man and a woman. Who had both made promises to other people. It mustn't happen again. He'd make sure of that.

So why did his decision leave him feeling hollow, with an ache around his heart?

Leo determinedly thrust all thoughts of Ella from his mind and concentrated on getting the motor home to Mr Deane in one piece.

Chapter Twenty-Five

Eventually Ella had composed herself sufficiently to return to the house – or so she thought. For when she bustled in saying, 'Time to get some dinner ready then,' Conrad eyed her suspiciously.

'You've been crying.'

'Hardly surprising, is it?' she said shortly. She had no intention of giving away what it was that had been the final straw. 'Where's Jeannie?'

'Gone up to her room. I think she wants to change her blouse – I saw her trying to rub out a dirty mark on it.'

'Well, that's an improvement.' It was the first time Jeannie had shown the slightest interest in her appearance since she'd retreated into herself. 'Perhaps seeing Leo has done her good. She seemed to be actually taking an interest in whatever he was talking to her about instead of just staring into space.'

'Hmm.' Conrad's expression was grim and she knew he was still worrying about what Jeannie might say if Leo persuaded her to begin talking.

'That's got to be a good thing,' Ella said firmly, fetching bread and cheese from the larder. 'She must be going through hell with all that locked up inside her, and sooner or later the truth has to come out.'

Jennie Felton

'I suppose.' Conrad sighed. 'But what I can't understand is how he could get through to her where we've both failed.'

He sounded a little put out, Ella thought, that a stranger had elicited more response from the girl he loved than he had been able to.

'Perhaps he made her feel safe,' Ella ventured. 'She associates both of us with what happened, while Leo has no connection to it as far as she is aware. And when we were in the workhouse he was always there for us. He made sure we weren't bullied, and of course he helped us to escape.'

'There is that, I suppose,' Conrad said, somewhat mollified, but anxiety still written all over his face.

'Look, Conrad, whatever she has to tell us when she's ready, we'll deal with it. Leo is coming back tomorrow to see if he can make any more progress with her. I for one hope he can. I want my sister back. And I don't want to see Martha jailed, or worse, for something she hasn't done. I can't believe you really want that either.'

Conrad didn't reply, just picked up the bread knife and began hacking off the crust of the loaf with vicious swipes.

'Don't, please, Conrad,' she cautioned him. 'We've got to try and keep calm in front of Jeannie. She'll sense it if you're in a bad temper, and it won't do her any good at all. Now, can you help me carry this through?'

She picked up the cheese and butter dishes, balanced them on three stacked plates, and went through the bar where she called up the stairs.

'Jeannie! Dinner's on the table.'

As instructed, Conrad was bringing the rest of the food, and Ella hoped he'd take notice of what she'd said about calming down in front of Jeannie. They took their places at the living room table and a few minutes later Jeannie appeared, still

382

tucking a clean white blouse into the waistband of her skirt. Then she sat down, reached for a chunk of cheese, and began nibbling on it, another positive sign. For the last couple of days she'd had to be coaxed into taking every mouthful.

'It was nice seeing Leo again, wasn't it?' Ella said, and to her surprise, Jeannie actually nodded. 'I think he's coming back to see you again tomorrow,' she went on.

Jeannie's eyes brightened and her lips moved, but no sound came.

'Oh, I forgot to tell you,' Conrad said suddenly. 'We had a couple of visitors while you were in Bath. Dr Blackmore popped in to see Jeannie and left some more medication to help her sleep.'

'That's good. We don't want to run short, do we, Jeannie?' Ella smiled at her sister.

'And he also wanted to let us know it's going to be at least another week before Lewis is allowed to come home – they're still concerned about his shoulder.'

'Right.' Ella couldn't help being relieved about that. She had enough to deal with as it was without having another invalid in the house. But the thought only made her feel guilty.

'Someone really ought to go and visit him,' she said. 'He won't know anything of what's been going on here, and he'll think we've forgotten him.' She cast a quick glance at Jeannie, hoping she hadn't upset her again by mentioning 'what was going on', but her sister seemed to have retreated back into her dream world.

'I was thinking the same,' Conrad said. 'He's had visitors, masters and boys from the school, Dr Blackmore said, but if you're going to be here with Jeannie I could ride over to see him either today or tomorrow.'

'That would be nice. I'm sure he'd be pleased to see you.'

Ella reached for the butter and spread some on a slice of bread. Though she wasn't in the least hungry, she knew she must try and eat something. 'And who was the other visitor?' she asked.

'A policeman from Hillsbridge. Apparently Garth's employer has offered to arrange the funeral and pay for it once his body is released.'

Again Ella glanced sharply at her sister, annoyed that Conrad had told her this in front of Jeannie. Why did men never stop to think before they spoke! But Jeannie still seemed to be lost in her own world and hadn't registered what had been said.

It was good news, though. Arranging a funeral was just one of the things she'd worried about in the wee small hours when she couldn't sleep. Not only was it something else to be arranged, but the cost of it would be yet another drain on their resources along with the solicitors' and barristers' fees. If Garth had been a much-loved brother she would have argued that all that should be in the hands of the family, but as things were, the less she had to do with it the better she'd be pleased. And from the casual way he'd spoken of it she imagined Conrad felt the same way.

A knock at the back door startled both Ella and Conrad but before either of them could go to answer it the door opened and slammed shut and a moment later a familiar figure appeared in the living room doorway. She was red in the face, her hat was askew, and her hair, come loose from its pins, hung in straggles down her neck.

'Aunt Ivy!' Conrad sounded both shocked and guilty, realising that in all the upset he hadn't thought to let Martha's sister or brother know what had happened.

'What's this I hear?' Ivy demanded. 'It can't be true, surely? I only went into Hillsbridge for some dried fruit to make a cake, and Mrs Robinson in the grocery shop starts asking me about our Martha and Garth. With Mrs Flower, the biggest gossip-monger going, standing at the counter right next to me, and a queue waiting behind, all getting their ears full. And me, Martha's own sister, not knowing what the dickens is going on. So you'd better explain, quick sharp! It isn't true, is it? Garth dead and our Martha arrested?'

'I'm sorry, Aunt Ivy, but it is,' Conrad said sheepishly, as if he was to blame for the whole thing, not just his aunt's ignorance of the awful events.

'Well why ever didn't you let me know? Fancy me having to hear it from the woman who serves in the grocery shop!' Ivy was outraged.

'I'm sorry,' Conrad said again. 'It's been all go here ever since—'

'You found the time to let Ella know, by the look of it.' Ivy glowered at Ella.

'Sit down, Auntie Ivy, and I'll make a cup of tea. You've had an awful shock,' Ella said, getting up. 'Jeannie, why don't you come and help me?'

Jeannie, who had been staring wide-eyed at her aunt, didn't move.

'What's up with her?' Ivy asked shortly, and Ella answered her with a tiny shake of her head.

'Come on, Jeannie.' She touched her sister's arm and beckoned, and to her relief Jeannie got up and followed her as if in a trance. In the kitchen Ella sat her down on one of the cane chairs while she put the kettle on to boil and set out cups, saucers, milk and sugar. It would give Conrad the chance to fill Ivy in on what had happened out of Jeannie's earshot, she thought, though how much Jeannie would have taken in she didn't know.

'Well, this is a tidy how d'ye do and no mistake,' Ivy said

when they returned with the tea. She looked badly shaken, as well she might, and was fanning herself with her handkerchief. 'I don't suppose our Ernie knows about it either if he hasn't been into town.'

'I'll ride over to the farm and put him in the picture,' Conrad said.

'I should think so too! So what happens next?'

The discussion was far from over, Ella realised. She touched Jeannie's arm.

'Let's go and have our tea in the kitchen,' she suggested, and to her relief Jeannie acquiesced.

'In here.'

The prison warder gave Martha a shove. She stumbled into the cell and the door clanged shut behind her. Drained physically and emotionally, she sank on to the hard bunk, let her chin drop to her chest and pressed her fingers to her aching temples. No need now to keep up appearances, no need to hold herself erect and maintain a defiant stare. Now there was no one to see, she could let down the guard that sustained her through what had been the most humiliating experience imaginable.

Handcuffs. A seemingly endless journey under the surveillance of a guard who never once took his eyes off her, contempt written all over his face. The sickening procedure of being booked into the prison, relieved of the few possessions she had been able to bring with her, stripped of her clothes, made to sit in a tin bath while her head was checked for lice, her hair washed with carbolic soap, and every inch of her body scrubbed with a loofah. Made to dry herself with a small coarse towel and dress in a rough prison smock. Escorted along a corridor with cells on either side, the inmates rattling the bars at the small high-up hatches through which food and water could be passed and shouting obscenities as they heard the tread of heavy boots and the clank of keys outside. Martha's guard bellowed at them to be quiet, or they'd get what was coming to them.

Martha was cold, hungry and thirsty. She wondered if she had missed dinner and would have to wait until the next meal time to get anything to eat or drink, or whether someone would bring her something. Her head throbbed unbearably, pain pulsing around one eye and blurring her vision. But still she could not regret what she had done. She'd bear all this, and more, willingly, if it meant saving Jeannie from this hell-hole. She wouldn't last five minutes here. She'd be broken, completely and utterly, her sweet childishness crushed, her fragile hold on reality destroyed for ever.

She couldn't – wouldn't! – let that happen to the girl who had become, to her, the daughter she had lost as a toddler. And besides, it was her son – her own son – who had taken advantage of Jeannie's innocence and trusting nature, who had defiled her, and driven her to the edge of madness. Regretfully, there was nothing Martha could do about that now, but it was in her power to save Jeannie from having to face the consequences of her actions. And do it she would, no matter what it cost her. She'd had her life, and on the whole it had been a good one. Now she would ensure Jeannie was free to live hers, and hopefully to be blessed with some peace.

Ella and Conrad would look after her. Ella was a good girl, dependable, kind, and fiercely loyal. And Conrad was in love with her. Perhaps between them they could steer Jeannie back from the brink. Help her to find happiness.

It was what Martha must cling to. That in the end the sacrifice she was making would not be in vain.

That alone would make it all bearable.

* * *

She'd got Jeannie away from the talk of Garth's murder not a moment too soon, Ella realised. She hadn't touched her tea and her hands picked ceaselessly at the folds of her skirt, whilst a variety of expressions flickered across her face as if she was having a bad dream.

'Jeannie?' Ella said anxiously. 'It's all right, darling. You're quite safe. I'm here.'

No response. Ella wondered if she should give her some of the tincture Dr Blackmore had left for her to try and calm her down. But most likely it would make her drowsy, and if she slept in the middle of the day she'd have to have another dose to make her sleep tonight. Ella didn't quite trust that she wouldn't become addicted to the stuff, whatever it was, and she didn't want that.

If only Aunt Ivy hadn't turned up, blurting out what she'd heard in the town in front of Jeannie. But to be honest, it was hardly surprising. Really, either she or Conrad should have thought to let her know before she heard the news in the way she had. Small wonder that she had been upset and indignant; it must have come as a dreadful shock. Ivy and Martha were close; she'd willingly helped out in the pub when she was needed, although she had family commitments of her own, and she had every right to know that her sister had been charged with the murder of her son. But she and Conrad had been too wrapped up in trying to deal with everything that was happening and hadn't given it a thought.

Jeannie whimpered softly, her thumb going into her mouth, and Ella made up her mind. It would have to be Dr Blackmore's tincture, and if taking it had any adverse effect she'd deal with it when the time came. At present the most important thing was to get Jeannie back on an even keel. She fetched the bottle and a teaspoon.

'Have this, Jeannie,' she said. 'It will make you feel better.'

She carefully poured out a spoonful, removed Jeannie's thumb from her mouth and slipped the spoon between her lips, making sure she had swallowed the tincture.

'Good girl. There you are, that wasn't so bad, was it?' She dropped the spoon into the sink and eased Jeannie on to her feet. 'Why don't you go and lie down for a bit? Have a little nap? You'll feel much better afterwards.'

Obediently, Jeannie got up and allowed Ella to propel her through the bar and up the stairs. In her bedroom she lay down on her bed and Ella pulled the covers up to her chin.

'Think nice thoughts, Jeannie. Imagine you're out in the meadows, with the sun on your face. Picking pretty flowers. For Mammy.'

She didn't know why she'd added that last bit. It had come out automatically, as if Jeannie were still a child, but Ella hoped that somewhere in the dark recesses of her mind it would strike a chord and comfort her.

Jeannie's eyelids were already drooping. Perhaps, delicate as she was, the previous dose of sleeping draught was still in her system. Whatever, Ella felt relieved to see her sister quiet and still at last. She crept softly from the room and went back downstairs to try and help Conrad mollify and reassure Aunt Ivy as far as was humanly possible in the face of the awful news she had just received.

'So – how did you get on with the Packer family?' Mr Deane asked, removing his spectacles and polishing them with his handkerchief.

He had been out of the building when Leo had returned, taking a lunch break, the clerk in charge of the reception office had said, and after that he had spent a good hour with an important client. Now that the appointment was over he'd sent for Leo, who'd thought from his employer's slightly glazed expression that the lunch had most likely included a glass or two of his favourite tipple, and hoped that it hadn't affected his judgement.

'To be honest I don't have a great deal to add to what we already know,' Leo said. 'It's as we were told – Conrad Packer claims to have been in bed and asleep, and Jeannie Martin is still in a state of shock and as yet unable to communicate anything she might know.'

'I see. And what about the young lady who spoke up for Martha Packer in court? Do you think it's possible she knows more than she's saying?'

'Absolutely not. She only got home from London yesterday and is as much in the dark as we are. But going back to Jeannie. I did spend some time alone with her and I believe I was getting through to her where no one else has been able to, though I must stress I kept well away from the subject of the murder for the time being. I've said I'll go back tomorrow in the hope I can build on what I was able to achieve today.'

Mr Deane still looked sceptical. 'How so? If she refuses to open up to her own sister?'

'She doesn't associate me with what happened at all,' Leo said. 'She remembers me as the boy who did his best to look after her and Ella when we were in the workhouse together.'

'Hmm.' Mr Deane considered. 'I assume you think she knows more about what happened than she's let on so far?'

'I don't think she would be in quite the state she is otherwise. I'm pretty sure she witnessed the killing and does know who is responsible, and if I can tease it out of her we should be able to discover who it is that Mrs Packer is lying to protect, and why.'

'You seem very sure she *is* lying,' Mr Deane said, replacing his glasses on the end of his nose and giving Leo a straight look over the top of them.

'Ella is convinced of it, and I trust her judgement.' Leo took a chance. 'You must think so too, otherwise why are you defending her?'

'Everyone deserves proper legal representation, whether guilty or innocent,' Mr Deane said, a little pompously. 'It is my responsibility to get her as light a sentence as is possible. That doesn't mean I have to disbelieve her confession and look for another scapegoat.' He paused, and Leo knew better than to interrupt when he knew there was more to come.

'There's no harm in you trying to elicit further evidence, I suppose,' Mr Deane said eventually, 'but it can't be tomorrow. I've arranged to meet with Mr Rupert Coulson, the barrister. I am going to brief him with regard to the defence, and you should be there.'

'Oh . . .' Leo's face fell. Though he felt awkward about coming face to face with Ella again, that didn't mean he wasn't anxious to do his best to help her with the dreadful situation she found herself in.

Mr Deane sat up straight in his tooled-leather captain's chair, imposing his authority on the young man who had been his articled clerk until he had gained all the necessary qualifications to make him a solicitor.

'Leo. If we are ever to make a good criminal defence lawyer of you it's imperative you gain as much experience as possible in the field. And it isn't every day that a case of murder drops into our laps.'

'No. I quite understand.'

Much to Leo's chagrin, he did. Mr Deane was quite right, he knew. He was a long way from being experienced enough to manage such cases by himself. Moreover, Mr Deane was not only his employer, but his prospective father-in-law. On all fronts, it would be unwise to argue, and in the end would do no good.

'We'll talk about this again.'

With that, Mr Deane dismissed him and Leo returned to his own office, ready to deal with the correspondence that he had been delegated to handle, but knowing that in reality he would still be thinking about Ella, Jeannie, and the woman who had taken them in, loved and protected them.

He owed her. And he would do his best to repay the debt that in reality was too great to ever be wiped clean.

When Leo had left the office, Mr Deane lifted the telephone from its ornate brass holder. After his liquid lunch, all he really wanted was to fall asleep, and in a minute or two he would, informing the clerk he was not to be disturbed and sinking into the leather wing chair that stood beside the window waiting for him.

But first there was something he must do. When the switchboard clicked through a connection he had only to check his diary for the number he required. And carefully choose his words when he spoke to the person on the other end of the line.

He was there again, the menacing shadow lurking behind her closed eyes. Jeannie shrank away from him, terror making her heart race and her stomach clench. He followed her, closing in, and she felt the wall solid against her back. Nowhere to go. No way of escape. She threshed about, sweat running from every pore, as his hand reached out and he towered over her, his face twisted and ugly, the mask of a monster hiding his identity. Panic consumed her, obliterating every rational thought, and she cried out, her own screams bringing her little by little through the layers of sleep to consciousness.

The last thing she saw before she woke properly was blood. Blood everywhere. Streaking the menacing grey shadow like a vivid sunset against a darkening sky. Spreading until there was no grey left at all, nothing but a sea of scarlet. Dripping from her own hands. And from the knife she held.

Jeannie shot bolt upright in the bed, eyes wide and staring, clutching at the sweat-soaked fabric of her blouse, and still screaming.

She felt arms going around her and fought like a crazed thing, twisting, turning, beating at the body that loomed over her with both hands.

'No! No! No!'

And then, as if from a long way off, a voice she recognised.

'Jeannie! Jeannie, darling! Shush! Shush! It's me, Ella.'

Though her sobs began to quieten she still couldn't bear to be touched, even by her sister. She backed up against the headboard, wrapping her arms around herself. The words were there, inside her. '*He was here!*' But still she couldn't speak them.

They would, in any case, have been useless. If she was asked 'Who?' there was no answer she could give. His face had receded behind the mask, into the shadow. And who he was, she didn't know.

Elliot replaced the telephone in its stand and sat staring at it, deep in thought.

He didn't like what he had just been told. Didn't like it one little bit. If Jeannie was to recover her memory and be able to speak out, the reputation of Marsh's was at risk. His life's work in danger of facing ruination. His own character smeared in the eyes of the whole city, including the dignitaries he was proud to count among his friends.

He rose from his chair, left the office, and went out into the passageway. A maid with a feather duster was flicking it over the marble bust that stood on a plinth beside the door to the salon. He called to her.

'Missy! Find Aaron and tell him I want to speak to him. Now, if you please.'

The maid bobbed a curtsy. 'Yes, Mr Marsh, sir.'

Elliot nodded, and returned to his office to await Aaron's answer to his summons. Much as his opinion of his long-time minder had deteriorated over the last months he was, Elliot thought, the only one who could avert the catastrophe that was of his making.

Chapter Twenty-Six

'Are you sure you and Jeannie will be all right if I go to Wells?' Conrad asked.

'Yes. You go. We'll be fine. There's nothing more you can do here, and Lewis will be so glad to see you.'

'Only if you're sure . . .'

It had been a relatively quiet day. Aided by Dr Blackmore's sleeping draught, Jeannie had spent a peaceful night, though Ella had made a bed up for herself on the floor of her sister's room so as to be on hand should she waken distressed. Ella's own sleep had been fitful. Not only was she unable to relax for worrying about Jeannie, the cushions she'd used to build a mattress were lumpy and kept shifting when she turned over and this morning she had woken with a stiff neck and aching back to add to the heaviness of fatigue.

Jeannie, however, seemed a little better, or at least, she'd returned to the silent disengagement that characterised her state of mind until Leo's visit had stirred something in her. Ella had been banking on him coming back today as he'd promised and working his magic on her sister again, but now it was late afternoon and she'd given up hope of him turning up.

There was no reason, though, why Conrad should not go to visit Lewis in hospital as he'd planned.

'How much will you tell him?' she asked now.

'I honestly don't know,' Conrad admitted. 'It all depends on how he is. The trouble is, I can't tell him half a tale – it's all or nothing – and though I don't want to worry him while he's stuck in there and away from us, it doesn't seem right to keep him in the dark.'

Ella nodded. 'I agree. I think he'd be really hurt – offended even – to think we'd deliberately kept it from him. And you never know, he might have some idea as to what we do next. He's cleverer than both of us put together.'

'I can't see that even he can come up with something we haven't already thought of,' Conrad said glumly. 'Until Jeannie remembers something – and you know the reservations I have about that – we just have to leave it up to the lawyers and hope they can make a good case for going easy on Mam.'

'I think I'll write to her,' Ella said. 'She'd like to get a letter so that she knows we're thinking of her.'

'As long as they give it to her,' Conrad said doubtfully.

'Oh, they will, surely! And you never know, she might have thought better of what she's claimed now she can see just what she's let herself in for.'

'I doubt it. You know Mam – stubborn to a fault.'

It was only a confirmation of what Ella knew deep down. Martha with her mind made up was a force to be reckoned with. She was unlikely to change her story now, however horrible prison would almost certainly be.

'I'd better be getting off then if I'm to get to the hospital for visiting time,' Conrad said.

'I'll have some supper ready for you when you get back, seeing as how you'll have missed your tea,' Ella said.

'If I'm late – and I probably will be – don't wait up for me.'

Conrad found his bicycle clips in the dresser drawer and tucked his trousers into them. 'I'll take a key.'

'No need for that. I shall want to know how Lewis is, and how he took the news, so I wouldn't sleep anyway,' Ella said. 'The door will be open.'

Conrad put on his cap. 'I won't disturb Jeannie. She was fast asleep again in her favourite chair the last time I looked in on her.'

'I know. That sleeping stuff really does seem to knock her out and last even the next day. But I suppose that can only be a good thing.'

'Take good care of her,' Conrad said unnecessarily.

'And you take care of yourself! We don't want anything else bad happening.'

'I think we've had our share for the time being,' Conrad said, and headed for the door.

'Too true!'

From the kitchen window Ella watched Conrad cycle away, then went into the living room where Jeannie was indeed asleep again, her head nestled into the curve of the big wing chair.

She found a pad of writing paper and a pen and ink and settled down at the table to write a letter to Martha, satisfied for the moment that she would be undisturbed.

'I thought I'd find you here, or somewhere like it.'

Aaron looked around with distaste. The dingy, windowless room was stuffy and smoke-filled, the gaming tables stained and ring-marked by countless beer glasses, whilst the gas lamps positioned over them flickered in their dirt-encrusted shades. This, he supposed, must be what Marsh's had been like before Elliot had transformed it.

At one of the tables, where a game of pontoon had just

finished, Pounds was pocketing his meagre winnings. Time to get out before he lost it all again, he'd decided. But Aaron was the last person he wanted to see. He'd been avoiding him since the bungled attack on Lewis Packer. Aaron might pay well, but he was bad news. And there could be only one reason why he'd come looking for the disgraced policeman.

'The boy's still in hospital,' he said shortly. 'Won't be out for another week at least.'

'So you said before. That's not why I want you.' Aaron jerked his thumb in the direction of the door. 'I've got another job for you.'

'Perhaps I'm not interested.'

'Too bad. You'll do it if you know what's good for you.'

Wearily Pounds rose and followed him. Aaron had too much on him, that was the trouble. A word from him in the ear of one of his erstwhile colleagues and Pounds might well find himself behind bars.

'What is it this time?' he asked bad-temperedly as they emerged on to the street.

'We're going for a ride.' Aaron indicated a motor drawn up at the kerb, with that spotty son of his behind the wheel. 'I'll tell you on the way.'

Pounds didn't like it one little bit. But he knew he had no choice.

Ella had finished her letter to Martha, popped it in an envelope and affixed a stamp. Then, tired out from so little sleep the night before, she settled herself in the chair opposite Jeannie's, and was dozing when she was suddenly awakened by the sound of breaking glass. For a moment she sat wondering if she'd dreamed it when it came again, splintering this time rather than cracking, and a tinkling as it fell to the flagged floor.

Instantly she was awake, adrenalin rushing through her veins and making her tremble. She leaped up, hurrying towards the bar before stopping short as she heard the creak of the back door and a man's voice.

'You needn't have bothered breaking that window. The door's not locked.'

Someone was breaking in. More than one person. Hastily Ella looked around for something to protect herself with, dived across the room and grabbed one of the fire irons. Grasping it firmly she ventured into the bar and called out.

'Who's there?'

For a heartbeat there was silence, then two men burst in from the kitchen. In that split second before they were on her she recognised one of them as the man who had confronted her and Martha when they had gone to Marsh's club. Aaron. Garth's father. The other, thick-set and bewhiskered, was a stranger to her. Before she could raise the fire iron to strike out at him he had her forearm in an iron grip, jerking, squeezing, until she was forced to drop it. Then, in a single fluid movement, he twisted first one arm behind her back and then the other, pinning her wrists together.

'What are you doing?' she squealed, her voice high with panic.

Aaron's lips curled into an unpleasant smile. He thrust her down on to a chair, where the other man held her with one big hand on her chest. Aaron pulled a length of thick twine from his pocket, then went behind her so she could no longer see what he was doing, bound her wrists tightly with the twine and knotted it around the bars of the back of the chair. Then he came around to face her.

'Where's Jeannie?'

So it was her sister they wanted. To take her back to the club, presumably. She couldn't allow that to happen.

'She's not here.'

Aaron raised his hand and slapped her across the face so hard that her head jerked back, jarring her neck.

'Come on. You can do better than that.'

Ella's mouth stung from the fierce blow, and blood trickled down her chin from where her teeth had bitten into her lip. But she was as determined as ever. She couldn't give Jeannie away.

'I told you – she's not here.'

'She's here, all right.' Aaron jerked his head at his companion. 'Go and find her.'

'You're not taking her back to that place!' Ella cried defiantly. 'I won't let you!'

Aaron laughed harshly. 'And how are you going to stop me, trussed up like a chicken ready for Christmas?'

He was right, of course. Even were she not tied up she would have been no match for these two burly men.

Vainly, she struggled with her bonds. 'You bastard!'

'You know what? You talk too much.' He took off his white silk scarf, testing it between his hands, and for a terrible moment Ella thought he was going to strangle her. Instead he put it over her mouth, tugged it so tight that her poor sore lips were stretched back at the corners, and knotted it at the back of her head. 'That should keep you quiet, my dear.'

From the living room came the sounds of a scuffle and Jeannie's screams of terror. Aaron's accomplice had discovered her. Ella jerked her head round to see them in the doorway, the man dragging Jeannie so that her slippered feet scuffed across the floorboards. Her eyes were wide with terror above the big hand that covered her mouth.

'Ah, Jeannie.' Aaron's tone was one of satisfaction.

'Well, we've got her,' the other man said. 'What do you want to do with her?'

'Once I've had my way with her, get rid of her to make sure she keeps quiet, of course. And this little hellcat too. Can't leave her here to tell tales, can we?'

Ella's blood ran cold. Did he really intend to kill Jeannie – was that the reason he had come here? But why? What was he afraid she might say if she regained her memory?

'No!' Gagged by Aaron's silk scarf it came out as a muffled, guttural sound yet pitched with desperation.

And in that moment, everything happened at once.

The man holding Jeannie must have loosened the hand that covered her mouth, maybe only a little, but enough to give the girl her chance, and she took it, sinking her teeth into a finger. The man let out a yell, instinctively jerking his hand away and putting it to his own mouth.

'Run, Jeannie!' Ella tried to say, but her words were indecipherable, and in any case, Jeannie was rooted to the spot, her eyes on Aaron. They blazed, those eyes, not so much with fear now, it seemed to Ella, as white-hot fury. Her lips worked soundlessly. And then, to Ella's amazement, she spoke for the first time since Garth's murder. Just one word. But full of meaning.

'You!'

'Come on, let's get going,' Aaron said abruptly.

'Where to?' Pounds had hold of Jeannie again, his hand streaming blood on to her blouse as he gripped her shoulder. He wasn't going to risk putting his hand over her mouth again, and in any case, if she screamed there was no one but them here to hear her.

'Somewhere their bodies won't be found in a hurry.' Aaron jerked Ella to her feet, stepping to one side as she kicked out wildly but ineffectively, and pushed her towards the kitchen door. 'Kelvin knows a good place. Come on!'

He bundled her through the kitchen and out on to the pub forecourt where his son was in the driving seat of Elliot's car with the engine running. Both girls were struggling but they were no match for the two men. Aaron manhandled Ella into the rear seat and grabbed Jeannie.

'You take care of her, I'll have this one.'

As Pounds climbed in beside Ella, Aaron lifted Jeannie bodily before heaving himself into the front passenger seat and plonking down with her on his knees, his arms pinning hers to her body so as to contain her desperate struggles.

'Go, Kelvin,' he instructed the lad, who was looking nervously at Jeannie. 'Now!'

The engine roared and Kelvin swung out on to the road. The motor rocked perilously as he struggled to correct the oversteer, narrowly avoiding another motor which was coming up the winding hill.

'Watch it!' Aaron ground out. 'A smash now is all we need.'

'I know. I know. I'm not used to this. If it were the pony and trap—'

'Well, it's not. Just get on with it. Bloody useless, is what you are.'

'Sorry.'

'Never mind sorry. Just think what you're doing.'

At the bottom of the hill Kelvin slowed to a crawl, then, after checking the road was clear, pulled cautiously across and into a lane almost hidden by thick hedges on either side. Aaron relaxed a little, his heartbeat returning to normal.

So far, so good. Kelvin might not be much good as a driver, but he knew the countryside that surrounded Bath like the back of his hand. He'd described the spot to Aaron, a wooded area straddling a river, well-hidden, but also easily accessible from the road. Perfect for their purpose. The two girls could be disposed of so they would be of no more threat to him or to Marsh's, and the fresh earth of their grave would be concealed beneath a thick layer of dead leaves, last year's and maybe the year before that. But not before he'd had his fun with Jeannie and satisfied the lust that consumed him every time he looked at her.

Smirking with anticipation, he shifted his hand to cup her breast, feeling her squirm beneath his touch. He was going to enjoy every moment of this. It was a pity she had to die, a lovely girl like her, but he couldn't risk her talking any more than Elliot could risk the reputation of his club. After all, he had a great deal more to lose than Elliot.

He was excited now, excited just as he had been that other night, when he and Kelvin had followed Jeannie and Garth to the Feathers. His original intention had been to bring her back and regain favour with Elliot, but when he'd seen her there, alone in the cottage, fragile, unbelievably beautiful, soft white flesh inviting yet somehow vulnerable above the plunging neckline of that enticing scarlet dress, he hadn't been able to resist the urge to satisfy his lust first.

That night, subsequent events had thwarted him. But this time . . . this time it would be different. He was among friends: his son, who was afraid of him, and the erstwhile policeman who was also afraid, not of him, but of the trouble he could land Pounds in if he dared to go against Aaron.

Trapped like a pinned butterfly, Jeannie dropped her head to her chest, her eyes shut tight. Behind her closed lids a horrifying scene was playing. Memories that had been buried deep in the recesses of her traumatised mind were resurfacing. Snatches had appeared to her in nightmares from which she had woken screaming, crying, but never the whole horrific picture. Tonight, seeing Aaron for the first time since Garth's death, standing there in the bar of the Feathers, had been the key that had unlocked those suppressed memories and forced a single word from her lips.

'You!'

Recollection had not come all at once, but was unfolding gradually, made clearer by the smell of whisky and cigar smoke on Aaron's breath as his chin rested on her shoulder and the repulsive touch of his hand on her breast. And her whole body shook, one muscle after the other tensing and pulsating, as she remembered.

The scarlet dress. Garth taking her down to the salon where the elderly, paunchy alderman was waiting for her. Her delight as he kissed her hand – 'Beautiful, my dear! Beautiful!' – there was nothing that pleased her more than such praise. And then the first pang of misgiving when Garth showed them into the private room with its crimson drapes and crimson velvet chaise glowing in the light of the candles in the chandelier. Clutching at Garth's hand, pleading silently with him not to leave them alone together. The door closing behind them. Her growing panic as it became clear what she was expected to do. Running from the room, gown awry, straight into Garth. The man she loved and had given herself to willingly, the man who had betrayed her. Her hands flexed and clenched now as she recalled how she'd thrust him away and fled up the stairs, knowing that he was following her.

Everything became a little blurry after that. She thought she remembered trying to close the door of her room and failing, but nothing more until she was in the motor. Perhaps she'd fainted from sheer terror. Now he was repeating over and over that he was sorry, that he would make sure something like that never happened again, that he loved her, but how could she believe him after what he'd done – offered her to a man old enough to be her grandfather, never mind her father. 'Be nice to him.' Those words kept echoing and re-echoing in her head and she cowered away against the side of the motor, not able to bear his touch, the touch that had taken her to the heights of delight.

When he drew up on the forecourt of the Feathers, however, she realised that at least he had not been lying when he said he was taking her home, and when he came around to help her out of the motor she let him. The place was in darkness, and that puzzled her. It wasn't closing time, surely? But the kitchen door was locked, and so was the main door into the bar, and there was a notice pinned to it. 'Closed Due to Unforeseen Circumstances.' What did that mean? Was it something to do with her?

Although Garth had covered her with his coat, she was shivering, and close to tears again.

'Where are they?' she asked, her teeth chattering.

'I don't know. But we'll try the skittle-alley. That's often left unlocked. We can wait there.'

But for once it wasn't. There was only one other option – the cottage, which would be far more comfortable anyway. Garth let her lean against the wall while he went to work on the lock with his penknife. 'I haven't lost my touch then,' he said, pleased with himself when the door gave.

Inside, the cottage had been barely touched since Seb's parents had both died. Martha had always been too busy to clear it out as she intended. Garth lit an oil lamp and settled Jeannie in what had been Granny Packer's favourite chair, tucking a blanket that he found in the bedroom around her.

'I'm so sorry, Jeannie.' He said it over and over. 'You're safe now. Mam will look after you until I can find a way for us to be together – but not at the club. No one will ever touch you again, I promise.'

The blanket – and his words – were warming her, and her fear of him receding. But her mouth and throat were still dry as dust.

'I'm thirsty,' she said, a little hoarsely.

'I'll go for some water.' There was no running water in the cottage; it had to be fetched from the well in the garden.

'There might still be tea in the caddy,' Jeannie said hopefully.

Garth looked, but it was empty. 'Mam must have taken it and used it up. Never mind, you can have some nice fresh water.' He fetched a jug. 'I won't be long.'

'Don't be, please!'

For some reason she suddenly felt afraid again, though no longer of Garth. It was as though some unknown terror lurked in the shadows and she didn't want him to leave her for as much as a second.

When she heard the cottage door open relief flooded through her. He *had* been quick. But it wasn't Garth who came bursting in. It was Aaron.

She shrank back in her chair, trembling again. 'What are you doing here?'

'Come to take you back to the club, of course.' He crossed the floor in a few easy strides and caught at her arm, jerking her to her feet.

She struggled to free herself. 'No! I don't want to go back there!'

'Well you are, and Garth won't interfere if he knows what's good for him. Where is he anyway?'

'In the garden, fetching water.'

'Ah. Right. Well, you're coming with me.'

The lines of his face were set in grim determination, and there was a look in his eyes now that she didn't like at all. Gloating. Lascivious. The same look as had been in the

406

alderman's eyes when he had seen her in her daring scarlet dress. She knew then he didn't only intend to take her back to the club but satisfy his lust as well.

Shaking with terror she wrenched her arm free and made a dash for the dresser where she knew Granny Packer had kept her knives in a wooden block. She snatched up the carving knife, holding it out in front of her.

Aaron laughed. 'You've got some nerve after all then.' He took a deliberate step towards her, reached out, and gripped her arm. 'Come on, drop it. You won't use it, anyway.'

She held on to it tightly.

The cottage door opened. 'What the . . . ?'

Garth was back. He slammed the jug of water down on the table, then charged towards them, grabbing Aaron from behind, yanking him away from her.

'Run, Jeannie!'

The knife fell from her shaking fingers, clattering on to the flagged floor, and she ran.

Now she felt again the rush of cold air on her face as she fled out into the night, stumbling on the cobbled path. The pony and trap was drawn up beside Elliot's car, a shadowy figure in the driving seat. Kelvin. Jeannie doubled back around the corner of the cottage and dived behind a water butt that stood there. Then she crouched down, her hands pressed against her mouth to stifle her hysterical sobs, terrified of being discovered.

How long she remained there she didn't know. At one point she heard voices followed by the engine of the motor cranking to life, the creak of the carriage and then the clip-clop of the pony's hooves on the cobbles, but still she remained where she was, afraid to believe Aaron had gone, unable to gather the strength to get to her feet.

But eventually she must have done, because she knew what

she'd found when she dared to venture back to the cottage. She'd seen it often enough in the nightmares from which she woke screaming. The blood. So much blood. Swimming all around Garth, a dark grey shadow in the fitful light of the oil lamp. The knife, still protruding from his chest. Sinking to her knees beside him, calling his name. The knife. She had to get the knife out of his chest. Then he'd speak to her, wouldn't he? Everything would be all right.

Tugging it free. Another rush of blood. His sightless eyes looking up into her face. It wasn't her Garth any more. Just a shell of scarlet and grey. Scrambling to her feet, backing away . . . An eternity, or so it seemed, crouching in a corner of the room . . . and then – oblivion.

It was there that Martha had found her, unable to speak, barely able to move. Everything that had happened had faded away, like a dream on waking, once so clear in every detail, then, in a few minutes gone, only the flavour of it remaining.

But now, as Aaron held her fast and the motor carried her and Ella heaven only knew where, it all came flooding back.

And Jeannie knew she would never be able to forget it again as long as she lived.

Chapter Twenty-Seven

By the time the meeting with the barrister was over it had been late afternoon, and Leo was fuming inwardly. It was almost as if Mr Deane had deliberately prevented him from going to the Feathers. There would have been plenty of time for him to have gone there and back again and still been in good time to meet Mr Coulson. As it was, he'd been barely able to concentrate on what was being said. He'd managed to make a few notes to give Mr Deane the impression he was listening, but in fact his mind had kept wandering away from the case they were defending – a churchwarden accused of appropriating the collection money – and back to Garth's murder. He believed Ella when she said she was convinced of Martha's innocence, but the only hope of keeping her out of prison was if he could somehow get Jeannie to talk about what had really happened that night.

'Will you join us for dinner?' Mr Deane had asked when the meeting was over. 'I'm sure Marigold would be pleased to see you.'

It was a regular occurrence; already Leo was being treated as one of the family. He never particularly enjoyed dining with them, though, sometimes feeling that Mr Deane's pontification and his wife's ceaseless chatter would drive him mad, but he knew he really had no choice but to accept the invitation, and at least Marigold, with her witty repartee, might take his mind off the subject that was tormenting him.

Not so. Tonight he had found himself irritated by her flippancy. What was funny about a churchwarden stealing money meant for the upkeep of the church and the poor of the parish? Marigold was determined to find it hilarious. Or a man's hat being blown off into the road where it had been run over by a horse-drawn carriage? That, it seemed, had been the highlight of her day when she'd witnessed it while on a shopping trip in town. Thankfully, though, the subject of Martha's incarceration did not arise. If it had, and Marigold had made some silly joke about it, Leo thought he would have been stung into saying something he'd later regret. As it was he brooded his way through three courses, and by the time coffee was served he could stand it no longer.

'Do you think I could borrow the motor so I can go out and see Jeannie now?' he asked Mr Deane.

'Jeannie? Who's Jeannie?' Marigold shot him a suspicious look.

'She's a potential witness in one of our cases.' Mr Deane had poured cream into his coffee over the back of a teaspoon so that it floated on the surface like a yellow crust.

'The problem is she is still suffering from shock and unable to tell us what happened.'

'The murder case?' Marigold asked, her interest piqued.

'Yes. Leo thinks he might be able to get her to open up, and tell us something that might be of use to us.' He turned to Leo. 'Must you go tonight? There's plenty of time, after all, before the case goes before quarter sessions.'

'Meanwhile, Mrs Packer is locked up in prison. The sooner we can find out what really happened and get her out of there the better.'

'Oh! Can I come with you?' Marigold cried, her eyes shining with excitement.

To Leo's relief, Mr Deane's reaction was swift and decisive. 'Certainly not. It would be quite wrong professionally and in any case I don't want you going to public houses.'

Marigold pouted and looked at Leo with big pleading eyes, though she must have known this was one occasion when she was not going to get her own way.

'Mr Deane?' Leo prompted his employer, who sighed resignedly.

'Oh, I suppose so. If you must.'

As he set out on the Hillsbridge road Leo was shocked to find himself comparing Marigold with Ella. Marigold might be prettier and wittier, but set against Ella she seemed shallow and empty-headed. There was no way Marigold could have survived the things Ella had; she would have stumbled at the first hurdle, while Ella had fought fearlessly for Jeannie, and was fighting now for Martha. The little girl who had been his friend had grown into an amazing woman, just as he had never doubted she would. She was strong, loyal, caring, all the things Marigold was not. And she had risen like a phoenix from the ashes of her life in the workhouse to be employed by a Member of Parliament, and engaged to the son of a baronet.

Leo's stomach twisted at that thought, and there was a bitter taste in his mouth. He'd found her again, only to lose her, this time for good. And all he could do for her now was fight for the freedom of the woman who had come to her and Jeannie's rescue.

Just as he rounded the last bend in the hill before the Feathers, another motor came off the forecourt so fast that it crossed on to his side of the road right in front of him. Leo jammed on his brakes, swerving towards the nearside bank and avoiding a collision by mere inches. But it wasn't just the near-miss that made his blood run cold. In the split second it had passed right beside him he'd recognised that motor! It belonged to Elliot Marsh, and the driver was the lad who usually drove Elliot's pony and trap. Beside him, he was sure, was Jeannie, sitting on a man's lap. And in the rear seat another man and a girl who he thought was Ella, though her face was half hidden by a swathe of something white. He turned in the driving seat, his eyes following the offending vehicle.

What the hell were they doing in Elliot's motor? Jeannie might have been persuaded to go back to the club, but Ella – never! Something was desperately wrong.

His thoughts racing, his breath coming shallow and fast, Leo swung on to the forecourt of the Feathers, turned, and headed down the hill in pursuit. Remembering his near-accident of the day before, he slowed at the last sharp bend, and when he came out of it there was no sign of the other motor. They were headed back to the club, he guessed.

He floored the accelerator and drove as fast as he dared, hoping he could catch them before they got there. It never occurred to him that the motor might have turned into the lane leading into open countryside at the foot of the hill whilst they had been out of sight.

Pounds was growing more and more uncomfortable with every passing minute. He hadn't liked this from the outset – he'd never have gone along with it if he didn't know that Aaron had him over a barrel – and he'd liked it even less when he'd seen the two young ladies he and Aaron were supposed to dispose of on Elliot's instructions. He only hoped Aaron wasn't expecting him to be the one to do the deed. Setting out to clobber a lad over the head was one thing, and when push came to shove he hadn't even been able to do that. But this was a step too far. Whatever the consequences he faced he wouldn't be party to Aaron raping that poor little lass, and he certainly wouldn't be party to murder.

Surreptitiously he removed the gag from Ella's mouth, putting a finger to his lips to warn her not to say a word, then got out his pocket knife and sawed through the twine binding her wrists. She was a canny one; apart from shifting so as to bring her arms back to their natural position and chafing her hands to bring some life back into them, she remained perfectly still, and though he couldn't see her eyes he could feel her looking at him, silently asking what he meant to do.

Truth to tell, he hadn't had time to work that out yet. But he was going to have to, and soon. They were already driving along the track that led to the spot Aaron had called 'the perfect place', and he couldn't imagine it would be very far or they'd run into civilisation again.

Whether Aaron was carrying a weapon he didn't know, but in any case the man was younger than he was, and fitter. If it came to a fight, Pounds knew he wouldn't stand a chance. And there was Aaron's son, Kelvin, too. Not that he was much of a threat, but there was advantage in numbers.

At least he had his trusty truncheon. His fingers closed around it in his trouser pocket as he considered his options. Aaron was a good bit taller than him; he wouldn't be able to get a good swing at his head unless he did it now, while Aaron was sitting directly in front of him. But he'd have to take Aaron completely by surprise, or he might end up clobbering the poor lass instead.

Stealthily he withdrew his truncheon, again signalling silently to Ella and hoping she understood what he was about to do. The motor jolted from side to side as it ran into a rut in the lane and sweat poured down Pounds' forehead. It was now or never.

He took a deep breath and steeled himself. Then he raised the truncheon and brought it down on Aaron's head as hard as he was able.

The crunch as hard wood connected with bone might almost have been the knocking of the engine, but the vibration of it travelled into Pounds' hand and up his arm so he knew he'd hit his target. Aaron's head and shoulders slumped forward with a guttural groan and almost simultaneously Jeannie screamed and disappeared from view into the footwell of the motor.

Disaster was moments away. The motor suddenly surged forward as a startled Kelvin turned to see what had happened and his foot inadvertently floored the accelerator pedal. Neither was he looking where he was going. The motor jolted violently as it hit another rut and swerved across the lane, careering into the high bank. At the moment of impact Pounds was thrown forward, so that his head hit the seat in front of him, jarring his neck, and the truncheon fell from his grasp. The motor was rearing up at a crazy angle, tipping so violently that for sickening moments it seemed it was going to turn over. Miraculously it did not, but somehow remained the right way up, though it still rocked alarmingly.

For what seemed like an eternity all was silent and still but for Jeannie's soft sobs coming from the front footwell and Kelvin's moans as he lay twisted somehow between the steering wheel and the front passenger seat. Ella had been thrown across Pounds' legs; as she tried to sit up the motor rocked again perilously. And a seemingly unconscious Aaron hung halfway out of the car.

'Jeannie!' Ella was trying to climb over Pounds now, presumably anxious to get to her sister. He gathered his senses.

'Wait! You'll have us over.'

Moving with caution, he managed to climb out of the car himself and without his bulk weighing it down it seemed a little steadier. He hoisted Ella out and held her hand while she scrambled down on to the track. Then he edged his way to the front of the motor and yanked on an unresisting Aaron so that he could reach Jeannie and pull her free. The moment Ella saw her sister she began climbing up the bank towards her, and Pounds supported the sobbing girl until her sister reached her.

'Beat it, you two!' he yelled to them.

He saw Ella grasp her sister's hand and then the two of them disappeared into the darkness.

Pounds scrambled down on to the track himself. His legs felt weak beneath him, but somehow he forced them to move, albeit slowly, away from the crashed motor. Kelvin would have to look after himself. As for Aaron, Pounds didn't know what damage he'd inflicted on him, but if he was only stunned, Pounds didn't want to be in the vicinity when he came to.

And if he was dead . . . Pounds shuddered to think of the consequences for himself.

But at least if he had committed murder, he'd killed a man who thoroughly deserved it. Not two innocent girls. At least he wouldn't have them on his conscience, if – when – he went to the gallows.

At the end of the lane Jeannie came to a halt, breathless, her trembling legs refusing to take so much as a single step more.

Ella tugged on her hand. 'Come on, Jeannie. You can do this.'

Jeannie shook her head, sinking down on to the bank.

'Well, at least get into the hedge and hide,' Ella urged, realising she couldn't drag her sister any further for the moment, and she was certainly too big to carry now, unlike that long ago night when they'd fled the workhouse.

To her relief Jeannie did as she was told. Twigs and a bramble or two caught at their clothes and hair, and carved deep scratches in their hands and faces, making Jeannie cry out, but at last Ella was satisfied that at least they were well hidden.

After a few minutes she heard footsteps and heavy breathing. Motioning Jeannie not to move or make a sound she inched forward and peeped out. It was the burly man, the one who'd helped them escape, but she made no move. In spite of what he'd done, she still wasn't sure if she could trust him.

'Are you all right, my love?' she asked Jeannie when he'd gone, up the hill in the direction of Bath.

She didn't expect an answer, but to her surprise Jeannie spoke in husky, strangled tones, not just a single word, but two whole sentences.

'It was him, Ella. It was him that killed my Garth.'

'Who?' Ella asked, staggered to hear her sister speak.

'Aaron Walters. I had Granny's knife and he was trying to take it from me and then Garth came back and I dropped it and ran. And then he came out and I went back in and Garth . . .' her voice faltered, 'and Garth . . . Oh, Ella, there was so much blood!' She broke off, tears flowing again, her body wracked with sobs.

Ella reached for her, held her tight. 'It's all right, my love. It's all right.'

She didn't really understand yet. It was all so confused. But at least Jeannie seemed to have remembered what had happened, and was able to talk about it. In her own good time she would. For the moment the most important thing was to remain hidden until she was sure it was safe for them to make their way home.

* * *

Leo was growing more and more desperate. He'd gone all the way into Bath at top speed and not seen hide nor hair of them. He'd then driven round to the club, expecting to see the motor parked outside, but there was no sign of it either there or in the surrounding streets.

Where had they been taken? Was it possible the motor had turned off somewhere when he'd momentarily lost sight of it? The road to the workhouse, perhaps? But why hadn't he seen it ahead of him on the long straight at the top of the hill? Suddenly Leo remembered there was a lane forking off in the dip before the road wound up again on the Bath side of the valley – he'd noticed a small wooden signpost though he'd never bothered to read it. Could they have turned off there? If they had, he wasn't hopeful of finding them – they had too good a start on him now – but he'd try it anyway. It really was the only thing he could think of, a long shot or not.

Hoping none of Mr Deane's friends had seen him cruising the streets of Bath, he headed back to the main Wells road for the second time that day, still keeping a good look out as he drove. As he left the environs of the city he saw the headlamps of another motor coming towards him and he slowed, his heart racing, so as to get a good look at it. But it wasn't Elliot's motor, it was a two-seater, and the driver was a man in a deerstalker hat. He slowed again to look along the road that led to the workhouse, though he was fairly certain that wasn't where they had been headed, and then put on speed again along the long straight before descending once more into the valley.

About halfway down the hill he passed a man walking up, but didn't give him so much as a second glance. Just someone making their way home after a late-night drinking session, he imagined.

In the curve of the road he pulled into the turning to the lane, slowing to a halt so as to try to read the signpost and find out where it led. Back into Bath, perhaps, by a circuitous route through a few outlying hamlets. His headlamps weren't angled high enough to see what it said, but the lane was really the only thing that seemed worth trying. If it did lead to Bath he'd go back and search there again. He reversed a little so as to be at the right angle to turn into the lane and as he turned back the headlamps illuminated a portion of the hedge and he thought he saw something move. Just a fox or a badger, he told himself, but he waited anyway and called out: 'Is anybody there?'

Again he thought he saw the leaves move and heard a branch crackle.

'Who's there?' he called again. 'Show yourself!'

And to his amazement and overwhelming relief first Ella and then Jeannie emerged from the shadow of the hedge.

He leapt from the motor, ran towards them, and they threw themselves into his arms. Bedraggled and shivering, but alive.

'What happened? Are you all right?'

Ella tried to answer but her teeth were chattering too much for her to make any sense.

'Never mind. You're safe, that's all that matters. Come on, let's get you home.'

Ella nodded. He helped the two of them into the motor and set off up the hill to the Feathers.

While Leo ensured all the doors were locked and bolted and pinned a sheet of brown paper over the broken pane in the kitchen window, Ella persuaded Jeannie to take a dose of Dr Blackmore's potion and poured stiff drinks to steady her own and Leo's nerves.

'How did you come to find us?' she asked, taking first a sip and then a gulp of her brandy.

418

'I was coming out to visit you and saw the motor with you and some men in it. It nearly ran into me. It was Aaron Walters and his son, wasn't it?' Ella nodded. 'I've been looking for you ever since.' He, too, took a healthy drink from his glass. 'But more important, what was going on, and how did you come to be hiding in the hedge?'

'It was terrible,' Ella said. 'They were going to kill us. And they would have done if the man Aaron had brought with him hadn't clobbered him, why I don't know, and Aaron's son who was driving lost control and crashed the car—'

'Slow down,' Leo said. 'You're losing me. Just start at the beginning – how did you come to be in the car with them in the first place?'

Trying to downplay the horror of it all so as not to upset Jeannie again, Ella related the awful story while Leo listened, and interrupted every so often with a question.

'So the same man who hit Aaron then helped you to escape?' he asked when she'd finished.

'Yes. If it wasn't for him . . .' She broke off, unable to complete the sentence.

'Where is he now?'

'On his way back to Bath, I think, walking. I saw him go past after we hid in the hedge.'

'And Aaron and his son?' Leo asked.

'I don't know. Still with the car, I should think. They both looked badly hurt – neither of them were moving after we crashed, and the man who helped us to escape did hit Aaron awfully hard. He could be dead for all I know.'

'I'd better go into Hillsbridge and report all this to the police,' Leo said. 'They'll call the ambulance to attend the men, I expect, and they'll certainly want to take a statement from you, and Jeannie too, if they can get anything out of her. Do you want to come with me, or will you and Jeannie be all right here?'

'We'll be all right,' Ella said. 'Jeannie's been through enough already tonight and I don't think we'll be in any danger now from Aaron or his son. Even if they managed to right the motor and get it back on the road I'd be surprised if either of them was in a fit state to come back here. You go, Leo. The sooner the better.'

'Just as long as you're sure.' He covered her hand with his, his eyes looking deep into hers. 'Don't answer the door to anyone except me or a policeman.'

'Don't worry, I won't,' Ella said with feeling, then added: 'I'll have to let Conrad in when he gets home. He rode his bike over to Wells to see Lewis.'

'Well, yes, obviously, but just make sure he's alone. And make sure you lock the door properly after me.'

'Leo, if they wanted to break in again it wouldn't be so difficult with nothing but a sheet of brown paper over the kitchen window,' Ella pointed out. 'But they're not in a fit state for that, I'm sure of it.'

She went to the door with Leo, watched him get the motor going, locked and bolted the door, and went back to Jeannie.

In the silent house the creak of every settling beam set Ella's taut nerves on edge but she told herself she was just imagining things. Thankfully the potion seemed to have calmed Jeannie. Although she was still huddled in her chair, her fingers working incessantly at the folds of her skirt, she had made some effort to clean her face with her handkerchief and a small pile of bits of twig that she'd picked out of her hair lay on the table beside her.

'How are you feeling, my love?'

Jeannie's eyes came up to meet hers. 'What I said . . . about Aaron . . .'

Ella had deliberately not mentioned it to Leo. She hadn't wanted him to start questioning her tonight, and she didn't think she should press her now.

'You don't have to say any more until you're ready, Jeannie.'

'But I want to.' Jeannie's voice was still hoarse from disuse, but urgent. 'Now I've remembered I have to! For Martha's sake . . .'

And suddenly the words were tumbling out, one on the other, and surreal as the story sounded, Ella was convinced she was telling the truth. No wonder she'd been left traumatised! But now she'd recovered her memory – thanks to the shock of coming face to face with Aaron again – and been able to speak about it, perhaps she would begin to heal.

It was a huge relief to know that Conrad's fears about Jeannie's part in the murder had been unfounded. They'd been right to suspect Martha was lying to protect her. But when Martha had found her with the knife in her hand and covered in blood she'd jumped to the wrong conclusion. What a wonderful, selfless thing to do, and so typical of Martha. Hopefully her ordeal would soon be over and she would be released.

Then Ella went cold again as something else occurred to her. Would the police believe Jeannie's story? Or would they think she was making the whole thing up to hide her own guilt? If so, she could still well end up in prison, or a lunatic asylum.

Determinedly she pushed the awful thought aside. She couldn't face it now, and she wouldn't have Jeannie questioned tonight.

'I think you should go to bed now and try to get some sleep,' she said. 'Come on, my love.'

She led an unprotesting Jeannie upstairs, helped her to undress, put her to bed with a second good dose of her sleeping draught, and stayed with her until her eyes closed and her breathing became even. Then she went back downstairs, poured herself another stiff drink and sat down to await Leo's return, and with him, presumably, the police.

She'd scarcely settled in the chair when a rap at the door announced that Conrad was home from Wells.

'What's all this?' he asked, indicating the broken window,

'Oh, Conrad, it's been terrible. Let's go and sit down and I'll tell you. But get yourself a drink first. Believe me, you're going to need it.'

Conrad listened aghast as Ella related the events of the evening, and his first thought was to go to Jeannie, but Ella stopped him.

'If you go up there you'll probably wake her up and that's the last thing she needs,' she said firmly. 'She's fine, I promise you. And there's more. She's told me what happened the night Garth was stabbed. It wasn't her or Martha, it was Aaron.'

'Aaron? What was he doing here?'

Ella launched into Jeannie's story and this time Conrad's overriding emotion was relief.

'Well, at least that's good. When your friend gets back with the police we can tell them that too. It'll put Mam in the clear, and Jeannie too.'

Ella didn't mention her fears that Jeannie's story might end up incriminating her, and she didn't think it was a good idea to tell the police about it tonight.

'Leave it until tomorrow,' Ella said firmly. 'If we say anything now they'll want to speak to Jeannie, and the last thing she needs is to have to go over it all again tonight.'

Conrad considered. 'Perhaps you're right.'

'I know I am.' She cocked her head at the sound of a motor

outside. 'That sounds like them now. Remember – not a word!'

'Look – whatever you say, I'm going up to sit with Jeannie. I'll be careful not to wake her – just make sure she's all right. And there's nothing I can tell the police about what happened earlier.'

Ella nodded, and went to open the door.

She didn't recognise the man who came into the house with Leo but she assumed he was a policeman. Though he was wearing a smart coat, waistcoat and tartan check trousers rather than a uniform, there was an air of authority about him.

'This is Detective Inspector Bowen,' Leo said. 'I went to Bath rather than Hillsbridge – I thought they'd be better equipped to deal with something like this.'

'I thought Mr Turner was the inspector—' Ella began but the policeman cut her off.

'Inspector Turner is not on call tonight – I am,' he said briskly. 'Do you know him?'

'Yes . . . He's the one who's been investigating Garth's murder. But . . .'

'Ah, the murder. Yes.' Inspector Bowen looked a little put out, as if there was professional rivalry between him and his colleague.

'Have you found Aaron Walters?' Ella asked urgently.

'Your abductor? Two uniformed officers have been despatched to what you claim was the scene of the accident. They will deal with whatever they find there, and this man will be taken into custody – if he's in a fit state. I'm here to get your side of the story first, and determine what charges, if any, should be brought against him.'

Ella didn't like this man, she decided. She hadn't been very enamoured of Inspector Turner either, but he hadn't been quite so pompous and objectionable, and she was glad she'd made up her mind not to talk about Jeannie's revelation tonight.

'You say your sister was abducted with you,' he said brusquely. 'Where is she? I'll need to speak to her too.'

'I'm sorry, but that will have to wait until tomorrow. She's in bed and asleep, hopefully. There's nothing she can tell you that I can't, and she's in no fit state to have to relive what happened tonight.'

The inspector pulled himself up to his full height, puffed up with pomposity.

'Madam, do you realise you are obstructing the police in the course of an investigation and that is a serious offence?

'Inspector Bowen.' Leo stepped forward, very much the lawyer all of a sudden. 'Miss Martin and her sister are the victims here. I'd advise you to cease harassing this young lady.'

The inspector turned on him. 'Just who do you think you are, eh?' His tone was heavy with sarcasm.

'I am a solicitor with the old established Bath firm of Churchill and Deane, Inspector. I am Miss Martin and her sister's legal representative. And if you do not desist with these bullying tactics I shall be registering a complaint with your senior officers.'

The inspector snorted impatiently. Some of the wind had gone out of his sails, but he wasn't going to admit it.

'I'll take a statement from you, Miss Martin, which will perhaps suffice for now. And I'd like one from you too, sir, if you have no objection,' he added sarcastically.

Somehow Ella managed to retain her composure until the inspector had left, having taken the requisite statements. As the door closed after him, however, she sank forward on to the drawing room table, trembling violently and burying her face in her hands.

'What a bastard!' Leo said with feeling. 'It's officers like him who get the police force a bad name.'

Ella raised her head a little, cupping it in one hand, and heaved a deep sigh. 'Can things get any worse?'

'They very easily might have.' Leo took the chair that the policeman had vacated and reached over to cover her free hand with his. 'I thought I'd lost you just when I've found you again.'

Something warm and sweet twisted in Ella's stomach. She turned her hand over so that her fingers intertwined with his and managed a weak smile.

'You don't get rid of me that easily.'

For a long moment they remained that way, neither speaking, as little tingles like the electricity generated by a lightning bolt passed between them. Then, abruptly, Leo stood up.

'I should be getting back. I'm going to have some explaining to do as it is.'

'Wait – just a little longer. There's something I haven't told you . . .' Ella caught at his sleeve. 'Jeannie has remembered what really happened to Garth. She's told me everything.'

'Really?' Leo sat down again, looking at Ella intently. 'She's talking?'

'Yes. It was Aaron Walters who was responsible, and I think the shock of seeing him again triggered her memory. And when she started talking, she couldn't stop. It was a huge relief to get it off her chest, I think, rather than bottling it all up inside.'

'So how did it come about?' Leo asked, his professional side coming to the fore once more.

Ella related everything Jeannie had said. 'I didn't want her to have to go over it all again tonight, though, which is why I didn't say anything in front of that policeman. And I'm worried that suspicion might fall on her too. Clearly Martha thought she'd done it, and wanted to protect her. But supposing they think that the reason Martha did what she did was because she *knew* she was guilty?'

Leo rubbed his eyes with his fingers. They felt gritty and sore, and a headache was beginning to throb behind them.

'I can't deal with this tonight, Ella. I'm too tired to think straight. And obviously the way forward has to be Mr Deane's decision. Now, I really must go. He'll be wondering what the hell has happened.'

'Yes, of course. You don't want to upset your future father-in-law,' Ella said evenly, though she felt as if her heart was being torn in two.

'We'll be in touch tomorrow. I'll come out and collect you and Jeannie and take you to the office. In the meantime, just take care, Ella.'

At the door he laid a hand lightly on her arm, stroking it gently, and briefly it was there again between them, that connection that neither could deny. Then he was gone, the motor pulling away from the forecourt, and as its lights disappeared into the darkness, Ella felt utterly bereft.

Jeannie was sleeping. Conrad took the chair beside her bed. He wouldn't leave her tonight. He'd get what rest he could in the chair. He stroked her hair where it lay tangled on the pillow and thought that out of this nightmare at least some good had come. She'd been besotted with Garth; now he was gone. And Conrad was going to make sure that he would look after her from now on. She might never feel about him the way she had felt about Garth, but he'd accept that. Just as long as he could be by her side, caring for her, hopefully one day making her happy again. He acknowledged that in the end Garth must have cared for her too, if he had given his life for her. His brother could not have been all bad.

* * *

Pounds huddled on a bench outside the railway station, the collar of his coat pulled well up in case anyone should recognise him.

He hadn't waited to find out if Aaron and Kelvin were alive or dead. Either way he was done for. He'd followed the girls along the lane and headed up the hill towards Bath. But he had no intention of remaining there. Best to get as far away as he could from all the trouble that might come to his door – and from his miserable carping wife. London beckoned. He could lose himself there, find work of some kind and start a new life.

But he wouldn't be using his experience to get on the wrong side of the law again, that much was certain. He'd learned his lesson. He'd be steering well clear of rogues like Aaron Walters and Elliot Marsh.

Shivering at the narrowness of his escape, Pounds settled down to wait for the milk train.

Chapter Twenty-Eight

'I'm sorry, Leo, but I'm afraid I can no longer represent the Packer family.' Mr Deane tapped his desk blotter with his pen to emphasise the point as he spoke.

'But why?' Leo asked, dismayed and bewildered.

This was the first chance he'd had to update his superior on the latest developments. He'd tried last night when he'd returned the motor, but an irate Deane, clad in his nightshirt, nightcap and slippers, had informed him testily that it would have to wait until morning. He was of no mind to listen to Leo's news at this ungodly hour.

Mr Deane sat back in his captain's chair, twirling the pen now between his fingers.

'Conflict of interest. Elliot Marsh has been a client of mine for many years, and is also a personal friend. Representing Mrs Packer in the matter of the murder of her son was one thing, but this is quite another, since Aaron Walters is a long-standing employee of Elliot's. It may even be that Marsh's is dragged into this whole unsavoury business. I simply cannot continue with the case, let alone become embroiled in this new debacle.'

'But—' Leo opened his mouth to argue, but his superior interrupted.

'I'm sorry, but that is my final decision. The Packer clan will have to find another solicitor.'

It was useless to argue, Leo realised, and unpalatable as it was, he could see Mr Deane's point.

'How are you going to let them know this?' he asked, an idea already beginning to take shape in his head.

'I'll write to them immediately. There's no time to be wasted in disassociating myself with these cases.' His eyes levelled with Leo's. 'Please ask my clerk to come in on your way out.'

Although the dismissal was crystal clear, Leo made no move to leave. 'At least let me go out and tell them myself. We owe them that much, surely.'

Mr Deane considered, then nodded. 'Very well, provided you don't take as long about it as you did last night. I expect my motor to be back in little more than the time it takes you to drive there and back.'

'Thank you, sir.' Now Leo did get up and move to the door, before Mr Deane could change his mind. 'I presume you won't need your clerk now?'

'You presume wrongly, my boy. It is always advisable to have written evidence of something as serious as this. Send him in.'

Leo found the clerk, then went out to where the motor was parked outside the office, got it started, and set off. As he headed through town towards the road that would take him to the Feathers he realised this would be the last time he would drive it.

The idea that had occurred to him in the office had turned to a firm decision. His mind was made up. If Mr Deane would no longer act for Martha, or take on the case of Ella and Jeannie's abduction, then he would. It would almost certainly cost him his position, but he was qualified now. He'd find another. And if it meant the end of his relationship with Marigold too, then so be it. He couldn't care less about that. The marriage would have been more one of convenience than anything else, on his part at any rate. He wasn't in love with her and never had been, and since meeting Ella again, he had realised that. He might have lost her to a man with a title, but that didn't mean he would settle for second best. And he didn't have to any more. If he was no longer employed by Churchill and Deane he need not worry about upsetting his superior.

As he sped away from Bath with the wind in his hair, Leo felt the chains dropping away from him, and he experienced the same feeling of freedom as he'd had when he'd walked out of the workhouse for the last time all those years ago. In spite of all the difficulties that still lay ahead, for the first time in a long while Leo felt truly happy.

In the sitting room of the Feathers, Inspector Turner was occupying the same seat as Inspector Bowen had last night, and another, younger, policeman sat across the table, a pen poised over a statement pad. Between them sat Jeannie. Her head was bowed, her face tear-stained, and from time to time her thumb strayed into her mouth, but she seemed relatively calm. Ella had been right. Being able to talk at last about the events that had been locked away inside her had certainly brought some relief.

From the other side of the room Conrad kept a watchful eye on proceedings, whilst Ella had retreated to the kitchen, supposedly to boil the kettle for tea, but in fact so that she could watch out of the window for Leo. He'd said he'd come this morning to take them to Bath, and she wished desperately that he would hurry up. She didn't like the policemen questioning Jeannie without a solicitor present, but she'd raised no objection in case it made it look as if they had something to hide. Besides, the sooner this was over with, the sooner Martha would be released from jail.

Just as she left the window to set out cups and saucers she heard the sound of the engine, and swivelling round so hastily she almost knocked a cup over she saw the motor pulling on to the forecourt. Breathless with relief, she flew out of the door.

'Oh, Leo, thank goodness! The police are already here, and Inspector Turner is talking to Jeannie. Is that all right, without Mr Deane? Will he be cross we didn't call for him?'

'Wait, wait, wait.' Leo turned off the engine and climbed down.

'But will he be? I hope we haven't done the wrong thing.'

Leo took her by the forearms. 'Ella, there's something I must tell you. Mr Deane won't be representing you or Martha any more.'

'What do you mean? Why not?' Ella was horrified.

'Because apparently Elliot Marsh is a client of his and also a friend. It's a conflict of interest, he says. But don't worry. I'm stepping in. I'll be acting for you from now on.'

'Oh – can you do that?'

'I'm going to, whether or not he's agreeable. Fill me in on the latest developments, and then I'll decide on the best course of action.'

'Oh, Leo – thank you!' Ella tried to compose herself. 'Well, as far as I know, Jeannie is telling them the same story as she told me. We haven't got around to last night yet. But one thing Inspector Turner did tell us is that both Aaron and his son were found alive. Aaron is badly hurt, his son not so much. So at least the man who intervened for us won't be facing a charge of murder, or not yet, at any rate, though it does seem that Aaron is in a bad way.'

'I can't say I'd cry any tears for the bastard, but I'd like to see him stand trial for Garth's murder and what he put you through last night,' Leo said with feeling. 'But terrible as it was for both of you, it will provide back-up evidence for Jeannie's story. Without it, it could well have been argued that she was lying to save her own skin as well as Martha's. As it is there can be no doubt that they took you for a reason – to stop Jeannie from revealing what really happened. And they had to act fast when they learned she was beginning to recover.'

'But how would they know that?' Ella asked.

'I told Mr Deane I was making some progress with her, and I suspect Mr Deane had a word in Elliot Marsh's ear,' Leo said grimly. 'Come on, let's go in and see how it's going.'

'Oh, there is one more thing,' Ella said. 'The policeman also said the white silk scarf Aaron gagged me with was found in the back of the crashed motor. That's more evidence to support our story, isn't it? I told the inspector who came last night about it and it was included in my statement. And if it wasn't recovered until later, I couldn't have known about it, could I?'

'Good.'

'And they did ask me if I could describe the other man, the one who helped us, and I said I couldn't. Is that perjury?'

Leo smiled. 'If it is, I think it can be excused. After all, he did save your life, and Jeannie's.'

And for that I shall always be truly grateful to him, he added silently.

As they entered the living room Inspector Turner had just finished reading Jeannie's statement aloud to her.

'Ah, the solicitor. You're just in time to witness your client's signature.'

Leo held out his hand.

'I'd like to see it myself first, if you don't mind.'

'As you wish.' Inspector Turner handed it to him and waited

expectantly while Leo read the statement.

'And Miss Ella Martin too. It was she who was the first to hear Jeannie's story. I'd like her to confirm there are no discrepancies.'

He passed the statement to Ella, who read it through and nodded. 'Yes, that's exactly what she told me.'

'Good.' He handed his own pen to Jeannie, who signed in a rather shaky hand, then placed the statement in his briefcase. 'Now, I am going to the hospital in Bath to see if Walters is fit to be interviewed. I'll keep you up to date with developments, Mr – ah . . .'

'Fisher,' Leo supplied. 'But I'm afraid you won't be able to contact me at Churchill and Deane. I am no longer with them. Mr Deane may well be representing Walters, and looking after Elliot Marsh's interests too, or so I believe.'

The inspector looked surprised. 'I see. Then perhaps you could contact us later this afternoon so that I can let you know where things stand.'

'I'll do that.'

'Don't you want to ask me about last night?' Ella asked.

Inspector Turner was already preparing to leave, as was the other officer.

'That won't be necessary at present,' he said. 'I have the statements you and Mr Fisher gave last night to Inspector Bowen, and they will suffice for the present.'

When the two policemen had gone, Leo turned to Ella.

'It's going to be difficult letting you know what's happening, too,' he said. 'After this I don't suppose I'll have the use of Mr Deane's motor. In fact, if I don't soon get it back to him I might very well find myself on a charge of theft.' Seeing Ella's horrified expression, he smiled. 'Don't worry, I don't think it will come to that.'

'I sincerely hope not! Oh, Leo, I don't know how we can ever thank you.'

Leo smiled briefly. 'Don't worry. I'll think of a way.'

Conrad, who had been occupying himself with Jeannie, looked up.

'We're in your debt, no doubt about that.'

'I was joking,' Leo said swiftly.

Ella went with him to the motor. 'I could always come into Bath on the train,' she suggested.

'Or I could come out on one. It all depends what happens. But I will keep you posted, and that's a promise.'

'I know you will.'

Once more there was a moment when their eyes met, conveying what they could not put into words. Then Leo started the motor and was gone.

Pounds had reached London and wasted no time in finding himself a room in a cheap lodging house near Paddington Station. Then he went out and looked for a shop selling stationery, bought a writing pad, envelopes and a pencil, and took them back to his room.

For the duration of the rail journey he'd been thinking about Aaron Walters and the awful crimes he'd committed, and about the woman who was in jail awaiting trial for something she hadn't done. He knew Jeannie might well have recovered her memory by now, but he wasn't sure what the police would make of it if she did. From what he knew of her she wouldn't make the most reliable of witnesses, and might even end up charged with Garth's murder herself. He wouldn't have been able to live with himself if that happened. Aaron might well be dead – he'd given him a pretty hefty thwack on the head – but if he wasn't, he should be the one to answer for his crimes.

There was no way Pounds was going to present himself at a police station to reveal what he knew. If he did he'd no doubt find himself arrested for assault at best, and, if Aaron was dead, charged with his murder. But if he put his story in writing it would at least corroborate Jeannie's story.

As a former policeman himself he was well used to writing statements. Sitting at a table in a down-at-heel coffee house he opened the writing pad and began by heading it up with his real name and address in Bath, so as to give it the necessary authenticity. He wasn't worried about the police looking for him there and they could hassle his bitch of a wife as much as they liked. He was gone and wouldn't be going back, and he intended to create a new identity for himself here in London. He then set out all the facts. He hadn't been there when Aaron had knifed Garth, but Aaron had told him what had happened when he'd asked him to go with him to silence Jeannie, and if necessary, her sister too. Having signed the statement he wrote a covering note of explanation on a fresh sheet of paper, put the whole lot in an envelope, and went in search of a police station.

It didn't take him long to find one – Paddington Green. He pulled his cap well down over his eyes, marched in, put the envelope down on the counter, and hurried out again, stuffing his cap into his pocket and quickly merging into the crowds thronging the pavement.

A weight seemed to have been lifted from his shoulders. He was ashamed of many of the things he'd done for Aaron Walters and Elliot Marsh, but he wasn't sorry he'd clobbered Aaron, and he felt he'd redeemed himself somewhat by putting the weight of his evidence behind those who were innocent of any crime.

He'd find himself an honest job here in London, he decided, be it labouring, window cleaning or sweeping the streets. He couldn't afford to do anything to draw attention to himself for the time being, at least. And whatever it was, it would be a relief to be a law-abiding citizen after the long years of dabbling on the seedy side.

Satisfied, Pounds found a tea room and ordered himself a much-needed beef and ale pie and a cup of strong tea.

Back in Bath, Leo made straight for Mr Deane's office, entered without knocking, and threw the keys to the motor down on the desk.

'I think I should tell you that I am going to represent Martha Packer, and Ella and Jeannie Martin if Aaron Walters survives to face trial for their abduction.'

The solicitor looked up, his face reddening with an angry flush. 'What are you talking about? I told you this morning, they are no longer clients of this firm.'

'Which I am leaving. You'll have my letter of resignation as soon as I've cleared my desk and written it. I'm sorry, sir, but I can't be associated with the scoundrels who have done the things they have. Ella and Jeannie Martin are lifelong friends of mine and that creates a conflict of interest, as you pointed out with regard to Elliot Marsh and Aaron Walters.'

'Have you taken leave of your senses? You'd throw away a promising career for girls who are almost certainly no better than they should be?' Mr Deane removed his spectacles, gesticulating with them as he spoke.

'They are thoroughly decent young women. And I won't be throwing away my career. I'm a fully qualified solicitor now.'

'Trained by us. No other firm in Bath will take you on. It's not the done thing to poach articled clerks from the solicitor who taught them.'

'Then I'll find someone elsewhere who will. Or set up my own business.'

'Leo.' Seeing he was getting nowhere by threatening, Mr Deane adopted a softer, more reasonable tone. 'Don't act in haste, my boy. You'll never be able to find another position as advantageous to you as this one. You'll be a partner soon, and when I am ready for retirement you will become the *senior* partner. Your future here is assured. As for the young ladies, they will have no difficulty in finding representation elsewhere. Now, tell me you won't do anything so foolish as turning your back on such an opportunity.'

'I'm sorry, sir,' Leo said, 'but this goes much further than you simply representing Walters, and maybe Elliot Marsh too. I believe you warned them that Jeannie was beginning to recover so that they could do something about it before she talked about what goes on at the club, and implicated Aaron Walters in the murder of Garth Packer.'

'How dare you!' His attempt at sweet-talking Leo forgotten, Mr Deane brought his fist down hard on his desk, so that paper scattered and flew. His eyes were bulging with fury, showing a network of tiny red veins. 'How dare you suggest such a thing!'

'Because you did, didn't you? I told you I was making headway with Jeannie, and you told Marsh. And then you tried to stop me talking to her again until they'd had a chance to get to her, first by insisting I went with you to see Mr Coulson and then by inviting me to supper.'

'Balderdash!' Deane blustered. 'I let you borrow my motor to go and see her.'

'Only because you thought you'd bought them enough time to deal with her. And you had. It was only thanks to Walters' accomplice that they escaped. If he hadn't done what he did they'd both be dead. You are every bit as guilty as Marsh and Walters, Mr Deane.'

'Get out!' A pulse throbbed visibly in Deane's temple and he had turned puce with fury, making Leo fear that he was about to have a heart attack or stroke. 'Don't bother to write a letter of resignation – you are fired. I don't ever want to set eyes on you again. And as for marrying my daughter – you can forget that. My consent is withdrawn.'

'Don't worry about that, sir,' Leo said evenly. 'I certainly won't, and I'm sure it won't take you long to find someone more suitable. Marigold is a very pretty young lady but I'm afraid I was never in love with her, so I'm sure it's for the best.'

Then, before Deane could respond, he marched out of the office.

It was late afternoon when a wardress opened the door of Martha's cell. Her heart sank. What now? It wasn't yet time for the evening meal, such as it was, and they'd already had their turn in the exercise yard for today.

The wardress, Neeson, a big brute of a woman, tossed a bag containing Martha's own clothes on to the bunk, her ugly face as forbidding as ever.

'Get dressed and get your things together.'

'Why? Where am I going?' Martha asked, summoning every ounce of her natural dignity.

'Back to Bath. Look lively. We haven't got all day.'

Back to Bath? But why? The warder stood in the cell doorway, arms akimbo, while Martha took off the prison issue smock and put on the dress she'd been wearing when she'd been arrested. She knew better than to ask any more questions. Neeson wouldn't give her any answers, and would more than likely give her a quick pinch for her trouble.

As the outer doors of the prison were unlocked she was surprised to see that it was not the transport she'd been brought here in that was waiting for her, but a motor car, and beside it one of the male guards was leaning on the bonnet and smoking a cigarette. He straightened when he saw Martha, tossed the cigarette butt down and trod it into the gravel.

'Come on then. In you get.' Unlike Neeson and so many of the other warders he had a pleasant, open face, and there was no malice in his smile. 'You're being treated like royalty tonight and no mistake.'

Martha climbed up into the motor and the warder got up beside her. The engine was already running, with a man in chauffeur's uniform in the driving seat.

'Let's go then, Wally,' the warder said, and the motor pulled away, down the drive, out through the gates which a doorman opened for them and closed behind them.

Martha felt able to ask this warder a question without fear of reprisal. 'Why am I going to Bath?'

'Search me. All I know is they want you back there quick sharp, and we weren't to use restraints on you.'

'Thank goodness for that.' Martha still had red weals on her wrist from the handcuffs they'd put on her when she'd been remanded in custody.

The remainder of the journey passed in silence, but when they reached Bath police station Martha was taken straight to an interview room, where she was shortly joined by Inspector Turner.

He took his place at the table opposite her, opened a file and shuffled papers. Then he looked up, straight into her face.

'I think it's time for you to tell us the truth, Mrs Packer.'

Martha stiffened. She hadn't known what to expect, but certainly not this. 'I've told you the truth,' she said wearily.

'Not according to new evidence.'

Martha could have sworn that she saw the merest twitch of a smile, but thought she must be mistaken. His next words, however, sent a chill down her spine.

'Your adopted daughter, Jeannie Martin, who was previously unable to recall the events of the night of your son's murder, has recovered her memory and has made a statement as to what actually happened.'

'No!' The denial was sharp and perhaps a little desperate. 'She had nothing to do with it. I killed my son. I've told you so over and over again.'

'You confessed because you believed she was responsible, didn't you?'

'Of course not! Why would I—'

'I'm sorry, Mrs Packer. I don't for one moment believe your story. Jeannie Martin claims that the murder was committed by Aaron Walters, and we have received a wire from Paddington Green police station in London to the effect that a former accomplice of Walters has made a statement to them which corroborates Jeannie Martin's contention. There are other matters, too, which we need not go into just now, which would also seem to show that Miss Martin is telling the truth when she says the killer was in fact Aaron Walters.'

All the colour had drained from Martha's face. She just couldn't take it in. Aaron Walters. The man whose dark shadow had blighted her life.

'But why?' she managed. 'What was he doing there?'

The inspector didn't answer her question.

'First, Mrs Packer, I would like you to reconsider your original statement and tell me what happened that night from your standpoint.'

'Jeannie's in the clear – really?' The words were out before she could stop them.

'She is, Mrs Packer.' That faint smile hovered once more around Inspector Turner's mouth. 'So, are you ready to begin?'

* * *

At a special sitting of the magistrates' court next morning, all charges against Martha were formally dropped. Leo was there, and when it was over and she walked from the building a free woman, he hailed a cab and took her home to the Feathers.

In all that had happened the previous night, Conrad had forgotten to tell Ella that Lewis was to be discharged from hospital, and she was both amazed and delighted when Dr Blackmore's pony and trap pulled up on the forecourt and the doctor came in with Lewis, whose arm was still in a sling, but who otherwise looked fit and well.

Jeannie, still very much on the edge of her nerves, burst into tears.

'That's a fine welcome for me!' Lewis teased her.

'She's just very emotional at the moment,' Ella said. 'She's pleased to see you really, aren't you, Jeannie?'

Lewis didn't question why that should be; he was used to Jeannie's highs and lows, and Ella didn't want to go into the awful story of last night's ordeal until the doctor had left and Lewis had had the chance to have a nice cup of tea. Conrad had prepared him for the situation at home when he'd visited, but he hadn't known, of course, about the abduction. And Lewis didn't know either of Martha's imminent release – Sergeant Love had called early this morning to inform them.

'And we're expecting Mam home today too,' Conrad told him. 'I must ride over and let Auntie Ivy know.'

He'd scarcely spoken when the cab Leo had called drew up outside.

The family reunion was joyous. Everyone was hugging everyone else, laughing and crying at once. Martha was home. Lewis was home. And Leo had told them he'd heard at court this morning that Aaron had died. It was over. Everything was going to be all right.

Elliot Marsh replaced the telephone receiver on its stand and sat at his desk deep in thought.

The call he'd just taken was from the hospital. Aaron Walters had passed away during the night.

In many ways it was a relief. He'd dreaded a trial when everything would come out in open court – the goings-on at his club which had led to Aaron's crimes. He wasn't out of the woods yet; there might well still be investigations, but he thought he had enough friends in high places to help him cover up what went on behind closed doors. None of them would want the truth of it broadcast, many were clients who would do anything to prevent their peccadillos becoming public knowledge and would be none too pleased if the club was closed down either. But even if it did come out it wouldn't generate the same damaging headlines as a murder trial. Though Aaron's death had saved him from that Elliot still felt a certain amount of regret, if not grief, that his minder had met his maker. They'd been together a long time, even if in recent years he'd become impatient and intolerant of Aaron's ways, and he'd miss him.

So, who would he name as his heir now that both Garth and Aaron were dead – if there was anything left to leave after the police investigation? Elliot wondered. Perhaps he'd close the club, retire, and enjoy the fruits of his labours. He had plenty of money salted away.

Elliot smiled suddenly. Really, that was a rather attractive prospect. Perhaps this whole unfortunate business was a blessing in disguise.

* * *

'Can we talk somewhere quiet?' Leo suggested to Ella.

She nodded. Happy as she was to have Martha home again in the bosom of her family without a stain on her character, the noisy celebrations were beginning to make her head ache.

A chilly wind was blowing scuds of rain into their faces as they crossed the yard to the skittle-alley.

'It's a shame it wasn't raining last night,' Ella said. 'They might have thought twice about driving out here in an open motor.'

'I doubt it. They were desperate to stop Jeannie from telling anyone what really happened.'

Leo lifted Ella up to sit on the bales of hay, leaned back against them, his hands in his pockets, and told her about the statement Pounds had made corroborating Jeannie's version of events.

'He really saved our bacon, didn't he?' she said. 'He can't be a bad man at heart. I hope he isn't caught and charged with killing Aaron.'

'I doubt he will be if he keeps his nose clean. London's a big place. But you know that.' He turned to look at her. 'I suppose you'll be going back there now this is all over.'

'I suppose.' Much as she loved her job, happy as she had been with the Hendersons, the thought of leaving Somerset made her heart sink. All the people she loved most in the world were here. 'And I suppose you'll marry your Marigold and live happily ever after,' she added wistfully.

'That's one thing that's not going to happen,' Leo said. 'I've parted company on very bad terms with Mr Deane and he made it very clear he doesn't want me as a son-in-law.'

'Oh, Leo – I'm sorry!'

'Don't be. I don't love her. Never have. I just got swept along. She's pretty and amusing, I'd have been assured of a

443

senior position in the family firm, and it seemed like a good idea at the time, though I'm not proud of that . . .' He hesitated and then went on: 'There's another reason, too, why I went along with it. A girl I couldn't forget and thought I'd never see again.'

A jolt like a lightning bolt shot through Ella's veins. Another girl?

'Who . . . ?' she asked, wary of what the answer might be.

'Can't you guess?' Leo smiled, but it was a sad smile. 'I found her again, but she's promised to someone else.'

Colour flooded into Ella's cheeks; though she still couldn't believe it, her heart was almost daring to sing.

'You don't mean . . . ?'

'Yes, you, Ella. But I don't suppose I stand a chance against the son of a baronet.'

'Oh, Leo!' She covered her mouth with her hands for a moment, overwhelmed with joy. Then she reached for his hand.

'I'm not going to marry him, Leo. It's really odd . . . because it was just the same for me as you say it was for you. I'd never forgotten you – never. I thought about you all the time. And when Monty asked me to marry him I wished it were you. I said I needed to think about it because I never expected to see you again either and thought perhaps I'd be crazy to pass up the opportunity. But I couldn't do it. I still have the ring he gave me but I've never worn it, and I'd made up my mind to give it back to him when I got back to London.'

'Really? So there is a chance for me?'

'More than a chance. I love you, Leo. I think I always have.'

'Oh, Ella!' He swung her down from the hay bales. She was in his arms, bodies entwined, hungry lips finding the only ones either of them had ever wanted.

The events of the past days had been appallingly dreadful,

but out of them had come this wonderful reunion that they had both given up on as an impossible dream.

And neither of them was going to let the other go ever again.

Martha had retired to the quiet of her room, drawn the curtains to shut out the miserable afternoon weather, and sunk down on to the bed she had shared with Seb throughout their long and happy marriage. How good it was to feel a soft mattress and feather pillow after the hard bunk of the prison cell.

She'd been wrong to believe that Jeannie had killed Garth. But who could blame her, when she'd found the girl too distressed to speak, covered in blood, and with the knife in her hand? And she still couldn't regret taking the blame. The Lord only knew what would have happened to Jeannie if she hadn't. Martha would have lost her, as surely as she had lost little Lily, and it would have been more than she could bear.

In the strange half-light the faces of all the children she had lost flickered just beyond her line of sight. Lily, of course, always Lily. Teddy and Dicken. And now Garth. She had loved them all. For all that he had caused her so much worry and heartache, he was still her son, and always would be. It was really not his fault that he had taken after his father. He'd been born damaged and she'd always known it, the reason she'd tried to protect him for as long as she could. Poor Garth. He'd never stood a chance.

But in the end he'd given his life for Jeannie.

A brief smile lifted the corners of Martha's mouth. At the end, against all expectations, he had made her proud.

Postscript

Eighteen months later

'All ready then?

Leo popped his head around the door of the bedroom where Ella was getting their little daughter ready for her christening. She was three months old now and was, in their opinion at least, the most beautiful baby ever, with her strawberry-blonde hair and big blue eyes fringed with thick dark lashes. They had named her Lilah after Ella's mother, and when Ella was feeding her she seemed to feel Mam's presence as if she were in the room with them, smiling proudly at her granddaughter.

'Almost.' Ella smoothed a few imaginary creases out of the skirt of the christening gown and reached for the matching bonnet. She had bought the gown and bonnet specially for the occasion – neither she nor Leo had any heirlooms to hand down, and although Martha had offered the gown her own children had been baptised in it had yellowed with age, and in any case Ella wasn't comfortable dressing her precious daughter in it considering that Martha had lost three of her babies in infancy. It wasn't that she was really given to being superstitious, but she wasn't going to take any chances. 'Is everybody else here?'

'Yes. They're all in the bar, having a celebratory glass of sherry.'

'Just the one, I hope,' Ella said wryly. 'We don't want anyone falling into the font.'

'Don't worry. Martha didn't open the bottle until the Hendersons arrived,' Leo reassured her.

'I'm so glad they were able to come.' Ella gave Lilah's gown one last stroke and got up. 'I feel like they're our very best friends. I could always talk to Mrs Henderson about anything, and now . . . Well, you wouldn't have your new position if it wasn't for Mr Henderson.'

'Yes, I owe it all to him,' Leo said.

It was the truth. When Ella had returned to London and told her employers what had happened, Mr Henderson had offered to speak to a friend who was head of a firm of solicitors in the city. He had offered Leo a position, a junior one for the present, but with very good prospects, and Leo had jumped at the opportunity.

'How can I ever thank you?' he'd said to Mr Henderson, and the man had smiled benignly.

'My pleasure. At least it means Sylvia won't lose Ella just yet – at least I hope not.'

'She won't leave you in the lurch, I promise,' Leo had said.

Ella had indeed remained with the Hendersons until she and Leo had married six months later and then she was still able to help out with the Henderson children every day as the apartment they were renting was within easy walking distance. It was only when her pregnancy with Lilah was well advanced that she had handed over her childcare duties, and by then Myra, the maid who had been chosen to replace her, was well trained in what was expected of her. Ella was confident things would work out well: she loved the children, and they loved her.

Ella had seen Monty only once, when she returned the engagement ring he had tried to put on her finger and explained as kindly as she could that she was now promised elsewhere. At least she was able to soften the blow with a good reason for turning down his proposal rather than having to tell him she just didn't fancy him! And strangely Monty seemed almost relieved. Perhaps, while courting her to annoy his parents was one thing, facing their opposition to marrying her was quite another.

To begin with she'd worried about leaving Jeannie, but she knew Martha and Conrad would look after her. A woman who would risk her freedom for Jeannie's sake would certainly make sure she was safe and well cared for, and Conrad adored her. In fact, when she, Leo and baby Lilah had arrived at the Feathers yesterday, Ella had been delighted to see that they had become very much a couple, with Jeannie hanging on to Conrad's arm as she had once hung on to Garth's.

The best surprise of all had come when she had asked Jeannie and Conrad if they would be Lilah's godparents, along with Mrs Henderson, who had already consented.

'Of course!' Jeannie had said instantly, then slipped her hand into Conrad's, smiling up at him and blushing a little. 'Shall we tell them our secret?'

'What's that?' Ella had asked, though from the way they were looking at one another she thought she already knew.

'We're going to get married,' Conrad had said. 'After tomorrow, the next time we're in church will be to hear our banns read.'

'Oh that is wonderful news!' Ella had hugged them both, and Leo shook Conrad by the hand.

'I second that.'

Now, on the day of the baptism, Ella tucked Lilah into her shoulder and ran her hand over her own hair to make sure no stray ends were escaping her combs.

'I'm ready then.' She smiled at Leo who stood holding the bedroom door open for her. 'Just think – that boy and girl in the asylum all those years ago – and look at us now!'

'There was never anyone for me but you, Ella,' Leo said.

'Nor anyone but you for me.' She dropped a kiss on to Lilah's silky hair, bright as a new-minted gold sovereign. 'We are so, so lucky. Together again, and now Lilah too.'

A breath of air fragrant with the scent of lavender whispered in through the window, open to the warmth of late summer, seeming to kiss Ella's cheek and her eyes sparkled suddenly with unshed tears. Mammy. Mammy was here with her, just as she always had been down the years.

'Thank you, Mammy,' she whispered silently.

Then she followed Leo down the stairs towards a future brighter than she could ever have dreamed of.

The family were gathered around the font, sunshine slanting in through the stained-glass windows above it casting a warm glow on their faces and turning the water that the vicar was sprinkling on little Lilah's forehead to sparkling droplets. His voice rang out strong and clear, echoing around the centuries-old stone walls and pillars and soaring up to the heavy wooden beams that crisscrossed beneath the arched roof.

'Lilah Martha, I baptise you in the name of the Father, and of the Son and of the Holy Spirit.'

Discarding the little cup and dipping his finger once more into the holy water, he made the sign of the cross on the smooth pink forehead, signifying that the baby was now part of the family of Christ, and would remain faithful unto her life's end. Throughout the ceremony Lilah had not so much as whimpered, and Martha smiled to herself, remembering how her children had all yelled lustily at the shock of the cold water on their bare heads, even if they had been quiet until then.

The priest returned Lilah to Jeannie's arms, lit a small candle from the fat paschal candle and handed it to Ella. Leo's hand closed over hers so that they held it together, yet another bond, if any were needed, between two hearts that had always been meant to be as one.

As the priest uttered the words of the final prayers Martha looked at her beloved sons and adopted daughters, their heads bowed respectfully. At Leo, who had brought Ella the happiness she so richly deserved, and at their darling little baby. My family, she thought, with a rush of love and pride. For a moment she thought too of Seb – how she wished he could have been here today! – and of all the children she had loved and lost. She would never forget any of them. But their loss had also in some way been her gain, for it made the living all the more precious.

How lucky I am, Martha thought, and as the priest spoke the final blessing she whispered her own prayer of thanks to a God she had not always believed in, and who had sometimes seemed so distant, even cruel.

Now it was as if the hymns and prayers of centuries of worshippers were imbued in the walls, lingered in the very air of this ancient church, giving it an aura of holiness and joy Martha had never experienced before.

In spite of all the hardships and losses she had endured, Martha knew she was truly blessed.

As the family emerged into the sunshine, baby Lilah, still in Jeannie's arms, was the focus of attention.

'She smiled at me!' Jeannie cried suddenly, her face a picture of delight. 'That's the first time she's smiled, isn't it, Ella?'

Ella exchanged an amused glance with Leo. She suspected

the 'smile' was most likely nothing more than a bout of wind, but she wasn't about to burst her sister's bubble.

'Because she knows you're not only her auntie, but also her godmother,' she said.

And seeing Jeannie happy and smiling after all she had been through was all she needed to make this perfect day even more perfect.

Look out for Jennie Felton's next tumultuous
and heartrending saga . . .

The Lost Sister

Coming soon from

HEADLINE

Try another of Jennie Felton's
gripping and emotional sagas . . .

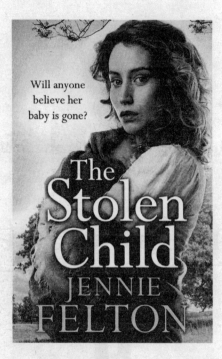

Will anyone
believe her
baby is gone?

The
Stolen
Child

JENNIE
FELTON

'Brimming with high drama, anguish, love, loss,
tragedy, and gripping twists and turns, this is an
absorbing and poignant story'

Lancashire Post

Have you met the Families of Fairley Terrace?

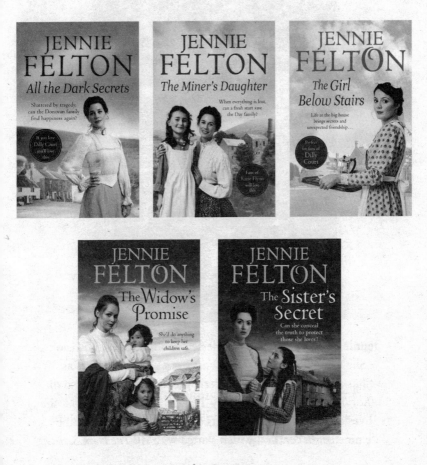

Jennie's compelling saga series
is available now from

HEADLINE

Jennie Felton grew up in Somerset, and now lives in Bristol.
She has written numerous short stories for magazines as
well as a number of novels under a pseudonym. She is also the
author of the Families of Fairley Terrace Sagas series, about the
lives and loves of the residents of a Somerset village in the
late nineteenth century, which started with *All The Dark Secrets*.

Stay in touch with Jennie!

Visit her on Facebook at
www.facebook.com/JennieFeltonAuthor
for her latest news.

Or follow her on Twitter @Jennie_Felton